"Moore has somehow managed to make a story filled with monsters and moldering corpses wholesome and cozy. Fans of comedic horror with heart, like *Hocus Pocus* and *The Addams Family,* will find plenty to love within these pages. The beating heart of this book is a tale of radical self-love and friendship in a world that seems determined to sow hatred and discord. If you're looking for a book that feels like a warm hug, you've come to the right place."

—M. J. KUHN, internationally bestselling author of *Among Thieves*

BY MARSHALL J. MOORE

SON OF A SAILOR SERIES

Son of a Sailor

Prisoners of a Pirate Queen

Enemy of the Empire

RITES OF RESURRECTION SERIES

The Pale City

The Ashen City

The Awoken City

Postcards from a Lake Monster

PRAISE FOR

THE HENCHPERSON'S GUIDE TO UNIONIZING

"Quirky and hilarious but also with depth and heart, *The Henchperson's Guide to Unionizing* is an unforgettable and fantastic story about being human. I loved it!"

—SARAH BETH DURST, *New York Times* bestselling author of *The Spellshop*

"A sweet, cozy adventure with *Haunted Mansion*–level horror about found family, loving oneself, and breaking free of chains, be they psychological, physical, vampiric, or . . . tentacled."

—DELILAH S. DAWSON, *New York Times* bestselling author of *Guillotine*

"Cozy, creepy, and full of heart (among other body parts) . . . a charming tale of found family that comes alive in its examination of responsibility, power, and what happens when we band together to decide enough is enough . . . An absolute delight of a book."

—EMILY KREMPHOLTZ, *USA Today* bestselling author of *Violet Thistlewaite Is Not a Villain Anymore*

"Charming and heartfelt . . . the most fun I've had in ages. Do I want to know more about how henchmen end up with their respective villains? Do I want to see them unexpectedly victimized by the underused 'there's only one castle' trope? Do I want to see them compare notes on their respective bosses? Yes, yes, and yes!"

—ANDREA STEWART, *Sunday Times* bestselling author of *The Bone Shard Daughter*

"Flips everything you thought you knew about classic monsters and their sidekicks on its head—then holds your hand while you file a worker's comp claim with your union rep . . . Moore's witty prose had me laughing out loud as I fell head over heels for Igor and his ragtag group of friends (tentacles and all). Brimming with creativity, magic, and a touch of the absurd, *Henchperson* is a heartfelt and hilarious tale of finding your people, acknowledging your own worth, and standing up for what's right—even when surrounded by an angry mob brandishing pitchforks."

—LAUREN THOMAN, author of *You Shouldn't Be Here*

THE HENCHPERSON'S GUIDE TO UNIONIZING

MARSHALL J. MOORE

THE HENCHPERSON'S GUIDE TO UNIONIZING

A NOVEL

BANTAM
NEW YORK

Bantam Books
An imprint of Random House
A division of Penguin Random House LLC
1745 Broadway, New York, NY 10019
randomhousebooks.com
penguinrandomhouse.com

A Bantam Books Trade Paperback Original

ISBN 979-8-217-37416-8
Ebook ISBN 979-8-217-37417-5

Printed in Canada

2 4 6 8 9 7 5 3 1

BOOK TEAM: Production editor: Ted Allen • Managing editor: Saige Francis • Production manager: Angela McNally • Copy editor: Emily DeHuff • Proofreaders: Melanie Gold, Barbara Stussy, Nicole Ramirez

Adobe Stock illustrations: Kat (bats), Edwards (trees behind author's name), Pixot (haunted house), radigrafis (trees behind haunted house), Gian (raised fist), dieno productions (lightning bolts below chapter numbers), Yanka (cat), SAJID (lightning bolt icon behind cap initials)
Sprayed edges art: John Viet-Triet Nguyen

Book design by Jo Anne Metsch

The authorized representative in the EU for product safety and compliance is Penguin Random House Ireland, Morrison Chambers, 32 Nassau Street, Dublin D02 YH68, Ireland. https://eu-contact.penguin.ie

For the unappreciated,

the overlooked,

and the unsung.

I see you.

THE HENCHPERSON'S GUIDE TO UNIONIZING

1

IT'S ALIVE

IN IGOR'S CONSIDERABLE experience, the Subject was one of the finest corpses he had ever assembled.

It lay upon the great stone slab which dominated the tower room that Igor's master had converted into his laboratory. Naked save for the sheet draped across its lower regions, the Subject was better than six feet of stiff muscles and ever-so-slightly mismatched limbs. Igor had done his best to pair them, but if there was one thing that his long and informal study of anatomy had taught him, it was that virtually no two human beings were exact matches for one another.

The natural exceptions, of course, being twins, but, as the Doctor had despairingly remarked upon more than one occasion, twins rarely had the decency to leave the world in as synchronized a fashion as they had entered it. So, like many other craftsmen, Igor had done his best with the materials available.

At least the stitches were scarcely visible. No one would ever accuse the short, hunchbacked manservant limping around the Subject's slab of an overabundance of grace, but Igor was a deft hand with a needle. One would have to look closely to distinguish the fine dotted lines demarking where the Subject had been opened up to install a fresher set of organs than those it had been buried with.

"Is the Subject ready, Igor?" the Doctor called from the upper floor of the laboratory, where he stood perusing the collection of arcane schematics and anatomical diagrams scattered across his worktable one final time. Behind him, conical electrical conductors towered like monoliths reaching towards the open sky above.

"Almost, Master!" Igor shouted, just as a lightning flash bathed the world in stark white, a tremendous thunderclap drowning out his reply. Igor blinked rapidly to clear his vision of the lightning's afterimages.

"Answer me when I ask you a question!" the Doctor yelled.

"Sorry, Master." Igor rounded the end of the table, inspecting the Subject one last time before the experiment truly began. Not for the first time, he caught himself envying the smooth muscles of its calves, one of which had once belonged to a champion distance runner. Igor's own legs were considerably more mismatched than those of the grafted-together corpse, one being nearly two inches longer than the other. This combined with his humped back to give him an ungainly, shuffling gait that was never quite fast enough to appease his master's limited patience. "Nearly ready. Just have to insert the—"

"The brain, Igor!" The Doctor jabbed a gloved finger at the corpse. The upper hemisphere of its skull hinged open at the occipital bone, exposing an empty cranium. "Maybe you can function without one, you cretin, but I hardly expect the ideal specimen of mankind to do the same. Do you?"

"No, Master!" Igor said, already heading for the great oak doors of the laboratory. He knew better than to take his master's insults personally. Like most geniuses, the Doctor was possessed of a mercurial temperament, his agitation inevitably growing the nearer he drew to an experiment's completion.

Grunting, Igor pushed open the heavy doors and hurried down the spiral staircase as swiftly as his shuffling gait permitted. Not for the first time, he silently bemoaned whatever wisdom or caprice had led his master to settle them in a ruined castle. An abandoned church would have been more to Igor's liking. They'd set up the laboratory in several of those down the years, and Igor had always enjoyed the way sound echoed and magnified in such spaces, how the broken panes of stained glass bathed the dusty floors in strange and wonderful colors.

Best of all, none of them had as many stairs as this accursed castle.

"Master knows what he's doing," Igor consoled himself, coming at last to the landing where the tower joined the ruined castle's keep. Safely out of his master's sight, Igor leaned against the nearest windowsill, listening to the rain pattering against the glass as he caught his breath. Just for a minute, he told himself.

Then it was back to work.

Another lightning flash, followed by a thunderclap that rattled the windowpanes. Igor peered out, hoping he might glimpse the next lightning bolt to go arcing through the sky.

Instead, a distant line of tiny lights came flickering in and out of sight along the steep and winding mountain path leading to the castle. Even from this distance and through the rain, there was no mistaking the dancing red and yellow flames.

Torches.

"Pitchforks too, I shouldn't wonder," Igor muttered, turning from the window and hurrying towards the stairs leading down to the dungeons.

Time was of the essence now.

*　　*　　*

At some point prior to the castle's abandonment but comfortably after the fortification had ceased to be of any military value, its owner had decided that its dungeons would better serve as a wine cellar. They were cool and dark, ideal for the storage of rare vintages—or laboratory materials sensitive to heat and light.

Igor hobbled down rows of shelves bearing labels like CHIANTI and MERLOT, though most had been crossed out and replaced with Igor's untidy scrawl. Dexterous though he was with needle and thread, his handwriting remained scarcely legible. He passed LIVERS and TEETH, crossed into the aisle for SKULLS (PARTIAL), then slipped into the row he was searching for.

"Brains," Igor said aloud, licking his lips as he surveyed the rows of glass jars before him, each containing a lump of gray matter floating in a briny alchemical solution of the Doctor's own devising.

Under better circumstances, Igor would have been more circumspect in his selection, but neither the raging storm nor the angry mob making their inexorable way up the mountain permitted him the luxury of time. He plucked up the nearest brain: TAX COLLECTOR.

"Pristine condition." Igor tucked the jar safely under his arm. Patting its lid, he hurried out of the cellar and up the stairs as swiftly as his legs could carry him.

* * *

"Master!" Igor cried, the oak doors of the laboratory groaning with impressive vibrato as he pushed them open. "There's an angry mob coming!"

"When isn't there?" the Doctor muttered. "They've torches and pitchforks, I suppose?"

"Farming implements of every description," Igor confirmed, having taken another breather on the landing as he climbed the stairs, where, through the window, he'd seen the mob reach the top of the mountain. In moments they would be hammering on the castle's front gate, which Igor doubted would hold for long under a sustained assault.

"Plebeians and luddites," the Doctor sneered, pushing his shock of bone-white hair back from his face. "Far be it from us to let such simpletons stand in the way of scientific progress. The brain?"

"Here, Master." Igor indicated the jar. "You mean to continue the experiment, then?"

"Of course I do," the Doctor snapped, rounding his worktable. "It'll take more than a gaggle of illiterate peasants to keep me from realizing my vision. Not when the completion of the Great Work is so near to hand, Nature's fundamental secrets laid bare before my—"

The remainder of the Doctor's monologue was cut short when he stepped on one of the numerous discarded glass vials littering the laboratory floor. His lanky arms flailed as his feet went out from under him. Igor started towards his master but had gone only a few shuffling steps when the Doctor caught himself on the worktable railing. He slowly straightened, lips curled downwards with the expression of a man trying to resurrect his dignity after discovering that his trousers had been unbuttoned all morning.

"It's an awfully large angry mob, Master," Igor said, taking advantage of the interruption. Were the Doctor permitted to resume his former line of self-indulgent thought, Igor would never be afforded the opportunity to get a word in edgewise. "A hundred, from the looks of it. Possibly more."

The Doctor blinked. For the first time that night, his eyes, hugely magnified behind his bronze-rimmed goggles, betrayed a hint of uncertainty. "That's practically half the village."

"Could be the whole village," Igor agreed. "Wives and babes too. Little ones carrying miniature pitchforks and tiny torches."

"I suppose I should be flattered." The Doctor grimaced at the Subject on its slab. He hurried down the stairs leading from his worktable to the laboratory floor, stepping gingerly in case of more rogue vials. "Had I known we were to play host to such a crowd, I might have thought to charge them admission. As things stand, their arrival must accelerate our timetable."

Hardly pausing as he reached the bottom stair where Igor waited, the Doctor plucked the brain jar from his manservant's waiting hands. Its lid opened with an audible *pop,* the briny smell wafting from it eliciting a sudden craving for pickles in Igor's growling stomach.

"But, Master," he protested, following after him, "the mob—"

"Will be some time in breaking down the front gate." The Doctor set the jar down and carefully extracted the brain. "I shall have time to complete the experiment, if only just. In the meantime, get yourself to the coach."

A warm but confusing feeling stirred in Igor's heart. Surely his master could not be telling him to flee for his life while he himself stayed behind—could he?

In all their time together, across dozens of experiments and countless villages populated with superstitious, hostile peasantry, the Doctor had always put his work before the safety of either of them. Nor, being an unsentimental sort, had he ever displayed much concern for Igor's well-being. But Igor, who had suffered from a lisp that rendered him nearly incomprehensible until the Doctor had intervened, firmly believed that actions spoke louder than words. And if the Doctor was willing to stand in the way of an angry mob while Igor fled for his life—

"What are you waiting for?" His master scowled as he bent over the Subject's open cranium, carefully aligning the brain with the electrodes dotting the skull's interior. "Start packing. Unless you want us to begin the Great Work anew with no equipment?"

"No, Master." Igor pushed down the sinking feeling in his gut, locking it away in the same neglected basement of his heart where he stowed the rest of his master's disparaging words. "I'll be quick."

"See that you are," the Doctor said absently, his attention fully returned to inserting the Subject's brain. "We haven't got all night."

As if in agreement, a flash of lightning arced across the sky above, and thunder shook the stone walls around them.

* * *

The sole silver lining to being run out of town by angry mobs on a recurring basis was that Igor had refined packing up the laboratory to an art. Diagrams were furled up and schematics folded, vials and alembics stowed safely in padded carrying cases. Tottering under a double armful of essentials, Igor limped to the trapdoor at the laboratory's far end, nudged it open with his foot, and descended into the narrow passageway beneath.

A short time later he emerged into the abandoned castle's rear courtyard, sweat plastering his scant hair against his forehead. A coach stood waiting, its pair of horses already bridled, stomping their hooves and whinnying uneasily as the storm above flashed its ire across the heavens.

"Easy, girls," Igor crooned from behind his armful of lab equipment. "We'll be gone from here soon enough, don't you fret."

One of the mares let out a fretful whinny. That hardly bothered Igor; he was well accustomed to having his advice ignored.

Not that being ignored was always such a bad thing. It certainly made it easier to work discreetly—a valuable skill, given the sort of tasks the Doctor typically set him to. To say nothing of the various chores and errands he performed unasked, like labeling the organ jars in the cellar. Or, in this particular instance, ensuring that the coach was ready and packed for a hasty getaway.

Long years in the Doctor's employ had given Igor an intimate familiarity with the rhythms of small, isolated villages like the one their current laboratory loomed above. From the moment he and his master established themselves on the outskirts of town, they were regarded with wary suspicion, which gradually but inevitably escalated into fearful hostility before finally metastasizing into a frenzy of mob violence. How long this metamorphosis took varied according to a number of factors, including their proximity to town, the population of the village in question, and the grisliness of the Doctor's experiments, but the outcome was always the same.

"Torches and pitchforks," Igor muttered as he loaded the last of the lab equipment into the back of the black coach. He was just shutting the door when the breeze whipping through the courtyard shifted, assaulting his nose with a new and acrid smell.

"Smoke!" Igor's already bulging eyes widened at the sight of a wispy bluish tendril rising from the castle's far wall. His gaze climbed the tower, its stones now bathed from below by more firelight than torches alone could account for.

The mob had set the ruined castle aflame.

With the Doctor still inside.

Unhesitating, Igor raced across the courtyard as swiftly as his awkward gait allowed, heart pounding against his ribs. If he hurried, he could still save his master from the pitchforks and the flames.

And then maybe, just maybe, the Doctor might thank him.

2

TORCHES AND PITCHFORKS

ONE SECRET PASSAGE and an interminable number of stairs later, Igor burst from the trapdoor onto a familiar scene.

The storm roiled and surged far overhead, the heavens themselves raging against the mortal man who dared defy the natural order with his unnatural experiments. Lightning spider-webbed across the sky as the wind howled, gusts of rain blowing in from the open roof.

The Subject lay upon its slab, the Doctor having inexpertly stapled shut its cranium. Long cables ran from electrodes pasted to its forehead, snaking up the stairs to the two towering conical conductors meant to catch the lightning flashing across the sky. The Doctor stood with both hands on the enormous lever between the conductors, the ambient electricity of the mounting storm causing his hair to stand on end even more than usual.

"Igor!" he shouted. "Get into position!"

"But, Master!" Igor cried. "They've set the castle on fire! The smoke—"

"A mere distraction!" the Doctor scoffed, goggled eyes glued to the light show playing out across the clouds. "A plebian display of overexuberance—"

Thunder boomed. So did the laboratory's oak doors, shuddering beneath the weight of pounding fists. From the other side came a muffled clamor of angry voices.

"Master, we need to leave!" Igor hurried up the steps to the Doctor. "They'll break it down any—"

The door shuddered again, then splintered under heavy axe-blows from the mob's doughtiest participants. A crowd of yellow-toothed peasants surged into the laboratory, shouting incoherently. One, catching sight of the Doctor standing between the conductor towers, raised a crossbow.

"Master!" Igor howled, reaching out to pull him from the line of fire.

A lightning bolt hurtled down from the heavens. It struck the laboratory tower, bathing the room in violent, blinding white light.

Heedless of the mob of peasants and cackling with lunatic glee, Igor's master pulled the lever with both hands.

Electricity raced from the walls, the ceiling, the very air itself, coalescing around the two conductor towers—and the Doctor standing between them. The electrical current savagely jolted away Igor's outstretched hand and surged through the Doctor, clearly illuminating his skeletal system.

The force of the shock knocked Igor to the floor. The peasant's crossbow bolt flew through the space Igor's hand had occupied seconds earlier and was promptly disintegrated by the galvanic forces surrounding the Doctor.

"Witchcraft!" someone shouted—an accusation the Doctor would have certainly taken umbrage at, had his ears not currently been vomiting sparks. Other shouts echoed the sentiment but were abruptly silenced by a deep, cavernous groan.

Every eye in the castle tower turned inwards, towards the Subject writhing upon its slab. Arcing loops of electricity raced up the cables affixed to its head and burrowed into its skull, causing the limbs Igor had spent many a painstaking hour stitching together to jerk and dance.

Slowly, inexorably, the Subject rose from its slab, arms held out stiffly before it. Opening bleary eyes, it surveyed the chaotic world it had been thrust into with an expression of consternation.

"IT'S ALIVE!!!!" the Doctor screeched in triumph, before being cut off by another surge of electricity that set his teeth rattling.

As if to confirm this observation, the Subject stood unsteadily. Nearly seven feet tall, it reflected the Doctor's ideal of humanity, all carefully grafted muscles and broad proportions. Constructed predominantly from male corpses, it had a strong jaw, firm chin, and thick brows, all of which Igor had painstakingly selected.

Yet the harsh electrical light rendered its flaws all the more apparent: the subtle mismatch of skin tones, the faint but unmistakable lines where Igor had stitched its constituent parts together, and the confused, infantile look upon its patchwork face.

"Mother of God," one of the peasants murmured, crossing himself.

"Rrraggh?" the Subject moaned inquiringly as the sheet draped across its lower regions slipped free. For reasons Igor could not guess and preferred not to speculate over, the Doctor had insisted on total anatomical accuracy.

"Mother of God," one of the peasant women said, in quite a different tone.

"Rrraggh?" the Subject said again. It took a step forward, arms extended straight out before it, the trailing cords of the electrodes still dangling from its head. As one, the throng of peasants retreated a step, their torches and farming implements insufficient weapons against the fear and awe the Subject inspired.

"Behold!" the Doctor shouted from his place above them all, still clinging to the lever even as arcs of ambient lightning danced across his body. "From cold flesh, new life! From death, rebirth! By the twin lights of science and alchemy, I have driven out the dark of supersti-sti-sti—"

A particularly powerful jolt of electricity racked his thin frame, clattering his teeth and illuminating his skeleton in minute detail. Steam issued from his ears.

It had to be killing him, Igor realized. His master had been electrocuted plenty of times, but never for so long or at such a high voltage. He must be in terrible pain, if the lightning coursing through him was powerful enough to rob him of the power of speech.

"Master!" Igor cried, finally pushing himself back onto his feet. Below, the Subject took another tottering step forward.

"Back, fiend!" one of the braver peasants cried, thrusting a torch towards the creature.

The Subject's eyes widened. A hoarse animal bellow of panic clawed out of its throat as it lashed out with one massive fist.

The blow caught the torchbearer in his middle, knocking him clear off his feet. The sudden violence shocked the mob from the fearful spell that had held them. With a wrathful cry to rival the Subject's own they surged forward, meeting the Subject's flailing fists with pitchfork, spade, and scythe.

Igor caught all of this from the corner of his eye as he hastened to his master. Bracing himself against the inevitable shock, he reached out and seized the Doctor's shoulders with both hands.

A coppery taste filled his mouth, the lightning wreathing the Doctor arcing into Igor's gnarled fingers as they tightened about the white lab coat. Before the shock could register, Igor pulled with all the strength in his small, stout frame.

The Doctor's gloved hands slipped free of the lever, which jolted back into its former position. Still sparking, he fell limply backwards. Igor grunted as he hit the wooden floor for the second time in as many minutes, the brunt of the Doctor's weight atop him.

The fall saved both their lives.

Lightning leapt back and forth between the twin cones of the conducting towers above them in a mounting frenzy. Sparks burst from them in torrents, cascading like golden waterfalls. There was a *whumph* like a great dog letting out a heavy sigh as first one tower overloaded, then the other. Black smoke billowed from their tops like huge chimneys.

On the floor, the Subject held one of the pitchfork-wielding peasants aloft, its massive fist clenching about the unfortunate man's neck. Igor had a brief, unsettling premonition of the man's head popping off like a champagne cork before the electrodes affixed to the Subject's head sparked and died, as overloaded as the towers they were still attached to.

The Subject's eyes blinked once. Its grip loosened, the peasant falling free.

Then the Subject toppled forward with the slow inexorability of a falling tree, crashing to the laboratory floor so heavily that the stones shook. Or maybe that was just the latest thunderclap, following swiftly on the heels of a lightning bolt that had snaked down from the heavens like God's accusing finger to strike the castle tower.

Igor blinked, clearing his eyes of afterimages as the white light receded. In its wake he saw the crowd of peasants in a wary circle about the Subject's prostrate form. Bitter disappointment stirred in Igor's heart at the thought of his countless hours of labor gone to waste, all his work now no more than another cold corpse lying facedown upon yet another laboratory floor.

How did things always end this way?

It was a philosophical pondering for another time. One of the peasants nudged the inert Subject with her pitchfork. As soon as they'd determined it was no longer a threat, their wrath would turn upon its creators.

"Time to go." Igor grunted, hoisting his limp master onto his shoulders. The Doctor let out a moan not unlike his creation's but offered no resistance as Igor carried him to the trapdoor.

"The hunchback!" someone shouted. "Get him!"

This was followed swiftly by an outcry of things like "Seize the brute!" and "Don't let the hideous little cripple escape!" and "That Doctor still owes me twelvepence, get him!"

Ignoring them all, Igor threw open the trapdoor and clambered inside, the Doctor draped over his shoulders like a large and mostly hairless mink stole. He'd just slid the iron bar into place when fists began hammering at it, followed by muffled exhortations to turn both himself and his master over to the mob's justice.

But Igor was already gone, hurrying down the hidden passage as quickly as he could beneath the added weight of the groaning Doctor slung across his shoulders. Soon they would reach the castle's rear courtyard, the coach with its waiting horses.

Soon they'd be heading across the rugged countryside in search of someplace new to set up shop and start again. Someplace the Doctor could complete his experimentation without interruption from uneducated and violent neighbors, so that one day he might succeed in his Great Work. Then the world would finally see the Doctor for the unparalleled visionary that Igor knew he was.

And the Doctor would turn to Igor with one of his rare smiles and thank his faithful manservant for all the years of devotion and toil.

Igor smiled as he descended the secret passageway. Another thunderclap shook the stones around him.

He hoped wherever they went next would be someplace sunny.

3

ROAD TRIP

DAWN HAD JUST begun to climb the distant hills when the Doctor finally roused from his stupor.

"Igor?" he croaked, voice nearly as hoarse and scratchy as the Subject's had been.

"Here, Master." Igor sat beside him, hunched even more than usual over the coach's reins. They'd ridden through the night, far enough and fast enough to be reasonably certain they'd escaped pursuit.

The Doctor lay sprawled with his head lolling against the cab's roof. Under better circumstances, he would have sat comfortably inside while Igor drove, but at present the coach was crammed full of all their worldly belongings.

At least this meant Igor would have company on the drive.

"Igor," the Doctor repeated, as if attempting to connect the name with the person to whom it belonged. He turned his head without raising it, bleary eyes sharpening. "Wha—"

His voice died in his throat, as Igor had expected—electrocution dried a body out something fierce. One hand still on the reins, Igor gently pressed a waterskin to the Doctor's lips.

"Slowly, now," he cautioned, watching his master's Adam's

apple bobbing with each swallow. "Wouldn't want you to choke after the shock you've had."

"I remember." The Doctor raised a trembling hand to wipe at his lips. "What happened?"

"The usual." Igor recorked the waterskin. "The mob broke down the door, the Subject—"

"I said I remember," the Doctor repeated, his gaze sharpening even as annoyance filled it. "I meant after you interfered."

"Interfered?" Igor blinked. "Master, I—"

"You laid hands on me," the Doctor said accusingly, raising his own hands. His fingers twitched intermittently in a series of tremors which had nothing to do with his dehydration. He had been afflicted by them for as long as Igor had known him. They had been his primary reason for employing the hunchback, at least initially. "You tore me from my moment of triumph, undoing all that I'd labored and worked and strove for, after years—"

"The electricity was killing you," Igor protested, though he followed it up quickly with a deferential "Master."

"One man's life is insignificant when weighed against the common good of scientific breakthrough." The Doctor waved a dismissive hand. It was a sentiment he repeated often, typically while setting Igor to some particularly hazardous task. "Besides, I had everything under control. The Subject had achieved consciousness and ambulation. A few more minutes attached to the electrodes and I daresay it would have had accumulated sufficient galvanic charge to move fully under its own power."

Igor considered pointing out that a single minute more of exposure to those same galvanic forces would have reduced the Doctor to a particularly crispy cadaver, then discarded the idea. Long experience had inured his master to the hazards of electrocution, fostering a blasé disregard which was likely the root cause of the improperly grounded conducting towers.

The Doctor turned to Igor again, his expression sharpening

with a hungry eagerness. "I don't suppose the Subject *did* manage to move on its own? Without the electrodes?"

"No, Master," Igor said reluctantly, knowing that the Doctor was seldom a gracious recipient of bad news. "The electrodes fried out. As did the Subject's brain, I'm afraid."

"I ought to have stuck yours in its skull instead," the Doctor grumbled. "Had you been able to restrain yourself against your baser fears, the Subject would have . . . would have . . ."

The Doctor's face twisted into a grimace. His cheeks ballooned, a sudden light of panic dawning in his eyes.

"Here, Master." Igor offered him the wooden bucket he'd kept between them against just such an eventuality. Between the electrocution, the jolting carriage ride across poorly maintained backwoods roads, and his master's generally irritable constitution, he was surprised the bucket hadn't been needed earlier.

Tuning out the sound of the Doctor retching loudly beside him, Igor fixed his attention upon the countryside they now found themselves traveling through. They'd left behind the steep, craggy mountains the castle laboratory had been nestled amongst sometime during the night. Now the coach rolled along through thickly wooded hills, the lush canopy permitting only the faintest rays of the unseen dawn. What little light reached the forest floor bathed their coach in soft golds and warm pinks that put Igor in mind of stained glass. He imagined the forest as a sylvan church, its pillars tree trunks, its vaulted ceiling made of leaves.

They drove along in silence, save for the Doctor's intermittent noises of gastrointestinal distress.

"Igor?" the Doctor croaked, his nausea evidently having subsided. "More water."

"Oh!" Shaking himself from his reverie, Igor fumbled the cork from the waterskin and passed it over. "Sorry."

His master only nodded wearily, gulping down swallow after swallow until the waterskin crumpled in his hand.

"May I say something, Master?" Igor ventured. The Doctor's head jerked in what might have been either a nod or merely the rolling of the coach. Igor decided to assume it was the former.

"This is only a setback." Igor glanced over his shoulder, although the castle was many hours and dozens of miles behind them. "We came so close to achieving your aims last night."

The Doctor made a queasily noncommittal noise.

"I mean," Igor continued, encouraged, "the Subject came alive! It sat up of its own volition. It even spoke! Or it tried to, at least."

"Until that idiot put a torch in its face," the Doctor grumbled, though his expression grew less sour and more thoughtful. "Though I suppose that did reveal that the Subject possessed a rudimentary instinct for self-preservation . . ."

"Precisely, Master!" Igor nodded eagerly. "We still learned much last night. Things we can incorporate into the next attempt."

Like properly grounding the conducting towers, he almost said, but caught himself just in time. His poor master had already suffered enough, and Igor didn't have the heart to point out that it was the Doctor's oversight which had resulted in his own near-fatal electrocution.

"The next attempt," the Doctor mused, scratching his head. "Of course. There must be another. Last night was only a setback."

"Yes, Master," Igor said, too relieved that the Doctor's ire was waning to be bothered that he had repeated Igor's observation as if it were his own.

"I suppose I should thank you," the Doctor said, sending a feeling of contented warmth flooding again through Igor's chest. "After all, I can hardly fault you for seeking to preserve my genius when there yet lies so much to do and to discover."

Igor nodded. Gratitude filled him so completely that he didn't notice until much later that the Doctor hadn't actually thanked him.

"Now, then." The Doctor glanced at the gloaming forest all about them. "Whereabouts are we, precisely?"

"Some thirty miles east of the castle," Igor said, having gone as straight as the winding forest road permitted. "Though probably much less, as the crow flies."

"And our destination?"

"Err . . ." Igor's fingers tightened on the reins. "Truthfully, Master, I was just trying to put as much distance between us and the mob as I could."

"What a depressingly illustrative example of linear thinking." The Doctor sighed and massaged his temples. "Your lack of initiative is, as always, a disappointment."

A faintly rebellious spark, often quashed but never extinguished, stirred itself in Igor's breast. If he were as lacking in initiative as his master claimed, then the coach wouldn't have been loaded and saddled in expectation of their abrupt departure, and the Doctor would have been left to the mercy of the mob.

Igor clamped down on the thought as swiftly as it arose. Last night had been a setback not only to the march of science but to his master's pride. Being no great intellect himself, Igor could scarcely imagine how it must have stung the Doctor's ego to have what should have been his moment of triumph quashed by a riot of illiterate vandals. Again.

And that was without even taking the electrocution into consideration.

"Sorry, Master," he said contritely. "Is there someplace you'd prefer we go?"

"Anywhere but this dismal forest." The Doctor wrinkled his nose, looking disapprovingly at the tranquil trees surrounding them.

"A beach, perhaps?" Igor suggested, trying not to sound too hopeful. He'd enjoyed collecting seashells on those rare occasions when their work had taken them to the seaside.

"Sand is inimical to the processes used in the Great Work." The Doctor frowned. "Remember how the cogs in my Resuscitation Device jammed during our time in the desert?"

"I do," Igor admitted, wincing. His pallid complexion left him particularly prone to sunburns, and he'd spent most of their time in the desert swathed head to toe in layers of protective clothing. This had had the unintended effect of lending him a more than passing resemblance to the mummies which the Doctor had ventured there to obtain, leading to more than one regrettable case of mistaken identity.

"To say nothing of that pharaoh's curse," the Doctor muttered darkly, his train of thought evidently running along a parallel track to Igor's. "The last thing we need is to be assailed again by necromorphic servitors."

"Most people just call them zombies." Igor fought down a shudder at the memory of the grasping hands of the linen-wrapped undead deep beneath the pyramids. "Though I can't recall ever hearing of any at the seashore—"

"No beaches," the Doctor said firmly. "We need someplace more temperate. Distant enough that no one from the last village will think to come looking for us, but not so far that I'll have to learn a new language just to order bread from the local bakery."

Igor decided not to point out that the Doctor usually left their grocery shopping to him.

"Someplace remote," the Doctor mused, drumming his fingers on the edge of the bucket, having evidently forgotten about its contents. "Without any nosy neighbors. Can't be completely isolated, though. There must be a town or village nearby where we can acquire what supplies we couldn't bring with us. Preferably one with a cemetery . . ."

Igor furrowed his brow, considering the locations of their previous laboratories.

"Ashcroft Abbey, perhaps?" he suggested. There was no

beach within a hundred miles of Ashcroft, but it fit the Doctor's criteria readily enough. And the statues of the various saints had been pleasant to look at. "It was quite nice, once we dealt with the ghouls."

"Detestable things." The Doctor shook his head. "But no. Apparently the Church reopened the convent at Ashcroft once they finished exorcising the grounds. No, we require someplace more secular."

"What about that tower near Barrowdale? Surely the townsfolk will have driven off that necromancer by now."

"In which case they'll be all the readier to drive off anyone else who takes an undue interest in the contents of their cemetery," the Doctor snapped. "The last thing we want is a vigilant peasantry. Perhaps . . . Oh, what was the name of that country villa on the moors?"

"Stokely House," Igor supplied. "It burned down."

"Lightning strike, or arson?"

"Both."

"God and mankind both setting themselves against me," the Doctor said, with some satisfaction. "We'll see who has the last laugh. What about that old hunting lodge in Utrecht?"

"Exploded." Along with most of the surrounding forest, for that matter.

"Right." The Doctor rubbed one of his ears, which had been partially deafened in the explosion. "Or that mountainside château near Blicktenstein—"

"Burned down. Chemical fire that time."

"Calamity follows in my wake," the Doctor lamented. "Clearly none of our previous lodgings will prove viable. If only there were someplace like Harrowdale Castle, or . . ."—his lips puckered, as if someone had just gagged him with a lemon wedge—". . . or Ravenwald."

"Ravenwald?" Igor echoed the unfamiliar name. "Where is that, Master?"

"Someplace I haven't been in a very long time," the Doctor said, shortly. He had never been terribly forthcoming about his personal history, and Igor knew better than to press him for details. "Had hoped never to return to, in fact, but I suppose it can't be helped. Not if the Great Work is to continue without further interruption, safely away from prying eyes."

"But"—Igor gulped, a sound that seemed to echo in the still forest—"if this Ravenwald is someplace dangerous—"

"It's not." The Doctor pursed his lips. "Well, *probably* it's not. Depending on whether the former occupants are still haunting the place."

A faint unease prickled at the base of Igor's neck. "Ghosts?"

Of all the various preternatural beings lurking in the world's shadowed corners, the spirits of the unquiet dead most unsettled Igor. The thought of a disembodied entity invisibly observing all he did unnerved him greatly, and it was only by some stroke of fortune that he had not yet encountered such a phantasm.

The Doctor's laugh was breathy and faintly unhinged. "Not exactly. As to whether they'll take umbrage at our moving in, or whether they're even still in residence . . . well, there's only one way to find out. Give me those."

The Doctor took the reins from Igor's hands and flicked them. The horses snorted in protest as they broke from their easy walk into a canter. Igor clutched the coach's handrails as it lurched unpleasantly.

"How long will it take us to reach Ravenwald?" Igor asked, raising his voice over the clatter of carriage wheels.

"A fortnight or so." The Doctor turned sharply to him. "Well, Igor? Are you just going to sit there while I drive, or are you going to see to our breakfast?"

"Breakfast?" Igor looked at the road ahead. The Doctor had modified the coach to include an alchemically powered gas stove for use on long journeys, but Igor had been hoping not to use it this morning. "I . . . I was rather hoping we might stop at an inn along the way."

A break in the journey would do them all good. After driving through the night, Igor had given the horses a brief rest an hour or two prior before continuing on their way, fearful that the mob might still be in pursuit. Igor himself had not slept for nearly three days. Bringing a patchwork corpse to life was a monumental task for even a fully staffed laboratory, and a positively titanic one for their two-man operation. They had worked tirelessly for the past week, fueled by a potent mix of the promise of scientific breakthrough, liberal amounts of coffee, and certain alchemical stimulants.

"No time," the Doctor said briskly, eyes fixed on the road ahead. "We cannot let the cravings of the flesh stand in the way of scientific progress, Igor. Now, I'll want my eggs—"

"Over easy," sighed Igor, who preferred his scrambled. He rose, gripping the coach's guardrails with both hands as he maneuvered himself towards the coach's door. He paused before opening it, looking over his hunched shoulder. "Master?"

"Hm?"

"What is this Ravenwald place you're taking us to?"

"The end of our road, I hope," the Doctor said, in the distracted tone that typically meant his thoughts were fixated wholly on the future. "Someplace where we can start over anew."

"Someplace new," Igor repeated in an undertone, smiling up at the morning sun.

That suited him just fine.

4

THE HAIRY NAG

TWO WEEKS OF monotonous travel later they reached a fog-shrouded bridge over a river whose banks were swollen by the unremitting rains. On the far side lay a modest town, the last rays of the setting sun gleaming off its shingled rooftops.

"Is this the place?" Igor asked, relieved at the thought that they had finally reached the end of their long, soggy journey. "Ravenwald?"

"Not quite," the Doctor said, hugging his arms about himself. The rain had finally slackened off that afternoon, only to be replaced by a cold fog. "Ravenwald isn't a town, Igor. It's a house."

"There are houses *in* the town," Igor ventured.

"None half so grand as Ravenwald Manor," the Doctor said, giving the place its right name for the first time in Igor's hearing. The carriage wheels clattered beneath them as they crossed over the rickety wooden bridge and onto the high street. "That's a few miles on, outside Ravensburg proper."

It was a fitting name for the rather gloomy town. The buildings lining the street were tall but narrow, the dark eaves of their steep rooftops overhanging the walls like a raven's outspread wings. Farther down the street, Igor could make out the winking lights of lamplighters plying their trade, but here on the outskirts all was foggy darkness. The fog rolling in off the riverbank transformed the looming buildings into shadowy, misshapen giants lurking in the mist.

Igor shivered.

"Can't wait to get out of this blasted damp," the Doctor muttered, his teeth chattering as he turned up the collar of his coat and peered balefully into the fog. "A warm fire and something hot to eat will do me good. Perhaps some sherry, too."

"Of course, Master," Igor agreed, gripping the reins of the coach tightly in his numbed hands. "I'll see about lighting a fire as soon as we reach the manor. As for food, I think I can throw together a stew—"

"No," the Doctor said sharply, turning his still baleful gaze on Igor. "No, absolutely not."

"It doesn't have to be stew," Igor amended. Like his temper, the Doctor's gastronomical preferences were mercurial. "Perhaps a roast—"

"Not the food, you dolt," the Doctor snorted. "Ravenwald Manor. We're not staying there tonight."

"Oh," Igor said, feeling utterly wrong-footed. It struck him as odd to call a halt so close to the end of their journey. "It's no trouble, Master. You said it's only a few miles farther, and the horses have been going at a steady—"

"I'm not concerned for the brutes," the Doctor said, not even glancing at the team that had carried them so far. "I just . . . would prefer not to arrive at the manor after sundown."

That struck Igor as even more curious, as the Doctor tended to disregard typical diurnal rhythms, sleeping only when he worked himself into an exhausted collapse.

"I see," he lied, sensing that the Doctor would react poorly to his pressing the issue. "I suppose I'll keep my eyes peeled for an inn, in that case?"

"No need." The Doctor thrust a trembling finger at a side street. "Turn there."

Several streets over, they emerged onto what Igor supposed must be the town square, though its only ornamentation was a weathered statue of a severe-looking man with drooping mustaches. At the Doctor's direction, Igor halted the coach in front of a ramshackle old tavern. The signboard above the door, illustrated with a haggard-looking horse, proclaimed the place to be THE HAIRY NAG.

Their horses were housed in the stable out back, along with the coach, which the Doctor sternly warned the stableboy not to even think about taking for a joyride. Igor hoped the boy would heed the warning; the Doctor had devoted a fraction of his genius towards inventing security devices for the coach, most of which were highly painful when triggered.

Inside, the Hairy Nag was warm, if not exactly inviting. Smoke hazed the air nearly as heavily as the fog had outside, and while the atmosphere was raucous and lively, many of the raised voices sounded angry or distressed rather than jovial.

All of them quieted, though, as the heavy oak door slammed shut behind Igor and the Doctor. Several dozen heads turned their way, surveying the newcomers with expressions that ranged from wary curiosity to hostile suspicion. Something in the Doctor's dissecting, reptilian gaze never failed to put strangers on edge, and Igor was only too aware of his own social shortcomings.

"Full house tonight," Igor observed, casting his gaze about the crowded tables in search of an empty pair of seats.

"Greetings, g-gentlefolk," the Doctor proclaimed, affecting a genial manner that was somewhat undercut by his chattering teeth. He was met with a resounding silence.

Undeterred, he strode purposefully to the bar, unconcerned by the glowering eyes that followed him. Igor hurried in his master's wake, his ears burning at the crowd's muttered exclamations about his humpback and hobbling gait.

Try though he might to emulate his master's cool disregard

for the opinions of the masses, Igor could never quite shake the faint sting of others' judgment. It was the first stage of a metamorphosis he'd witnessed too many times to count. First came the revulsion, which was merely physical, and the easiest to shrug off. But suspicion followed swiftly on its heels, as those who judged books by their covers naturally presumed nothing good could dwell within a creature so outwardly unlovely—though if Igor was being charitable, he supposed that his penchant for grave robbery did somewhat vindicate that attitude.

Vindicated or not, suspicion eventually but inevitably gave way to hostility, which swiftly boiled over into physical violence. This was the natural life cycle of the angry mob.

"A room, if you please." The Doctor slapped a handful of silver coins upon the bar, shaking Igor from his brooding. "And a table for two."

The barkeep, a pretty young woman with curling blond hair, scrutinized them both as she swept the coins into the pockets of her voluminous apron.

"I'll have one of the lads make up a room for you upstairs," she said, jerking a thumb at the ceiling. "As for a table . . . well, we're a bit full tonight, what with the cold and damp. See if you can't find a pair of empty chairs."

"A pair of—" the Doctor started, outrage at the lack of hospitality clouding his face. The barkeep flinched as he leaned in close. "Listen here, you scurrilous—"

"I'm sure we can scrounge something up," Igor said, hurriedly interposing himself. "Many thanks, miss . . . ?"

"Ruth," the barkeep said.

"Ruth," Igor repeated, ignoring the Doctor's peevish *harrumph* behind him. "We've had quite the long journey, and it's left us a bit out of sorts. But I'm sure we'll find someone willing to share a table. Would you mind terribly seeing to our room yourself?"

"Of course." Ruth flashed him a faintly grateful smile, looking relieved to have an excuse to get away from the Doctor. "I'll see to it that you get one of the nicer ones."

"Thank you." Igor turned to survey their prospects, doing his best to avoid the Doctor's glower. His gaze roved the smoky tavern, but as the barkeep had said, tonight was a full house, and every table seemed to be packed with townsfolk seeking refuge from the cold and fog.

The two nearest barstools were unoccupied, while the ones beyond them bore a trio of bearded men, identifiable as hunters by the crossbows hanging from their backs and the furs draped around their shoulders, as well as their smell.

"Pardon," the Doctor said, shaking off his irritation to fix the nearest of the hunters with what was likely meant to be an ingratiating smile. "But if you're not sitting in these—"

Without so much as a glance the Doctor's way, the hunter drew a knife the size of Igor's forearm and buried its tip in the barstool the Doctor had been eyeing. "Taken."

"So I see," the Doctor said, hurriedly backing away.

"What about that one?" Igor tugged on his master's sleeve and pointed at a small table at a corner booth. Its sole occupant was a dark-haired woman with a woolen shawl draped about her shoulders, bent over a steaming bowl of soup. Though she sat alone, much of the rest of the booth was taken up by a collection of bags and suitcases that had the look of being hastily packed, and more than a few rather water-damaged.

"She's probably less likely to stab me, at any rate," the Doctor allowed.

"Soup spoons are poorly suited for stabbing," Igor agreed, speaking with the wisdom of experience.

"Begging your pardon, madam," the Doctor said as they drew to a halt before her. A cane lay on the seat beside her, its ivory head carved in the likeness of a leering human skull. "But if I may be so bold as to say, it's a shame that a woman such as yourself should have to dine alone."

The woman paused with her spoon halfway to her mouth, appraising them with a critical eye. Those eyes were a brown so deep they were nearly black, and would have been a perfect match for her hair, were it not for the few streaks of silver in her tangled bun.

"A woman such as myself," she repeated, raising an eyebrow. "You mean half-drowned and homeless?"

The Doctor's smile faltered only momentarily. "I've always had rather a soft spot for derelicts and castaways."

Largely, Igor knew, because no one asked questions when they went missing.

"Castaway's the word for it," the woman agreed, somewhat bitterly. "Bloody rains washed away my cottage and damn near everything in it."

"That makes us rather a pair, then," the Doctor said, evidently forgetting Igor was standing at his elbow, "seeing as I've also been recently displaced. May I sit?"

"I shan't stop you," the woman said, shrugging. Which wasn't exactly an invitation, though the Doctor readily took it as one.

"Most indebted to you," he said, moving aside the woman's cane and sliding into the booth on her left side. Since much of its middle was occupied by her remaining worldly possessions, that left the opposite side for Igor, who settled himself atop the booth's cushioned seat. "This is my associate, Igor. And I am Doctor—"

A screeching yowl like the wails of the damned split the air, issuing from directly beneath Igor. What he'd taken for a cushion had sprouted knives and sunk them directly into his posterior.

Yelping, Igor sprang from his seat, clutching both hands to his bottom. A furry gray streak jumped down from the booth and raced across the tavern floor, leaping onto the bartop. The hunters sitting there hastily relocated to the far end of the bar, making signs to ward off evil.

"Well done," the woman said, pursing her lips. "Now you've gone and sat on my cat."

The cat in question was a gray tabby, her back arched and ears flat against her head, striped tail lashing wildly behind her. Her fur stood on end, more than doubling her apparent size, and when her yellow eyes caught Igor's brown ones she opened her mouth and hissed.

"I—" Igor started, heat rising in his cheeks. "I hadn't—that is, I thought—"

"Igor!" the Doctor snapped, his own cheeks similarly flushed, though his mortification was blended with rage. "Apologize to the lady this instant!"

"I'm so very sorry," Igor said contritely. The cat was still staring furiously at him, and he had the queer impression that if he turned his back to her she would immediately seek revenge. Swallowing this irrational fear, he returned his attention to the cat's owner, though he was unable to meet her eyes. "Sorry, Miss . . ."

"Devereaux," the woman supplied, and to Igor's immense relief she sounded more bemused than angry. "Margaret Devereaux, though most folk round here just call me Auntie Mag." An ironic tone colored her voice. "On account of my nurturing disposition, of course."

"Of course, Miss Devereaux," the Doctor said, voice turning positively oily. "Though such a matronly address surely misses the mark. Why, you can't be a day over—"

Something small but surprisingly heavy struck Igor from behind, followed a moment later by the now unpleasantly familiar sensation of claws sinking into his back. Shrieking, he launched himself clear of the table, arms flailing as he spun about, trying to dislodge his feline attacker. This effort proved fruitless, as she'd buried her claws deep in his hump.

"Grimalkin nurses grudges as if they were her kittens, I'm

afraid," Mag told the Doctor conversationally. "Hopefully the same can't be said of your . . . associate. Ivor, was it?"

"Igor!" the Doctor shouted, his face now fully red. "For heaven's sake, just stand still—"

Igor tried to, he really did. But balance had never been one of his stronger physical attributes, his legs being what they were, and so instead of coming to a stop his weight went out from under him, and he fell. For a brief, panicked moment, he thought he was about to land atop the cat, which with his luck would only enrage the beast further.

Fortunately for them both, the cat's sense of self-preservation outweighed its thirst for blood. It sprang free of Igor's back, bounding nimbly onto the tabletop. A fresh wave of pain shot through Igor as he landed roughly against the wooden floor.

"Are you all right?" the Doctor asked, his voice dripping with such concern that Igor nearly forgot the stinging pain where claws had pierced his skin.

"Fine," he muttered, acutely aware that every eye in the tavern was now fixed squarely on him as he pushed himself to his feet. Only then did he realize that the question hadn't even been directed at him.

"Oh, it's nothing," its intended recipient answered. Auntie Mag held up a hand, where a line of bright red blood stood out like a ruby teardrop against her milky wrist. "Grim's scratched me plenty worse than this before, you can be sure."

The cat had wrapped her tail protectively around her legs and was grooming herself frantically, her pink tongue smoothing down her still-raised hackles.

"Oh," the Doctor said, sitting back in his chair with evident relief. "Good. Though if it had been more severe than that, I do have some small skill in the medicinal arts—"

He trailed off abruptly, finally becoming aware that every soul in the tavern was paying them close attention. The Doctor's face went from ruddy to pale with remarkable alacrity, for reasons Igor knew only too well.

Across every village they'd been chased out of, every laboratory razed to the ground, every angry mob howling for their blood, there had been a single recurrent theme: The earlier Igor and the Doctor drew attention to themselves, the more foreshortened their stay. Rural townsfolk were suspicious and insular as a rule. The more interest they took in the newly arrived scientist and his hunchbacked assistant, the sooner they caught on to the nature of the Doctor's plans, and the quicker they reached for their torches and farming implements.

"On second thought," the Doctor said, clearing his throat and waving to the barkeep, "we'll take our meals in our room."

5

RAVENWALD MANOR

FOG STILL HUNG heavily over Ravensburg as their coach trundled past the town limits early the next morning, every jolt over the uneven cobblestones causing the scratches on Igor's back and bottom to smart anew. Having been forced by his injuries to sleep on his stomach, he was stiff and aching as they drove into the thickly wooded countryside.

Despite both the weather and the events of the previous evening, the Doctor seemed in good spirits as they neared their destination. After their frosty reception the night before—to say nothing of the spectacle he had made of himself—Igor had to admit that he'd be glad to return his attention to assisting his master in the Great Work. Better to focus his energy on their noble aspirations than to waste time brooding upon past failures.

He did feel a little bad about sitting on the cat, though.

After an hour's drive through the woods, the Doctor directed them off the main road and onto an even more neglected country lane, which soon began to climb steadily uphill. Through the faint fog blanketing the woods, the dim outline of a grand manor house began to take shape.

The closer they drew, the more details emerged from the

fog, like a rough sketch being filled in before their very eyes. The venerable old mansion was all carved stone walls and gabled rooftops, graced by the occasional gargoyle. In the days of its full splendor it must have been an imposing sight, with its towers and flying buttresses, but it had clearly fallen on hard times. Thick strands of ivy climbed the walls to frame broken windows, the shards of glass still clinging to their frames like jagged teeth in a hungry mouth. No light shone from inside, and as the coach rattled to a halt, no one emerged from the towering double doors to greet them, or to drive them away.

"Master?" Igor asked, his voice hushed. "Is this the place?"

"Ravenwald Manor." The Doctor's feverishly bright eyes swept back and forth across the decrepit old building. "Albeit somewhat worse for wear than I was anticipating."

That was quite the understatement. Igor shivered, wondering if the manor house's interior was in any better condition than its exterior. Somehow the prospect was doubtful, as the rain-worn faces of the gargoyles lining the roof seemed to snarl down at them.

"And who lives here?" Igor asked, his voice trembling slightly as he recalled the Doctor's ominous comment about Ravenwald's being haunted. Angry mobs, resurrected corpses, even the occasional warlock were all well within Igor's experience. Ghosts were not.

"As of today," the Doctor said, "we do."

* * *

Within, Ravenwald Manor was much the same as without: disheveled grandeur sinking slowly into decay. The front doors opened onto a foyer that would have been more impressive had its central chandelier not fallen at some point, cracking the ornate marble floor where it had landed and scattering shards of crystal everywhere. Cobwebs crowded every corner, and the air was thick with a stale, musty attic smell. What furniture there was had been draped with thick white cloths, which were themselves draped in an even thicker layer of dust.

"Well." The Doctor rested his hands on his hips, surveying the ruin. "This place has seen better days."

"How long has it been since you were here?" Igor asked, following carefully after the Doctor as he picked his way through the shattered crystals littering the floor.

"Long ago," the Doctor said, pausing beside the fallen chandelier. "More years than I care to recall. Admittedly, it wasn't quite so neglected under my great-great-uncle, the previous Count Ravenwald—"

"Wait a minute," Igor interrupted, an act which was in itself so unprecedented that the Doctor paused long enough for Igor to catch up to him. "You're a count?"

The Doctor had always been reticent regarding his personal history, in particular his family, though both his refined accent and apparently limitless funding had led Igor to assume his master was the product of generational wealth. Correctly, it seemed.

"Debatably," the Doctor said, resuming his trek across the foyer. "That inheritance is contingent upon which of my relations are still clinging to this mortal coil. Depending on who died and when, the title should belong either to me or to one of several cousins."

"So," Igor said, adjusting to this new information, "should I address you as Count, then, or—"

"Absolutely not," the Doctor snapped, whirling sharply on his heel. Igor took a step back, crushing a fallen bit of crystal into fine powder beneath his heavy boot. "Any title that can be earned through mere accident of birth is one I've no interest in claiming. Earning a doctorate, on the other hand, requires actual work!"

"Of course, Mas—err, Doctor," Igor said, craning his neck as far as his hunch allowed. Near the ceiling, a pair of bats fluttered about the dangling chain from which the chandelier must have hung. "But if this place isn't actually yours, then . . . should we be using it as our laboratory? I mean, shouldn't we ask one of those cousins you mentioned?"

"I haven't time to waste on those dithering inbred morons," the Doctor said coolly, evidently choosing to overlook his relation to said inbreds. "The nearest of them lives in the capital, on the far side of the mountains, and clearly hasn't paid this place any mind for the last half century or so."

"And the townsfolk?" Igor asked, trailing along behind the Doctor as they reached the far end of the foyer, where a grand set of double stairs led to the manor's upper floors. "They'll notice that we've taken up residence, sooner or later."

"If any of them ask, tell them Cousin Wilhelmina sent me here to do some maintenance on the place," the Doctor said, putting a finger to his temple. "That should be sufficient to allay the villagers' suspicions while we devote ourselves to the Great Work."

Igor had to admit that it was one of the Doctor's more plausible cover stories. It even had the added bonus of not requiring either of them to pretend to be members of the clergy, something they'd had to resort to on surprisingly many occasions.

"There's an observatory just off the north wing that will serve for a laboratory, as I recall," the Doctor said, opening an inconspicuous door to reveal a set of servants' stairs leading downwards. "But first, we need to ensure that we won't be disturbed. Now come along, Igor. I haven't all day."

"Yes, Master." Sighing, Igor relinquished his hopes for a ground-level laboratory.

* * *

The basement was, unsurprisingly, a crypt. Its walls were of a marble similar to that of the floor above and lined with paneled niches in which the various members of the Ravenwald family lay interred, their names and dates displayed on stately brass plaques.

"You'll be doing most of your work down here, Igor." The Doctor's breath plumed before him in the light of the lantern he'd carried down.

Igor rubbed his gooseflesh-prickled arms and looked dubiously about the crypt's dim confines. "It's a bit chilly."

"The ideal temperature for storing bodies." The Doctor trailed a hand idly over the engraved names of his deceased relations as he stalked down the length of the crypt. "You'll grow accustomed to the cold."

A pair of freestanding coffins stood against the far wall, carved from dark stone that looked much older than the pale marble surrounding them. The Doctor peered down at the larger of the two. Its lid was carven in the likeness of a man with an aquiline nose, slicked-back hair, and drooping mustaches. The other coffin bore a woman's likeness, though the carven bridal veil over her face made her features difficult to discern.

"Are we going to be making use of . . ." Igor gestured vaguely at the coffins, and at the niches in the walls. "You know, for the Subject?"

"Certainly not." The Doctor ran a finger along the coffin lid, then examined it by lanternlight, revealing surprisingly little dust. "Everyone down here's been dead far too long to be of any use in the Great Work."

Igor licked his lips, relieved. "Where will we get the bodies, then?"

"There's a cemetery just a mile or two down the road where we can procure our raw materials," the Doctor said. "And the gravekeeper is quite deaf, as I recall. Assuming the old coot hasn't joined his tenants by now."

That struck Igor as exceedingly likely, given how long it had evidently been since the Doctor had last set foot inside Ravenwald Manor.

"Any other nearer neighbors we need to be mindful of?" he asked, wondering why this clammy crypt had been the first stop on his master's tour of their new abode.

"Not exactly," the Doctor said, patting the coffin's stone lid with something that almost resembled affection before turning and heading for the basement stairs, taking the lanternlight with him. "You'll let me know if one of the coffins moves, won't you?"

Igor's blood dropped to the frigid room temperature. "You said there weren't any ghosts."

Or had he? The Doctor's response to that line of questioning had been distinctly evasive. Nor did he seem likely to answer now, retreating as he was towards the stairs.

"What do I do if one of the coffins *does* move?" Igor asked, hurrying after him. At the foot of the stairs he glanced over his shoulder, half-expecting the coffins to have shifted positions while his back was turned. The fact that they had not failed to fill him with relief.

"Scream," the Doctor suggested from several steps up, not pausing or looking back.

"But you said the laboratory would be all the way over in the north wing!"

"Scream loudly, then."

* * *

"Oh, now *this* should do nicely," the Doctor said as he pushed open the double doors of the manor's observatory.

Igor concurred with his master's assessment. Clearly a late addition to Ravenwald's architecture, the observatory adjoined the north wing, attached to the main body of the manor house by an open-air covered walkway leading to the fourth floor. The only other means of egress was a winding stone staircase wrapped tightly about the outside of the observatory tower, which should serve as a useful delay against the inevitable pitchfork-wielding mob.

Nor was the observatory's suitability limited to its defensive advantages. Its center was taken up by a large dais which Igor supposed had once housed a telescope but would serve very well as an operating theatre. Surrounding it was a set of low balconies, where Igor could easily imagine the Doctor conducting his alchemical experiments.

"We'll have to do away with these," the Doctor said, frowning at the collection of astrolabes and orreries by the door. "My great-great-aunt collected them. She's the one who commissioned the place. Old bat always had her head in the clouds." He gave the nearest orrery an experimental push. It crashed to the floor in a jumble of bronze planets. "Though in her case I suppose they were nebulae."

Igor winced. "Isn't astronomy one of the noble arts?"

"All the astronomers say so," the Doctor said, adjusting his glasses and surveying the observatory proprietarily. "We'll bank the generators across that far wall. Dissection will of course be handled in the crypt, but we'll need several tables for assembling the Subject, to say nothing of those required for the necessary chemical and alchemical processes . . ."

Igor was only half-listening to his master's muttered plans for their new laboratory. Trailing after him, Igor turned in a slow circle, his head craned as far back as his hump permitted, peering up at the constellations painted upon the domed ceiling. The telltale seam down the middle indicated it could be cranked open by a pull chain, affording an unrestricted view of the night sky—or easy access to lightning storms, as the case might be.

Dark and musty as it was now, even years of neglect could not fully diminish the observatory's stately majesty. Igor's mind reeled at the thought of long hours spent peering through telescopes at the starry sky, charting the courses of the heavenly bodies in their long dance, divining secret meanings from—

"Igor!" The Doctor snapped his fingers in Igor's face. "Have you caught a word I've been saying?"

"Of course, Master!" Igor squeaked, a guilty flush climbing his neck. The Doctor narrowed his eyes. "Err, except for the last thing . . ."

"Sometimes I wonder why I even bother," the Doctor muttered. "Pray try and keep your brain from wandering as much as that lazy eye of yours, will you?"

"There's no call for that, Master," Igor said, more shortly than he'd meant to. He was only a very slight bit walleyed, though that did not stop the Doctor from calling attention to it.

"It's a good thing I took you in," the Doctor said, as if Igor hadn't spoken. He let out a long-suffering sigh. "Heaven knows where you'd be without my guidance."

Someplace with a beach, a traitorous voice whispered in Igor's mind, but he quashed it almost instantly. The Great Work was of far greater consequence than his selfish desire to vacation someplace warm.

"Still in the orphanage?" Igor offered instead, vaguely hoping that a reminder of the Doctor's initial kindness in taking him in might soften his regard for Igor in the present.

"Likely so," the Doctor agreed, not sounding remotely mollified. "Sometimes I wonder if it wasn't a mistake to pluck you from that dreadful place."

"No, Master!" Alarm coursed through Igor at the thought of what his life might have been like had the Doctor not taken him in. "Of course it wasn't!"

"Wasn't it? Heaven knows I'd do better with a more attentive assistant." The Doctor made a show of sweeping his gaze about the forlorn observatory, as if hoping a replacement Igor would materialize from its darkest corners. "One who shares my passion for the Great Work. Who understands the importance of the undertaking he and I are striving together to achieve."

"But I *do* share your passion, Master," Igor said, his voice somewhere between panicked and whining.

The Doctor pushed his shock of bone-white hair back from

his brow in a gesture that Igor would have thought melodramatic, had his attention not been wholly focused on atoning for his lapse in attention. "Do you? Because that is far from the impression you've given me so far."

"I'm sorry . . ."

"In fact," the Doctor said, with a gleam in his eyes often mistaken for madness by lesser intellects, "one might think you have lost sight of the lofty aims to which we aspire. The triumph of rationality over primitive fears, the victory of man's will over nature's indifference, the defeat of death itself at the hands of science! The brave new world ahead, in which men shall walk as gods, unwearied by age, unafflicted by disease, untroubled by . . . by . . ."

"Calamity?" Igor suggested timidly.

"Calamity!" the Doctor cried, snapping his fingers. "These are the things for which I strive daily, Igor. For which I have forsaken the fleeting pleasures of the flesh and turned my back on more worldly ambitions."

"Of course," Igor agreed eagerly. "You are above such paltry temptations, Master."

"I am, aren't I?" the Doctor sighed. "Yet sometimes I feel . . . undervalued."

"By me?" Igor squeaked.

"Who else?" Another sigh, this one loud enough to echo in the observatory's impressive acoustics. "You seem not to appreciate the sacrifices I've made. The lengths to which I have gone, the depths of knowledge I've plundered. Sometimes, Igor, I feel as if you take it all—take me—for granted."

"Of course not, Master!" Igor dropped to his knees, bracing his hands against the floor. "It is my life's great joy and purpose to help you along in the Great Work! To do those things too trivial to occupy your great genius, to serve as your hands while your mind is engaged else—"

"Good!" the Doctor said, suddenly turning brisk. His arm

twitched in an abortive gesture, as if he'd been about to put his own hand on Igor's shoulder, only to realize that doing so would have required him to touch Igor's hump. "And speaking of hands, Igor . . ."

"Yes, Master?"

"We're running quite low on parts." The Doctor stepped back without helping Igor up. "Be a good lad and fetch me some, won't you?"

"Of course," Igor said, wincing as he rose unsteadily, "Master."

"And remember," the Doctor said, showing his teeth, "the fresher, the better."

6

THE CEMETERY

FRESH, IGOR CONSOLED himself as he threw open the lid of the wooden casket he'd just spent the last hour unearthing, was a relative term.

The Doctor's preference was for donors to the Great Work to be so recently deceased that rigor mortis had yet to set in. But acquiring corpses that had been dead for less than a handful of hours was always a tricky proposition, one that usually meant running afoul of the local constabulary, the families of the deceased, or both.

For a while they had tried their hands at stealing from the frigid storage basements of medical universities, a practice the Doctor maintained was the only reason he'd been denied tenure during his brief stint in academia. These specimens were of consistently high quality, and they possessed the added bonus of their various organs' having already been labeled. But such institutes of higher learning were few and far between, and they were rarely located in the smaller, more isolated settlements the Doctor preferred for setting up his laboratory.

There had also been the brief but memorable period when the Doctor had elected to manufacture fresh donors, reasoning that any idiot with a knife and a flexible moral framework could accomplish as much. But that had proven far more troublesome than it was worth. Igor had been relieved when they'd returned to the tried and true method of grave robbing. Corpses that had already been buried seldom screamed, even when cut open.

* * *

Finding a suitable grave had been easy enough, as had been accessing the cemetery. Spread out over several acres and bordered on all sides by the dense forest surrounding Ravenwald Manor, the place had the rambling, half-wild feel common to many rustic graveyards. Many of its headstones were overgrown with moss, and the tall iron fence surrounding it was choked with thorny brambles. Igor found it all comfortingly familiar.

True to the Doctor's recollection, the cemetery lay a mile or so up the road from the manor. But when Igor had knocked at the cemetery gatehouse, he'd been greeted not by a half-deaf old gravekeeper, but a tall, robust young woman with an untidy mop of brown hair.

"Help you?" she asked, peering down at Igor from her considerable height. Muscles strained against the sleeves of her plaid shirt, which had been rolled up to show off an impressive pair of forearms. She looked better suited for a career in blacksmithing or lumberjacking than gravekeeping.

"Delivery," Igor said, jerking a thumb over his shoulder at the wooden cart he'd hauled from the manor himself. A plain oaken casket sat within it, the lid securely fastened. Igor had taken it from the Ravenwald crypt, reasoning that it was always handy to have a spare casket or two lying about.

"A delivery," the gravekeeper repeated, her gaze shifting from Igor to the casket. "The next tenant isn't due until tomorrow, as I recall."

"Folk have a tendency to die unscheduled," Igor said, giving a resigned shrug. "Terribly inconvenient of them, I agree."

"Uh-huh," the brawny gravekeeper said, still looking at the casket. "This tenant of yours have a name?"

"John Smith," Igor said, pressing a quartet of copper coins into her calloused palm. Typically, the cost for burial in a parish as remote as this one was only a single copper, but Igor always paid four when he went to collect materials. The second coin was to buy the gravekeeper's silence, the third compensation for any trouble that might arise if Igor's activities were discovered, and the fourth—well, it wasn't as if guarding a cemetery was a particularly lucrative career, was it?

"Ah." The gravekeeper disappeared the coins into a pocket without comment. No fool this one. "You got a particular plot in mind?"

"I'll know it when I see it," Igor said, which wasn't a lie.

The gravekeeper grunted and moved to the cemetery gate, which was tall and iron-wrought, as Igor had expected it to be. Nor were the statuary depictions of saints and angels to either side a surprise. One cemetery was much like another, and Igor had long since stopped counting how many he'd plundered.

"I'll keep it unlocked until sundown," the gravekeeper said. "You'd best be on your way before then."

"Of course." Igor nodded as she wrenched the gates open. Their rusted hinges screeched like the damned in protest, a sound which struck the same welcoming chord Igor imagined most people felt upon hearing their dog barking behind their front door when they returned at day's end. Not that the Doctor would ever permit Igor something as indulgent as a pet, of course.

"Thank you," Igor said, picking up the handles of the cart and pulling it through the gate. The coffin's contents rattled as the wheels churned over the uneven paving stones.

"Sure." The gravekeeper waved at the foggy rows of headstones. "You'll want to keep to the path, if you know what's good for you. Man's liable to trip and break his neck in this murk."

"Don't worry," Igor assured her, surveying the misty cemetery before him. "I know my way around."

* * *

Years of grave robbing had given Igor a keen eye for recently disturbed earth, and it took him less than a quarter of an hour to find a suitable grave. Its headstone had been carved with the figure of an angel weeping, her face obscured behind the cradle of her arms, her wings draped over the headstone's sides. The sight stirred something in Igor's chest, and for the first time in longer than he could recall he felt a twinge of misgiving about what he'd come here to do.

"Needs must," he muttered in a half-hushed tone, putting his back to the weeping angel. Silently, he resolved not to look at it again, and under absolutely no circumstances to read the name or dates engraved between her wings. Easier that way.

Igor opened the casket he'd brought into the cemetery. Within lay not a corpse, but a collection of tools: a pair of spades, one long-handled and the other short, a hooded lantern, jars of varying sizes, and—in their own special case—an assortment of surgical tools that the continent's foremost chirurgeons would have envied.

Igor's hands practically itched to hold them, to feel the gentle parting of skin beneath blade as he worked with methodical, patient surety to cut cold organs free from the flesh that imprisoned them. It was a pleasure he knew well and empathized with wholeheartedly: the satisfaction of a tool being put to the use for which it was intended. To take those pieces of a body, flawed and imperfect as his own was, and join them to one another—and in so doing, to create something new and wonderful, greater than the sum of its parts.

Not yet, though.

First, he had to dig.

* * *

For about a year prior to meeting the Doctor, Igor had been apprenticed to the butcher who owned a shop across the street from the orphanage. The butcher had been a gruff, taciturn man, but he'd taught Igor the essentials of his trade. From him Igor had learned how to slaughter a hog so quickly and cleanly that the animal never realized it was dead, how blood drained from a body more swiftly when it was hung upside down, and the precise places to make the incisions to remove the useless organs while preserving the choicer cuts of meat.

The butcher had died before Igor's apprenticeship was complete, and Igor had abandoned butchery when he'd entered the Doctor's service, but those early skills had proven good practice. The first time the Doctor had laid a human corpse on a slab and told him to get to cutting, Igor had hesitated only a moment before picking up the knife.

As with most things, the first time was the hardest. But Igor swiftly adjusted to his new role as a dissector, which differed from butchery primarily in that the inedible organs like the slippery spleen and fiddly little kidneys were the ones he was meant to keep, not discard. On the inside, a dead pig and a dead person looked much the same.

So long as he avoided looking at the faces, of course.

* * *

Once he'd uncovered the coffin and smashed the lock on its lid, the rest was easy.

Humming snippets of a half-remembered aria, Igor made the necessary Y incision in the donor's chest, peeling away the skin with practiced ease. He was pleased to see that most of the internal organs appeared to be in good shape; the funeral must have occurred within the week.

Using retractors to hold open the incision, Igor dived into the delicate business of separating body parts from body. He worked steadily, methodically, making a small cut here, breaking an obstinate bone there. He unspooled intestines, extracted a gallbladder, freed the cold heart from the prison of its ribs. Each organ went into one of the glass jars he'd brought, which had been filled with a preserving agent the Doctor had concocted.

During his decades-long pursuit of the Great Work, the Doctor had attempted various means of bringing dead tissue to life. In the earliest years of Igor's service, his obsession had centered on the resurrection of a single body, perfectly preserved. These efforts had begun promisingly enough but had borne little fruit as time drew on, and the Doctor's fixation had gradually shifted from singular pristine corpses to amalgams, their parts sourced from a variety of donors. The resulting creations were inarguably unlovely in appearance, but what would physical beauty matter in a future where death itself might be undone?

Hands occupied with the steady rhythms of familiar work, Igor allowed his mind to drift towards that imagined future. Someday soon, the Doctor would complete his Great Work. The Subject, its constituent parts drawn from a dozen different donors, would draw its first breath. Oxygen would rush down its reconstructed esophagus and expand to fill the lungs Igor had painstakingly pried free of their native ribs. The eyes he'd spent hours carefully selecting would flutter open, the brain behind them taking its first view of a world forever changed by the newborn creature that dwelt within those newly sparking synapses.

The Subject would stand under its own power, breaking free of the trailing electrodes which had provided it that first burst of motive energy, discarding them like a prisoner casting off his shackles. Blinking eyes would rove its brave new world, settling at last on its creator. Igor could so easily picture the exaltation on the Doctor's face in his moment of triumph, and it was only a little bit more difficult to envision the smile of gratitude on his face as he turned towards Igor, about to thank him for all his help in bringing this new being into existence—

"Ow!" A sharp pinprick of pain jolted Igor from this pleasant fantasy: He'd accidentally sheared off the smallest tip of one of his knuckles. Hissing, he pressed it to his lips, the familiar coppery taste of blood filling his mouth.

It was his own fault for allowing himself to become distracted, he silently chastised himself. For letting his mind drift indulgently to an imagined future rather than remain focused on the present task. A little pain was a sharp reminder, but not an unearned one.

"Idle hands," Igor muttered, pulling his knuckle from his mouth and examining it in the late afternoon light—dissecting a corpse was no swift task, and he'd lost most of the day to the work. Fortunately, the cut was small and had already almost stopped bleeding.

He only hoped the Doctor would not notice the injury. Igor's hands, as he was often reminded, were the most valuable part of him.

Sighing in relief, Igor paused to take inventory of the organs he'd harvested thus far, now neatly arranged in their jars within the casket he'd brought.

"Heart, spleen, liver, kidneys, lungs," he murmured, allowing a faint swell of pride despite the earlier mishap as he compared the collection of parts against the mental list he'd had memorized well before he'd ever been taught the alphabet. After all his work, the donor's body was little more than a hollowed-out husk. All that remained were—

"The eyes." Igor's stomach gave an uneasy lurch. The Doctor had always insisted that he harvest the eyes first, as they were exceedingly delicate, and the only organs his master was adamant *must* come as a matched set.

"No one will know a mismatched pair of lungs to look at them," he said in Igor's memory. "Nor kidneys, or any of the other paired bits. But if one eye doesn't match the other, it's hardly of any use, is it?"

In Igor's opinion, this assessment was hardly fair to people with heterochromia. But as with many such quibbling details, he knew better than to argue with the Doctor over it.

"Eyes," he repeated to himself, clambering awkwardly in the confines of the open grave over to the corpse's head. Even disregarding the Doctor's particularities, the eyes were his least favorite body parts to harvest. They were so small, so delicate, so *squishy.*

Worst of all, there was no way to collect them without looking into the donor's face. To confront the fact that the body he'd spent his day defiling had once been a living, breathing person with their own dreams and fears and inner life. It made the rest of the work harder, which was why Igor always saved the eyes for last.

This donor's face was smooth and unlined, the first flush of youth supplanted by death's waxen pallor, skin stretched tight across cheeks that must have been rosy in life, now grown sallow. The hair, stiff and brittle, had not lost its warm honey-gold color. The ghost of a smile hovered about the stitched lips, as if on the verge of laughing at some private joke.

Too young. Igor banished the thought as he knelt, gently prying open the eyelid, willing himself to see an object rather than a person. Beneath its lid, the eye was glassy and unmoving, its bloodshot cornea forming a reddened halo about the clear blue iris. The black hole of the pupil stared unseeing and unmoving at the misty sky above.

Igor found this morbid sight perversely comforting. If eyes were the windows to the soul, then the lights were out and no one was home.

Sweat from his labors beaded on Igor's brow, the chill of the fog sending a shiver down his bent back, but his hands remained perfectly steady as he gently inserted the tip of the scalpel between the eyelid and the outer membrane of the eyeball—

"Mrrp?"

It was a testament to his muscle memory that Igor's hands remained statue-still even as the rest of him twitched in surprise at the animal sound shockingly close at hand. He craned his neck to see a pair of yellow eyes peering down at him from the lip of the grave.

"Oh," Igor said, withdrawing his scalpel as carefully as he had inserted it. "It's you."

The gray cat from the tavern stared down at him, her tail lashing. Igor wondered whether she remembered his inadvertently sitting on her the night before, and if so, whether cats could hold grudges. Something in the tabby's unblinking yellow gaze hinted that the answer to both questions was yes.

"Go on." Igor waved at it. "Go on, get out of here! Shoo!"

The cat—Grimalkin, she'd been called, or Grim—yawned, revealing sharp teeth and a pink tongue. Settling onto her haunches, she curled her tail about her legs, still staring at Igor.

"Creepy," he muttered. "Going to jump on my back again as soon as it's turned, are you?"

Her answer was an aggravated yowl, as if to remind him that she had only been paying him back in kind for sitting on her in the first place.

"You just stay back," Igor said, brandishing a fist at her—the fist holding the scalpel, he realized belatedly. Grim's hackles rose, and she spat out a hiss.

"Sorry," Igor said, wincing. "Just . . . leave me be, won't you?"

The cat made no answer to that, which Igor supposed was the greatest assurance he could expect. Still a little wary, he turned slowly back to the corpse, expecting at any moment to once again feel the unpleasant stab of claws digging into his hump.

To his relief, Grim did not attack, though he still sensed her yellow gaze watching him with unnerving intensity. After a fortifying breath, Igor resumed his work. Taking great care not to apply too much pressure, he gently levered the eyeball with the tip of the scalpel until it popped free of the socket with a satisfying squelch.

"Nearly done," Igor breathed, exchanging the scalpel for a pair of scissors. A quick snip, and the eyeball was dangling from the trailing optic nerve pinched between his fingers.

"Now," he said, allowing himself to feel the slight swell of satisfaction at a job deftly done, "for the other—"

Grim made no sound as she jumped. Her claws dug into his back—not his hump, this time, but the opposite shoulder, clinging to him with all fours, twenty sharp pinpricks burning along his back. Igor hissed as he stumbled backwards. But the pain was inconsequential compared to the more pressing concern of keeping the eyeball safe. If he dropped it—or heaven help him, crushed it—the Doctor's rage would be apoplectic.

Grim lunged, biting Igor's hand. His grip on the eyeball slipped, but before it could fall more than an inch the cat caught the optic nerve neatly between her teeth.

"No!" Igor howled, grabbing for her. She slipped out of his reach in that curiously liquid feline fashion and leapt nimbly up from the grave and onto the graveside, tail held high as she trotted off into the mist with her prize.

Cursing, Igor hauled himself up from the grave, slipping and sliding on the loose dirt he'd unearthed only that morning. Half-climbing, half-crawling, he crested the graveside just in time to glimpse Grim disappearing behind a row of headstones.

"Come back!" Igor shouted, taking off after her as fast as his hobbling gait allowed. The cat glanced over her shoulder, ears flattening and eyes narrowing. The eyeball dangling from her mouth wobbled from side to side, nearly brushing the cemetery grass.

Igor slowed, deciding to try a different tack. He extended a hand—not holding a scalpel, this time. "Here, kitty kitty . . ."

Grim's tail lashed, but she held her ground as he drew nearer, one slow, careful step at a time. "Just give it here . . ."

Warily, she leaned away from his outstretched hand as Igor took another step, then another. "Just . . . a little . . . Gotcha!"

He lunged, only to be rewarded with a searing pain as Grim's claws raked the back of his hand. She shot away, a gray streak in the fog.

Igor followed, breathing heavily as he gave chase. Grim wove between headstones and darted around standing plinths, the eyeball still hanging from her mouth. Igor had nearly caught up to her when she shifted course abruptly, taking off like a shot towards a looming mausoleum.

"Not—getting away," Igor panted as the cat darted behind the mausoleum, disappearing from view, "—that—easily—"

He rounded the corner of the mausoleum and took one step towards Grim, who'd halted not ten feet away—

Igor's foot landed not on damp grass but on empty air. He toppled forward, into the fog.

His fall was cushioned by damp dirt, half a dozen feet down. The impact was still enough to knock the air from his lungs. For a moment Igor could only lie at the bottom of the grave, wheezing softly. The slate-colored sky looked oddly peaceful from down here, framed on four sides by dirt.

The uniform gray sky was broken by the silhouette of a small, grayer head peering down from the head of the grave. Cats always looked pleased with themselves, in Igor's opinion, but this one looked downright smug. The eyeball, he was dismayed to see, was now held with surprising delicacy between her front paws.

"You tricked me," he said stupidly.

Grim licked her lips, then yawned.

"Well," she said, in a voice that was as condescending as it was unexpected, "it wasn't exactly hard to do."

Then she was gone, taking the eyeball with her and leaving Igor alone at the bottom of an empty grave.

"Huh," he murmured to himself, once the shock of hearing a cat talk had worn off. "That could have gone better."

He only hoped the Doctor wouldn't be too upset about the eyeball.

7

NEW NEIGHBORS

"WHAT IN THE name of Darwin do you expect me to do with a single eyeball?" the Doctor demanded, tossing the offending oculus at Igor.

"I did harvest both, Master," Igor protested, catching the eyeball in both hands. Its gelatinous texture was unpleasant against his palms, but he forced himself to swallow his discomfort. "Only—"

"You squashed the other one." The Doctor pinched the bridge of his nose. "I assign you only the simplest tasks, and yet you still find a way to fumble them."

"You could still use this one," Igor grumbled, placing the eyeball carefully back in its jar. Ordinarily he'd never behave so snappishly towards his master, but ordinary days seldom included being robbed and lured into an open grave by a talking cat.

The Doctor blinked owlishly behind his spectacles.

"That is," Igor amended, before the Doctor's own temper could rise in retaliation, "is it really so bad if the eyes aren't from the same donor, so long as they've a similar level of sightedness?"

"Sightedness," the Doctor repeated, shaking his head as he bent over the manor's dining room table, which he'd wasted no time in covering with anatomical charts and arcane alchemical recipes. “I am striving to create a being in which the human form is brought to its ultimate incarnation. My Subject is to be the ideal specimen, the pinnacle of decades of painstaking work, the avatar of mankind’s conquest of death. And you want it to have mismatched eyes?”

“Plenty of people do,” Igor said, pointing to his own slight walleye. “Remember that village where it seemed that every fourth person was a heterochromatic?”

“Genetic abnormalities,” the Doctor sniffed. He tapped his finger on an evolutionary chart on which an ape knuckle-walked its way to upright humanity. “Nature’s mistakes, which I intend to correct.”

“Just use the one eye, then,” Igor said, looking down at the jar in his hands.

“I am trying to make a new Adam, not some misshapen, sputtering, cyclopean monster.” The Doctor brushed aside a pile of disorganized papers under which lay a particularly yellowed sheet of parchment that had been burned at the edges. “Speaking of which . . .”

He held the parchment up to the oil lamp, turning it partially transparent. Through its backside Igor glimpsed dense lines of script in an alphabet he didn’t recognize, along with stark silhouettes of bat-winged human figures.

“Grab those, will you?” the Doctor said, furling the parchment and gesturing with it to a pile of kindling stacked beside the hearth. “As many as you can.”

“But what about the eyeball?”

“Throw it out,” the Doctor called over his shoulder as he swept from the room. “Or add it to the spare parts collection. I truly could care less, Igor.”

Could not *care less,* Igor thought, but did not say. He put the eyeball jar carefully on a shelf, already thinking of the uses he might put it to if the Doctor truly didn’t want it. In fact, it was just the thing he'd been looking for to complete an experiment of his own . . .

Brightening, he followed in his master's footsteps, pausing only to collect the kindling sticks. Curiously, each of their tips had been sharpened to a point.

"These are awfully sharp," he observed, hurrying to catch up.

"I should hope so," the Doctor said, making his way down the manor's dusty halls towards the foyer. "I spent an hour this afternoon whittling them to a point—even got a callus on my thumb—while you were out gallivanting."

That wasn't exactly how Igor would have characterized his day.

"I don't suppose you've had a chance to check the pantry, have you?" the Doctor asked before he could say as much.

"I have, actually." Igor enjoyed cooking even more than he did needlepoint, and hadn't been able to resist a brief inspection of Ravenwald's kitchen, which was impressively spacious and outfitted with an acceptable collection of cutlery. "Mostly preserves and pickled vegetables, but if you want me to head into town for proper provisions—"

"We've more pressing concerns," the Doctor said as they reached the grand foyer, his gaze darting to the floor-to-ceiling windows. These were mostly boarded up, though near their tops, long rays of dying sunlight stretched across the manor ceiling. "Was there any garlic in the pantry?"

"None that I could see, though maybe—"

"Can't be helped, I suppose," the Doctor said, frowning up at the sunbeams. "Less than half an hour until sundown. We'll be cutting it close."

"Close to what?" Igor asked, despairing of following his master's winding train of thought even as he trailed after him across the crystal-littered foyer floor. "Where are we going?"

"To deal with—"

A resounding *thwack-thwack-thwack* sounded somewhere to

their left, barely muffled by the thick oak of the manor's front doors. Igor yelped in surprise. Momentarily distracted, he nearly lost his footing on one of the crystal shards. The sharpened sticks—no, stakes—went tumbling from his arms.

"—the neighbors," the Doctor finished.

Thwack-thwack-thwack. Belatedly, Igor recalled the manor's ornate bronze door knockers, each hanging from the beak of an equally ornate bronze raven.

"Someone at the door for you, Master," he said, because of course it wasn't as if someone would make the trek all the way to the manor to see *him.* Not unless someone had made the connection between the newcomers to town and the recently defiled grave . . .

"I don't have time for this," the Doctor muttered, genuine agitation in his voice. "Igor, would you be so kind?"

"Of course, Master." Igor hurried over to the door, pausing only to retrieve a heavy brass candlestick from its sconce on the wall. Positioning himself so that he'd be behind the door when it opened, he raised the candlestick over his head in both hands.

"Coming!" the Doctor called, inflecting his voice with uncharacteristic geniality as the impatient knocking repeated a third time.

"A thousand apologies," the Doctor said, plastering on his genteel smile as he opened wide the door. "But I'm afraid we weren't expecting—*you*?"

Igor nearly echoed the sentiment as the little gray tabby slipped between the Doctor's legs and strode boldly into the foyer. Grimalkin paused, tail flicking back and forth as she looked up at Igor, still standing behind the door with the candlestick held high. Hastily, he shoved it behind his back, earning an unimpressed yawn.

"Terribly rude of me to show up unannounced like this, I know," came Auntie Mag's voice from the other side of the door. "But it's the prerogative of nosy women to spy on their neighbors, you know, and when I heard that someone had moved into the old Ravenwald place, I'm afraid my curiosity got the better of me."

"Not rude in the slightest," lied the Doctor, who was at his most wrathful when unexpected demands were made upon his time. "But I . . . thought you said your cottage was—"

"Washed away in the rains, yes." Through the crack of the door's hinges, Igor glimpsed Mag jerk a thumb over her shoulder. Her other hand rested atop the handle of her cane, its ivory skull grinning out from between her fingers. "But it's been such a terribly long time since there's been a living soul in this place that I simply had to see it for myself. May I come in?"

"Of course." A muscle twitched in the Doctor's jaw as he stepped aside, permitting her entry even as he glanced over his shoulder at Igor. "Some light, perhaps?"

"Certainly," Igor croaked, putting the candlestick back into its sconce and trying to look as though that were the whole reason he'd been lurking behind the door in the first place. "Welcome to Ravenwald Manor, Miss Devereaux."

Auntie Mag touched a finger to her skirt in the world's most abbreviated curtsy as she crossed the threshold, her cane taptapping against the marble floor.

"You're lucky," she told the Doctor. "It's hard finding help with actual manners."

Grim yowled in protest, which Mag answered with an irritable hushing sound.

"Igor is the very soul of delicacy," the Doctor said smoothly, which was a far more generous compliment than any he'd ever paid Igor directly. He gestured at the foyer's cracked marble floor, its shattered crystal chandelier. "Though as you can see, you've caught us at rather an inopportune time. Perhaps you might pay a call later, when the house is more suitable for hosting . . . ?"

"Oh, no need." Auntie Mag waved one hand airily and raised

her cane with the other. Faint violet lights shone within the ivory skull's eye sockets. "I only needed you to invite me in the one time."

"Master!" A sudden jolt of fear shot through Igor as he connected the dots, too late. "She's—"

"A witch," the Doctor said, his eyes widening behind his spectacles as a nexus of purple energy coalesced about the skull. The crystals scattered across the floor rattled, the smallest of them flying towards Auntie Mag's cane as if drawn by magnetic force.

"Got it in one," Auntie Mag crowed, the unearthly light from her cane turning her grin savage. "Not that it'll help you much."

She brought her cane down in exactly the same manner in which Igor would have used the candlestick to cave in her skull, had he realized her true nature in a timelier fashion. A writhing, undulating ribbon of violet light streaked across the field of shattered crystal towards the Doctor. Horrified, Igor watched his master raise his forearm against the curse blazing towards him, the air filled with a briny smell and the cackle of Auntie Mag's laughter.

There was a flash of blinding white light, followed by a sound like a thunderclap. Lightning leapt sparking from the Doctor in every direction, but the man himself stood unharmed—save for where the curse had burned through the sleeve of his lab coat, revealing the complex gauntlet of brass and clockwork beneath. An elaborate jumble of grinding gears, tangled copper wires, and spinning gyros, the gauntlet was the Doctor's primary defense against physical danger.

Or mystical, as it happened.

"Nifty trick," he said, adjusting one of the gauntlet's knobs. "Fortunately, properly applied galvanic force is more than capable of countering sorcerous energies. Igor?"

Igor, who had been padding as quietly as he could towards Auntie Mag, lunged forward, swinging the candlestick. Mag whirled about, her eyes flashing with the same violet light as she raised her cane.

Not fast enough. Igor's hands tightened on the candlestick's haft, anticipating the reverberation of the blow striking home—only for something small and furry to slam into his shins hard enough to knock his feet out from under him. He went down hard, small chunks of crystal digging into his back as the candlestick went rolling away across the floor.

Igor found himself looking up at the ceiling, where the last rays of sunlight had finally disappeared. Ravenwald Manor lay dark, save for the flashes of blue and violet light that lit the foyer as Auntie Mag tested her magic against the Doctor's invention.

Help him, Igor told himself. But before he could push himself to his feet, a regrettably familiar set of claws sank into his chest, weighing him down.

"I'm up by three, if we're keeping score," Grim informed him, flexing her claws to accentuate her point. "You want to press your luck with number four?"

Igor opened his mouth to utter some witty rejoinder, but to his dismay what came out instead was the reaction he'd first had upon hearing the gray tabby taunt him, back in the graveyard. "You can talk."

Grim licked her lips. "I see you're as smart as you look."

It was something the Doctor might say.

A whistling split the air as a bolt of magic bounced off the sphere of arcing electricity surrounding the Doctor and rebounded directly into the fallen chandelier. A rattling noise filled Igor's ears as the crystals still dangling from it glowed purple, suffused with the witch's magic, brighter and brighter—

"Down!" Igor shouted, hugging the cat to his chest with both hands as the chandelier exploded, sending shards of crystal flying in all directions like an enormous, unspeakably expensive grenade. Grim let out a protesting yowl, her claws digging even deeper into his chest as he rolled over, shielding her from the blast. Igor gritted his teeth as shards of crystal peppered his back, but these were only minor hurts; by some stroke of rare fortune he and the cat were on the very outer edge of the blast field.

The sound of battle between the Doctor and Auntie Mag had stilled, replaced by a faint ringing in Igor's ears. Groaning, he pulled himself upright, looking over to where the inventor and the witch stood at an apparent impasse.

"That," the Doctor said, gesturing with his ungauntleted hand at the sad remnants of the chandelier, "was a family heirloom."

"Your next of kin can send me the bill," Auntie Mag said, leaning heavily on her cane. "Now get out of my way, before—"

A scream split the air, so high and keening it was impossible to imagine it had issued from any human throat. The sound sent a frisson of fear down Igor's spine, one tingling vertebra at a time. In his lap, Grim quivered and pressed herself against him, every hair on her body standing on end.

A second scream joined the first.

There was a rush of air, a gasp like someone's last breath. A shadow blurred into life atop the grand staircase, becoming a shockingly pale man in a high-collared cape—though something about him looked oddly familiar. His eye caught Igor's, and his lips twisted in a mirthless smile.

Igor turned towards the door, driven by a blind urge to run.

Another blur in the air, and a redheaded woman in a diaphanous white gown stood blocking his way. She was tall and inhumanly beautiful, and so pallid that Igor's hand twitched with the instinct to reach for his scalpel. But she was no inert donor; that was made abundantly clear as she took a step forward, her bare feet making no noise on the crystal-littered marble.

"Stay back!" Auntie Mag barked, thrusting her cane upwards, towards the tall man with the hooked nose and drooping mustache who stood above them on the marble staircase. He hissed at her, his full lips peeling back to reveal incisors as long as knives.

"Great," the Doctor said, glowering at Auntie Mag as the redheaded woman bared fangs of her own. "You've woken the vampires."

8

[VERY] OLD NEIGHBORS

"VAMPIRES?"

The word resounded through the foyer, echoing off marble and crystal alike in a rich, thickly accented basso profundo. It spilled from between the sneering lips of the mustachioed arrival, his diction crisp and not at all hampered by the overlong canine teeth.

"What you call vampires are common vermin," he continued, punctuating the words with slow, deliberately imposing steps down the marble staircase. Neither his flowing cape nor his feet made any noise against the stair. "I and my bride are as far beyond such pitiful creatures as you think yourselves beyond the crude ape."

"Ah!" The Doctor leaned forward, ignoring the bared teeth of the redheaded vampire. "I'd no idea you had any familiarity with the evolutionary sciences, Lord—"

"Count," the vampire corrected, his mustaches twitching in annoyance. Igor realized where he'd seen that facial hair before: on the statue in the Ravensburg town square. "If you dare spend what little life remains to you in addressing me, you shall do so using my proper title."

There was another blur in the air where the Count stood.

Suddenly he was within arm's reach of the Doctor, leaning in so close that even Igor, at the Doctor's elbow, could smell the cloying, coppery stink of dried blood on the creature's breath.

"I am Count Heinrich Karl Edouard Ferdinand von Ravenwald, lord and master of Ravenwald Manor, Defender of the Woods and Vanquisher of the Steppelanders, Prince of Blood, Defiler of Baldonia, Ravager of—"

"Oh, will you *stop*?" The Count's wife tossed her curling red mane over one shoulder, rolling her eyes. "You can give yourself all the titles you want, Karl, but they don't have quite the *oomph* that you think they do."

Her words hung in the still air between the vampires and their prey.

"Oomph?" the Count asked, in a much less bombastic tone. Even his accent was less pronounced. "What do you mean, Cornelia?"

"I mean," she said, "people aren't terribly impressed by someone calling himself the Defiler of Baldonia when there hasn't been a Baldonia in six hundred years."

"Of course there isn't," the Count protested. "I defiled it."

"I know," Cornelia said tiredly. "Now, will you stop playing with your food? Some of us are thirsty."

The Count growled something inarticulate, but as he turned his attention back to the cornered group, the Doctor was already speaking.

"While I can't fault you for being in such an ill humor after we woke you so rudely—and prematurely—might I be so bold as to venture a supposition that you and your sort are . . ."—he swallowed audibly as the Count leaned in, his fangs drawing nearer to the Doctor's jugular vein—". . . that is, you wouldn't feed upon a relation, would you?"

Wariness entered those red eyes, though the fangs retreated only a matter of inches. "You claim to be my living kindred?"

"I am, in fact," the Doctor said, withdrawing a square of

parchment from his jacket pocket. Hands trembling more than usual, he unfolded it until it had expanded in his arms like a map, though a brief glance revealed it was in fact an ancient and tattered family tree.

"You see," the Doctor said, turning so that the Count could peer over his shoulder, in what was perhaps the single bravest action Igor had ever seen his master take, "here's you, at the top, with the bloody sword and the raven rampant beside your name . . ."

"My coat of arms," the Count nodded, leaning in. Behind him, his redheaded wife rolled her eyes. "And you claim . . ."

"This is me," the Doctor said hurriedly, jabbing his finger at a tiny nameplate at the extreme bottom right corner of the family tree, predeceased by nearly every other name within a radius of several branches. "Arguably, I've even a distant claim to inherit, given that the title passes to the eldest living member—"

The Count showed his fangs.

"—but happily, I've no interest in seeking to wrest the family title from you." The Doctor refolded the parchment and tucked it under one arm. "I assure you, on my honor . . ."

He put a hand to his chest as if greatly moved, a motion which caused a wooden stake to slip from an inner pocket of his jacket.

". . . that I mean you no harm," he finished, surreptitiously kicking the stake over to Igor. The vampire's faintly glowing red eyes followed the motion.

"Indeed," the Count murmured, sounding not at all convinced. "But if this is so, then why did you permit our greatest enemy to enter our ancestral home?"

The Doctor blinked in confusion. "Your greatest—"

"He means me," Auntie Mag sniffed, straightening from where she'd been standing heavily with both hands on her staff, as if drawing strength from it—or perhaps it was the other way around, Igor thought, as the eyes within the ivory skull winked purple. Mag's own eyes flickered from the Count to the Doctor. "Why do you think I was so keen to get past you?"

"You *used* me?" the Doctor asked, sounding far more offended at the prospect than he had at being magically assaulted.

"Magic fades past the threshold of another's dwelling," Mag said, tapping her cane against the marble. A burst of violet sparks issued from the contact, lighting her grim smile. "Unless you're invited in, of course."

"You used me," the Doctor repeated, sounding genuinely hurt.

"To get inside," Igor realized aloud, glancing between the witch, his master, and the pair of vampires. "You were after them, not us. We were just in the way."

"Clever boy," Mag said with an approving nod. Between her legs, Grim wrinkled her nose at him. "As for 'greatest enemy,' that's rather blowing it out of proportion, though I don't doubt they'd have tried the same if they'd ever managed to get past the wards on my cottage."

"A cottage which happens to no longer exist," Cornelia pointed out. "I passed by your place last night while I was hunting, Mag. Only it was just . . . gone. Washed away in the river?"

"Something like that," Auntie Mag said, her lips twisting sourly. "Fortunately, I found other accommodations before the sun went down."

That explained what she had been doing in the Hairy Nag, at least.

"Ravensburg not exactly being the sort of thriving metropolis one can simply disappear into," Auntie Mag continued, "I knew it'd only be a matter of time before the vampires tracked me down. So when I realized that the enigmatic gentleman who tried to charm me last night was planning to occupy Ravenwald . . . well, I saw an opportunity."

"Plus we needed a new place to stay," Grim added, causing everyone to look down at her. She peered brightly back up, tail wrapped about her front paws. "And at least the manor's dry."

The Doctor blinked. "Your cat talks."

"Alas, yes." Mag nudged Grim with her foot, earning an annoyed *mrrp.* "Even when no one's asked for her opinion."

"Everyone wants my opinion," Grim said primly, daintily licking one paw. "I'm a cat."

"You're a familiar," Mag corrected sourly. "Less an actual cat than simply a cat-shaped—"

"Enough of this," the Count said, massaging his temples with a long-nailed hand. "You have both invaded my home without my leave, and are both planning on killing me—yes, Doctor, I know that's a stake. I cannot tolerate such a bold attempt on my unlife, not when it threatens also the safety of my beloved bride—"

"Who said I was threatened?" Cornelia raised an eyebrow. "Mag's feud is with you, Karl. I've only ever gone along with it because you make such a fuss."

"Cornelia, love," the Count said in what Igor assumed was meant to be an aside, though at such close quarters it was clearly audible to all present, "I have asked you before not to address me by my forename in mixed company, let alone in the presence of my nemesis—"

"And I've asked you not to send me to harass the cranky witch across town," she countered, with a sidelong glance at Auntie Mag. "No offense."

Mag shrugged. "None taken."

"My dear." The Count rounded on her, his voice wavering somewhere between pleading and a whine. "I am trying to keep you safe, as outside forces threaten our home—"

"Keep me under your thumb, you mean." Cornelia folded her arms across her chest. The moonlight now streaming in from the high windows revealed a tracery of freckles along her forearms. "I've told you, this may be your ancestral home, but I've had enough. I want out."

"Not this again," the Count groaned, throwing a *See what I have to deal with?* look at the Doctor. The Doctor replied with a sympathetic grimace, which was a surprise; Igor was uncertain as to the exact nature of the Doctor's marital history, but certainly there had never been any mention of a Mrs. Doctor. "Have I not asked you to restrain these outbursts, Cornelia? Such behavior is unseemly within the bonds of marriage—"

"A marriage that's been dead for the last century," Cornelia said. "In every conceivable sense of the word. These nights we're barely even housemates."

"Housemates!" Igor exclaimed, clapping his hands as inspiration struck. The clap was unexpectedly loud, but perhaps that was just as well. Now he had everyone's attention.

"Look," he said, refusing to be put off by the vampires' red eyes, the Doctor's bespectacled ones, or Mag's faintly violet gaze. "Instead of fighting, why don't we simply share the manor? It's certainly large enough to accommodate everyone."

One corner of Auntie Mag's mouth twitched in a not-quite-smile. "Did you miss the part where the dear Count and I are trying to kill each other?"

"Why, though?" Igor asked.

"Real estate," Mag said, peering about at the manor's dusty furnishings.

"Principle, mainly," the Count said, tugging on his mustache. Cornelia rolled her eyes.

"So no real reason," Igor said, hoping that if the Count killed him for his temerity he'd at least do so quickly. But the elder vampire merely frowned in confusion, as if he hadn't considered matters from that angle before.

"Ravenwald Manor's big enough for all of us," Igor repeated, waving both arms about at the huge foyer. "Neither we nor Auntie Mag has any reason to stop you from drinking anyone's blood, other than our own."

"Which would be the height of unmannerly behavior between housemates," Mag pointed out, earning a glare from the Count.

"Exactly," Igor said, relieved beyond measure that *someone* at least seemed willing to hear him out. He glanced briefly down at Grim, who blinked as if encouraging him to continue. "I'm sure you and your wife have been feeding upon the townsfolk of Ravensburg without interruption for decades. Speaking for ourselves"—he looked at the Doctor, who was gazing at him with a curious, almost puzzled look, as if he were witnessing a family pet defend its doctoral thesis—"we have our own Great Work, which we've been pursuing for many years. Ravenwald would make an ideal setting to see it through to its completion."

"That reminds me," said Grim, tilting her head. "Why *do* you need all those body parts?"

"Nothing weird," Igor assured her, feeling himself color a little at the question. "Just bringing a corpse to life, is all."

"Hardly a challenge," the Count observed, with a smile that was all fangs.

"You're a necromancer, then?" Mag asked the Doctor, her face lighting with real interest.

"Only if you're being extremely technical about the definition of necromancy," the Doctor replied, plainly affronted. "The very nature of my Great Work—"

"Won't interfere with your drinking villager blood," Igor assured the Count, wresting the conversation back to his proposal of cohabitation. He nodded to Mag. "Nor will it interfere with your, err . . . cavorting with the Devil?"

"Please," Auntie Mag sniffed. "As if I'd ever dance with that old goat."

"Igor's right." Grim glided from between her mistress's feet to lean against Igor's leg. Her unblinking feline gaze swept across them all. "Our agendas don't actually conflict. And we've all got reasons to want privacy from Ravensburg and its villagers."

"Exactly," Igor said, bending to scratch between Grim's ears, which she graciously permitted. "I'm guessing everyone here has had some bad experiences in the past when it comes to pitchforks and torches?"

The identical grimaces on the faces of the Doctor, the Count, and the witch were answer enough.

"It's not the worst idea," Cornelia acknowledged, glancing at her husband.

"It is not," the Count agreed, smiling thinly. "Very well, then."

"All right." Auntie Mag raised her cane with both hands, the skull's eyelights blazing to violet life. The others tensed, but she merely began sketching arcane sigils in the air, each of which burned bright before fading, leaving only a searing afterimage. "Let's make it official."

"I recognize some of those," the Doctor said, blinking at the sigils issuing from the cane. "You mean to have us make a binding pledge?"

"How else is an agreement between three such as ourselves to be enforced?" the Count asked, smiling thinly. "Magic will keep us from violating the terms."

The Doctor still looked unconvinced. "Which are?"

"We three shall do no harm unto one another," Mag said. A faint line of sweat beaded on her wrinkled brow, as though pulling forth each of the burning sigils was costing her some effort. "Nor permit one another's harm through inaction, so long as we dwell within these walls. Nor interfere with one another's pursuits."

"Seems fairly comprehensive," the Doctor admitted. "And what do we swear by?"

"Blood, bone, and breath," the Count provided. "That is the typical offering, is it not?"

Mag nodded curtly. "If one of you would do the honors . . ."

"Happily." The Count raised a hand, palm outwards, into the space between himself, the Doctor, and the witch. A seam opened in his palm, as if cut by an invisible razor. A dark tendril of blood issued forth. "By my blood, I so swear."

Mag glanced at the Doctor. "Bone?"

"Right, hang on . . ." Behind his spectacles, the Doctor's eyes scanned the floor, all shattered crystal and broken marble. He darted downwards and then straightened, holding something between his thumb and forefinger.

"Ha!" he crowed, triumphantly holding a bloody tooth up to the glowing sigils. "Felt the damn thing come loose in the fighting. By my bone, I do swear."

The tooth leapt from the Doctor's hand, floating in the space between the three while the Count's blood orbited in ribbons around it.

"By my breath," Auntie Mag said, letting out a long exhalation, "I so swear."

Blood, bone, and breath hovered there a moment, then winked out of existence, replaced by a bright violet flash that lingered on the faces of those who had sworn to do one another no harm.

"It's done?" the Doctor asked, frowning a little. Mag nodded tiredly. "How will we know if it worked?"

"You could try breaking it," the Count suggested, giving him a mild look. "I for one will be quite amused when your blood comes streaming out your pores."

"That's one hypothesis I won't be testing," the Doctor said, putting both hands in his pockets. "Well, seeing that we're now neighbors, why don't we celebrate together over dinner?"

"No objections here," Mag said, leaning on her staff. "Do you cook, Doctor?"

"Igor does." The Doctor looked at Igor. "You said you already toured the kitchens?"

"Yes, Master," Igor said, plumbing his memory for something he could throw together from what he'd found in the pantry and what was left of their coach's supplies. "I'll have the table set for six in . . . two hours, say?"

"That shall be plenty of time for my bride to supply our dinner," the Count said, looking to his wife. "Darling, might I trouble you to go on a brief hunt . . . ?"

"Fine," Cornelia said. "It'll get me away from you, at least."

There was that curious blurring of Igor's vision, and a moment later she had vanished. The Count repeated the trick, though the faint rush of air left by his passage seemed to be heading in the direction of the crypt.

"I'll go fetch my things, then," Auntie Mag said, collecting her skirts about her and turning to stride towards the door. "Coming, Grimalkin?"

"Actually," Grim said from near Igor's leg, "I heard some rats in the walls. Do you mind if I . . . ?"

"Go wild," Mag said, waving a hand. "I'll see you in two hours."

"Leaving me just enough time for some autodentistry," the Doctor said, wincing as he rubbed his jaw. "There are some teeth in the spares collection, I believe, Igor?"

"There are, Master," Igor said, beaming up at him. Any moment now, the Doctor would congratulate him on his quick thinking in diffusing the situation, would thank him for so skillfully brokering a truce that left all parties, if not satisfied, then at least content with the new state of affairs. Any moment . . .

"Hopefully I find a molar that'll fit," the Doctor said instead, turning and picking his way across the shattered crystals. "I'd prefer stew if possible, Igor. Preferably with plenty of garlic."

"Garlic?" Igor furrowed his brow and pushed down the urge to tell the Doctor to fix his own damned stew. "I don't think the vampires would take kindly to that."

"Exactly," the Doctor hissed, leaning in close and lowering

his voice. "Magical oath or not, our new housemates are hardly to be trusted."

"Not even the cat?"

"*Especially* not the cat," the Doctor said with a shake of his head. "Be on your guard around them all, Igor, particularly the vampires. After all, if anything were to happen to you . . ."

Hope sprang anew in Igor's breast as he looked up at his master.

". . . I'd hate to have to go to the trouble of training a new assistant," the Doctor continued, "let alone hiring another cook. See you at dinner."

9

HOUSEMATES

DINNER TURNED OUT to be a rather tense affair.

They took their meal in the dining room, despite the Doctor's vehement protests that he required its massive table to organize his research notes. He relented only after the Count insinuated that it would be a dreadful shame if someone were to spill blood on the aforementioned notes. As crudely veiled a threat as this was, the Doctor clearly recognized it was made in earnest, and settled for spending the whole meal grumbling about the soup's lack of flavor.

"You've made this recipe before plenty of times," he told Igor after swallowing a spoonful. "Why doesn't it taste as good?"

"No garlic," Igor said, glancing at Cornelia and the Count sitting tersely side by side, each sipping from a goblet.

"I like the croutons," Grim put in, reaching a paw into her own bowl to bat one across the soup's cheesy surface. Igor wasn't sure why the feline familiar had insisted on having her own bowl of onion soup, given that her diet was assumedly carnivorous, but it would have been rude to refuse her.

"Stop that," Auntie Mag chided, dabbing her chin with a napkin. "Personally, I think the soup is rather tasty, garlic or not. You've a talented chef in your employ, Doctor."

"Igor does have his uses," the Doctor acknowledged, too determined to be put out to fully accept the compliment. "Truthfully, I find the body's continual need for sustenance exceedingly tiresome. So much time wasted replenishing our energy with food and drink, which would be better spent in unlocking the universe's grandest mysteries."

"It is the way of men to take what they have for granted," the Count said, swirling the blood in his goblet. Beside him, Cornelia coughed into her sleeve. "Nothing like eight centuries of a liquid diet to make you hunger for a prime rib."

"I've been meaning to ask about that, actually," Mag said, leaning forward with her elbows on the table. "You're Count Ravenwald, lord of Ravenwald Manor."

The Count's mustaches twitched as he sniffed. "Obviously."

"And you've been"—she waved vaguely as the Count sipped at his goblet, leaving his lips stained red—"a vampire. For eight hundred years?"

"Give or take a few decades," the Count said. "I fear I rather lost track after the second century or so."

"Right," Mag said, tapping her spoon thoughtfully against the side of her bowl. "I myself took up residence in Ravensburg only a few years ago. But the townsfolk say that there used to be people in the manor. Living people, I mean, within living memory."

"My descendants," the Count acknowledged, briefly making eye contact with the Doctor, whose curiosity seemed to be winning some inner battle against his petulant mood. "They dwelled here undisturbed for many years, yes."

"Until you decided to move back in." The Doctor jabbed his spoon towards the vampiric end of the table. "According to my third cousin Josephine's letters, you caused a stir."

"Mortals." The Count rolled his eyes. "You devour a few servants, and all of a sudden everyone starts complaining about how difficult you're making it to find decent help. Nobody in this century wants to work anymore."

"Where were you in the meantime?" Igor asked. He tried not to quail as the Count's red eyes turned on him. "I mean, if you moved *back* into the manor, where were you before?"

"Lots of places," Cornelia put in, drumming her fingers against her own bloody goblet. "Marovia for a few decades, and Cladbury. And Albaren before that . . ."

"I don't remember Albaren." The Count frowned.

"Maybe you should actually have gotten out to explore the Old City, then," Cornelia said, "rather than sitting around in that tower every night waiting for me to bring you dinner, then spending the rest of the night reciting poetry at me."

"Forgive me for wanting to introduce you to culture," the Count sniffed. "Some of those verses are hundreds of years old—"

"You *wrote* them!" Cornelia objected, scowling.

"Poetry is rather subjective, I find," Auntie Mag said, sipping her soup. "Though I must admit I'm rather partial to rhyming verses."

"That's just because most spells are in rhyme," Grim said, plucking a crouton from the soup with her teeth and dropping it onto the tablecloth. "At least, most of the ones that aren't in the Elder Tongue—"

Mag's eyes flashed violet as she gestured sharply. Grim's words abruptly trailed off into a series of chirps and trills, then an outraged series of mewls.

"You should watch your own tongue, kitty cat," Mag said primly. "Before something slips from it that ought not to."

Poor Grim let out a disconsolate meow. Igor was about to ask Mag to let her speak, but before he could, the Doctor leaned forward, eyes bright with interest.

"Did she say the Elder Tongue?" he asked Mag. "I must confess to a passing fluency in the language. It's used in a goodly number of the more esoteric alchemical manuals—"

"I'm quite aware of its provenance," Mag replied coolly, "as well as of the various uses to which it may be put. But," she said, raising a hand before the Doctor could interject further, "I'd prefer not to talk shop at the dinner table."

The Doctor's expression grew brittle. "I see."

An awkward silence fell over the dining room, broken only by a mewling complaint from Grim. Robbed of the power of speech, she'd resorted instead to furiously kneading at the burgundy tablecloth while making angry trilling sounds, a performance the Doctor and the Count were both observing with narrowed eyes. Belatedly, Igor realized that the tablecloth, like everything else in Ravenwald Manor, was likely a family heirloom.

"Could you . . ." Igor cleared his throat, and tried not to waver under Mag's gaze. Something about being fixed with her full attention made him feel like a beetle about to be pinned to a display board. "Err, if it isn't too much trouble, Miss Devereaux, I think Grimalkin has something to say."

"I'm sure she does," Mag muttered, pausing with her spoon halfway to her lips. Sighing, she waved a hand over Grim, along with a muttered imprecation that made Igor's eyeteeth hurt.

A gleam of violet light, and Grim's trills were replaced by more recognizable speech.

"—ing down your throat, I'll make a complaint to the Unsmiling King himself—"

"Grimalkin," Mag hissed, her eyes flashing briefly purple. "If you are so determined to abuse the gift of speech, I may be tempted to revert you to your true form."

Igor blinked. His knowledge of witches was scant, but evidently there was some truth to the rumor that their familiars were otherworldly beings bound into animal shapes.

Grim's tail stiffened angrily, and when she spoke next, her voice was cold. "We both know you wouldn't dare. I'd be useless to you if you turned me back."

"Try me," Mag murmured, glancing up and down the table at

their dinner companions. "Now, unless you'd like to have tentacles again instead of paws, I suggest you stop talking."

"Fine," Grim spat, ears flattening against her skull. She leapt down from the table and padded across the floor. "I smelled voles in the front yard, anyway."

A frosty silence descended over the dining table in the wake of her departure, interrupted only by Auntie Mag slurping loudly from her soup. Igor looked down at his own bowl and was mildly surprised to find it empty.

"There's plenty of soup left in the pot," he said, pushing his bowl away and rising from the table. "Would anyone care for seconds?"

No one did.

10

DIGNITY

RAVENSBURG WAS FAR less forbidding by daylight than it had been in the fading dusk.

The midday sun shone brightly down from a cloudless sky as the black coach trundled along the road into town. The sunlight glowing on their shingled roofs gave the tall, narrow houses a cheerful cast, as did the laundry lines strung between the upper windows.

Nor was this shift in mood limited to the architecture, Igor was relieved to note. Perhaps motivated by the change in weather, the townsfolk had taken to Ravensburg's streets, hustling industriously about the day's business or strolling leisurely across the way to chat with their neighbors. Igor caught himself wondering wistfully what it must be like to have dwelled in a single place for so long that folk would call to invite you onto their porch to share a drink, or into their home to share a meal.

Not that any such invitations would be forthcoming for him. A pall of silence seemed to shroud the black coach and its mares, quieting conversations and drawing wary gazes as it rolled along the narrow streets. Igor fixed his eyes on the road ahead, doing his best to ignore both the undisguised stares and the whispered speculations that trailed in his wake.

"... that odd professor fellow's manservant ..."

"... taken up residence in the old Ravenwald place, I heard ..."

"... stirring up things best left alone ..."

"... well if it *is* haunted, it's their heads ..."

At least, Igor tried to console himself, they were merely curious about the new arrivals to town. Curiosity was the first step along the long road that invariably ended in pitchforks and torches, but it was a far sight better than the suspicion that always followed. A grace period, of a sorts. It fell to him to make the most of it.

Igor put his head down and drove on.

* * *

Igor spent his afternoon perusing the stalls in the town square, where a market had sprung up under the watchful eyes of the statue at its center. The statue, as he had realized the night before, was carved in the likeness of the Count, down to the drooping mustache. He did his best to ignore it, instead turning his attention to checking items off his long list of groceries and laboratory supplies. Several items from the latter list would require more discreet inquiries—ones best made after sundown.

His grocery shopping concluded, Igor turned his attention towards greasing the palms necessary to ensure that nobody came poking about the site of their new laboratory asking untoward questions. A quick pop into the Hairy Nag with a small sack of copper coins landed Igor the names and addresses of several of the town's most prominent citizens, courtesy of the tavern's day shift bartender.

The sacks Igor conveyed to the town sheriff, burgomaster, and several other prominent or wealthy villagers were heavier, and the coins they contained were of gold and silver. Not for the first time, Igor found himself wondering whether his master's experiments in the noble art of alchemy had actually unlocked the secret of transmuting baser metals into gold. For all the travails and indignities the Doctor had suffered in his pursuit of the Great Work, he had never been in want of funds.

The town officials Igor spent his day bribing were not inclined to inquire after the provenance of their unexpected windfall, instead unanimously agreeing that Ravenwald lay too far outside the town limits to be worth paying close attention to, provided that its new inhabitants kept any potentially criminal activities confined to the manor's premises.

Gold, Igor reflected as the coach pulled up to the final address on the bartender's list, really was the most remarkable of all alchemical metals. What other substance could cause a man to willfully blind his own eyes, hold his own tongue?

"Guess this one will put the stuff to the test," he said, craning his neck to peer up at the church he'd parked the coach in front of. Its tall steeple was ever so slightly crooked, like a hat that hadn't settled quite right upon the wearer's head. No doubt this cant was due to some shift in the earth upon which the church sat, perilously close to the riverbank. Even from this angle, Igor could see the faint line of discoloration along its stone walls denoting the high-water mark of the recent floods.

"Maybe they're taking up donations for repairs," he mused. He patted the last sack of coins the Doctor had issued him, tucked snugly in the largest of his coat pockets. It would be nice to think that at least some of their palm-greasing funds might go towards a worthy cause.

Igor had been unsurprised when the Hairy Nag's bartender had named the local priest, one Friar Bernhard, as one of the key townsfolk he'd have to win over. Religious leaders were often even more influential than their secular counterparts when it came to swaying the masses of small towns like this one, and seldom any less vulnerable to the allure of gold. And according to the bartender, few of Ravensburg's citizens were as universally respected as Friar Bernhard.

The front doors of the church stood invitingly open, organ music issuing softly from within. Igor slipped inside, blinking as his eyes adjusted from the fading light of early evening to the dimness of the church.

When they did, he found that he was far from alone.

The wooden pews were crowded with townsfolk, though there were none of the chorused hymns or recited prayers indicative of a service in progress. Instead, the parishioners sat leaning forward with heads bowed, as though gravity itself bent them towards the altar. Following their collective gaze, Igor was met with the familiar sight of an open casket.

He'd interrupted a funeral.

Dread seized his heart. For a panicked moment he considered turning tail and sprinting back to the coach, only to realize with dismay that several of the nearest parishioners—no, he corrected himself, the nearest *mourners*—had turned in their seats to gaze at the latecomer.

At least, Igor consoled himself as he lowered himself into the nearest unoccupied pew, he was already dressed in black.

Igor had witnessed his share of funerals, typically while lurking out of sight and waiting impatiently for the casket to be buried and the bereaved to disperse. This was the first he'd attended inside a church, and he found himself enjoying the mournful wailing of the pipe organ and the strong, sonorous tones of the eulogy, delivered by a broad-chested man who must have been Friar Bernhard.

Igor was acutely conscious of the coins bulging in his coat pocket. To distract himself, he turned his attention to the stained glass windows. These usually depicted local saints, or stories from the scriptures, but whoever had cast these particular windows had apparently possessed a taste for more abstract art. Igor admired them anyway, tracing the contours of where the pieces of glass had been soldered together, appreciating how the fading sun refracted the light into a rainbow of different hues . . .

"Sorry to keep you waiting."

Igor only just barely kept from yelping as he turned about, discovering with a start that the funeral service had ended and that the majority of the mourners had filed out the door. A few of those still lingering cast a curious look at Igor, and at the priest standing above him. Up close, Friar Bernhard was not as tall as he'd looked at the altar, yet there was something in his craggy face and easy bearing that made him seem to take up more space than his stature alone could account for.

"Didn't mean to give you a start, lad," Friar Bernhard said, putting a hand on Igor's shoulder. Igor looked down, surprised both at the friendly touch and at the scars on the friar's knuckles. "Are you all right?"

"I was looking at the stained glass," Igor managed.

"An enduringly popular pastime within these hallowed walls," Friar Bernhard said, chuckling ruefully. The stained glass cast a faint rainbow halo across the bald dome of his head. "Particularly while I'm sermonizing, though I daresay I kept their attention tolerably well this evening. Did you know Matthias?"

"Matthias?" Igor asked, wrong-footed.

"Matthias Fleischer." Friar Bernhard glanced towards the altar. "That'd be a no, then."

Igor's stomach sank as he realized that Matthias must have been the donor—no, the *corpse*—lying in the casket. His cheeks colored. "I didn't mean to interrupt."

"There are no interruptions in this house, my son." Igor fought down a wince at the peculiar feeling those last two words summoned in him. "The Almighty and I both have time for everyone who steps through these doors, whatever the reasons that have called them here."

"Well." Igor cleared his throat and did his best to ignore the uneasy twist of guilt stirring in his gut, just beside the sack of coins in his pocket. He opened his mouth, intending to make some tentative overture on behalf of his master, but what came out instead was: "Who was he?"

"Matthias?" The lines of Friar Bernhard's craggy face deepened. "A young man, taken from us suddenly by mischance. We weep for his loss, even as we rejoice in what life he had."

"I'm sorry," Igor said. He plumbed his memory for a sentiment more appropriate to the moment. "Gone too soon."

Friar Bernhard surprised Igor by taking a seat beside him. He was a large man, broad-shouldered and big-bellied, and the wooden pew groaned as Igor scooted over to make room.

"Too soon," the friar repeated, leaning forward and folding his arms on the back of the next pew. "I suspect we all think as much, when our time comes. But there is something keenly unfair in a light as bright as Matthias Fleischer's being snuffed out when it had scarcely begun to shine. I expect that I'll shed more than a few tears when it comes time to bury the poor lad."

"I didn't see a churchyard out front," Igor said before he could stop himself.

"Nor will you find one out back. We're too near to the river. It'd be a disservice to the deceased if they were to wash downstream after the first heavy rainfall." He shook his tonsured head, which was no longer lit with rainbows, as the sun had gone down. "No, lad, the dead deserve to stay buried. They've suffered enough as it is."

"I . . ." Igor could think of no answer to that, or at least none that would not condemn him in the kindly friar's eyes. Instead, he reached into his coat. "I'd like to make a donation. To your church."

Friar Bernhard raised one gray brow. "Is that why you came here tonight, my son?"

Not trusting himself to speak, Igor nodded. He drew the bulging sack from his coat and wordlessly handed it over. Friar Bernhard took it carefully in both hands, his brows lifting slightly at its weight. He looked inside, then slowly back up at Igor.

"That," he said after a moment, "is probably more gold than has ever passed through these doors before tonight."

That was rather the point of a bribe, Igor thought. He forced what he hoped was an ingratiating smile. "It's meant to be a *generous* donation."

"The generosity of a gift is proportionate to the wealth of the giver," the friar said carefully. "The beggar who gives his only coin to a good cause is more charitable than the lord who parts with a chest of gold, then returns home to feast in his palace."

He set the sack gently down on the pew and slid it across to Igor. "Your offer is appreciated, but I cannot accept it."

"But . . ." Igor felt as if he'd been struck on the head. Never, in all the years he'd worked for the Doctor, had someone refused a bribe.

He looked about the church, taking in the mismatched wood of the pews, the threadbare altar cloth, the tarnished brass candles, the uneven walls. "This place is falling apart."

Friar Bernhard raised an eyebrow.

"I—I mean," Igor stammered, sliding the sack back towards the friar, "couldn't you use this to fix up the place? Especially if the river's eating away at the foundations?"

"I daresay I could," Friar Bernhard said softly, looking down at the sack. "Daresay that with what you're offering I could rebuild the old place. Shore up the foundations, erect a new bell tower, maybe even pay for new windows."

"You could," Igor agreed, though privately he thought the current stained glass was pretty enough.

"I could," Bernhard said, rubbing his scarred hand over his shorn pate. "And all it would cost me is knowing that I'd spent such a windfall on my building, while the poor of my parish struggle to feed their children."

Gold clinked as he pushed the sack back towards Igor. As he

did so, his sleeve rode up, revealing the barest hint of a tattoo, though it was covered before Igor could glimpse anything more than a handful of vaguely runic shapes.

"This old place has held up for better than three centuries," the friar said, looking up at the church's rafters. "Maybe it'll last through the next one, maybe it won't. My charge isn't to care for a building, but for the people who step through its doors. To treat them with kindness and dignity." Friar Bernhard turned his head towards the open casket lying on the altar. "In death as well as life."

"Then use this," Igor insisted, rising from the pew and putting the sack of gold directly into the friar's hand, "to cover the funeral expenses."

Bernhard hefted the sack and fixed Igor with a shrewd look. "This much would cover half a year's worth of funerals, I reckon. You some sort of serial murderer?"

"Certainly not," Igor said with a nervous laugh, studiously avoiding thinking about that brief but harrowing period when the Doctor had decided to create fresh donors to the Great Work. "Use the rest to . . . feed the poor, or however else you think it would best be spent."

Friar Bernhard gazed long at the sack of gold in his hands.

"That's a heavy purse to trust to one man's judgment," he said at last. "May what little wisdom I possess prove equal to the task."

"I'm certain it will be," Igor said, sliding past him in the confines of the pew. A weight had lifted from him upon handing over the gold, and he was eager to continue with the evening's tasks. He still had several items of more questionable legality to acquire, and finding a decent black market in a town as modest as Ravensburg would no doubt—

"Under whose name?" Friar Bernhard asked, freezing Igor in his tracks.

"Name?" Igor echoed, turning reluctantly from the open

church doors, beyond which Ravensburg's nighttime fog had already begun to gather.

"For your generous donation," the friar clarified, still holding the sack of gold in both hands. "Who should I say is making this gift?"

Igor hesitated. This was the whole point of having come to this house of worship in the first place. All he needed to do was name the Doctor and mention that he was residing at Ravenwald, and the friar's subsequent gratitude would be sufficient to allay any concerns his flock might have regarding their strange new neighbors.

Igor's gaze caught on the casket lying on the altar. For the first time, he allowed himself to look directly at the body lying within. A young man, scarcely older than Igor had been when he'd first entered the Doctor's service. His cheeks were beardless and unlined, his eyes closed. Peaceful, in a way that so few of Igor's donors ever seemed to be.

Dignity, Igor thought, echoing the friar's words, *in death as well as life.*

He turned to Friar Bernhard, who fixed him with a knowing gaze. Igor inhaled deeply.

"Make it anonymous."

11

THE APOTHECARY

IT WAS FULL night outside by the time Igor returned to the black coach. A thick fog had rolled in off the river to blanket the streets, restoring the sinister atmosphere of the night before. Shivering, Igor hugged his coat about him as he hurried towards the coach, eager to finish the day's tasks and return to Ravenwald, perhaps to a warm fire and a mug of something hot.

He hadn't quite made it to the coach when a lone figure came hurrying towards him from the fog, a voluminous cloak billowing out behind. Igor tensed, steeling himself for confrontation as he shrank against the side of the black coach.

The cloaked figure passed beneath one of the streetlamps, lifting her hood enough for Igor to catch a glimpse of the delicate, doll-like features and golden curls of Ruth, the Hairy Nag's nighttime barkeep. Only she was headed *away* from the tavern.

Nor had she seen him, Igor realized, as she passed from the circle of dim lamplight to stride briskly down a sloping side street towards the waterfront. Whatever the reason for her hurry, it had nothing to do with him—only his uneasy nerves had made him believe so.

Still pressed against the side of the coach, Igor breathed a sigh of relief. As soon as he returned to Ravenwald, he promised himself, he'd fix a strong cup of tea.

Movement in the fog ahead caught his eye. Another shadow, this one slinking along the walls of the nearest buildings with motions quick and furtive. Had Igor not already been looking in precisely that direction, they would have escaped his notice entirely.

Instead, as the figure turned down the side street, Igor caught the gleam of lamplight reflecting off a mass of long, curly red hair.

"Cornelia," Igor breathed. Out hunting for her dinner and the Count's, no doubt—and judging from the direction she was headed, Ruth was tonight's main course.

The sensible thing, Igor knew, would be to ignore what he'd just seen. To clamber onto the coach and resume searching for whatever passed for a black market in Ravensburg. Interfering in their vampiric housemates' dietary habits would endanger not only Igor himself but the entire Great Work.

But . . .

But Ruth had treated them as she might have treated any other customers, despite Igor's awkwardness and the Doctor's rudeness. As kindnesses went, it was a small one, hardly a step above common decency—but Igor had experienced precious little of either in his life.

"I won't be long," Igor said, giving the horses an affectionate pat.

Then he set off down the sloping side street, towards the waterfront and after the vampire.

* * *

Igor trailed Cornelia at a distance, trusting to the occluding fog and her focus upon her prey to keep her from noticing him. If the stalking vampire had any idea that she herself was now being pursued, she showed no sign, only followed doggedly after the barkeep as she entered Ravensburg's waterfront.

The fog hung even more thickly here, though the fog did little to dampen the shouts and raucous cries issuing from the dockside taverns, gambling dens, and other houses of ill repute of the district. Ruth made straight towards one of the latter, which stood so near the docks and quays that he could hardly believe it had been spared by the recent floods. Igor watched as she slipped inside, then shifted his gaze back to Cornelia—

She was gone.

Igor turned, scanning the fog, wondering if she'd performed the same disappearing trick she'd displayed back in the manor—

Chill fingers settled around his neck.

"Did your Doctor send you to spy on me, then?" came the vampire's voice in his ear, cold as her hands.

"No?" Igor squeaked. His fright gave the denial an upward lilt that transmuted it into a question.

"Very convincing," Cornelia said, hands still on his neck. Not squeezing, merely holding him in place. "Why else would you be stalking me, then?"

"The girl," Igor managed. He pointed at the doorway Ruth had disappeared into. "I saw you following her."

"And you decided to follow me, too?" Cornelia released him. Igor turned to look up at her, found she was looking down at him with a bemused expression. "To what end?"

"I . . ." Igor swallowed, embarrassed. "She was nice to me."

"She was . . ." A smile crept across Cornelia's face, broad and genuine and only a little bit frightening. "You thought I was going to drink her blood?"

"Well," Igor said, acutely conscious of her smile's gleaming fangs, "yes. I mean, you're on the hunt, aren't you?"

"I am," Cornelia said after a moment's consideration, glancing towards the door the barkeep had entered. The sign above it read ALEXEI'S APOTHECARY in a cheery handwritten font. "But that girl isn't my victim."

"Who is, then?" Confusion drew Igor's brows together.

Cornelia's fanged smile widened. "I'll show you."

* * *

The bell above the apothecary doorway jangled merrily at Igor's entrance. Behind him, Cornelia stood hesitating on the threshold, not yet having been invited inside.

"One moment!" boomed a basso voice from somewhere near the back of the shop. The speaker emerged a moment later from behind a beaded curtain, his arms laden with packages wrapped in oilcloth. Long white hair stuck out at all angles from beneath his tricorn hat, yet he moved with unexpected sprightliness as he set his burdens down upon the countertop, then turned to regard his visitors with an appraising eye.

"Do not stand there with door hanging open!" he said, waving them forward. "Come in, before the fog follows you inside!"

Igor did as he was bidden, Cornelia following close behind. If the proprietor was at all surprised at being visited after sunset by a walleyed hunchback and a beautiful redhead, it didn't register on his broad, shockingly pale face.

"Welcome," he said, wiping his hands on the front of his apron, "to Alexei's Apothecary! How might I be of service?"

"Are you a pirate?" Cornelia asked, seemingly unable to tear her gaze from his hat.

"A smuggler," Alexei said, touching two fingers to his tricorn's brim. "Piracy is rather a diurnal activity, I'm afraid. Besides, I've mostly retired from the more . . . active side of the trade."

Igor blinked. "You're a black marketeer?"

"Just so," Alexei admitted cheerfully. "People bring me things from far away. Sometimes things others might regard askance, were they to be bought and sold openly. Whereas I am more than happy to facilitate such transactions discreetly. Speaking of which, what brings you to my humble shop this fine and foggy eve?"

"Alchemical supplies," Igor said. His heart rose as he looked about at the jars of strange fluids, vials of exotic elixirs, and beakers of mysterious compounds lining the walls. Many of them he recognized by sight, and those few he did not were neatly labeled.

Yes, Igor decided, Alexei's Apothecary would provide nicely for the Great Work's needs—and Igor's more furtive ones. No more having to filch alchemical ingredients from the Doctor's stores.

Cornelia seemed quite taken with the sheer variety of merchandise on offer. Unsurprising, Igor supposed, when most shops closed well before sundown.

Alexei's pale face brightened. "Then you have come to the right place, my hunchbacked friend. I've bezoars and toadstones, metals and substances from antimony to calamine, vitriols of every color, aqua fortis . . ."

"All of that will do nicely," Igor said, consulting his mental list. He glanced about, looking for Ruth. "Do you mind if I browse?"

"Not at all." Alexei handed Igor a wooden shopping basket. "Call if you need assistance."

Cornelia trailed after Igor with an air of vague interest as he went to the wall of alchemical ingredients. The Doctor's last attempt at bringing a Subject to life had left their stores badly depleted, requiring Igor to restock many key ingredients.

"What's the use of all these things?" Cornelia asked, peering closely at a vial of clear liquid labeled ALKAHEST. "I thought you and your Doctor were bringing a corpse to life, not transmuting lead into gold."

"Very funny," Igor said, glancing over his shoulder to ensure that Alexei hadn't overheard. Fortunately, the albino shopkeeper had settled in behind his register with a tattered paperback. "There's more to the Great Work than stitching together a few body parts and zapping them with lightning."

Cornelia cocked her head. "Lightning?"

"Applied galvanic forces are integral to resuscitating the Subject," Igor said, quoting the Doctor by rote. "But that's only the final step. While I'm busy attaching the Subject's limbs and installing its organs, the Doctor is hard at work plumbing the mysteries of the alchemical arts . . ."

He glanced sidelong at her as he carefully plucked up the vial of alkahest and set it carefully in the shopping basket. "Sorry. I don't mean to bore you—"

"You're not." Igor was taken aback at the earnestness in Cornelia's tone. "Trust me, it takes a lot less than two hundred years to grow tired of having the same conversations with the same person. I'm quite starved for new topics of discussion."

"All right," Igor said uncertainly. "But stop me if you do get bored. The Doctor says I have a tendency to prattle on."

Something hard flickered in Cornelia's gaze, but Igor caught it only out of the corner of his eye as he returned his attention to the shelves. "Anyway, each of the Subject's limbs and organs receives multiple alchemical treatments. Most slow or reverse the natural pace of decay, while others are meant to improve the Subject's bodily systems—better cardiovascular efficiency, faster firing synapses, and so forth. To say nothing of balancing its humors—"

He turned down an aisle and nearly collided with Ruth, who was bent over inspecting the contents of a lower shelf. She hurriedly straightened and backed away.

"Oh!" Igor blurted. "I— Sorry, I didn't see you there."

"It's all right," Ruth said, hastily replacing a jar and turning it so that its label was facing away. Catching Igor's gaze, she looked quickly away—but not fast enough to hide the purpling bruise threatening to eclipse her left eye.

That hadn't been there the other night.

"I—" he started, but Cornelia had already stepped towards the girl. This close, Ruth looked hardly older than Cornelia, who must have been turned into a vampire well before she'd celebrated her twenty-fifth birthday.

"Can I help you?" Cornelia asked.

Ruth hazarded a sidelong look. "You're not— You don't work here, do you?"

"No," Cornelia said. "But if you're looking for . . ." She plucked up the vial Ruth had just placed on the shelf and held it to the light. "Arsenic?"

"I—" Ruth's swallow was loud enough that Igor wondered that Alexei didn't hear it from behind the register. "I don't. That is—"

"It's all right." Cornelia set the vial back onto its shelf with a soft *clink*. "I'm a friend."

Ruth's back stiffened beneath her oversized cloak. "I don't even know you."

"No, you don't." Cornelia shook her head gently. "But I've been where you are now, once upon a time. Who was it that blackened your eye?"

The other woman's lips pressed tightly together, as if she were afraid that the answer might come tumbling out if she opened them.

"Your husband?" Cornelia pressed, her voice softer than Igor had ever heard it. "Your father?"

Those lips trembled, parted. "Uncle."

"Ah." Cornelia's voice was flinty. "How many times?"

Ruth's reply was a whisper so hoarse that Igor had to strain to catch the words. "I don't know."

Cornelia nodded briskly, like this was precisely the answer she'd expected. Perhaps it was. "His name?"

Ruth looked up so suddenly that her hood slipped free from her head, revealing her shock of blond curls. "What are you going to do?"

"Make certain he never lays a hand on you again," Cornelia said firmly. "And save you the price of a bottle of arsenic."

Ruth's laugh was disbelieving. "What, you're the Angel of Mercy?"

Cornelia regarded her levelly. "What if I am?"

"You can't be." This time the laugh died on Ruth's tongue. "The Angel's just a folktale."

"Most such tales have a grain of truth to them," Cornelia said. "Some more than others. Your uncle?"

Ruth glanced furtively about the shop, then stood on tiptoe to whisper in Cornelia's ear. Cornelia listened, nodded, then lightly put a hand on the other woman's shoulder.

"Find a place to stay the night," she advised. "Someplace safe, with someone you can trust."

"I will," Ruth said, nodding. Then, daring to look Cornelia full in the face: "Thank—"

"Don't." Igor flinched at the sharpness in Cornelia's voice. "Only promise me that the next time you see someone in straits like yours, you remember this moment, and do what you can to help her. Promise me that."

A nod, and Ruth fled from the shop, the bell jangling merrily above the door as she departed.

"Will she be all right?" Igor asked.

"She will be once I'm done."

"With what?" Igor asked, though he suspected he already knew the answer.

"Come, Igor." Cornelia's smile was all fangs as she headed for the door. "We're going hunting."

12

HUNTING

"DO YOU DO this often?" Igor asked a short while later, as they lurked atop the tiled rooftop of a warehouse that looked to have been abandoned after the recent floods. "Hunting down men like . . . well, bad men?"

"I used to," Cornelia said, not looking at him. She sat crouched like a gargoyle on the edge of the rooftop, her gaze fixed upon the lamplit window across the way. "Years ago, back when I was first turned. When I thought I could use my curse for good. Less often, these nights."

This high above the foggy streets, there was less mist and more sky above them. In the moonlight, Cornelia looked not a day past twenty, but the jaded weariness in her voice belonged to someone far older.

"That must have been a long time ago," Igor ventured. "If you don't mind my saying so."

The barest hint of fangs peeked out from beneath Cornelia's upper lip. "It's been more than two hundred years since I last saw the sun."

Igor glanced upwards. "At least you still have the stars."

Cornelia's gaze followed his. "I suppose I do. Funny how the heavens are always there above us, yet we forget them so easily."

"Heavens," Igor repeated. "Back in the apothecary, Ruth called you the Angel of Mercy."

"She did." Cornelia's mouth twisted downwards in a wry expression that could have been either a smile or a frown. "Every village and hamlet has its local saints—the smaller the town, the more obscure the saints. I don't remember any longer if there was an Angel of Mercy before I was turned, but that's what the women of Ravensburg took to calling me, after the first few years of my feeding on the men who preyed upon them."

"That seems a poor way for a vampire to keep a low profile."

"I was always careful." Cornelia's red curls bounced as she shrugged. "Discreet. But folk caught glimpses of me now and again, and word began to spread. The women of Ravensburg whispering to one another that if your husband raised a fist to you, if your brother laid a hand on your daughter, then a prayer to the Angel of Mercy would see to it that he never did again."

"And you . . . answered their prayers?" Igor turned his gaze back to the window, waiting for some sign that Ruth's uncle was in residence.

"As many as I could. For as long as I could."

"What changed?"

"Nothing." Cornelia looked down at her hands. "Which was precisely the problem. Men like the ones who blackened that girl's eye kept appearing, year after year and generation after generation. Cropping up like weeds, and no matter how many I rooted out . . ."

Her gaze drifted downwards, watching the ebb and flow of foot traffic on the streets below. "There stopped seeming much point. So when Karl moved us to another of his estates, this one in distant Marovia, I hardly fought him on it. So the Angel of Mercy passed from local legend to an old wives' tale, to just another piece of half-remembered folklore."

"But you're here now," Igor pointed out. He gestured at the window across the way.

"Well." Moonlight shone off Cornelia's fangs. "Sometimes I get tired of venison."

"Oh." Igor cleared his throat. "Can I ask a question?"

Cornelia glanced at him. "You want to know why I'm the one who does all the hunting, not Karl. The Count, to you."

Igor ran a head over his scalp. "I don't mean to pry—"

"You're not." Cornelia looked back across the way, her smile fading. "How much do you know about vampires, Igor? Aside from the restrictive diet and the uniquely awful sunburns."

"You're quite polite when it comes to social calls," Igor said, thinking of how she'd had to wait to be invited inside Alexei's establishment. "Am I right in guessing that you're quite allergic to garlic as well?"

The fanged smile's ghost made a brief appearance. "Highly."

"Then I'm afraid we've exhausted my expertise on the subject."

"Allow me to fill some gaps in your knowledge, then." Cornelia rested a hand lightly on her neck. "For one thing, vampires are mystically bound to obey the commands of the one who turned them."

Igor stared at her, aghast. "You don't have free will?"

"Oh, I do, to some extent," Cornelia said bitterly. "Even though the very blood in my veins compels me to obey Karl's whims, I can resist. For a time, at least."

"What happens if you don't do as he tells you?" Igor asked, morbidly curious. He seldom found reason to disobey his master's orders, not when the Great Work was so self-evidently important, but there was something chilling about the idea of being unable to refuse.

"It hurts," Cornelia said quietly. "He's permitted me to leave before, sometimes even for weeks at a time. But the blood always calls me back to him in the end. I think it amuses him, like giving a hooked fish some slack before reeling it back in."

Igor shivered. "And there's no way to free yourself from him?"

"Not unless he releases me from our bond," Cornelia said quietly. "But he'll never allow it. Easier most nights to spare myself the indignity and do our hunting as he asks. Speaking of which . . ."

She pointed across the way. A man had appeared in the window, little more than a silhouette against the lamplight—albeit a silhouette that was holding a bottle and sported a short, goatish beard dangling from his chin.

"Is that him?" Igor asked.

"This is the address, and the beard matches the description she gave me." Cornelia stood and rolled her neck as though working out a kink. "I won't be long."

"Wait." Igor scrambled to his feet, acutely conscious of the rooftop's sharp slope and the long fall to the street below. "I want to help."

Cornelia's brows raised. "Why?"

"I . . ." Igor tried to identify the impulse which had led him to such a bold proclamation. Not some desire to avenge Ruth's mistreatment at her uncle's hand; whatever protective urge had led him to intervene in what he thought had been Cornelia's attempt to drain the girl did not extend so far as that.

No, what had propelled him to his feet was the same urge that had led him to follow the Doctor across all the years and miles, to labor unceasingly over another man's vision. The desire to be a part of something greater than himself. Not just to help, but to prove he *could* help.

That he was useful.

"Do you have any plans for the body?" he asked, looking at the silhouette framed in the window. "Once you've drained it, I mean. Exsanguinated donors are far easier to harvest from."

"Ah." Cornelia's smile returned, bright beneath the moonlight. "In that case, tell me, Igor . . . have you ever wanted to be an actor?"

Igor stared at her. "Have I ever wanted to *what*?"

* * *

At least the role Cornelia had cast Igor in hadn't required a costume.

Safely back on ground level, he crossed the narrow cobblestone street to the house they'd been surveilling, pulling a cloaked young woman after him.

"Not so gently," she muttered in his ear as they reached the doorstep. "You're supposed to be put out with me, remember?"

Igor swallowed both his answer and his mounting apprehension. He'd learned early on that he was no good at play-acting; the other orphans had wasted little time in pointing out that his distinctive physical attributes presented an insurmountable obstacle to the willing suspension of disbelief. Evidently it had lain beyond their powers of imagination to accept the possibility of a crusading knight or brave musketeer with a crooked back.

His hand had somehow become a fist, which was just as well. He rapped it smartly against the door, three times.

No answer.

Igor knocked again. Still nothing.

"Maybe he went to bed," he said after the third knock, but this supposition was immediately belied by the muffled echo of heavy footfalls and muttered curses from inside. Igor stepped back as the door slammed open, releasing a foul-smelling cloud of sour body odor and stale beer into the night.

"Give it a rest, you insufferable pieces of—" the goateed man at the center of the cloud was saying, gesticulating with the mostly empty bottle in his free hand. The other held the door open as he trailed off, squinting hard at the sight of a hunchbacked stranger and a woman wearing an oversized cloak upon his doorstep. "Wazzall this, then?"

"Begging your pardon, sir," Igor said, clearing his throat and tugging at his companion's sleeve, "but I believe I found your niece wandering the streets, alone and unchaperoned. May we come in?"

Those narrowed eyes shifted from Igor to the cloaked woman, whose downcast gaze kept her features obscured beneath her hood, then to the street behind them.

"Get inside, girl," he snarled, reaching out and grabbing her by the upper arm. She crossed over the threshold without resistance as the drunk shifted his gaze to Igor. "Much obliged t'ya, I'm sure. Now shut the door."

"Gladly," Igor said, stepping inside and closing it after him. The house smelled as much like a distillery as its owner, who scowled down at Igor in angry confusion.

"What d'you think you're playing at, showing up here having laid hands on my Ruth—"

Pale hands reached up and pulled the hood down, revealing not the barkeep's golden curls but Cornelia's red ones. And her even redder eyes, and her long white fangs.

"Thank you for inviting us in," she said, and sank those fangs into the drunken uncle's neck before he could scream.

Every fiber in Igor's being implored him to turn and run, yet he could not help watching as the man went limp in Cornelia's arms. She sank to the floor beneath his weight, her mouth still fastened to his neck and her hands supporting him like some blasphemous parody of a pietà. A faint sigh issued from the man's lips, and then he stilled.

"Cornelia?" Igor asked, clearing his throat. "Shouldn't you—"

Her head snapped up towards him, her eyes shining brightly scarlet, her lips and chin coated darkly crimson. She hissed, displaying reddened fangs as long as Igor's little fingers.

"I mean," he said, fighting down the urge to shrink away, "aren't you meant to bring him to the Count?"

Cornelia blinked and shook her head, pressing her lips together. When she opened them her fangs had retreated to the more modest length Igor was accustomed to.

"Sorry," she said, sounding a bit as though Igor had caught her filching from the cookie jar. "Nearly got carried away there."

"It's all right." Igor squatted to examine her victim. The man's chest still rose and fell, which Igor supposed was a good sign—for the vampires, at least. "What do you need me to do?"

"Grab his legs," Cornelia said, seizing him beneath the arms. Igor hurried to do as he'd been bidden and found that he was taking less of the man's weight than he'd expected. Cornelia's slender appearance belied her vampiric strength. "The coach is still around the corner?"

"It is," Igor said, having driven it to the address provided at her behest. "You sure nobody's going to see?"

"Even if they do," Cornelia grunted as they maneuvered towards the door, "nobody's going to say anything in this part of town. Now come on."

They stumbled out into the night, where the fog hung less heavily than it had nearer the docks. Still, none of the townsfolk spared so much as a second glance at the sight of a slight young woman and a hunchback with a limping gait carrying a dazed man down the street. Even the smallest villages had their seedier neighborhoods, and this was evidently Ravensburg's.

Igor grunted as they rounded the corner, hauling the vampire's stupefied victim towards the mews behind the house. The black coach stood waiting, the horses stamping restlessly at the cobblestones. Together they bundled in their semiconscious cargo alongside the groceries and alchemical supplies Igor had procured earlier in the evening.

"Going to be a tight fit," Igor noted, shutting the coach door. "Now, let's—"

"Wait." Cornelia pointed upwards as a shadow detached itself from the nearest rooftop, bounding nimbly down windowsills and balconies until it reached a fencepost. "Is that . . . ?"

"Grimalkin?" The little gray tabby hopped down from the fencepost. Tail held high, she trotted towards them. Something small, wriggling, and glowing faintly silver dangled from her mouth.

"What are *you* doing here?" Igor asked, perplexed.

"Mrrp," Grim said around her mouthful of . . .

"And what *is* that?" Igor asked, bending for a better look at the silvery creature Grim had caught. It was vaguely centipedal in shape, and it certainly squirmed like one—only ordinary centipedes didn't glow silver, and weren't translucent, and certainly didn't have tiny human fingers in place of legs.

"Mrrp," said Grim again, then dropped the glowing centipede thing. Its finger-legs flailed as it hit the cobblestones. "I followed you, obviously. Figured you could give me a lift back to the manor. Saw you park the coach just after I caught this ephemeral."

"But what *is* it?" Cornelia asked, looking faintly ill as the centipede thing began scuttling away with erratic sidewinding motions.

"A piece of a human soul," Grim said, leaning back on her haunches and wiggling as her eyes tracked the ephemeral's movements. "In this case, a miser's regrets."

She pounced, leaping through the air and landing with both paws on the ephemeral, which squirmed and writhed beneath her claws. "Could one of you get me a jar? I'd rather not carry this thing in my mouth all the way back to the manor."

"I suppose," Igor said, hurrying into the coach and retrieving one of the specimen jars he always kept there—there was no telling when he might come across a recent corpse with a perfect set of teeth or a mostly intact liver. Unscrewing the lid, he held it out to Grim, who plucked the many-limbed ephemeral up with her teeth and tossed it neatly into the jar.

"Thanks," Grim said, leaping nimbly onto the driver's seat beside Cornelia. Igor clambered up after them. "I've complained to Mag before, but regrets taste *terrible.*"

"She makes you fetch them for her?" Cornelia asked as Igor took hold of the reins.

"Along with all other sorts of ephemera," Grim confirmed, curling herself around the jar.

"What other sorts are there?" Igor asked, glancing down at the glowing finger centipede scuttling around in its jar. "You said this one was a miser's regrets?"

"Plucked from his dreams," Grim said with her characteristic tone of feline self-satisfaction. "There are as many sorts as there are human feelings and experiences. Last one I brought Mag before the rains was an orphan's hopes."

"So that orphan's hopeless now?" Igor asked, shifting uncomfortably in his seat as they turned onto the main road, the uneven paving stones jostling the coach from side to side.

"No more than any other orphan," Grim assured him. "Nor will that miser wake tomorrow with any fewer regrets. Ephemera are all dream stuff. They form and disperse while the dreamer sleeps, like the mind purging itself of waste."

"So your taking them doesn't hurt anyone," Cornelia said, and Igor wondered whether that was envy in her voice.

"Not directly," Grim said. "Though plenty of ephemera have gone into Auntie Mag's curses over the years."

"And she can't harvest them for herself?" Igor asked.

"That's right." Grim licked her paw and rubbed it against her ear. "Only familiars can touch them."

"She needs you, then," Igor said, thinking not of the strange little creature in the jar but of the countless hours he'd spent grafting body parts together while the Doctor watched with faintly trembling hands.

"To do the things she can't," Cornelia agreed, wiping a smear of blood from the corner of her lip. She didn't look as if she was thinking of Auntie Mag, either.

"It's that or let her turn me back into what I used to be," Grim said, wrinkling her nose. She gave Igor an appraising look. "What would you say to making a donation? I've never given her a hunchback's hopes."

"Nor will you," Igor said, flicking the reins. He had no desire to see what shape his own buried aspirations might take, not if the creepy little centipede thing was typical of its species.

"Alas." Grim stopped grooming herself. Her whiskers twitched as she looked dubiously down at the ephemeral scrabbling against the walls of its glass prison, then up at Igor. "I don't suppose you could bring me more jars, at least?"

13

GOING TO THE CHAPEL

"HOLD VERY STILL, Igor," the Doctor said a few days later, as he poured a beaker full of bubbling yellow liquid into the graduated cylinder Igor held between his hands, which already contained a gleaming silver concoction. "The resulting compound is *highly* acidic."

"Yes, Master." Igor's every muscle fiber strained to steady his hands even as he fought to ignore the droplet of sweat sliding slowly down his nose. Though the Doctor had forbidden Igor to develop the alchemical solutions and elixirs integral to the Great Work, he had no compunction against enlisting Igor's aid in his pursuit of the same. The tincture they were currently developing was one of the most fundamental, intended to revivify necrotic tissue.

"Steady," the Doctor murmured, pouring the yellow liquid from beaker into cylinder. "Nearly—"

Had his concentration been less absorbed in the immediate task, Igor might have caught the warning signs: the faint grimace about the corners of the Doctor's mouth, the shoulder twitch that rippled like a shock wave down through the arm to his fingers. But with his world winnowed down to the cylinder in his hand, Igor noticed his master's tremor only when the steady stream of liquid jerked violently from side to side, splashing over the cylinder's rim.

"Igor!" the Doctor shouted as Igor jerked the cylinder away, instinctively following the motion of his master's shakes. The burbling compound within the cylinder sloshed over the rim, spattering droplets everywhere. Some landed on Igor's thick leather gloves. Others splashed against the steel worktable, warping and dissolving the metal upon contact.

"You nearly spilled it on *me,* you oaf!" the Doctor yelped, backing away as the beaker of frothing yellow stuff slipped from his hand onto the laboratory floor, sending up a cloud of foul-smelling vapors. "You might have injured me!"

"Sorry, Master." Igor set the cylinder down on the worktable, stripping off his gloves before the acid could eat through them. "I only— Your hands—"

"Are unharmed, no thanks to you," the Doctor growled, tearing off his own gloves and examining his fingers. "Why in the blazes did you jerk the cylinder away like that?"

"Master," Igor said. "You had the shakes again. I saw."

That did not lessen the Doctor's outrage, but it did rob it of its momentum. Running an acid-free hand through his hair, the old scientist turned his back on Igor without a word.

"Master?" Igor asked, tentative. "Are you—"

"I had it under control," the Doctor said, his voice softer than Igor was accustomed to. "*Have* it under control."

Igor chose not to press.

"Of course, Master," he said, turning his attention to the worktable so that the Doctor would have time to compose himself. "Shall we begin again? I'll hold it steadier this time."

"I should hope so," the Doctor said, joining him to frown down at the acid-pocked worktable. "Unfortunately for the Work, the measurements involved in the compound are exactingly precise. And you just spilled the last of our quicksilver all over the table."

"I'll go back into town. The apothecary was out last time I went, but perhaps there's been a restock—"

"That'll waste the rest of the afternoon," the Doctor said. "You know we cannot afford to fall so far behind schedule."

"Maybe not, but—" A thought occurred to Igor. "We might ask our housemates."

The Doctor gave him a look. "You think the Count just happens to keep rare metals lying about?"

"No," Igor allowed, but stood his ground. "But Auntie Mag might. Didn't you say that there's a great deal of overlap between alchemy and spellcraft?"

"I wouldn't say a great deal . . ." The Doctor trailed off, a perplexed look creasing his brow as he realized that the solution Igor was offering to their problems might in fact work.

"There's no harm in asking," Igor said, seizing on the Doctor's indecision.

"No," the Doctor agreed, something almost like a smile tugging at his mouth. "Not so long as you're the one doing the asking, anyway."

Igor paled.

"Half a pint should do nicely," the Doctor continued. He strode over to the laboratory doors and opened them wide, hurrying Igor through them. "But come straight back here once you've acquired it, even if she turns you into a toad. Understood?"

"A toad?" Igor turned around in alarm. The wind on the exposed walkway between the observatory and the manor house tugged at his coat.

"Or a newt," the Doctor said, then shut the laboratory door in Igor's face.

* * *

Ravenwald's hallways were not quite as dusty as they had been when the Doctor and Igor had first arrived. Igor's many duties kept him preoccupied, but he'd still found a handful of minutes here and there for some light dusting and sweeping. It would be a long while before his efforts made the place anything approaching presentable, but most worthwhile things took time to achieve, and he took satisfaction in working to restore the decrepit old estate to a shadow of its former grandeur.

In his most private moments, Igor even allowed himself to hope that perhaps the Doctor would decide to settle here permanently after the completion of the Great Work. That Igor could turn his attention from digging up bodies and sewing their parts together to renovating the house properly, to planting a garden and baking fresh bread. To creating things that lived and grew without the aid of electricity. To building something that would last longer than a few short moments of ecstatic creation. To form relationships and bonds and community with their neighbors, knitted together as closely and lovingly as Igor's careful stitchery rather than being driven into the night time and again. To someday succeed at bringing new life into the world, and in so doing widen the circle that thus far had contained only himself and his master.

Of course, this imagined idyllic future was wholly dependent upon how long they were able to cohabitate with their housemates.

Over the last few nights, the inhabitants of the manor had settled into an uneasy rhythm. While the Doctor reassembled the laboratory equipment and consulted his schematics, Igor spent his nights raiding the cemetery for parts, and his days cataloguing them. Soon they would begin selecting which of the harvested limbs and organs were best suited for use in the Great Work. Following that was the main body, so to speak, of the Work: the construction of the Subject.

Even putting his daydreams aside, Igor was quite looking forward to that part. To taking the parts he had collected from disparate bodies and binding them together into a single whole, creating something new and functional from that which had been discarded. To reaching out to his creation and find it reaching back, its curiosity to know him equal to Igor's longing to be known.

Meanwhile, Cornelia continued hunting for herself and the Count. So far, Ruth's uncle had been the only townsman she'd abducted, with the remainder of the vampires' nightly meals consisting of deer and the occasional goat. Igor had a suspicion, bolstered in part by Cornelia's conspicuously long absences, that she was also spending a portion of her evenings venturing into town to scout for other, more deserving prey. And when the time came for her to enlist his help in carrying such victims back to the manor, well . . . that would spare him a trip to the cemetery, just as had the drunken uncle's exsanguinated corpse.

Auntie Mag was holed up in the manor's chapel, about as far from the observatory as it was possible to get. Igor occasionally glimpsed Grim prowling the halls or slipping in through open windows, a small and silvery bit of ephemera wriggling between her teeth. He had wondered more than once what use Auntie Mag intended for them; now it seemed he was about to find out.

Strange noises echoed down the hallway as Igor approached the chapel, an odd and discordant combination of chanting, music, animal grunts, and a softer, more rhythmic sighing that put Igor in mind of waves. Only they were hundreds of miles from the sea, and if Mag had been letting in any animals other than Grim, he would have noticed by now.

The inexplicable noises were not the only sign that something was amiss. As Igor approached the chapel door, its outline glowed dimly purple, as did the strangely elegant sigils carved into the door itself. Igor had never seen their like before, not even in the Doctor's alchemical treatises, but when he peered too closely at them he found himself afflicted with a sudden splitting headache, as if the sigils resented his attempt to read them.

Taking a deep breath, Igor rapped on the door. The sigils' glow intensified, causing him to belatedly hope that they weren't some sort of mystical ward. Maybe the Doctor was right, he thought, but before he could resign himself to life as an amphibian, the door swung open, seemingly of its own accord.

Auntie Mag had made some renovations to Ravenwald's chapel, judging by the scrimshaw talismans draped above the pews, the animal skulls mounted upon the walls, and the glowing vortex of violet light swirling inside a silver circle set into the floor.

Mag stood upon the altar, holding her cane over the vortex like an orchestra conductor. The eyes set in the cane's skull glowed brightly purple, but Mag's own eyes were closed as she chanted long, sonorous words belonging to no language Igor knew. The glow from the vortex lit her from beneath in a pale, unearthly shade of magenta.

Of Grim, Igor saw no sign.

Almost against his will, Igor found himself drawn into the chapel, the swirling vortex pulling at him like the whirlpool it resembled. Flashes of green and pink burst intermittently from its depths, like strange faraway lightning. Smoke and flame too rose from it, along with a cloying, rotten smell like drying seaweed.

As Igor's traitorous feet pulled him nearer, Mag's chanting rose in volume and pitch. She threw her head back, eyes still closed, as a blast of foul-smelling wind blew her hair back from her face. The echoing animal sounds issuing from the skulls mounted on the walls screeched and howled and hooted their reply, joining the witch in a macabre chorus.

The vortex shuddered violently, ripples coursing through it. The very walls of the chapel shook, as if at the approaching tramp of some unseen giant, or the knock of a vast hand upon the door. The air hung heavy with the taste of salt, and Igor sensed some vast presence looming.

A tentacle burst from the vortex.

Slimy and sickly green and thick around as a young tree, it writhed and undulated towards the ceiling, towering over Mag. Still chanting, she opened her eyes, gazing up at what she'd summoned with a look of equal parts terror and rapture.

For his part, Igor felt nothing but cold dread, and a vague sense of nausea. He must have made some sort of sound, though, because Mag's eyes dropped from the towering tentacle to him. The chant died on her lips.

"Sorry," Igor heard himself say. "If this is a bad time, I can come back—"

The vortex's glow faded. The tentacle shuddered, then was yanked downwards as if a titanic hand was pulling it back into the depths whence it had emerged. It writhed and thrashed, knocking a chunk of masonry from one of the walls, to no avail. More of the tentacle's length slipped back into the vortex, like a worm being dragged down a drain.

"No!" Mag screeched, waving her cane in what was either an incantation or mere desperation. The tentacle paid her no heed. It lashed out, throwing itself towards the chapel floor.

Towards Igor.

He took a step back, already knowing that he couldn't outrun it. Another step, and something small collided with his leg with surprising force. Igor's feet went out from under him, and pain shot through his rump as he fell.

"Move!" Grim shouted, nudging him with her head. Even as Igor's forebrain screamed in terror, his body obeyed, rolling to the side just in time to avoid being smashed into an Igor-shaped pulp by the tentacle slamming into the ground where he had just lain.

There was a gurgling sound from the vortex, followed by a protesting screech from the tentacle as it latched itself onto a pew inches from Igor's head. Revulsion coursed through him as he saw that the tentacle was tipped with a small, disturbingly human mouth.

"Rejoice," it said, and bit him.

Igor yelped, more from surprise than pain, as the tentacle's mouth dug into the shoulder of his lab coat, unable to penetrate the double layer of cotton.

"Get off!" Grimalkin snarled, batting at the tentacle with both paws, claws fully extended. Furrows of bright pink blood appeared along the tentacle's flanks, and the mouth released Igor with a plaintive whine.

Then it was gone, the force of whatever was pulling the tentacle back down into the vortex dragging it across the chapel floor and into the swirling pool of light upon the altar. Auntie Mag had abandoned her attempts to salvage her summoning in favor of cowering behind an overturned lectern. This quickly proved a shrewd choice, as the tentacle made one last abortive grab for her, its human teeth clacking together before it was dragged fully into the vortex, which promptly disappeared.

The light dimmed, leaving only the late afternoon sunlight filtering down through the stained glass windows. The animal noises faded, as did the otherworldly sighing and the distant music. Only the cloying seaweed stench remained, and the pain in Igor's shoulder.

Gingerly, Igor pulled himself to his feet. On the far side of the chapel, Auntie Mag did the same, leaning heavily on her cane and looking much the worse for wear. Her hair stuck out at all angles, and her face was drawn with rage.

"What," she bit out, "do you think you're doing here?"

"Err." Igor cleared his throat, suddenly wishing he had a more compelling reason for interrupting the profane ritual he'd just witnessed. "Borrow a cup of quicksilver?"

14

THE UNSMILING KING

"I EXPECT YOU HAVE questions," Grim said once they were safely out of earshot.

"You might say that," Igor said, his voice still trembling. He was no stranger to peril—a life of robbing graves and dodging angry mobs had inured him to mundane fears. But what he'd just encountered in the manor's chapel was so far beyond his experience that he found himself struggling to give voice to it. "Thank you for stepping in, by the way."

"With the tentacle?" Grim asked, tail swishing as she trotted beside him. "Or with Mag?"

"Both, I suppose," Igor admitted. "I don't think I'd much like being a toad."

Grim blinked up at him. "A toad?"

"Never mind," Igor said, resisting the urge to look back over his shoulder at the desecrated chapel. "You sure she's not going to . . ."

"Come after you?" Grim yawned. "She's much too focused on the summoning to waste time on vengeance. But I'll talk to her, just in case."

"Thank you," Igor said, the weight of dread lifting slightly from his shoulders.

Grim drew to a halt as they reached a hallway intersection, glancing surreptitiously to either side. “It wasn’t your fault, anyhow,” she added in a low undertone. “The portal was already unstable even before you walked in. Your interruption just hurried its collapse.”

“Portal,” Igor repeated, envisioning that terrible violet vortex. “So it’s a door? To wherever that tentacle came from?”

“Right,” Grim said, looking up at him with her bright yellow eyes as she turned and continued along a corridor. “To the Outside.”

“Outside,” Igor repeated faintly, following her. He’d heard the term, of course, but it was most often uttered in the same breath as similarly near-mythical places, like Faerie, or the Below. For Grim to speak of it so casually . . .

“That’s where you’re from,” he realized, looking down at the little gray tabby strolling along beside him. “The place Mag summoned you from. Outside, the realm of unspeakable horrors and torments unimaginable—”

“Don’t get hysterical about it,” Grim said, and to Igor’s surprise she actually sounded a little self-conscious. “You could say the same of Marovia.”

Igor, having never been to Marovia, could offer no comment.

“Besides,” Grim said, sounding a bit uncomfortable, “just because I’m *from* the Outside doesn’t mean I want to go back.”

“Then why are you trying to open a door to it?”

“Same reason you’re helping the Doctor with his Great Work.” Grim sounded as if she would have shrugged if her anatomy permitted it. “Mag’s my boss. She can’t compel me in the same way an elder vampire can their offspring, but I’ve still got certain . . . obligations to her, let’s say.”

“Like helping her open a portal to the Outside,” Igor said, clenching his hands to keep them from trembling. Now that they were safely away from the profane chapel, the shock of his encounter with something so wholly alien was setting in. To his surprise, discussing the matter with Grim kept the subject from overwhelming him, grounding the experience in something adjacent to his reality. "To let in . . . what, a really large octopus?"

"No," Grim said, pausing to lick a paw. "Auntie Mag intends to complete the Rite of Opening, and in so doing grant our lord and master the Unsmiling King, Devourer of Worlds, the Dour Prince, God of Blasphemy and Lord of Untruth, entry into your reality so that He may reign sovereign here forevermore."

Igor stared at her.

"Please don't make me say all that again," she said.

"So"—Igor struggled to wrap his mind around this revelation—"you and Auntie Mag are working to open up our world to an evil god from the Outside?"

"He's not all bad," Grim said, in the same tone Igor himself had often used when justifying the Doctor's behavior. "Just wants to remake reality in His image."

"Which is what, exactly?" Igor asked, thinking of the animal skulls profaning the chapel.

"More tentacles, mostly." Grim hopped onto a plinth bearing a bust of someone Igor surmised was one of the Doctor's distant ancestors, given the similarity of the nose.

"And what does Mag get out of this exchange? Besides tentacles, I mean."

"Apotheosis." Grim's gaze flickered back down the way they came. "In appreciation for letting Him into this reality, the Unsmiling King has promised to . . . change her. Make her into something other than human. Something better, at least in His view, and hers."

"But why would *she* want that?" Igor asked, desperately searching for some shred of sense in this increasingly unhinged conversation. "To be transformed like that?"

"Igor." Grim gave him a look that was almost pitying. "Can you honestly tell me that you've never resented the body you were born into?"

"I . . ."

Of course he couldn't.

"Mag's older than she looks," Grim said, lowering her voice. "But even her magic has its limits, and the human body can incur a debt of only so many years before time comes to collect."

"So the King's offered her immortality?" Igor asked.

"Or something near enough as to make no difference," Grim said. "But listen, Igor. You don't have to worry—"

"About the eldritch god looking to reshape reality?" Igor asked, hearing his voice climbing towards hysteria but unable to slow its ascent. "Or the witch who's hell-bent on helping Him to do it? Whyever would I worry?"

"Mag has been trying to complete the Rite of Opening for years," Grim said. "And she's never come close to succeeding."

"The thirty-foot tentacle back there would indicate otherwise."

"*One* tentacle," Grim countered. "Had the Rite been successful, there would have been dozens. It's the difference between poking a finger through a door that's open just a crack and walking through it."

"Okay." Igor saw her meaning but was not quite assuaged. "And her other attempts?"

"Last time, all she managed to summon was a rainstorm," Grim said. "Albeit one that got rather out of hand."

"That's why you were in the Hairy Nag that first night," Igor realized aloud. "Mag washed away her own cottage?"

"Not intentionally."

"Uh-huh." Igor raised an eyebrow. "So what's to stop her from flooding the manor?"

"Location, mostly." Grim turned and blinked up at the sunlight streaming in through the floor-to-ceiling window. "Ravenwald Manor sits on a convergence of leylines, which give Mag considerably greater . . . let's say, finesse, when it comes to ritual magic. Why do you think she was so hell-bent on getting into the place that first night?"

"So you're saying she'll succeed, now that she's moved in?" Igor asked, unmollified.

"No," Grim said, too quickly. "Not when she's still missing certain . . . components."

"Components," Igor repeated. "So that's what all the ephemera are for? Ingredients for this Rite of Opening?"

"As well as physical components," Grim admitted reluctantly.

"Like an eyeball?" Igor suggested, thinking back to their encounter in the graveyard the week before.

"Maybe." Grim hopped down from the plinth and sidled up to him. "Listen, Igor. I *like* this reality. I like being a cat. I even like you, for some reason."

Igor blinked. "You do?"

"You're more tolerable than most," she said, flicking her ear. "My point is, I'd rather not have to go back to the place where I was before. To being *what* I was before."

"Which was what, exactly?" Igor asked, thinking of how Auntie Mag had threatened to turn Grim back over dinner that first night.

"Something much less cute," she said. "Just like we'd all be if the ritual were to succeed. Fortunately, Mag hasn't a chance at successfully completing the ritual without the Eye of Anthomset—"

"The what?"

"Big old amethyst from down south," Grim explained. "Supposedly the subject of a pharaoh's curse—that'd be the Anthomset in question—and the object of more than a few holy quests, thefts, treasure hunts, and even a war or two."

"We're a long way from the desert," Igor observed, recalling the months he and the Doctor had spent raiding tombs, desecrating mummies, and getting sand in unpleasant places.

"The Eye has traveled a long way," Grim said. "Legend has it that a crusader from Ravensburg brought it back home, though Anthomset's curse caught up to him not long after."

Igor considered that. "How would you rate the likelihood of the legend's being true, on a scale from 'the king under the mountain returning' to 'coelacanths are actually still swimming around in the southern seas'?"

"Definitely on the fishier end," Grim said. "But Auntie Mag and I moved here in search of the Eye years ago, and we haven't found a trace of it. If it was ever actually here, it must have disappeared long before we came here."

"That's an awfully big assumption to gamble the end of the world upon."

"The world's always almost ending," Grim said, in what Igor thought was intended to be a comforting tone. She hopped onto a window ledge, through which the late afternoon sun poured like liquid gold, turning her gray coat silver. "That's what makes it special."

"Still," Igor said, "I'd rather it not end while I'm still in the middle of it."

"Don't worry, Igor." Grim curled herself into a ball on the window ledge and looked at him sleepily. "Auntie Mag's never going to find the Eye."

"How can you be so sure?" Igor asked.

"Because," Grim said, closing both eyes and lifting her chin to the sun, "I won't let her."

15

STOLEN HEARTS

THE DOCTOR'S REACTION to discovering that their housemate was attempting to open a portal to a hellish otherworld was startlingly prosaic.

"Of course she's consorting with extradimensional beings," he said when Igor informed him that morning, dismissing his assistant's concerns with a shrug. His narrow arms worked vigorously as he ground a fistful of yellowish crystals into a fine powder, the scrape of mortar against pestle setting Igor's teeth on edge. "Her familiar's very existence is proof of that. Where did you think Miss Devereaux summoned her from in the first place?"

Until the appearance of the massive tentacle, Igor hadn't given the question much thought. "So the Outside is real, then?"

"Incontrovertibly so," the Doctor said. "Nor is it the only realm besides our own." He waved the mortar at the orrery by the laboratory door. The clockwork device looked like an inverted infant's mobile, bronze planets slowly orbiting a gold-plated sun.

"Worlds upon worlds," the Doctor said. "Not mere planets, but other dimensions of reality entirely. Some nearer to ours, and thus more alike, others farther away, and correspondingly stranger."

"But they can still reach us?" Igor frowned at the bronze spheres. "I mean, if Mag's trying to summon her god—"

"The barrier between our world and the others is permeable," the Doctor said, returning his attention to the mortar and pestle. "Miss Devereaux is attempting to breach it from our side, judging by what you've told me transpired last night. Such an occurrence is rare, but hardly unprecedented. Though I must admit to some surprise at the orientation of her summons. It's my understanding that the Below is the easiest of the otherworlds for a witch to access."

"Below?" Igor squeaked, looking down at his feet, then back at the Doctor. "That is"—he lowered his voice, hardly daring to speak the dread realm's name—*"Hell?"*

"Peasants' superstition." The Doctor sneered down at the pestle, mashing the crystal fragments with renewed vigor. "I very much doubt that the Below is the eternal destination of all souls damned by an absent Almighty, given the lack of concrete evidence that either even exists. But by all accounts it certainly matches the popular conception of the place. Fire and brimstone and a decidedly unpleasant local populace."

Igor thought of the more lurid bits of stained glass he'd seen in various churches, and shuddered. "Demons, you mean."

"Oh, get hold of yourself," the Doctor snapped. "Miss Devereaux's allegiance is to the Outside, not the Below."

"But she's trying to end the world," Igor protested, baffled by the Doctor's cavalier attitude. "Shouldn't we be concerned?"

"The world has a funny way of persisting despite the best efforts of witches, gods, and kings," the Doctor said. "And by your account, Miss Devereaux's patron deity seeks to reshape the world, not annihilate it."

"That's not terribly comforting to those of us living here."

"No," the Doctor agreed. "But should she succeed . . ."

He poured the crystals into a decanter of bubbling red liquid. The resultant explosion bathed his face in lurid light. "Then at least the results will be interesting to observe."

* * *

The surprisingly brawny gravekeeper failed to answer Igor's knock at her door when he returned to the cemetery that night. Igor presumed she was asleep, or perhaps had gone into town for a drink at the Hairy Nag—and saints only knew when she might return, or in what state.

That was little trouble, as Igor habitually kept a set of lockpicks in his coat.

The cemetery gates groaned comfortingly open as he slipped inside, the coffin cart trundling along behind him as he navigated the foggy rows of headstones. Igor hesitated before a newly carved stone bearing the name FLEISCHER. Certainly, Matthias Fleischer would make an ideal donor; the young man's untimely death had left all his organs undamaged.

The Doctor had always maintained—and Igor had always believed—that grave robbing was a victimless crime. After all, why let the bodies rot when they could serve to further the cause of human knowledge?

Yet somehow Igor could not bring himself to plant his shovel in the freshly tilled earth. Not after having attended the funeral. Not when he could no longer ignore that Matthias Fleischer had been a person before he had been a cadaver, with dreams and fears and longings unique to him alone. He'd had friends, a family, a community—a large one, judging by how well attended his funeral had been—all of them still mourning his loss.

Igor's hands tightened on the shovel as he turned away from the headstone, his cheeks flushed and his breathing shallow.

Matthias Fleischer's grave, at least, he refused to desecrate.

* * *

After some searching, Igor settled upon a shallow pauper's grave near the edge of the cemetery, so close to the wrought iron fence that the branches of the surrounding forest overhung it. Nor was there a headstone to further trouble his uneasy conscience.

For several hours he was able to lose himself in the work, drawing satisfaction from the bite of spade into earth, the prying open of the casket lid, the careful precision of parting flesh with scalpel, and the even more delicate extraction of the organs from the body that had housed them. Galled by his previous failure, Igor even forced himself to do the eyes first, which he harvested without any interruptions, feline or otherwise.

Igor was so absorbed in his labors that he almost didn't notice the sound of someone weeping nearby.

He paused, one hand bracing himself against the damp earth of the grave wall, the other elbow deep in the donor's chest cavity. For a moment, he thought that he'd imagined the sound, that it was one of those curious nighttime noises so near to a human voice that the unwary might mistake it for such, like a whippoorwill's call or the sighing wind.

Then it came again: the ugly, braying sound of someone weeping without restraint, with no one around to hear, or see, or judge. Igor shifted uncomfortably in the grave, acutely aware of his unintentional voyeurism.

Whoever it was must only be a few graves over for him to hear them even through the fog. Igor thought about calling out, or whistling a tune. But acknowledging that he'd heard would only make things even more awkward. And didn't folk wisdom warn against whistling in a cemetery at night?

His musings were cut short by the realization that his arm had gone numb—the one he'd been steadying himself with, fortunately, not the one rooting around in the donor's sternum. Wincing, he adjusted his grip on the organ he'd been in the process of removing when he'd first heard the weeping, and slowly withdrew it.

The fist-sized muscle in question glistened pinkly in the foggy night, hardly desiccated at all. Moving with even greater than usual care so as not to disturb whoever was sobbing a few graves over, Igor began to clamber out of the one he'd just desecrated.

His foot slipped.

Igor scrabbled desperately at the walls of the grave with his free hand but found no purchase in the wet dirt. He tumbled backwards and only just had the presence of mind to clutch his prize against his chest before he landed in the coffin. Something squelched wetly under him.

"Oof," he breathed, staring up at the mist-shrouded sky framed within the rectangle of the grave. He looked down at his chest, reassuring himself that the organ he'd been laboring over for the last quarter hour remained undamaged.

A snakelike hiss cut through the night directly above him. Igor looked up to see a pale face staring down at him, red eyes aflame, mouth opened wide to reveal gleaming fangs. A curtain of hair haloed it, faintly red in the dim moonlight.

"Cornelia?" Igor croaked.

"Igor?" Cornelia blinked, dousing the fiery gleam in her eyes. Her fangs retracted to a less intimidating length. "What are you doing down there?"

"I thought that would be obvious," Igor said, raising the organ demonstratively. To his surprise, Cornelia giggled.

"I've heard of coming to someone with your heart in your hand," she said, sniffing a little. "But I thought it was just a saying."

"Well." Igor looked down at the donor's heart resting on his palm. "It's not *my* heart, really. Help me up?"

Cornelia nodded and offered him a hand. Igor took it, then yelped in surprise as she lifted him bodily from the grave, depositing him neatly beside his cart.

Vampires, he thought, not unappreciatively.

"Thanks," he said once he had his feet back under him. Cornelia nodded, then turned quickly away. Not quickly enough that he missed the tear tracks streaking her face, though.

"Guess you heard me, huh?" she asked, as Igor busied himself rummaging through the jars of preserving fluid he'd brought.

"Heard what?" Igor asked, unscrewing the lid of one and inserting the heart neatly inside.

"Igor."

"Sorry." He screwed the lid back on and turned around. "I wasn't meaning to eavesdrop, I promise. I just . . . was in the middle of something."

"Or someone," Cornelia said, glancing downwards. Igor tried not to look; for all his careful incisions, he'd made rather a mess of the poor donor when he'd landed on top of it.

"Right," he said, hesitating. It was none of his business, he knew, but he couldn't help asking, "Are you all right?"

"Oh, fine." Cornelia shrugged. "Most women you find crying in cemeteries are."

"Sorry," Igor said again.

Cornelia exhaled, which Igor supposed was a habit left over from her mortal days. "No, that was rude of me. You were only trying to help."

"I . . ." Igor looked at his feet, unsure of where to go from here. He was used to being yelled at for his thoughtlessness, but being apologized to afterwards was new territory for him. "Is it . . . Were you crying because of the Count?"

"Karl?" Cornelia's laugh was disbelieving. "Saints, no."

"Oh." Igor racked his brain for another reason but came up empty. "Why, then?"

Cornelia stared at him thoughtfully.

"Come on," she said abruptly, then turned and strode through the graveyard, her bare feet making no sound on the dewy grass. "I'll show you."

A few moments later they stood before a pair of timeworn

graves, headstones so badly eroded that the names and dates carved into them had been rendered completely illegible.

"My parents," Cornelia said, nodding first to one, then the other. "Mom, Dad, this is Igor."

"Hello," Igor said dubiously, glancing up at Cornelia. "Are they, err . . ."

"They're dead. The normal kind of dead, I mean. Not getting up unless there's a necromancer about, and even then all he'd manage to raise is a handful of dust."

"I'm sorry," Igor said, privately wondering whether a more useless pair of words existed in any language. "They . . . must have died a long time ago?"

"Oh, hundreds of years." Cornelia's voice was detached despite the tear tracks she hadn't yet wiped away. "Fever took them. Back when I was still alive."

"Oh." Igor digested this. "I . . . didn't know you were from here. Ravensburg, I mean."

"Born, raised, and turned," Cornelia said, waving vaguely about the cemetery, as if the entirety of the town and its populace were contained within its bounds. Igor supposed one day they would be. "I was only seventeen when Mom and Dad went. Or maybe eighteen. It gets harder to remember, the longer I've been around."

"Not that hard, it seems," Igor said quietly. Not if she was here tonight, crying over a grief that was older than any living soul.

"It's odd," she said, nodding her agreement. "You'd think that as time goes on, the hurt would fade. And maybe in some ways it has, but . . ."

She inhaled sharply, and for a moment Igor feared she'd start crying again. "I heard once that the grief doesn't ever get any smaller, your heart just grows bigger around it as more people come into your life. And that's probably true. Only . . ."

"Only you've been stuck with the same person for hundreds

of years," Igor finished. Cornelia shot him a grateful look, and a small nod.

"The Count," Igor said, struck by a horrible thought. "He's not . . . he didn't . . ."

Cornelia laughed without mirth. "He didn't have anything to do with my parents' deaths, if that's what you're asking. Although . . . maybe losing them is why I fell for him so easily. It was only a year or two later that he turned me."

"You were lonely," Igor said softly.

"I was." Cornelia hugged herself, her shoulders hunching. "My parents were . . . they were good folks, on the whole, but I was their only child, and they were always protective of me. Perhaps a bit too much, I can see now. Without them, I was alone. Lost. Until . . ."

"Until the Count."

Cornelia nodded. "He doesn't bother much these nights, but Karl can be charming when it suits him. Make you feel as if you're the only person in the world, as if his whole attention's fixed on you and only you. Impress you with his education, his depth of culture, the breadth of his travels. Doubly impressive to a young maiden who'd never been more than thirty miles from where she was born."

"Courtship is one thing," Igor pointed out. "An eternity of vampirism is another."

"Tell that to me at twenty," Cornelia said with a bitter laugh. "Not that I'd have listened, when Karl made it all sound so darkly glamorous. Perhaps my parents would have set me right, had they been there."

Igor swallowed, unwilling to allow himself to fall back upon the crutch of those two useless words again. Instead, he offered up the only solidarity he could think of. "You know, I grew up in an orphanage."

Cornelia looked at him. Without speaking, she put a hand on

his shoulder, not flinching when she brushed his hump. Igor shivered, still unused to the feel of a friendly touch.

Were they friends now?

"I don't know what happened to my parents," he said, clearing his throat. "Or even whether anything happened to them."

"What do you mean?"

"Sometimes parents would leave their babies on the orphanage doorstep," Igor explained, shifting uncomfortably on his uneven legs. He disliked dwelling on his past, but Cornelia had been open with him, and she deserved the same in return. "Babies who were blind, or deaf, or who'd been born missing a hand. Sometimes a toddler whose legs didn't work right."

"I'm sorry." Cornelia squeezed his shoulder. Somehow the words didn't sound as useless coming from her.

Igor nodded, looking down at the weathered headstones beneath which Cornelia's parents had been laid to rest. "I'm glad you could know yours. For all I know, mine are still out there someplace."

"So the Doctor isn't . . ." Cornelia tucked a red curl behind her ear, frowning a little. "I thought maybe he might be a relative."

Igor shook his head.

"You're awfully devoted to him." Cornelia's tone was one of studied neutrality. "I guess your wages must make up for how he treats you?"

Igor cocked his head to one side. "Wages?"

"Holy night," Cornelia swore softly. "He doesn't even *pay* you?"

The Doctor had always cited the high operating costs of the Great Work as prohibitive to either of them drawing a salary. Only now that Igor considered it, if they had enough gold to bribe a town's worth of officials, then surely there was enough to pay him . . .

"He's good to me in other ways," Igor said, a little more defensively than he meant to.

"Such as?"

"He took me in. Taught me to read. And . . ." Igor touched a finger to his lip. "I had a terrible lisp, growing up. No one could understand a word out of my mouth. Until the Doctor."

Cornelia raised a brow. "He fixed it?"

"Misaligned jaw," Igor said, rubbing his chin. "Hours of surgeries, and the recovery was far from pleasant, but . . . for the first time in my life, I could speak clearly. Be understood. Can you imagine how that felt?"

"I—"

Cornelia's next words were cut off by the sound of a snapping branch behind them. They whirled around, Igor's heart pounding as a shadow loomed large in the fog.

"Hey!" The shadow drew nearer, resolving into the tall form of the gravekeeper, holding a hooded lantern at shoulder height. "Who's—"

Her words died away as the lanternlight fell on Cornelia, bathing her in its warm glow. The gravekeeper stared at the redheaded woman in her graveyard, barefoot and wearing a filmy white gown.

Igor had never been stirred by the great passions by which playwrights and poets made their living, but even he had taken note of Cornelia's considerable beauty. Evidently, so too had the gravekeeper.

"I . . ." she started, finding her voice. "I must have left the gates unlocked."

"You did," Igor lied, looking at Cornelia. She was staring at the gravekeeper, her own expression an odd mix of shyness and hunger. Igor hoped she wasn't planning to drink the other woman's blood; that would make future visits to the cemetery awkward for all involved.

"Well." A smile crinkled the corners of the gravekeeper's

eyes, which were still fixed on Cornelia. "I suppose I should leave them unlocked more often, if it means the likes of you come wandering through."

Cornelia cocked her head. "Was that . . . poetry?"

The gravekeeper's smile grew confused. "Poetry?"

"The likes of you / Come wand'ring through," Cornelia said. "It even rhymed."

Igor counted off the syllables on his knuckles. Sure enough, it was in perfect iambic tetrameter, once the gravekeeper's accent was taken into account.

The gravekeeper's brows drew together. "Do you . . . like poetry, miss?"

"I used to." Cornelia's pale cheeks did not exactly flush, though they might have, were she still alive. "Though I'm afraid I've somewhat soured on the subject in recent years."

The gravekeeper barked out a laugh. "Just as well, seeing as that's the most verse you're likely to get out of me." She thrust out a hand. "I'm Laura."

"Cornelia," she replied, placing her slender hand in Laura's calloused palm. Igor inched away, sensing that this was hardly the moment to reintroduce himself.

"Cornelia," Laura the gravekeeper repeated slowly, savoring each syllable. "I'm quite sorry I wasn't at the gate tonight to let you in."

"Don't trouble yourself over it," Cornelia said, turning her gaze to her parents' graves.

"Kin of yours?" Laura asked, nodding at the worn headstones.

"Yes," Cornelia said, then added quickly, "distantly."

Thick brows drew together. "You're from here, then?"

"Originally," she admitted. "But I haven't been back to Ravensburg since I was little more than a girl."

Igor silently applauded this technical truth as he took another step back, nearly tripping over a funerary urn as he did so.

This moment was growing more private by the moment, and both Cornelia and Laura appeared to have forgotten his existence.

"Me as well," Laura said, nodding. "Got word a few months back that my old grandpap had passed, and that his vacancy left the folk of Ravensburg in need of a new gravekeeper."

"And you took them up on it?" Cornelia was faintly incredulous as she gave Laura a slow and—in Igor's opinion rather indulgent—look up and down. "I'd think stonemasonry or woodcutting more appropriate to a woman of your . . . stature."

"Who's to say I haven't tried my hand at both?" Laura countered, teeth gleaming white as she smiled. "But I like the work well enough, and the cemetery. It's . . . peaceable, here. Gives me space to think. To breathe. You know?"

Cornelia nodded, though Igor guessed from the faint crease of her brow that she was trying to recall what breathing had felt like.

"Anyhow . . ." Laura cleared her throat and tugged at the collar of her flannel shirt. "I don't mean to keep you, nor to intrude. My sympathies for your loss, Miss Cornelia."

She turned and began to pick her way back amongst the headstones.

"Wait!" Cornelia called after her. Laura halted, turning around, and in her eyes Igor saw a gleam of something like hope.

"Thank you for letting me visit," Cornelia said, "Laura."

Laura nodded, touched her hand to her chest. "You're welcome anytime, Miss Cornelia."

Then she was gone, disappearing into the fog like a particularly solid phantasm. Cornelia watched her go, eyes shining.

"I'm pretty sure I've got a scalpel on me," Igor said, patting his pockets.

Cornelia started as she turned to him. "What for?"

"Cutting the tension," Igor said, grinning as Cornelia's jaw fell open. He held up a hand. "Don't tell me you weren't about to take her by the flannel and pull her into the first empty coffin you found?"

"I don't . . . I wasn't . . ." Cornelia sputtered.

Igor folded his arms over his chest and fixed her with his good eye, waiting.

"All right, fine," she admitted, brushing a strand of auburn hair from her face. "She is . . . quite striking. Polite, too, in a rough way."

Igor nodded. "So what are you planning to do about it?"

Cornelia shot him a quizzical look.

"Your marriage to the Count is essentially over," Igor reminded her. "If you wanted to court someone new—"

"Court?" Cornelia's laugh was incredulous. "I've only ever been courted once, Igor, and that relationship has lasted two hundred years. I wouldn't even know where to start with someone new. And besides . . ."

She looked past Igor, to the dark forest beyond the graveyard's tall iron fence. "My marriage isn't over yet. I'm supposed to be hunting dinner for Karl at this very moment."

Igor wanted to protest further but decided against it. "I'll see you back at the manor, then?"

"You will," Cornelia said. "And . . . I'm sorry about your parents, Igor. You deserve better."

"I . . ." Igor swallowed the lump which had mysteriously obstructed his airways. "So do you."

They stood there a moment, neither of them speaking. Yet somehow Igor knew that things had shifted between them.

Cornelia nodded, smiling a little, as if she was thinking the same. Then her form blurred and dissolved into the mist, off to seek her sanguinary supper.

Alone in the graveyard, Igor peered down at the headstones where Cornelia's parents lay buried. She *did* deserve better—better than the Count, certainly. And perhaps he could help her find it.

It seemed like something a friend would do.

A broad smile broke across Igor's face as he made his way through the fog back to his cart, the germ of an idea blossoming into something in the rough shape of a plan. Cornelia's hesitancy about thrusting herself into the messy world of courtship and romance was understandable, but that was hardly an insurmountable obstacle. She just needed a little encouragement, and perhaps a helping hand.

That Igor himself had absolutely no romantic experience was hardly a problem. After all, he reflected as he returned to his cart, surveying the organs packed neatly away in their jars, he'd stolen plenty of hearts at the Doctor's behest.

What was one more, for Cornelia's sake?

16

INSPIRATION

"I'VE BEEN THINKING, Master," Igor said the following afternoon, as they labored atop the manor rooftop.

"I thought I smelled something burning." The Doctor made an adjustment to one of the support struts of the lightning rod they'd spent most of the day erecting. "Yet no smoke seems to be issuing from your ears, so I trust that whatever's on your mind isn't too mentally taxing."

"No," Igor said, ignoring the jab. The Doctor was always edgy at this phase of the Great Work, professing a pronounced dislike of heights. Yet the installation of the lightning rod was a crucial step in the process, and a two-person job. Igor had briefly entertained the possibility of enlisting Cornelia's help, but had decided against it on the grounds of keeping their newfound friendship a secret. Somehow he didn't think either the Doctor or the Count would approve.

Only that morning he'd discovered a freshly drained corpse awaiting him in the wine cellar he'd been using to store the collection of organs he'd accumulated. A note tied to the fresh corpse's big toe, signed with a heart and the letter C, had assured Igor not to worry his conscience over the man's death, as he'd been both a barrister and a philanderer.

"Well?" Igor's master frowned at him from the other side of the lightning rod's support strut. "Was I wrong about the effort of cognition shorting out your synapses?"

"You don't have to talk to me like that, you know." The words tumbled from Igor's lips of their own accord, having failed to consult his brain beforehand. Hastily, he added, "Master."

The Doctor gaped at him, mouth working silently but no words forthcoming.

"I mean," Igor said, his urge to apologize warring against his desire to explain himself, "you don't need to treat me like I'm stupid. I'm not."

The Doctor continued to stare.

"That is," Igor said, the urge to explain beginning to win out, "I know I'm not brilliant, like you. Not a genius inventor or alchemist or any of the things you are. But I'm not stupid."

His hands tightened around the lightning rod, and he wondered where this burst of courage had come from. Or whether it was not courage but some hitherto unknown breed of madness, if there was any difference between the two. "And I'm tired of you talking down to me like I am."

"I see." The Doctor glanced at the ground far below, then back at Igor, his gaze hard. "Given that you've elected to wait until you had me in a rather precarious position to express your dissatisfaction, I suppose I am obligated to ask: How, precisely, would you prefer I speak to you? As an . . . equal?"

"Of course not," Igor said, sensing he was treading on dangerous ground. "I'd just prefer you assume my understanding, rather than my ignorance."

"A novel proposition," the Doctor said, rather testily. He returned his attention to the lightning rod, which had begun listing to one side. "Is there anything else you intend to extort from me, while you have me atop this godforsaken roof?"

In for a penny, in for a pound, Igor supposed.

"Well," Igor said, drawing in a breath and tightening his fingers about the lightning rod for support. "I think that I deserve a wage."

The Doctor blinked. "A what?"

"Wages," Igor said, now fairly certain that his grip on the lightning rod was the only thing keeping him upright. "For all the work I do. Finding donors, cataloguing organs, stitching, trips into town—"

"I thought you *liked* the needlework," the Doctor interrupted, aggrieved.

"I do." Igor nodded. "But just because I enjoy it, doesn't mean it's not work. And I think I should be paid for it, and for everything else."

The Doctor looked at him, his eyes magnified behind his spectacles. "And here I thought you were a believer, Igor."

Igor frowned. "We haven't been to a church service in—"

"Not in superstitious folktales of capricious gods smiting down the infidel from on high," the Doctor said, which struck Igor as a perilously atheistic stance coming from a man currently holding on to a lightning rod. "In the Great Work, of course. The noble destiny of all mankind, which you and I have labored towards all these long years. Together."

"But—" Igor started, but found himself unable to refute the Doctor outright. The Great Work had been their shared goal for longer than Igor could recall.

"All we have ever done," the Doctor said, making that abortive one-handed gesture that meant he'd nearly worked himself up to giving Igor a friendly touch before thinking better of it, "has been in pursuit of that Work, with its deep mysteries and tremendous importance. And you are the hands acting in pursuit of that solemn quest, as I am the eye fixed upon it."

"Master, I . . ." Confusion and pride both stirred in Igor's chest. This was the closest the Doctor had ever come to complimenting him, and the effect was mildly disorienting—particularly this far off the ground.

"Would you turn your back on all our efforts, now that we stand poised upon the precipice of true greatness?" the Doctor asked. "Over something so paltry as *money*?"

Igor clung tight to the lightning rod, his mind spinning. "If the Work is so important to you, Master, then surely it's worth parting with a few coins."

The Doctor's lips became a thin line. A muscle twitched in his jaw. Igor waited, wondering what had come over him that he'd dare to question his master this way.

Wordlessly, the Doctor reached into his lab coat pocket and tossed a small pouch at Igor. Coins jingled inside as Igor caught it one-handed, his other still gripping the lightning rod.

"There," the Doctor said coldly. "Wages. Now let us return to the task at hand, before—"

"I want more," Igor said, forcing the words out before his courage could fail him.

In all the years he'd worked for the Doctor, he had never asked for so much for himself. But now that he had, he seemed unable to stop—as if he'd opened the floodgates for all his wants and desires to come rushing out in a single torrent before their source could run dry.

"To do more, I mean," he clarified, before the Doctor could turn apoplectic. "For the Work. Not just finding the parts or putting them together, but the rest of it."

The Doctor's gaze became caught somewhere between scorn and pity. "Alchemy, you mean."

"Yes." Igor hoped it was a good sign that he hadn't been refused outright. "I don't just want to build the Subject's body. I want to mold its mind, balance its humors, calibrate its—"

The Doctor scoffed. "You've had no formal schooling, Igor, let alone in a subject as complex and esoteric as alchemy."

"We've built dozens of Subjects together." Igor felt something worryingly like anger stirring in his breast. "I've helped you prepare elixirs hundreds of times, and I can mix some of the less complex ones myself—"

"It's not a question of capability." The Doctor pushed his hair back from his head—evidently his agitation had eclipsed his discomfort with their current elevation. "If there's one thing you certainly excel at, Igor, it's following directions. What you lack, I'm afraid, is vision."

Igor blinked. "Vision?"

"Of the creative variety," the Doctor said. "Alchemy is as much art as it is science—and thus necessitates a certain creative genius which you are sadly lacking."

"I—" Igor began to protest, but the Doctor merely shook his head in what he probably thought was an avuncular fashion.

"It's hardly your fault," he said. "None of us bear responsibility for the shape in which nature fashions our minds, any more than our bodies. Which is why it falls to us, in our Great Work, to correct nature's mistakes."

He gave the lightning rod a shake, then nodded in a vaguely satisfied way. "I trust you can finish up here on your own."

"But, Master—" Igor protested, the lightning rod leaning sharply to one side as the Doctor began to pick his way across the roof to the ladder they'd climbed up.

"Join me in the lab once you're done." The Doctor turned and started down the stepladder, as Igor tried to simultaneously right the listing lightning rod and tighten the bolts of its support struts. "But first, stop by the spare parts collection, will you? I want to evaluate pancreases."

He descended the stepladder without waiting for an answer, leaving Igor to strain against the weight of the lightning rod. As he wrestled it back into place, his mind raced, spurred on by the Doctor's casual reference to their spare parts collection.

There was an easy way to disprove the Doctor's misapprehension that Igor lacked the necessary creativity for the alchemical half of the Great Work. All he had to do was create something new, something wholly his own, something unlike anything anyone had ever seen before.

Little did the Doctor know, Igor had already been hard at work doing exactly that.

17

SPARE PARTS

BY EARLY THE following morning, Igor had nearly finished creating a Subject of his own.

"It looks a little runty," Grimalkin said dubiously from her perch atop a wine rack. With the crypt occupied by the vampires, Igor had commandeered Ravenwald's wine cellar for the storage of body parts, though he hadn't yet gotten around to relabeling the shelves.

"It's not supposed to be full-sized," Igor said from where he stood bent over a battered wooden table, carefully applying electrodes to his secret project's cranium. "That would take too much time and effort away from the Subject upstairs."

"And your *master* would notice you pulling double duty," Grim said scornfully.

Igor winced. He'd already told her about his confrontation with the Doctor on the roof, which Grim had effusively approved of. She'd taken to hanging about while he performed his tasks for the Doctor, often commentating on his work. Igor was somewhat surprised to discover that he rather welcomed her company. It was nice to have someone to talk to during the tedious hours of cataloguing organs, even if Grim did occasionally indicate her boredom with a given topic by conspicuously grooming herself in unmentionable places.

"It would certainly be harder to pull off if this one was any larger," he said, setting down his scalpel and moving to the far end of the table, where he'd gathered an assortment of alembics, burners, beakers, vials, and alchemical ingredients. Igor had needed to wait until the Doctor dropped into an exhausted sleep well after midnight to smuggle these out of the main lab, and would have to see that they found their way back there before the Doctor awoke sometime that afternoon.

Plenty of time for what Igor intended.

"So what's the point, then?" Grim prowled along the top shelf as Igor organized his makeshift alchemy station. "To prove to your boss that you can do whatever he can do?"

"Not exactly," Igor said, unstoppering a vial full of dark yellow liquid and carefully pouring it into a decanter. "How much do you know about alchemy?"

Grim sniffed. "I know that it isn't real magic."

"I've also heard that it's not real science. Really, it's somewhere between the two, I think." Satisfied with the amount of bile he'd poured into the decanter, Igor picked up another vial, of which he poured in only a smattering of droplets. "The alchemists hold that there are hundreds of different humors or fluids that make up the human body, and that each of these various fluids corresponds to a different personality trait. People with more than the usual amount of blood were more energetic, those with too much phlegm overly timid, and so on."

"Uh-huh." Grim sounded unconvinced, but the swishing of her tail betrayed her interest. "So, human personality just comes down to whatever fluids you've got sloshing around inside?"

"Not all," Igor said, shaking his head. "You can't make a person more sanguine by injecting more blood into them. People are more complex than that. They defy easy categorization, and the correlation between the body and the mind remains unclear. A murderer's brain looks much the same as a saint's."

"You would know, I suppose." Grim glanced at the racks of brains floating in their jars on the aisle opposite her. "Then what's the point of what you're doing now?"

"The humors may not dictate personality," Igor said, pouring the contents of the last of the vials into the decanter, which he stoppered and began shaking vigorously. "Not for a person, anyhow. But for an empty vessel, they can provide a template."

"An empty vessel," Grim repeated, settling onto her haunches and peering down at Igor's miniature Subject. "What sort of personality are you hoping to impart upon this little guy, then?"

"They're genderless," said Igor, who'd long been of the opinion that endowing a Subject with reproductive parts was merely an invitation for unnecessary complications. "As for the personality . . . helpful, and inquisitive, and energetic, and creative. Someone who'd be good help around the lab."

"An assistant to the assistant," Grim mused. "Creating your own little Igor, Igor?"

"Whatever do you mean?" Igor asked, returning to his Subject while the alchemical concoction heated.

"I've been watching you," Grim said, staring unblinkingly at him. "Whatever your Doctor orders you to do, you do. Even if it's difficult or unpleasant, or something he could easily do himself. He bosses you around, and bullies you when he's in a bad mood. And no matter what you do for him, it's never quite enough. He *uses* you."

"I . . ." A thousand denials sprang to Igor's mind, yet died somewhere on the way to his tongue. Similarly traitorous thoughts had occurred to him on occasion, but he'd always quashed them as swiftly as they'd arisen. To hear them spoken aloud . . .

"You're afraid I'll treat this one the same way," he said instead, looking down at his own Subject, then back at Grim. "Do you really think I'm capable of that?"

"You're bringing a thinking being to life without its consent," Grimalkin pointed out. "For the express purpose of working as your slave."

"I don't want to enslave them!" Igor protested, aghast.

"So you'll pay them for their work, then?" Grim pressed, clearly unwilling to let the issue rest. Belatedly, Igor realized the parallels to her own summoning. "And give them the option to say no, if they don't want to?"

"Yes and yes," Igor said, looking down at his inert creation. "Although that latter might be a touch difficult."

Unlike the Doctor's Subjects, there was no mistaking Igor's creation for a human. A little under a foot tall if they stood upright, they had a bulbous head dominated by a single oversized eye socket, which left only just enough space behind it for enough gray matter to constitute a rudimentary brain. Regrettably, this afforded no room for a mouth, only vestigial vocal folds.

"How're they going to eat?" Grim asked, sounding genuinely concerned. "And how did you find a corpse so small?"

"I didn't," Igor said, deciding to answer the second question first. "I grew them."

"You grew them?" Grim sounded at once horrified and impressed.

"In a jar," Igor said, waving at the dozens of jars placed upon their racks. "Alchemy has more applications than just balancing the humors. It's about transmutation. Turning one thing into another."

"You grew this in a jar," Grim repeated, looking down at the Subject. "Overnight?"

"Longer than that," Igor admitted. "As for the mouth . . . well, I put some plant material in the jar as well. Enough that they should be able to photosynthesize, rather than eat or breathe."

"That explains the green skin," Grim said, fixing him with her unblinking yellow stare. "So. You put the necessary organs into a jar, along with—what, a head of cabbage?"

"Spinach, actually," Igor said. "Then I filled the jar with the necessary alchemical compounds—"

"And grew this little fellow," Grim said, hopping down onto the table to land beside the miniature Subject. "How long have you been planning this, Igor?"

Igor had never possessed any talent for lying. Besides, Grim deserved an honest answer.

"Over a month," he admitted. "Since before we came to Ravenwald."

"And the Doctor never noticed some of his store of parts going missing?"

"There's a lot he doesn't notice." The words slipped from Igor's lips with a bitterness that surprised him. "And I only ever took the spare bits, the ones he'd already passed over for inclusion in the Work."

"Why?"

"I . . ." Igor hesitated. He'd never given that fear voice before, had scarcely even acknowledged it to himself. "After the Work. The last time, I mean. We were nearly successful. And I was afraid . . . I thought that, if we got it right, and the Doctor had a living, thinking, talking Subject . . ."

He looked down at his hands. "What use would he have for me, once the Work was complete?"

"So that's why you started building your little creation?" Grim cocked her head to one side. "So you'd have a purpose, if the Doctor decided he was done with you?"

"So I'd have a friend," Igor said softly.

"Oh." Grim's tail brushed softly across the tabletop. "I . . . see."

Igor nodded, not trusting himself to speak. Silence hung heavy in the frigid wine cellar.

"So, then," Grim said, looking up at the stone ceiling, "do you need to wait until a thunderstorm to get your little spare up and walking about?"

"Spare," Igor repeated, smiling a little. It was an apt name. "Not exactly."

* * *

Rejuvenating the tissues of a human-sized Subject required a tremendous amount of galvanic force. Perhaps one day mankind might be able to generate such high voltage artificially, but until technology caught up to the Doctor's vision, the Great Work would remain reliant upon fierce thunderstorms to generate the necessary power.

Igor was under no such constraint when it came to his own creation. Being significantly smaller than a human being, Spare required only a modest electrical charge to bring their inert form to life.

"I didn't know you knew how to ride a bike," Grim observed, having resumed her place atop the cellar shelving.

"It's a difficult skill to forget," Igor panted, wiping sweat from his brow with the back of his wrist. His legs worked mechanically at the pedals of the stationary bike, which was mounted on a pair of wooden struts. Its wheels were affixed to a crude metal battery, which was in turn attached to the electrodes Igor had placed on Spare's cranium. Each revolution generated a small amount of electricity, which would compound over time, the longer and harder Igor pedaled.

"How much more time do you expect this will take?" Grim asked, yawning wide. "Not that I have anywhere to be, but—"

The air filled with the sharp stench of ozone. Yellow sparks burst like fireworks from the electrodes affixed to Spare's cranium. On the table, the little Subject jerked upright like a marionette being hauled to its feet.

"It's alive!" Igor shouted, having always wanted to be the one to say that. He stumbled from the bicycle, nearly fell, righted himself. Ignoring Grim's look of disdain, he hurried to the table and peered down at the small green humanoid lying upon it, its single large eye closed.

"Must have passed out from the shock," Igor said sympathetically as he carefully removed the electrodes from Spare's head. "Grim, I think there's some camphor among my—"

Spare opened their eye, revealing a bright sky-blue iris. It rolled about, then fixed on Igor staring back down at it from a distance of a few inches.

"Hey," Grim said from somewhere above and behind him. "Isn't that the eyeball that—"

Spare's eye widened. They shrieked, a high and keening sound made all the more impressive by their lack of mouth.

Then they slapped Igor across the face.

"Ow!" he yelped, a hand rising to his cheek. He was more surprised than hurt; Spare probably weighed about as much as Grim. "What—"

They slapped him with their other hand, then sprang from the wooden table, landing with unexpected nimbleness on the dusty floor. Turning round, Igor just glimpsed their bare green feet disappearing around the far end of the nearest wine rack.

"Wow," Grim remarked from atop that same rack. "You made the little guy *fast*."

"They're genderless," Igor reminded her, hurrying down the aisle past organ jars and wine bottles alike. "Spare, come back! I—"

From somewhere in the depths of the wine cellar, Spare shrieked again, the sound echoing faintly as they got farther away. Heading, Igor realized with stomach-sinking dread, towards the staircase leading up to the rest of the manor. If Spare got out—or worse, if the Doctor discovered what Igor had been misallocating spare organs for . . .

"Stop!" Igor yelled, panting as he raced after his fleeing creation, already winded from his exertions on the stationary bike. "Just wait a minute—"

He rounded a corner and was immediately greeted with a full bottle of wine hurtling towards his head. Thankfully, dodging thrown objects was another skill at which Igor possessed considerable practice. Nimbly sidestepping, he barely slowed in his pursuit as the bottle smashed into the wall behind him.

"It's all right!" he yelled after the little cyclopean creature, which was now racing headlong towards the stairs. "I don't— No one's going to hurt you!"

Spare answered that with a dubious trilling sound, but Igor had no time to wonder at his creation's unexpected capacity for vocalization, not when they were nearly to the staircase. He chased after them, cursing his uneven gait and the painful stitch in his side in equal measure.

Spare mounted the first stair.

A flash of gray fur. Grimalkin, bounding down from the shelves, across the floor, past Spare and up the stairs. Roughly the same size as the little creature, she stood with her hair on end, blocking their flight up.

"Hi," she said, showing her teeth.

Spare shrieked and turned around, only to find Igor standing there.

"You're all right," he said, making an abortive grab for them, but Spare slipped from his grasp and ran between Igor's legs, disappearing back into the depths of the wine cellar.

"Igor," Grim said calmly, padding down the stairs. "The door."

"Right," Igor nodded, pushing the door to the stairway closed as Grim returned to the cellar floor. Dazed, he touched two fingers to his reddened cheek. "I . . . he slapped me!"

"Genderless," Grim reminded him. "What were you expecting?"

"What do you mean?" Igor asked, double-checking that the door was securely closed. Would Spare understand how to operate doors? Like a newborn gazelle, they had begun running almost instantly, and had been smart enough to try to slow his pursuit with the thrown bottle. Could they understand how to work a doorknob just as instinctively?

"Imagine you wake up and the first thing you see is some giant looming over you," Grim pointed out. "How would you react?"

"Not well," Igor admitted. "Especially if it looked like me."

"Don't say that," Grim said, shouldering his leg with surprising force. "I scratched Mag when she summoned me, you know. Kind of set the tone for our relationship, in retrospect."

"I can see how it might have." Igor smiled despite himself. He looked around the wine cellar, the pattering of Spare's footfalls fading, then ceasing altogether. "Now what?"

"Now," Grim said, almost gently, "you try again. Go and introduce yourself properly this time."

"But what if they won't come out?" Igor asked, then voiced what was really troubling him: "What if Spare doesn't like me?"

"They probably just need time," Grim advised. "Let them hear your voice, get used to you. Cats take a while to decide whether we like someone, too."

"Oh?" Igor looked down at her. "How long did it take you to decide about me?"

"Jury's still out," Grim said, her tail brushing his leg. "Go say hello, Igor. I'll watch the door."

Igor knelt and gave her a grateful scratch between the ears, which Grim deigned to accept. Then he strode off down the rows of wine racks, turning his head slowly from side to side in search of movement.

"Spare?" he called softly. "It's all right. You can come out."

There was no answer, but Igor hadn't really expected one. It wasn't as if Spare would recognize their name, when they didn't even know they had one.

"Spare," Igor repeated, moving slowly through the wine cellar. He was determined not to spook them this time. "My name is Igor. I'm your . . . well. I'm not sure what you'd call me, exactly."

He paused, ears straining, and a moment later was rewarded by a faint scuffling.

"I'm the one who made you," Igor said, heading in that direction, careful to keep his voice gentle. "I'm not saying that to . . . brag, I guess, or claim ownership, or anything like that. I just thought you should know that I brought you here, into this world. Which I guess makes you my responsibility."

There was a squeaking sound to his left. Igor turned and found Spare's single blue eye staring back at him from the depths of one of the little diamond-shaped wine rack alcoves, flanked by bottles on all sides.

"Hey there." Igor offered what he hoped was an encouraging smile. "Hey, Spare."

The eye stared back at him, then narrowed.

"You can stay there," Igor assured his creation. "If it makes you feel safe. I don't want you to feel trapped. No one should feel they're being forced to stay someplace."

He turned and leaned against the shelf, hoping Spare might grow bold enough or curious enough to venture from the little nook in which they had hidden themself.

"I know there's probably a lot you don't understand," he continued, closing his eyes. "About me, or the world, or yourself. And I'll try to teach you as best I can about all of it. If you'll give me that time. But . . ."

He opened his eyes, and nearly jumped to see Spare's one huge eye looking back at him as they leaned out from their niche.

"Hey," Igor said, not daring to move. "I just . . . wanted you to know, I guess. Why I brought you into this weird, confusing world."

He hadn't said it before, not aloud. Not even to Grim.

Spare stared at him, their blue eye wide, guileless, curious.

"I made you," Igor confessed to his creation, "because I was lonely."

18

INCISIVE

SPARE GREW GRADUALLY less reticent over the course of the next several nights, though to Igor's relief they seemed content for the time being to confine themself to the wine cellar. Pleased though he was with his creation, Igor had resolved not to introduce Spare to either the Doctor or the world before he felt the little construct was ready.

Besides, with the selection of body parts finalized, Igor was kept so busy by the construction of the Great Work's full-sized Subject that he had hardly time for anything else.

At first, the Doctor's intended paragon of the human form was little more than a limbless and headless torso, its chest cavity and midsection hollowed out like a turkey awaiting stuffing. Into this empty chassis Igor placed the organs he'd harvested, starting with the long and ropey maze of the lower digestive system, a step which always inspired in Igor a perverse craving for haggis. From there he'd add the other necessaries: kidneys, spleen, liver, and the like, before working his way up to the lungs, heart, and similar respiratory parts.

Once the torso was mostly assembled came the comparatively easy task of attaching the arms and legs, the most troublesome aspect of which was ensuring that the nerve endings were properly aligned. This required frequent testing via the application of galvanic force, and for several days Igor's own limbs ached from long hours spent pedaling the stationary bike.

"These are kidneys," he told Spare one evening, not quite a week after assembling the lightning rod. He handed the jar containing the two bean-shaped organs to the little cyclops, who held it in both hands for closer inspection. "They turn water into waste."

Spare trilled inquisitively.

"You don't have any," said Igor, who'd made considerable progress in interpreting his creation's various vocalizations. "You get all your nutrients from sunlight, remember?"

Spare made a dissatisfied *mrrp* sound that Igor suspected they had picked up from Grim.

"I'll start taking you outside more often soon," he promised, taking the jar of kidneys back. "Just have to wait until I've introduced you to the Doctor, that's all."

"And when are you planning on doing that?"

With all the practice he'd gotten from his housemates, Igor was by now almost totally inured to being snuck up on.

"Soon," he assured Grim as she hopped down from a wine rack.

"That's what you said two nights ago," Grim said. She sniffed Spare in greeting, which they returned by scratching her head. Igor still felt a touch sore that his creation had warmed up to Grimalkin more quickly than they had to him.

"And the night before that," Cornelia added, stepping out from the shadows. Newly returned from hunting, judging by the faint smear of red at the corner of her mouth.

"I'm waiting for the opportune time," Igor said, a touch defensively. He tapped his lip. "You've got something right there, by the way."

"Ah." Cornelia wiped the blood away with her thumb. "Damn sheriff put up quite the struggle."

Igor nearly dropped the kidney jar. "You drained the sheriff of Ravensburg?"

"He was abusing his station," Cornelia said darkly. She cocked her head. "I'm surprised you'd be put out about it. You've made no bones about my choice of victims before."

"I'm not upset," Igor said, though that was only half true. If Cornelia's strong sense of justice had decreed the sheriff's punishment, he'd no doubt earned it. But the sheriff was also one of the officials Igor had bribed to keep attention away from Ravenwald Manor. Deserved or not, his removal meant one less delay against the inevitable mob. "Just surprised me, that's all."

"Influential men are just as likely to be villains as the common sort," Cornelia said, misunderstanding his surprise. "More, really."

Evidently growing bored, Spare wandered towards the worktable on which they had been given life, which was presently occupied by another of the vampires' exsanguinated victims. Igor took small comfort in the knowledge that at least that one wasn't someone he had bribed.

"So." Grim settled onto her haunches. "When's this opportune moment of yours going to come?"

"I'll know it when it arrives," Igor said, returning his attention to the task of locating an appendix from their stores—as so often happened, that particular organ had been overlooked while he and the Doctor had been in the planning phase.

If he was being honest with himself, Igor wasn't quite ready to introduce his creation to his master. He could not quite shake the feeling that the Doctor would be less impressed with Igor's inventiveness and proficiency in alchemy than irked at his misappropriation of laboratory materials.

"Look," he said to the others. "The Doctor's getting on in years. I can't just spring a surprise like Spare on him."

"I watched him electrocute himself yesterday," Grim said. "More than once."

Cornelia frowned. "Again?"

"My point being," Igor continued, turning back towards the worktable, "that I can't just wait for him to notice that Spare's around—"

On the worktable, Spare stood holding a scalpel with both hands in a manner that reminded Igor less of a surgeon than of a night watchman shouldering his halberd.

"Spare," Igor started, "don't—"

Spare made a high, trilling sound. The scalpel flashed as they cut into the side of the donor laid out upon the table. Igor winced, grateful that the body in question had already been fully drained of blood.

"Barbaric," Cornelia said, wrinkling her nose.

"Aww," Grim said, tail brushing against Igor's side as she watched with undisguised amusement. "They want to help."

"That's one term for it," Igor muttered, wanting to reach out and pluck Spare from the table but knowing better than to do so while they were wielding the scalpel. "Guess that's another donor gone to waste—"

Letting out a high, victorious trill, Spare flung the scalpel away. Igor ducked as it flew towards him, burying itself with a resounding thrum in the wine rack just behind him.

"Spare!" Igor shouted as the construct reached both hands into the opening they had carved in the donor, narrowing their eye in concentration as they rooted around. "Don't—"

There was a faint, wet tearing sound as something came loose. Spare toppled backwards, tottering on the edge of the table. This time Igor threw himself forward, catching his one-eyed creation before they could hit the floor.

"You could have gotten hurt!" Igor said, his voice thick with some emotion he couldn't quite place as he cradled Spare against his chest. They made a throaty purring sound, one they had *definitely* picked up from Grim.

Gingerly, Igor set Spare down. They looked down at the

thing they had pried loose from the donor—two things, really—then held them up to Igor in offering.

"Kidneys," Grim said, blinking slowly.

Cornelia looked down at the organs in question, bemused. "Huh."

"Thank you," Igor said, taking them carefully from Spare and plopping them into a waiting specimen jar. He looked over at the donor, in whose side Spare had cut a surprisingly precise square incision.

"Kid's a fast learner," Grim remarked.

"So it appears," Igor said faintly, as Spare ran over to the wine rack and began jumping for the scalpel they had accidentally embedded there, which was mercifully too high for them to reach. Somehow their eagerness reminded Igor of his own early days under the Doctor's tutelage, which had been as informal, haphazard, and slapdash an on-the-job training as could be imagined. Igor had been forced to learn quickly, puzzling out those things he hadn't yet learned on his own lest he risk the Doctor's displeasure.

"Here," he said, walking over to the wine rack and pulling the scalpel free. Spare reached up both hands for it, cheeping plaintively, but Igor shook his head.

"Not yet," he said, returning to the worktable and rummaging through the tray of tools he'd placed beside it. He selected a scalpel small enough for Spare to hold in one hand.

Spare clambered onto the worktable. Igor handed them the scalpel he'd selected, then held up his own full-sized one in demonstration.

"First," he said, recalling his own harried instruction from the Doctor all those years ago, "I'm going to teach you how to hold it properly."

Spare narrowed their eye in concentration, then adjusted their grip on the miniature scalpel to resemble Igor's.

"Good," Igor said, smiling. "Almost right. Just let me . . ."

He reached down, adjusted Spare's grip so that their index finger would have greater control over the blade. Something warm and unfamiliar stirred in Igor's heart as Spare turned their unblinking gaze up to him, expectantly awaiting his next instruction.

It took Igor a moment to realize that what he was feeling was pride.

He had created Spare intending them to be a friend and helpmate in his own tasks. And to their credit, the little cyclops seemed eager to learn. But not all skills could be learned by observation alone; the delicate arts of dissection and stitchery required a patient teacher.

In that regard at least, Igor felt confident he could do better for Spare than the Doctor had for him.

19

MIDNIGHT SNACK

"I'M SURPRISED THE Doctor let you out of the lab," Grim remarked a few nights later, trotting along beside Igor as they made their way down the lane towards the cemetery. "Aren't you in a big rush to get the Subject all stitched together before the next time it storms?"

"The Doctor likes to say that you can't rush art," Igor said, shrugging as he pulled the corpse cart along behind him. "And I might have told him we were out of algaroth."

"Which is some sort of dreadfully important alchemical tincture, I presume?"

"It's a powder, actually. But yes."

Grim fixed him with her yellow-eyed gaze. "And *are* you out of it?"

"No," Igor admitted. "But the Doctor doesn't know that."

"Who are you, and what have you done with Igor?" Grim asked, but she sounded pleased, as well as amused.

"Someone who needs a break." He'd installed the last of the Subject's internal organs earlier that night, then sewn up its chest cavity. It still needed a head, not to mention limbs, but those were relatively easy compared to what he'd just achieved. "I think I've earned one."

"Whether or not the Doctor agrees," Grim said approvingly, then cocked her head. "So you're spending it . . . going back to the cemetery for more parts?"

"Not quite," Igor said, as the cemetery's wrought iron gates loomed ahead in the mist. "Hold on a moment."

As he set the cart down, Grim leapt nimbly onto a tree stump. "I want to thank you. For keeping an eye on Spare when I can't."

Grim blinked. "You know about that?"

"Doesn't take a genius," Igor said, throwing her a rueful smile. In fact, Spare had grown brave enough to venture from the wine cellar a few nights ago, and had even begun observing Igor's work on the Subject in the laboratory during those rare hours when the Doctor succumbed to sleep. But there had also been times when he'd been obliged to leave the inquisitive little construct unattended—times that seemed to mysteriously coincide with Grimalkin's disappearing from sight for a few hours, and not for her usual ephemera gathering.

"So," Igor continued, fumbling in his pocket, "I made this for you."

He produced the collar he'd sewn together from an old leather coat. He'd even stitched Grim's name into it in gold thread, which he'd thought would nicely match her yellow eyes.

"I'll understand if you don't want to wear it . . ." he began, holding it out for her to sniff.

"Let's see how it fits first," Grim said guardedly. "Go ahead."

She held patiently still as Igor fastened the collar around her neck, mindful to keep it from being too tight. "How's that?"

"Tolerable, I suppose," Grim said, flicking one ear.

Anxiety roiled in Igor's stomach at her cavalier tone. Should he have wrapped the collar before giving it to Grim? Or worse, what if the choice of gift had inadvertently offended her? Mortified, he recalled how she'd likened his creation of Spare to slavery. Would she think that giving her a collar was meant to signify the same?

"It's all right if you don't like it," Igor blurted, unable to contain his anxiety any longer. "I can help take it off, you don't have to—"

"I like it," Grim said. Then, more quietly: "It makes me feel like a real cat."

"You are a real cat," Igor said, relief flooding through him. He scratched her reassuringly between the ears. "In every way that matters."

Grim leaned into his hand, purring. "Thanks, Igor."

Igor smiled.

The sound of a door slamming open echoed through the fog. They both turned to see a tall shadow detach itself from the graveyard gatehouse to trudge towards them, holding a hooded lantern high.

"Who goes there?" Laura's voice rang through the mist. "I warn you, if you've come this way looking to make trouble—"

"It's me!" Igor's voice came out in something of a squeak. "Igor!"

"The hunchback?" Laura asked, drawing nearer and lifting her lantern higher. "What're you doing out here so late? And who were you talking to just now?"

"Myself," Igor lied, while out of the corner of his eye Grim hopped onto the cart. "Bad habit, I'm told, but when you spend long enough working on your own—"

"You needn't tell me twice," Laura said, a smile creasing her face. Her gaze shifted to somewhere past Igor's shoulder, eyes narrowing. "Who's that?"

"Igor?" came Cornelia's voice from behind him as she materialized from the fog—in the normal fashion, thankfully. "You said to meet you at— *Oh.* Hello, Laura."

"Miss Cornelia." Laura tucked one of her unruly strands of hair behind her ear. "Why—err, that is, what brings you here this evening?"

Cornelia gave Igor a pointed look. "As a matter of fact, I'm wondering the same thing."

"Well," Igor said slowly, as this was the part of his scheme which required the most delicacy, "for starters, Laura, I wanted to thank you for your forbearance and discretion this last fortnight or so."

"You've already expressed your gratitude," Laura pointed out, patting the bulging coin purse hanging from her belt. Coins jingled merrily inside. "Rather eloquently, in my book."

"Then you won't object to one more token of appreciation," Igor said, turning and retrieving a wicker basket from the corpse cart. He handed it to Laura, whose nostrils flared even before she opened the basket and peeked inside.

"Sandwiches?"

"Also some apples and a tin of biscuits," Igor added. "And two bottles of wine."

"You must think me some kind of lush," Laura said. She glanced upwards at the waning crescent moon just visible through a gap in the fog. "Bit late for a picnic lunch, though."

"A midnight snack, then," Igor said, turning to Cornelia. "Provided you share it with Cornelia, of course."

It was difficult to tell in the moonlight, but the color seemed to drain from Laura's face.

"That's what you brought me out here for?" Cornelia asked, frowning down at Igor. "You know I can't—that I'm on a liquid diet."

"Of course," Igor said smoothly, having already anticipated this objection. "One of the wine bottles is for you. The red, naturally."

"Naturally," Cornelia said tightly, turning her attention to the gravekeeper. "Laura, I must offer a thousand apologies. I had no idea Igor had this in mind when he asked me to meet him here, and you're under no obligation—"

“I’d be happy to,” Laura said, then cast her gaze towards her feet. “Err, that is, so long as *you* don’t feel obligated to—”

“I don’t,” Cornelia said, just as hurriedly. She glared at Igor, who grinned widely. “Though I must beg your pardon in advance for what I’m sure will be absolutely atrocious manners, as it’s been a long time since I’ve enjoyed a meal in company.”

“That,” Laura said, seeming to regain some of her confidence, “is an unspeakable shame, if I may say so.”

“You may,” Cornelia said, hesitating. “My h—that is, my family—they’re rather controlling, I’m afraid.”

“Ah.” Laura nodded sympathetically. “Family’s always a tricky matter. I wouldn’t want you getting in trouble with them for being out here with me, of course—”

“No,” Cornelia said, red curls bouncing as she shook her head. Something defiant gleamed in her eyes. “No, I . . . I want to. Have a picnic here. With you.”

“You’re certain?” Laura asked.

“I am,” Cornelia said, in the tone of someone who had just emerged victorious from some internal debate. “It’s been—well, a dreadfully long time since I’ve had the pleasure of decent company.”

“You might be waiting a mite longer, then,” Laura said, rubbing the back of her neck self-consciously. “Can’t say there are many folk who’d count me as such.”

“I doubt that very much.” Cornelia smiled slightly. “I must confess that I’ve returned in my mind to our last conversation often.”

Laura barked out a laugh. “Then you must really be starved for conversational partners, miss. I’m not what most would call the talkative sort.”

“That’s no bad thing,” Cornelia said, her smile widening. “Sometimes it’s nice to be listened to.”

“I’d certainly like to.” Laura looked shyly down at her feet. “Listen to you, I mean. To what you have to say.”

Cornelia took a step nearer. "On what subject?"

"Can't see it hardly matters, with a voice like yours." Laura dared a glance at Cornelia through her tangled hair. "You could read from the dictionary and I'd hang on every word."

Cornelia laughed. "I'm sure we can settle on more interesting topics." She rested her hand on Laura's flannel-clad arm. Laura looked down at it, then at the woman it was attached to. Between her bangs, Igor saw a wolfish hunger gleaming in those brown eyes.

"Well," he said, clearing his throat. Cornelia jerked her arm away from Laura as if she were a hot stove, both of them resolutely looking anywhere but at each other. "I think it's time Grimalkin and I were on our way, then. Laura, you'll have her back to Ravenwald Manor by night's end?"

"Of course," Laura said, clearing her throat. She offered Cornelia her hand. "Shall we?"

"A moment," Cornelia said, turning to take the picnic basket from Igor.

"Thank you," she murmured in his ear, and gave him a quick cold kiss on his cheek.

"Would you like to come inside?" Laura asked, gesturing at her little gatehouse cottage as Cornelia joined her, picnic basket under one arm. "Or—"

"Actually," Cornelia said, looking up at the stars twinkling overhead as the fog began to dissipate, "let's stay outdoors."

She glanced briefly at Grim and Igor, smiling. "It's turning out to be a nice night after all."

20

ASSISTANCE

IGOR SPENT THE next several nights attaching the Subject's limbs. Though less technically demanding than installing organs, this work was so labor-intensive that he hardly ventured beyond the observatory turned laboratory for days on end.

The work was not only hard, but lonely. The Doctor had absented himself from what he dismissed as the tediously mechanical process of grafting limbs to torso, grandly declaring that he would be pursuing the far nobler art of alchemy in one of the manor's upstairs bedrooms. This left Igor with many long hours of solitary stitching, and though he found the work itself soothing in its repetitiveness, he soon wished for more company.

"Why not take Spare?" Grim suggested when he voiced this complaint a few nights into the process, during one of the rare breaks when Igor ventured down to the wine cellar for replacement parts. "They may not be much of a conversationalist, but any company's better than none, if you're feeling lonesome."

For her part, Grim had been too preoccupied with her own responsibilities to spend much time hanging about the lab. Auntie Mag, Grim confided, was gearing up for another attempt at the Rite of Opening, and consequently nearly all of Grim's time was taken up with forays into town to acquire ephemera.

Cornelia's visits too had become more infrequent, as her nightly hunts seemed to mysteriously take up more time than they had previously—the difference, Igor was almost positive, being those hours spent visiting a certain brown-eyed gravekeeper.

"I'd have to explain where they came from if my master discovers us," Igor pointed out, browsing a shelf full of severed hands preserved in jars. The phalanges of the one he'd intended to attach to the Subject had turned out to be broken, necessitating a replacement.

"Wasn't that the point of creating Spare, though?" Grimalkin asked, glancing over to a corner of the cellar where Spare was busy arranging a collection of eyeball jars according to size. "Showing the Doctor your capabilities?"

"It was," Igor admitted. "Only . . ."

He trailed off as he inspected one of the hands for damage. He had anticipated that the Doctor might be displeased with him for creating a Subject of his own, though that fear hadn't been enough to stop him from going through with the plan. Only after bringing Spare to life had Igor realized that he had more to fear than his own standing with his master. What if the Doctor took out his frustrations with Igor upon Spare? Or what if the Doctor decided he actually preferred a servant who wouldn't talk back, wouldn't ask questions, wouldn't demand a wage?

Igor glanced over his shoulder at Spare, who'd begun grouping the eyeballs according to color, and wondered whether he was looking at his replacement.

"You said you wanted Spare to be your assistant, right?" Grim sauntered up alongside Igor. "Let them assist you, then."

Still Igor hesitated. "I—"

"Think of it this way," Grim pointed out. "It'll make the stitching go more quickly."

"I suppose it would." Igor watched as Spare rearranged the eyeballs yet again. He was well aware that the little construct was capable of more. Given how quickly they had absorbed his lessons on anatomy—did it feel stifling, he wondered, to be kept from more engaging work?

"Spare," Igor said, clearing his throat.

Spare looked up from their task, their eyeball widening hopefully.

"How would you like to come upstairs," Igor continued, "to help me with—"

Before he could finish, Spare let out a high-pitched squeal and threw themself at his leg, knocking over several of the eyeball jars along the way. They hugged Igor's leg tightly, their eye closed and creased at the corners in what Igor presumed was a smile.

"I think," Grim said, her tail lashing happily, "that's a yes."

* * *

In the laboratory, Spare proved to be as quick a learner of the delicate craft of stitchery as they had been of physiology and dissection. Still, Igor thought it best to give his cyclopean creation some additional practice before allowing them to work on the Subject proper.

"Now," he said, holding up a skull and resisting the urge to soliloquize about jesters, "obviously the first step in attaching the jawbone is ensuring that the mandible is properly aligned to the temporal bone. Go on, give it a try."

He lowered the skull to Spare, who held the waiting jawbone. Igor again felt that odd stirring in his heart as his creation carefully slotted the jawbone into place with a faint *click*.

"Very good," he said encouragingly. Spare curiously hinged the jaw open, then shut, turning the skull into a macabre puppet. "Now, since this jawbone came from this skull, the two fit together perfectly. But when attaching parts from two separate donors, you might need to make some adjustments. Shaving down bone or filing teeth until they fit properly. The last thing you want is a Subject with snaggleteeth—"

Spare squealed with sudden fright. Their huge eye growing wide, they yanked the skull from Igor's grip and hurled it at him. Startled, Igor jerked away, the skull flying past him—

—and smacking directly into the Count, who'd been leaning towards Igor with fangs extended. The vampire recoiled, hissing like an irate cobra.

"Back!" Igor shouted, fright turning his voice into a falsetto squeal as he plunged his hand into his pocket, where he'd been carrying a vial of garlic powder ever since that first night. He popped out its cork and brandished it at the Count. "Get back!"

The Count shrank away, mustaches twitching as he wrinkled his nose, but his retreat carried him back only a few paces before he mastered himself.

"It'll take more than a pinch of seasoning to keep me at bay," he spat. Fleetingly, Igor wondered whether that had been intended as a pun. The Count advanced towards him again, grasping hands outstretched, his face contorted in a rictus of what was either fury or a barely suppressed need to sneeze.

"Stay away!" Igor squeaked, backing up until he bumped against the hard surface of the Subject's slab. Before he could dart away, the Count swooped in, his black cape fluttering.

"Now," the vampire said, his voice dripping with both venom and phlegm as Igor brandished the garlic powder, "you will tell me what you have done with my— Ow!"

His cape fluttered as he looked down to where Spare had just driven one of Igor's scalpels into the vampire' ankle. Snarling, the Count kicked at Spare, but the construct dodged aside nimbly enough for Igor to fling the entire vial of garlic powder into the Count's face.

"Gah!" the Count gasped, doubling over. "Gah—ahh—ahhch!"

A small explosion in the guise of a sneeze burst from the vampire's nose, echoing like a cannon blast. The Count's shoulders shook as he scrunched up his face, mouth hanging slack as he tried and failed to stop a second sneeze from following on the heels of the first. And another, and another.

Igor watched in horrified fascination as the Count held his clawlike hands to his face, striving to contain both the sneezes and the dribble of snot dangling from the tip of his nose. A high trilling at Igor's side pulled his gaze downwards. Spare was tugging frantically on his sleeve. They pointed the scalpel in their other hand at the Count, still sneezing, and piped out something urgent.

"Oh," Igor said, realizing that the garlic had bought them only a few seconds. "Right."

He reached under the Subject's table and pulled free the wooden stake he'd loosely nailed to its underside, then barreled into the Count shoulder first. They fell to the laboratory floor in a tangled pile of limbs, cape, and something wet Igor preferred not to think about.

Perhaps the Count had been rendered vulnerable by the garlic powder, or maybe he just hadn't been in a physical altercation these last few centuries. Either way, Igor quickly gained the upper hand. A few moments later he was sitting atop the Count, who'd been rolled up like a cigar inside the folds of his own cape.

"Now," Igor said, surprised at how calm he sounded when his heart was beating loudly enough that the Count must surely hear it, "you're going to explain to me why you attacked me just now."

"Or what?" The Count sneered, or tried to—the bubble of snot in one nostril rather undercut his scorn. "You'll drive that sharp bit of wood into my heart?"

"Or whatever you have that passes for one," Igor said, raising the stake in question. He wondered if his brain hadn't been swapped with one from his collection, presumably one with more bravado and a less developed sense of self-preservation.

"You're bluffing," the Count spat. "I have seen how soft-hearted you are, hunchback. How gently you treat your master, and my wife, and that thing that claims itself a cat. And you expect me to believe you could destroy me in cold blood?"

"I probably couldn't," Igor admitted, handing the stake to Spare. The little construct took it in both hands, their eye narrowing at the Count. "Spare here, on the other hand . . ."

Spare slapped the blunt end of the stake against their hand, like a constable with a sap. This wasn't exactly the impression Igor had intended, but the Count's widening eyes betrayed a flicker of uncertainty.

"Now," Igor said, "are you going to talk, or is Spare going to have to make Cornelia a widow?"

"My wife." The Count's eyes narrowed. "Yes, you would be eager to curry her favor, wouldn't you?"

Igor blinked. "I would?"

"Of course you would," the Count said, half to himself. "She is beautiful, and powerful, and not without her own cunning. What mortal man, even one such as you, would not seek to do her bidding for a chance at the immortality she promises?"

"You think Cornelia's offered to make me a—to make me like you?" Igor laughed shakily at the sheer absurdity of the idea.

"Everyone desires this," the Count said, nodding down at himself, though the effect was rather spoiled by the puffiness of his cheeks, the flecks of snot clinging to his mustaches, and his ignominious mummification in his own cape. "Why do you think I have gifted my immortality to only one, after so many mortal lifetimes?"

Igor wetted his lips. "Your wife seems inclined to return it, were that an option."

"It is not." The Count sounded, for a moment, almost sad. "I have tried, you know. To find a cure. There is none."

A pang of sympathy twinged in Igor's chest. "Is that why you turned Cornelia? So you wouldn't be alone?"

"Not that she has ever been terribly appreciative of the gift."

The Count scowled. "And now I ask again: What have you done with my bride?"

Igor blinked. "What do you mean?"

"Do not dissemble," the Count scoffed. "I know that she has been leaving the remnants of our prey in that basement where you keep your grotesquerie. For a time I thought it mere convenience—what better way to dispose of unwanted bodies?"

The Count licked his lips, pink tongue lingering about his gleaming fangs. "But these last nights she has lingered away from the manor for many, many hours, not returning until the sun has nearly risen. Far longer than necessitated by a night's hunting."

"Maybe she's losing her touch," Igor suggested.

"Cornelia?" The Count showed his fangs, smiling with something that was almost like pride. "Never. She has always been clever and resourceful, just as she has always been headstrong and obstinate."

"I wouldn't think those were traits you'd admire in her," Igor said, the words slipping free before he could stop them.

"On the contrary." The Count's smile grew all the more repulsive for its sincerity. "Cornelia's willfulness is one of the things which drew me to her in the first place. The challenge of taming her, you know."

Igor's fingers curled into fists. He was perversely grateful that he'd handed the stake over to Spare. If he'd held it now, he wasn't certain that he'd have been able to resist the urge to plunge it into the Count's heart.

"And this has what to do with me?" he growled.

"I want to know where she has been disappearing to," the Count said, eyes narrowing. "Whether she is planning another attempt at escaping the manor and our marriage."

"You think she'd tell me that?" Igor scoffed, hoping he sounded appropriately scornful. "Leaving me your leftovers doesn't make me her confidant, *milord*."

"No," the Count said slowly, and Igor was relieved to hear the first hint of doubt creeping into his voice. "No, perhaps not. But what else could have prompted this change in her, if not your arrival to this house? Particularly when she is so overfond of you."

Igor's admiration of Cornelia's beauty did not extend to physical attraction, yet even so his cheeks grew hot. "Overfond?"

The Count blinked owlishly up at him. "You really don't know, do you?"

"Know what?" Igor demanded, feeling wrongfooted and testy about it.

"The lengths to which my Cornelia has gone to ensure your protection," the Count said, smiling thinly. "Perhaps it is better that way. Now, if you would kindly let me up—"

"So you can try to drink my blood again?" Igor demanded.

The Count rolled his eyes, as if Igor's accusation was thoroughly unreasonable. "So that I may discover what, exactly, my dear bride is plotting. Pray be quick about it; I haven't all night."

Spare made an inquisitive sound, offering Igor the stake. Though a darker part of him was tempted by the offer, he shook his head and pushed it away—not so much out of squeamishness, moral or otherwise, but because the Count was Cornelia's to deal with, not his.

"Get out of here," Igor said, standing and backing away to the other side of the Subject's table. Spare hopped onto it, standing with stake at the ready between their creator and the Count as the latter unwound himself from his cape.

"Well." The vampire stood with the air of a man attempting to reclaim what shreds remained of his dignity. "This has been most . . . enlightening, I suppose. I shall even leave you with a bit of advice."

"What's that?"

"Not to interfere again in another's marriage," the Count advised, brushing dust from his shirtfront. "Such meddling rarely ends well for anyone involved." He showed his fangs. "Particularly the interloper."

He turned to go, cape swishing dramatically behind him.

"Don't come back here," Igor called after him. "I won't hesitate to stake you next time."

"Next time," the Count said, letting out a huff of breath that might have been mistaken for laughter, were it not so cold, "you'll be asleep."

Igor shuddered, and resolved to wreath the door of his sleeping quarters with garlic at his first opportunity.

The doors slammed behind the Count. Igor slumped over the worktable, his body trembling as if he'd just run a long race at a dead sprint.

He had to inform Cornelia of the Count's suspicions, of course. But it was late enough at night that he wasn't sure where to even begin looking for her—not to mention that doing so would only confirm the Count's accusations.

"I'll ask Grim to talk to her next time they cross each other's paths," he said, half to Spare and half to himself. He had a vague sense that Grimalkin and Cornelia had been venturing into town together while he was cooped up in the laboratory. He rather hoped the three of them might be able to visit Ravensburg together, but that would have to wait until after he'd finished the task at hand.

"So to speak," he muttered.

He gave Spare a wan smile. "Ready to get to work?"

Spare trilled their agreement, setting down the stake and taking up a position near the Subject's head, beside the metal rolling cart where Igor kept his tools.

A short time later, Igor was fully immersed in the rhythms of the Great Work, taking his careful time threading the selected severed hand to the Subject's wrist stump. Spare stood beside him, their eye trained on his hands as they observed his stitches.

"Scissors, please," Igor said, eyes fixed on the two tendons he'd just artfully sewn together, holding out a hand. Spare turned towards the tool cart, but before they could take hold of the scissors, the laboratory doors creaked open on their ancient and unoiled hinges. Igor had a momentary horrifying vision of the Count returning in wrath, before the far worse reality asserted itself.

"What in the blazes is *that*?" came the Doctor's astonished voice.

Beside Igor, Spare whimpered.

21

THE SINCEREST FORM OF FLATTERY

"THAT'S OUR SUBJECT," said Igor, deciding in a moment of panic that his only defense was to play dumb. He kept his gaze fixed on the tendons he'd just sewn and held out his open palm. "Scissors?"

Spare chirped in answer and began rummaging around in the tool cart.

"Not that," the Doctor said, his voice strained. "I meant the odd little creature handing you the scalpel."

"Scalpel?" Igor asked, then bit back a yelp as Spare pressed the wrong end of the wrong instrument into his palm.

"Thank you," Igor hissed at Spare, earning a cheerful trill in reply. He flipped the scalpel around, then trimmed the thread with one deft cut before turning around on his stool to look at his master.

"This is Spare," he said, nodding down at his creation, which was now holding up a surgical mirror like a shield between themself and the Doctor. "Spare, this is the Doctor. Say hello."

Spare made no answer, just lowered the mirror enough to glare at the Doctor over its rim.

"Spare," the Doctor repeated, scratching his head. "What

is— Where did this curious little creature come from, precisely?"

Igor straightened his posture as much as his hunched back allowed. "I made them."

The Doctor stared. "You what?"

"I created them," Igor said, putting the hand not holding the scalpel gently on Spare's shoulder. "I grew Spare in a jar, using an alchemical solution and body parts from our collection. The ones we'd already passed over as unsuitable."

The Doctor blinked owlishly behind his spectacles. "You made him out of spare parts?"

"Them," Igor corrected. "Spare is not gendered. Some of the parts from the spare collection, yes. Muscle tissue, a discarded lung, an appendix. That sort of thing."

"An appendix," the Doctor repeated, still staring dazedly at Spare. "What a useless organ. Why is it dressed like that?"

"I didn't want them to have to run around naked." Even if there was nothing between Spare's legs, it had struck him as undignified not to give the creature something to wear.

"No, I mean . . ." the Doctor gesticulated weakly at the miniature white lab coat Igor had stitched together, and at the single-lensed goggle which magnified Spare's already huge eyeball into something positively enormous. "Why is it dressed like *you*?"

"Oh," Igor said, setting his scalpel down but keeping his hand firmly on it, in case Spare got any ideas. "Well, seeing that Spare is going to be helping me in my work—"

"Oh, saints." The Doctor sank into a cushioned chair Igor had dragged from the parlor at his behest. "Tell me you're not going to try to strongarm me into paying this one too."

"No," Igor said. Spare trilled indignantly. "I mean, yes, but don't worry, I'll pay out of my own wages—"

"I should think so," the Doctor said, cracking one eye open.

"Given that we certainly haven't the budget for an additional employee."

Igor had severe doubts about that, but decided not to press.

"Listen, Master," he said, clearing his throat. He'd been waiting for the opportune time, but this appeared to be the best he was going to get. "I've been thinking hard, and—"

The Doctor put his head in his hands and groaned, so loud and long that Igor worried he must be in considerable pain. He was about to take a step forward when the Doctor sat up, leaning forward with his fingers steepled, elbows resting on his bony knees.

"I should have known this day would come," the Doctor said, his voice thick with weary resignation. "In truth, I'm surprised it didn't arrive sooner."

Igor consulted his mental calendar. "Tuesday?"

"Not the day of the week, you dolt," the Doctor snapped. Then, resuming his melancholic tone, continued: "The day when you would decide to supplant me. The night when your hubris would whisper that you'd learned all that I can teach. When you bear out the sad cycle of history and rise against me, the apprentice deluding himself into believing he can outstrip his master—"

"Apprentice?" Igor repeated, latching on to that one word so strongly that the rest of the Doctor's monologue almost didn't register. Almost.

"Metaphorically speaking," the Doctor amended. "As I was saying . . . I suppose I should have realized that it was inevitable you would seek to emulate me. To attempt the creation of life yourself. Prolonged exposure to genius breeds admiration, yes, but also envy, and—"

"Hold on." Igor frowned. "You're saying I created Spare because I was *jealous* of you?"

"Well," the Doctor hedged, "doubtless you were also seeking to curry my favor. Imitation being the sincerest—"

"Doctor," Igor said impatiently, causing the Doctor to give him a strange look. "I made Spare myself, without any help. To prove that I could create a living, conscious being from dead flesh and alchemy. And I succeeded."

He gestured at his creation. Spare had apparently grown bored with the conversation and was now arranging the implements on the tool cart in order of sharpness. "And I . . . I think I'm ready to do the same on a larger scale."

The Doctor digested this. "With the Subject, you mean. Balancing its humors and such."

"Yes." Igor resisted the urge to look over his shoulder at the inert, half-assembled amalgam lying on the table beside him. "When it wakes up—when we bring it to life—it's going to be a person. I want to help shape what kind of person it will be."

He had never voiced his desires to the Doctor so forcefully before, and did not expect an immediate answer to such a speech. Nor did he receive one. For a long time the Doctor merely stared unblinkingly at Igor through the thick frames of his spectacles. There was no sound in the laboratory save for the quiet clinking of metal on metal as Spare amused themself with the surgical instruments.

"Perhaps," the Doctor said at last, with a calm that immediately set Igor on edge, "you have lost sight of the aim of the Great Work to which we aspire, my dear Igor."

Igor's back stiffened. The Doctor only ever addressed him that way when he was truly displeased. "What—"

"We are engaged," the Doctor continued, unfolding himself from his chair and crossing slowly to the worktable, "in the greatest pursuit ever attempted by mortal man. Guided by the light of natural philosophy, we endeavor to bring forth a new breed of humanity. One neither begotten by nor beholden to some absent god, but fully aware of its provenance as the noble successor of its baser progenitors."

He leaned over the tool cart, fixing Spare with a look of pure contempt. Spare squeaked and jumped onto the table to dart behind Igor.

"If I am to create a superior race of beings," the Doctor said, turning his contempt upon Igor, "then I am to start with the creation of the ideal human specimen. Not some misshapen cyclops you've wrought in your own image. Do I make myself clear, Igor?"

Igor swallowed. "But—"

The Doctor slammed both fists against the metal tray. Tools clattered across the laboratory floor. "Do I make myself clear?"

Spare let out a frightened trilling sound. Igor sucked in a shuddering breath and forced himself to look up at the Doctor towering above him like an enraged scarecrow in a white coat.

"Yes," Igor said, then, hating himself for saying it: "Master."

The Doctor said not a word, only jerked his head sharply before turning on his heel and marching from the laboratory. The double doors slammed behind him with an air of finality.

Igor slumped against the worktable, his eyes closed. They stung faintly at their corners, a sensation he could scarce recall feeling since he'd left the orphanage.

A metallic scraping pierced the silence. Igor rubbed at his eyes, then opened them to see Spare retrieving the tools scattered across the laboratory floor. Igor watched as the little construct selected a pair of scissors and lifted them, though their diminutive stature prevented them from actually putting them back onto the cart, even standing tiptoe.

"Don't!" Igor snapped, snatching the scissors from Spare before they could hurt him or themself in the process. "Don't bother. I've got them."

Spare squeaked as Igor knelt and began tossing the fallen tools back into the cart, not bothering to organize them. His eyes still stung with shame and wounded pride and bitter disappointment.

How could he have been so foolish as to think that the Doctor might be pleased—let alone impressed—with his creation of Spare? Why, after all their years together, was he so naïve as to think that his master would view Igor's ambitions as anything other than a threat?

A soft *meep* from the tool cart drew Igor's attention. Spare peered out from behind it, their wide eye brimming with an unshed tear.

Igor's shame took on a wholly different tenor. He had endured years of the Doctor's berating and browbeating and bullying, yet he had taken out his frustrations upon Spare in exactly the same manner at the first opportunity.

"Spare," Igor said, reaching out to the construct. "Spare, I—"

Spare shrank away from their creator, hiding behind the leg of the cart. They eyed him dubiously, much as they had upon their first encounter. Wincing, Igor decided to heed Grimalkin's early advice and give Spare the space they needed for him to regain their trust.

"I'm sorry," he said, voice hoarse. Still kneeling, he picked up a pair of metal tweezers, holding them out for Spare's inspection. Spare peered shyly around the corner of the cart, not quite ready to come closer.

That was all right, Igor assured himself. Spare just needed time. Igor could give them that much.

"These are forceps," he explained, holding the tweezers up to better catch the lamplight. "They're for removing small objects from the Subject. Do you want to hold them?"

Spare chirped cautiously, darting forward and snatching them from Igor's grasp. They turned the forceps over in their hand, eyeball narrowing in concentration, then experimentally opened and closed them.

"Very good," Igor said, packing as much gentle approval into the words as he could muster. "Would you like to put them back on the cart?"

Spare nodded. Igor lifted his creation so that Spare could

gingerly set the forceps back atop the metal cart. When he set Spare down, they turned to Igor, hands outstretched.

"We'll put them all back," Igor promised, smiling. "But only after I show you what each one is, and how to use it. Does that sound good?"

Spare chirped what Igor could only assume was an affirmative.

Working together, they put the tools back into place, one at a time. As they worked, Igor thought hard on what his master had said.

The Doctor had never been shy about professing the ultimate goal of his Great Work. Whatever else anyone might say of him, he was fanatically earnest in his zeal to create a new and superior race of human beings, of which the Subject was to be merely the first.

Yet, for the first time in his long service to his master, Igor found himself wondering what sort of world would remain for those who had been brought into it in the normal fashion. What place there might be for those, like himself, who were less perfect and more human.

He was still mulling the question over when the screams began.

22

LATE NIGHT VISITOR

IGOR RACED THROUGH the labyrinthine halls of Ravenwald Manor, Spare clinging to the collar of his lab coat and chirping in alarm. Weird lights pulsed and raced along the ceiling, while ahead in the distance a strange and dissonant choir sang in voices unlike any Igor had ever heard. Chill winds caught and tore at the edges of his coat despite the manor's closed doors, grasping at him like ghostly fingers.

"Grimalkin!" Igor yelled, but the unnatural gale rose and snatched her name from his mouth. He kept calling anyway. "Cornelia!"

Atop his shoulder, Spare echoed him, though their trilling voice could hardly shape their names.

Somehow Igor crossed the length of Ravenwald in a fraction of the time it normally took. It was as if the very hallways had warped and twisted around him, the architecture of the manor itself conspiring to bring him nearer to his goal. How else could he have found himself so suddenly standing outside the chapel door, the protective runes carved into its face blazing a bright and venomous purple?

Wards or no wards, Igor wasted no time in knocking. Accepting whatever fate might befall him for doing so, he pushed the door open, Grim's name hovering on his lips.

It died there.

The chapel itself was much unchanged from when he'd last seen it, save that the scrimshaw trinkets hanging from the rafters now danced and juddered in the whirling vortex of wind that had overtaken the room, and save for the sickly greenish light emanating from the towering figure standing inside the silver summoning circle.

Clad all in rags, it stood three times as tall as even the Doctor, yet its frame was not proportioned to match. What Igor could see of its long limbs and slender torso were gaunt to the point of being skeletal, like a stick insect enlarged twentyfold. The flesh glimpsed beneath its rags was pruney and bloated like that of a drowned corpse. Its hooded head was turned away from him, a fact for which he was perversely grateful.

Terror wrapped its icy claw about Igor's heart. Had Auntie Mag succeeded at last in fully summoning her otherworldly liege from Outside? Was this her Unsmiling King's true form—and if so, where were the witch and her familiar?

Movement near the impossible thing's feet drew Igor's eye and gave him his answer. Auntie Mag knelt there, prostrate, just outside the silver circle. Grimalkin stood at her mistress's side, back arched and fur puffed out to a degree that might have been comical under circumstances less dire.

"Grim!" Igor shouted, taking another step into the chapel.

The vortex of wind abruptly stilled. Dread filled the pit of Igor's stomach as the impossible giant slowly turned, fixing him with its terrible gaze.

It had no eyes.

Nor a mouth, nor nose, nor any other discernible features. Beneath the ragged fringes of its hood lay only skin, somewhat wrinkled and mottled but otherwise smooth, and without mark or blemish of any kind.

It looked, Igor thought with an edge of hysteria, like his thumb after he'd spent too long in the bath. A choked, gargling sound rose in his throat at the absurdity, though whether it would emerge from his lips as a laugh or a scream was anyone's guess.

The faceless head stared at Igor, if a being with no eyes could be said to stare. It raised its disproportionate arms to grasp the neckline of its shabby robe with slender seven-fingered hands. Gently it pulled at its décolletage, baring its chest like a bride upon her wedding night.

Only the giant's chest was as narrow as the rest of it, and nearly as featureless—save for a ragged slash running from one side to the other, just below the jutting collarbones. A dull dark red against the pale flesh, Igor took it for an old scar badly healed.

That is, until the slash opened wide and began to speak.

"Be welcome," the horrid mouth said in a low, gurgling voice, "cringing servant and half-formed slave. Rejoice and tremble at your fortune in being one of those few living to lay eyes upon the Duke of Want."

Not the Unsmiling King, then, though the thought gave Igor no consolation when faced with the unremitting terror before him. He wanted desperately to move, to run, though whether towards Grimalkin or away from the chapel entirely he couldn't say. But his feet refused to move in either direction, and his only comfort was Spare's trembling presence atop his shoulder.

The air before him blurred. The Count appeared, standing between Igor and the towering Duke of Want, his cape draped about his shoulders.

"Witch!" the Count spat in Auntie Mag's direction. "What manner of devil have you summoned into my abode?"

The Duke of Want cocked its faceless head as Cornelia too blurred into existence, crouched atop a pew in a pose reminiscent of the gargoyles adorning the manor's roof. Only those sad stone grotesques had never looked half so fearsome as the red-haired vampire did now, all gleaming fangs and savage beauty. Igor was surprised to see her there rather than out hunting or trysting with Laura, until he realized that by now it must be close to dawn.

"I—" Mag started, but a sharp movement from the Duke drove her head against the stone floor with an audible *crack*. Grim mewled and nosed at her mistress, tail quivering.

"You labor under a double misapprehension, young parasite," the Duke told the Count, tilting its eyeless face down to the silver summoning circle in which it stood, then back to the vampires. "I am no devil dragged screaming up from Below, but a high prince amongst powers for which you have no name. Now fall upon your knees and do homage to me, if you value at all the nocturnal half-life to which you have consigned yourselves."

The Count sneered. "Do not insult me with idle threats, you misbegotten fiend. I am lord here, and you the intruder. Within this manor's bounds, you have no power beyond the circle into which you have been summoned."

"The witch did not summon me into this decrepit dwelling." The hideous mouth upon the Duke's chest made a horrible croaking sound. It took Igor a moment to realize it was laughter. "I invited myself."

It stepped out of the circle in a single stride of its stilt-long legs, unhindered by any magical barrier. Snarling, Cornelia leapt at it, her fangs bared.

Igor's throat constricted as the Duke of Want raised its hand almost lazily. Thick bands of something black and oily wrapped themselves about Cornelia, pinning her arms against her sides and suspending her in midair, slowly rotating.

"Do you tire of your stolen unlife, little leech?" the Duke asked in its drowned man's voice. "Does guilt stir in your breast at the lives you have sacrificed upon the altar of your own misery? Have you wept for the ocean of blood you have spilled?"

Cornelia opened her mouth as if to spit out an answer. Instead she screamed as the black bands tightened around her middle.

"I will help you to weep," the Duke of Want said, and bloody tears began leaking from Cornelia's eyes.

Somehow the ghastly sight unstuck Igor's feet. He stole furtively towards the altar, Spare close behind him.

The Count let out a furious snarl but took only a single step nearer, red eyes flickering between the Duke of Want and Cornelia. On the altar, Grimalkin was pressing her body against Auntie Mag, who sat cowering with her back against the lectern, heedless of the bloody cut across her brow. Igor and Spare joined them, just as the Duke of Want turned its attention upon the Count.

"Do something!" Igor hissed, shaking Auntie Mag. She roused from her stupor enough to turn her head and watch as the Count hesitated, just as Igor had. He took an uncertain step forward, then another in the opposite direction.

And another. His edges began to shimmer, as if in a heat haze. But before the Count could blur away, the Duke crossed the distance between them in two long strides, its clammy hands seizing the vampire around his middle.

"Help them!" Igor pleaded, gesturing at Cornelia hanging in midair, blood streaming from her eyes and splattering against the pews below.

"I—" Mag's dark eyes turned to the towering figure as it lifted the Count from the floor, cradling him to its chest like a child with a doll. "I don't—"

"Century upon century, devouring the souls of the living," the mouth across the Duke's chest was saying, inches from the Count's face. "Have you never wondered what your many victims felt, in their final moments?"

The Count merely groaned as the awful mouth widened, revealing teeth like a lamprey's.

"They let you stay in their home!" Igor practically shouted at Mag, shaking her harder. *"Help them!"*

Grimalkin put both her paws on Mag's knee and meowed, long and loud and plaintive.

The witch sucked in a shuddering breath, then stood. "My lord!"

The mouth did not close, but neither did it devour the Count. The Duke of Want turned slowly, taking a long step towards the altar. "You object to my sport, priestess?"

"Of course not," Mag said hurriedly, wiping away a droplet of blood threatening to trickle into her eye. "But the leech and his progeny are—are useful to my aims, and I fear their loss may delay the coming of our dread sovereign."

"The Unsmiling King," the Duke said, its mouth grimacing. "Whose coming you yourself have more hindered than hastened, Margaret Devereaux."

Auntie Mag nodded so emphatically that Igor worried she might do further damage to her skull. "I will admit to setbacks, and will do whatever penance our lord demands upon his apotheosis. But I assure you, the Rite of Opening is nearly complete."

"Yet you have succeeded in opening the portal only a fraction," the Duke of Want said, nodding down at the silver circle whence the gargantuan tentacle had burst forth mere days ago. "Not nearly wide enough to permit our King entry to this realm."

"I need only a handful more components," Mag said, a hint of desperation creeping into her voice as she rattled them off. "A glutton's shame, the teeth of a usurer, the Eye of Anthomset—"

"All of which can be acquired without the aid of these parasites," the Duke said, stroking the Count's hair with its seven-fingered hand as if he were a favored pet.

"They're security," Grimalkin said, coming to stand beside Auntie Mag.

The faceless head tilted. "You dare address me, servitor?"

"I do," Grimalkin said primly, though her tail's frantic lashing from side to side betrayed her true feeling. "You accused my mistress of delay, but before we came to this town her prior attempts to open the portal were thwarted by mortal men and women who banded together to drive the witch from their midst."

"I see," said the eyeless one, holding the Count before them. "And these leeches are your protection against such rabble?"

"My lord," Auntie Mag broke in, her voice trembling, "if you will just—"

"Enough!" The Duke of Want dropped the Count unceremoniously to the chapel floor. Behind the gaunt monstrosity, the oily black bands restraining Cornelia dissolved into nothingness. She blurred from sight before she could hit the floor, her vampiric powers restored.

"The Unsmiling King grows impatient, priestess," the Duke warned Mag, reaching out one of its too-long arms. It brushed the backs of its seven fingers gently down her face in a grotesque parody of a lover's caress. "And so do I."

"A little more time," Mag said, looking as if she wanted very badly to close her eyes but feared what might happen if she did. "I just need—"

"You have until the night of the next full moon," the Duke said, its awful mouth a grim smile. "If the Rite is not completed by then, I shall drag you Outside so that you may personally offer your excuses to the Unsmiling King."

Then it was gone, and with it the unearthly winds and eerie green light. On the chapel floor the Count groaned, then vanished, blurring away. Igor let out a long, unsteady exhalation as the rush of terror and adrenaline faded, replaced by an exhausted sense of dread.

"The full moon," Mag said, slumping exhaustedly to the floor. "Saints, that's less than two weeks away. How am I . . . what . . ."

She looked up at Igor, who shrugged helplessly. Purring loudly, Grimalkin crawled into Mag's lap, blinking her yellow eyes up at her mistress.

"Not now," Mag snapped, hoisting her familiar from her lap. Grim's purr turned into a protesting yowl. "There's no time to play kitty any longer. We have work to do, you and I."

She cast an unfriendly gaze at Igor. "And unless you'd like to donate a hunchback's agony to the cause, I suggest you take your leave."

Igor took a step backwards, then hesitated, not wanting to leave Grimalkin alone with her mistress, who seemed more than willing to vent her fear and frustration over her shrinking deadline upon her hapless familiar.

"Leave!" Mag snapped, pushing herself to her feet with the aid of her cane. She brandished it—not at Igor, but at Grimalkin. "Unless you'd like to see what this one *really* looks like. She and I are going to have a proper face-to-face, and I promise you that her real countenance isn't nearly so fuzzy."

That struck Igor as a deeply ungrateful attitude towards someone who'd just helped mollify the ire of the Duke of Want, but before he could express the sentiment Grim twined herself about his legs, yellow eyes looking up at him.

"Go, Igor," she said, her voice scarcely louder than her frightened purring. "I'll be fine."

"But—"

"Go," she repeated, biting gently at his ankle. "I'll see you later. If I'm . . . if I can."

Igor swallowed his own concern and his outrage for his friend. Pausing only to scritch Grim briefly between the ears, he scooped up Spare and fled, not wanting to see Auntie Mag force Grimalkin out of the cat's body she so loved and into whatever malefic shape she'd had Outside.

If he was being wholly honest with himself, his concerns were not entirely for his feline friend. With the threat of the

Duke of Want's attention hanging over them like a headsman's axe, Auntie Mag would be considerably more determined to complete the Rite of Opening before the next full moon. How could Grim hope to delay the world's end in the face of such pressure?

In his arms, Spare made a soft *meep.* Igor looked down. In his creation's eye, stained glass shone dimly reflected, untainted by the chapel's desecration. The sight gave Igor pause.

Perhaps there was another way. A means not only of safeguarding the world against the Unsmiling King, but of ensuring that Grimalkin could remain a cat. Of guaranteeing the success of the Great Work, perhaps even of breaking the Count's hold over Cornelia. Accomplishing any one of those endeavors would constitute a herculean undertaking on its own. To achieve them all in one fell swoop would require nothing short of a miracle.

A good thing, then, that Igor knew exactly who to talk to.

23

NIGHT OUT

THE DOCTOR, HOWEVER, refused to permit Igor to go into town. He would not put off the Great Work for hell or high water, both of which were encroaching upon Ravenwald with the return of the tempestuous rains and Auntie Mag's redoubled attempts to complete the Rite of Opening. Igor's next two days were spent painstakingly attaching the Subject's limbs to its torso.

By the end of this marathon effort, Igor was practically cross-eyed from the hours of fine detail work. Even so, he could not help but feel a stirring of pride upon tying the final thread of the Subject, which was now complete from the neck down.

"Not that I'll be ready to choose a head until I've finished balancing the humors," the Doctor said, carefully measuring out several drops of natron into an alembic. "The last Subject was too choleric. Small wonder it burned through its initial galvanic charge as quickly as it did."

This was hardly the time for Igor to mention that the previous Subject had burned out because the Doctor hadn't properly grounded the conductor towers. The atmosphere between Igor and his master had remained markedly chilly following the latter's introduction to Spare.

"How much longer until you've finished with the humors?" Igor asked.

"Several days," the Doctor said, lighting a burner beneath the alembic. "A week, on the outside. To say nothing of the various compounds and elixirs that still need applying, now that you've finished stitching the limbs on."

"If you need someone to assist with the elixirs while you focus your attention on the humors," Igor said, striving for a casual tone, "I could—"

"No, Igor." The Doctor watched as the natron within the alembic began to boil. "I haven't changed my mind. Perhaps, if you'd merely done the tasks you were instructed to, and not spent your time in pilfering our spare parts . . ."

"You would've let me perform alchemy?" Igor was unable to hide his surprise.

"Who can say?" The Doctor shrugged. "Instead, you chose to sneak about behind my back, appropriating laboratory resources for your own ends. That trust will take time to rebuild."

"I'm sorry, Master," Igor said, deflating. Only he wasn't, really, or at least not as sorry as the Doctor plainly thought he should be. Not when his illicit experiment had given him Spare.

"Sorrow's an unproductive feeling," the Doctor said, watching as the bubbling natron began flowing down the long tube of the alembic into the receiving vessel. "Do better instead."

"At what?" Igor just barely bit back the bitterness in his tone. "I've finished with the Subject's limbs, and its organs, and its torso. The only thing I have left to attach is the head, and you're still holding off on that—"

"If I trusted your aesthetic sense, then perhaps I'd let you choose our Subject's head." The Doctor broke his gaze from the alembic to scowl at Igor. "Your little monocular homunculus is a living indication that you have no eye for such things, if you'll pardon the pun. Besides, there's still plenty of work to be done about the lab. Ensuring that the electric cables running from the lightning rod are securely attached to the generator, modulating the Tesla coil, grounding the conducting towers—properly, this time . . ."

A small explosion in the alembic lit the Doctor's face a lurid green, accentuating the hollows in his cheeks, the bags beneath his eyes. For a scientist of his advanced years, the Doctor was as robustly energetic as a man half his age. This was due at least in part to his willingness to subject himself to his own experimentation, but even the regular consumption of alchemical elixirs to slow the worst effects of age upon the human body were no substitute for adequate sleep and nutrition.

"Master?" Igor asked, softer this time. "When was the last time you had a meal?"

"A what?"

"Something to eat."

"Oh." The Doctor gestured over his shoulder at the coat rack near the door, which bore several identical white lab coats. "I had some carrots last night, I think. Or maybe the night before. Kept some in my pocket in case I got peckish."

Some rifling through the lab coats produced a trio of carrots, one half-eaten and all three practically crawling with mold.

"Last night or the night before?" Igor asked, his own stomach growling. Lost in the depths of his stitching, he too had subsisted on little more than snacks, but he was more used to going without than the Doctor was.

"Well," the Doctor said, glancing irritably at him, "what did you expect? With you wrapped up in lab work, I was left to fend for myself."

Igor nearly protested that he couldn't stitch dead limbs to their Subject and prepare the Doctor's meals at the same time, but he forced himself to silence. They were both weary with their respective efforts, and hurling accusations at each other would serve neither of them.

"I'll head into town for groceries, then," he said, pocketing the Doctor's ongoing list of needed alchemical ingredients as he headed for the door. This was exactly the opportunity to slip away to Ravensburg that he'd been waiting for.

"Watch out for Miss Devereaux," the Doctor said as Igor was about to depart. "She's been in a foul mood lately."

This was hardly news to Igor, who'd stayed away from the chapel ever since the Duke of Want's intrusion. He'd already overheard several arguments between Mag and the Count, who angrily asserted that the Duke's intrusion violated their mystical compact and was thus grounds to expel Mag from Ravenwald. Mag, for her part, contended that as the Duke's intrusion was not something she had intended, she was in no way in violation—a position the mystical agreement seemed to uphold, considering that nothing catastrophic had occurred to her yet. Whether that exemption would still apply if she succeeded in bringing the Unsmiling King into the world was anyone's guess, but Igor expected that they would all be beyond caring at that point.

"Anyhow," the Doctor continued, "I'd avoid crossing her path, unless you've reconsidered the life amphibian."

"I have not," Igor reassured his master as he closed the door behind him.

* * *

"Going somewhere?" came Cornelia's voice, just as Igor was about to clamber onto the driver's seat of the black coach.

"Thought I'd take the horses for a stroll," Igor said, turning to look at her. Cornelia was dressed in one of her customary gowns, but this one was more elaborate than the others he had seen, all silver brocade and delicate white lace. She'd tied her hair back with a ribbon and slipped on elegant gloves that came up to her elbows. There was something different in her posture, too, but Igor couldn't put his finger on precisely what. "Figured you'd be out hunting by now."

"Well." Cornelia wrung her gloved hands, looking—to Igor's

surprise—somewhat abashed. "I was hoping to go into town tonight. With Laura."

Understanding dawned.

"You're taking her out," Igor said, looking over Cornelia's dress with new eyes. "And you're looking for a ride?"

"If it's not too much trouble." Cornelia nodded. "I'd rather not make Laura walk all that way. But if you'd rather not—"

"I don't mind," Igor assured her, climbing onto the coach and patting the seat beside his own. "In fact, it would be my genuine pleasure."

"Thank you." Cornelia climbed up to sit beside him, and as she settled her skirts about her, Igor saw that her changed posture was due to a pair of impractical heeled shoes.

"Off we go," Igor said, flicking the reins. He turned to Cornelia, grinning. "Your paramour awaits."

* * *

"Well!" Laura said, looking impressed as the coach trundled to a halt in front of her cottage. "Don't you know how to make a girl feel special."

Igor touched a finger to his temple in greeting, which Laura returned with a nod. She too had dressed up for their night on the town, but unlike Cornelia, Laura had opted for tan trousers paired with brown leather riding boots, and a waistcoat and tailcoat both of forest green. Her yellow cravat had been tied rather inexpertly, and Igor's sharp eyes spotted fraying hems at her coat's edges, but the ensemble suited her tall frame better than any gown might have.

Cornelia did not seem to take any notice of the more threadbare elements of Laura's wardrobe, gazing at her as if she hung the moon as she gingerly stepped down from the coach. "Only the best for you, my dear."

"Too kind, my lady," Laura said, placing one foot behind the other and bending at the waist in a motion that seemed unable to decide whether it was a bow or a curtsy. Cornelia smiled and dipped her skirts in return.

"These are for you," Laura said, producing a bouquet of wildflowers she'd evidently been holding behind her back. "Seeing as this is our first real . . . Well, I thought you might like them."

"I love them." Cornelia stood on tiptoe to kiss Laura on the cheek. "You look quite dashing tonight."

"Do you think so?" Laura asked, tugging at her collar, to the further dishevelment of her cravat. "I don't have a dress, so I . . ."

"Wore your best," Cornelia finished for her, adjusting the cravat. "Here."

She plucked one of the flowers from her bouquet and fastened it through one of Laura's buttonholes, then stepped back to admire her handiwork.

"Well?" Laura asked, shifting her weight nervously. "How do I look?"

Cornelia gave her a wide smile that held no hint of fangs. "You're perfect."

24

MORE THINGS IN HEAVEN AND EARTH

IGOR DROPPED THE lovers off in front of Ravensburg's lone and somewhat shabby theatre, which was evidently playing host to a touring troupe.

"The VaudeVillains," Igor read, gazing up at the hand-drawn marquee.

"Don't judge," Laura said, her cheeks coloring. "I saw them a few years back, in Cladbury. They're quite the comic act."

"No doubt," Igor said, somewhat wistfully. Predictably, the Doctor seldom had time for such frippery as live entertainment. And tonight, Igor had more pressing business.

"When should I pick you up?" he asked Cornelia, as Laura sauntered over to join the queue at the refreshment stand. "And where?"

"You needn't trouble yourself," Cornelia said, patting him on the shoulder. "I appreciate the ride into town, Igor, but now that we're here, I think we can find our own way back to Laura's cottage."

Igor glanced at the gravekeeper. "Have you told her, then? About . . . you know."

"Not yet." Cornelia's smile faltered as she leaned in, lowering her voice. "I . . . don't know how she'll react. Finding out she's being courted by a monster."

"You're not a monster," Igor said, realizing as the words came out that he'd long since stopped thinking of Cornelia's vampiric nature as anything to be afraid of. It was just one facet of who she was, much like her red hair or her sense of justice.

"There are some bodies in your wine cellar who'd disagree," Cornelia said, glancing towards Laura. "I just . . . want to enjoy tonight. With her."

"You should," Igor said, giving her what he hoped was a reassuring pat on the shoulder. "Take all the time you like. And if you need me, I'll be stopping by Alexei's later on."

"Thank you," Cornelia said, bending down to give him a quick peck on the cheek. She straightened, then frowned. "What will you be doing until then?"

Igor gave her a crooked smile. "Seeking spiritual guidance."

* * *

"Let me make sure I understand you rightly," Friar Bernhard said, pouring a steaming pot of tea into Igor's cup. The two of them sat in the rectory of Ravensburg's church, a cozy little room that was well insulated against both the nearby river and the rain pattering against the windows. "You want to know if anyone's ever spoken to an angel?"

"Well," Igor said, measuring out a spoonful of sugar, "you seemed like the person to ask."

Bernhard huffed out a surprised laugh. "Suppose you've got me there. Are you a believer, my son?"

Igor hesitated. "I'm a man of science."

"One hardly excludes the other," Friar Bernhard said. He gave a contemptuous snort. "Though there's no shortage of fools belonging to either category who seem to think it does. Way I see it, the Almighty wouldn't have gifted us brains or afflicted us with curiosity unless we were meant to use the former and indulge the latter."

"I try to keep an open mind," Igor offered, which had the dual benefits of being true and seeming to mollify the friar. "And I've certainly seen things which defy easy explanation."

"More things in heaven and earth," Bernhard said, offering Igor a lemon wedge. "Thus your question about angels."

"Right." Igor accepted the lemon. "*Has* anyone ever managed to talk to them? Lately, I mean, not in the scriptures."

"I speak to them." Bernhard rested his forehead against his steepled fingers in an attitude of prayer. "Every night, in fact."

"I meant more"—Igor tried to think of how to put it politely—"directly."

Bernhard arched a shaggy brow. "I'd argue that praying's the most direct means of talking to the holy there is. But as far as I can say, no one's spoken face-to-face with an angel in living memory."

Igor nodded glumly and sipped his tea. Truthfully, he'd expected as much, but it was still disappointing to hear. He supposed he'd have to resort to means other than literal divine intervention to stop Mag from bringing the Unsmiling King into the world.

"Unless," Bernhard mused, "you're counting the Angel of Mercy, I suppose."

Igor choked on his tea.

"Sorry?" he sputtered, dabbing at his mouth with his sleeve.

"You've probably not heard of her," Bernhard said, handing Igor a napkin. "She's a local legend said to aid women in need. Lately some of my parishioners claim to have seen her. Ruth Dreyfuss even says she spoke to the Angel some weeks back, if you can believe it."

"I can," Igor said faintly.

Friar Bernhard rubbed his tonsured head thoughtfully.

"Though now that I'm thinking on it, Ruth's uncle did vanish the very night she claims to have met the Angel . . ."

"Maybe she prayed for him to vanish." Igor cleared his throat. "So if no one has credibly spoken to angels, then what about . . . other beings? Not from"—he pointed at the ceiling—"but"—lowering his gaze to the floor.

The craggy lines of Bernhard's face sharpened, something wary entering his gaze. "I should warn you, my son, that my order considers demonology a sin of particular malignance."

"I'm not—" Igor started, cheeks burning. "This is all purely theoretical."

It wasn't, of course, but Igor figured that whatever damnation he might incur by lying in a church was preferable to seeing all he had worked for burned down around his ears again.

"Theoretical," Bernhard repeated, looking as if he'd just bitten into one of the lemon wedges on the plate between them. "Did your Doctor put you up to asking about this, then?"

Igor started. "How did you—"

"I'm a priest, not a recluse." Bernhard began heaping spoonfuls of sugar into his teacup. "Small as Ravensburg is, it would be hard *not* to overhear rumors about the strange old man and his hunchbacked assistant taking up residence in our local haunted house. Is he up to some sort of witchcraft, then? Your Doctor?"

"No," Igor said, then decided to tell a partial truth. "But there *is* a summoning circle carved into the manor floor. I want to be certain that nothing comes through from the other side while the Doctor is conducting his research."

"A summoning circle?" Bernhard considered Igor through the steam rising from their teacups.

Igor forced himself to stare back evenly. "It was there when we moved in."

"I suppose I shouldn't be surprised." Bernhard's shoulders relaxed as he lifted his teacup to his mouth and blew on it. "The

Ravenwalds have always tended towards extremes of eccentricity."

"So I've heard," Igor said. The Doctor and the Count both were proof enough of that. "Is there a way to ensure that it stays closed? The circle?"

"My first suggestion would be to avoid conducting any profane rituals in its vicinity." The friar took a sip of the hot tea and winced.

"I'll do my best not to," Igor promised. A thought struck him. "Could the circle be used in a different direction? Not to summon a being from Below, but . . ."

He pointed at the ceiling.

Bernhard frowned. "Historically speaking, the Almighty tends to react rather severely to anyone attempting to reach the shining gates by means other than the natural course."

"I've no desire to be on the receiving end of a smiting," Igor assured the priest, even as his heart sank. So much for that plan. He glanced out the window, where the rain had finally slackened off. "Thank you for entertaining my scientific curiosity."

"Certainly," Bernhard said, sitting back in his chair. "So long as it remains in the realm of the strictly theoretical."

"Believe me," Igor said, and silently hoped he wouldn't be smitten for lying, "this is one hypothesis I never want to test."

25

FLOTSAM

DUSK HAD JUST fallen as Igor exited the church, the faint drizzle of rain turning the streetlamps into fuzzy halos, their dim lights penetrating only a handful of yards into the foggy gloom. Consequentially, Igor almost missed the vandalism done to the black coach.

Someone had painted the word FREEK on its side in wide, sloppy white brushstrokes. Frowning at both the audacity and the illiteracy of the culprits, Igor put a finger to the paint and found it was still wet—perhaps there was still time to wash it off.

"Good thing I'm heading to the waterfront," he muttered, climbing up into the driver's seat.

The haze of fog was not so dense that Igor missed the suspicious glances thrown his way, some of which bordered on hostility. Snatches of overheard conversation alluded to the curious activities of Ravenwald Manor's new tenants; evidently the erection of the lightning rod had caused quite a stir amongst the townsfolk, though most seemed to have little inkling of its purpose. Muttered rumors reached Igor's ear as he stabled the horses near the waterfront, hinting at a mysterious rash of disappearances amongst the men of Ravensburg: not only drunkards and vagabonds, but also lawyers, tradesmen, and other respected members of society.

"All gone without a trace," Alexei proclaimed cheerfully as he refilled a pail of soapy water. "Here one day, same as ever, then the next morning—gone! Like they just got up in the middle of the night and walked off into the woods, never to be seen again."

"You don't say," Igor grunted, putting his elbows into scrubbing at the coach with a sponge. For whatever reason, the letter F was proving particularly resistant to his efforts. Alexei's mention of the woods left him uneasy; how long until the townsfolk connected the string of disappearances to the goings-on at Ravenwald Manor?

"I do." Alexei didn't seem to catch Igor's discomfort. "But the most curious part is that several witnesses swear they saw the missing in the company of a beautiful redheaded woman on the night they disappeared."

"Most men tend to lower their guard around women." Igor grimaced, thinking back to the Doctor's brief flirtation with manufacturing donors, which had more than once necessitated that Igor disguise himself as an elderly babushka to lure the unwary.

"Too true." Alexei grinned at Igor, white teeth shining in his pale face. "Or maybe the Angel of Mercy has stepped out of folktales to walk the streets again, eh? Visiting the justice of wronged women upon the men she finds deserve it?"

"The Angel is a children's story," Igor said, now even more discomfited. "No different than a child wishing on a star for the Moon Maiden to whisk them off to Fairyland."

"And yet men continue to disappear." Alexei sounded wholly unbothered. "Speaking of beautiful redheaded women, why have you not returned with the one you brought to my shop that first night?"

"She's too busy dragging men off into the woods."

Alexei belted out a laugh. "So she is the culprit! You keep dangerous company, my friend Igor."

Igor forced a smile. "You don't know the half of it."

* * *

Igor had nearly finished his shopping when the bell above the apothecary door jangled, but he thought nothing of it—not until he heard the familiar *tap-tap* of a cane against the floor, or Alexei's bellowed greeting: "Miss Margaret, my dear!"

"Good evening, Alexei," came the horribly familiar voice of Auntie Mag, separated from Igor only by a few rows of shelves. Igor pressed himself against the nearest shelf, his heart and mind racing as he clutched the wooden shopping basket to his chest. He hadn't seen Mag leave the manor since she'd taken up residence there—had hardly seen her outside the desecrated chapel, for that matter.

So what was she doing here?

"What brings you here this dreary night?" Alexei asked, evidently wondering the same thing. "I have hardly seen you these past few weeks."

"Well"—Igor retreated further into the shelves as Mag closed the door, shutting the foggy night firmly on its other side—"it's been difficult for me to brew up my usual tonics and elixirs, lacking a fixed abode."

"I heard about your cottage," Alexei said, not without sympathy. "Is your cat all right?"

Mag sniffed. "Grimalkin's fine."

Was she? Igor hadn't seen Grim since the night of the Duke of Want's intrusion, after which he'd been so absorbed in the Work that he'd barely ventured outside the laboratory. He'd assumed that Grim was being kept similarly occupied, but now he wondered uneasily whether the truth was something more sinister.

He looked around the tall, narrow shelves, wondering if there was a way to purchase the alchemical supplies in his basket without drawing Mag's attention. Easier said than done, with a proprietor as gregarious as Alexei. Probably it was safer for him to make a stealthy exit, then come back once Mag had bought whatever she had come for and taken her leave.

Deciding on this reasonable course of action, Igor bent, gently placing his shopping basket on the floor. He straightened, turned around—

—and immediately knocked a decanter of something green and pickled off its shelf. He grabbed for it, but it slipped through his panicked fingers and shattered against the floor, bathing Igor's boots with green slime and glass shards. A briny stench rose to assault Igor's nostrils.

"Blast," Igor hissed. He took an unsteady step back as the green liquid pooled at his feet, but before he could turn and flee the apothecary shop, Mag's dreaded *tap-tap* drew near. Thinking quickly, he slipped a vial of fine black powder from his basket into his coat pocket.

"Igor." Auntie Mag appeared at the far end of the aisle, leaning on her cane in a rather rakish manner. If she was surprised to see him here, there was no sign of it in either her voice or her face. "Fancy seeing you here this evening."

"Mag." Igor swallowed his fear and apprehension. Curiously, what replaced them was a hot, righteous anger welling up in his belly. "Come here in search of kittens to drown?"

"I doubt Alexei has any in stock." Mag glanced down at the slimy, misshapen thing that had been pickling in the decanter. "Though I suppose you never know."

"Igor!" Alexei appeared over Mag's shoulder, towering over the witch as he surveyed the mess with a look of dismay on his face. "Are you hurt?"

"I'm fine," Igor said, flicking the worst of the slime from one of his boots. "Sorry about the mess. If you have a mop, I can—"

"Is no bother," Alexei said, waving a finger at him. "At least the cleaning is not. But I am afraid that in my store, you buy what you break."

"Oh," Igor said, patting his pockets. A glance at the price tag below the now empty spot where the decanter had stood caused his stomach to flip. "I . . . that is, I can come back with more—"

"I'll pay for it," Auntie Mag said. She was studying him with unnerving intensity, as if he were an interesting worm she'd just discovered beneath a rock.

"You'll what?" Igor squeaked. But Mag was already passing Alexei a surprisingly weighty purse.

"Let's take a walk," she said, *tap-tapping* her way down the aisle. She slipped her hand through Igor's arm, her grip surprisingly firm against his biceps as she steered him towards the door. "I've been meaning to find time to have a chat with you, as it happens. Just the two of us, someplace away from prying ears."

Away from the manor, in other words.

"About what?" Igor asked as Mag opened the door, revealing the foggy waterfront beyond.

Mag smiled as they stepped out into the night. A knowing smile, one without any trace of warmth. "The future, of course."

*   *   *

"Where are we going?" Igor asked. The lights of the riverfront district faded into the gloom behind them, giving way to a narrow, curving street of muddy cobblestones hugging tight against the river.

"You should be asking yourself that, my hunchbacked friend." Mag navigated the uneven road with surprising ease, the tapping of her cane muted by the mud. "How long is it that you've been in your Doctor's employ?"

"Years." Igor frowned at her seeming non sequitur. "Or . . . decades now, I guess."

"An awfully long time." Mag skirted around a puddle as the road wound past the last of Ravensburg's riverfront houses and into the lonesome dark between the water and the empty farmland surrounding the town. "And has your long service enhanced your prospects?"

Igor frowned. "What prospects?"

"For advancement," Mag clarified. She wiped perspiration and fog from her brow. "Unless you intend to remain a laboratory assistant forever?"

"It's a noble calling." Igor attempted an air of lofty disdain. "Helping to push the bounds of scientific knowledge. To usher in the light of progress and the dawn of reason upon a superstitious world—"

"You're like a trained parrot, the way the Doctor's words come out of your mouth," Mag said, unimpressed. She looked at him closely, her dark eyes searching. "But how much of it do *you* believe, Igor?"

"I . . ." Igor closed his mouth, a muscle working in his jaw. "All of it, of course."

"Of course," Mag repeated softly. She turned and ambled her way downhill, venturing farther from the lights of Ravenwald and deeper into the river's floodplain. Igor followed, wondering whether she'd brought him out here to kill him. Probably not; she'd had plenty of opportunities before tonight, and this seemed like more effort than he warranted. But he kept a close eye on her all the same.

"Where's Grimalkin?" He figured this was as good a time as any to ask. "I haven't seen her about the manor."

"Nor will you until she finishes the task I've set her." Mag's voice dripped with contempt. "One she ought to have completed long since."

Searching for the Eye of Anthomset, Igor supposed, though he couldn't say such a thing aloud in Mag's hearing. Instead he looked about at the fog rolling in off the river, so thick that he could hardly see the water. "It's been storming an awful lot lately."

"She's hardly made of sugar," Mag all but snapped. "Ah. Here we are."

At first, Igor took the pile of splintered timbers and collapsed beams lying between them and the water's edge for a shipwreck, one still half-submerged. Only a closer look as they drew nearer revealed the clumping tufts of straw that must once have been a thatched roof, and the scattered debris and detritus that had been furniture before disaster struck.

Igor surveyed the wreckage. "This was your cottage?"

"It was," Mag said. "Until I attempted to summon the Unsmiling King with undue haste, and nearly drowned in the process."

"I'm . . . sorry?" Igor ventured. Mag didn't sound particularly perturbed about it.

"I'm not." Mag's warmthless smile reappeared. "I have lived . . . a very long time, young Igor. Longer than you'd think to look at me. This is far from the first time I've started over after losing everything." She leaned heavily upon her cane and rubbed her bad hip. "Not even close."

Igor gazed down at the wreckage of her cottage. "Why show me this?"

"Because I *didn't* drown," Mag said. She looked at Igor, a cunning gleam in her eyes. "Because I'm a survivor. And I think you are too."

Despite the Doctor's best attempts, Igor nearly said. Then frowned, wondering what had prompted such an ungrateful thought.

"I've been through a few scrapes," he admitted. "But—"

"I've seen the sort of work your Doctor puts you to," Mag interrupted. "The dangers you risk on his behalf. The problems he presents to you, and the dedication with which you set about solving them. Your initiative. Your ingenuity."

"Thank you?" Igor ventured. Some treacherous part of his heart stirred at the compliments, even as the rest of him warned against their source.

"So much promise," Mag said, and to Igor's surprise she reached out and rested a hand on his hunched shoulder without a trace of hesitation or revulsion. "So much *potential.* All of it wasted on that vainglorious egotist."

"The Doctor—" Igor began, then trailed off, not knowing what he intended to say in the Doctor's defense. Unsure, perhaps, whether he even wanted to defend him.

"Is undeserving of your service," Mag said, seizing on his indecision. "But there are other masters who are worthy. Who will offer you greater rewards than jealousy and scorn."

She extended a hand to Igor, wrist limp and palm down. Less a proffered handshake than the gesture of a queen bestowing her favor.

"Saints preserve me." Igor looked incredulously up from the hand to its owner. "Are you . . . offering me a *job*?"

Mag raised one dark eyebrow. "Perhaps I was mistaken about your ingenuity, if you're only just now catching on."

Igor stared, dumbstruck.

"I see I shall have to spell things out plainly for you." Mag sighed and withdrew her hand. "Yes, Igor, I would like you to come work for me. I have need of an able assistant, and you have proven yourself both capable and reliable. Neither quality can be attributed to my current . . . associate."

"Grim."

Mag gave a curt nod. "In the early days I valued her independent nature. But the longer she has been with me, the more recalcitrant she has become. I need a more tractable partner."

A shudder tingled up Igor's spine at the word. "But . . . you're trying to end the world! Why would I want any part in that?"

"I would hardly think this world has been overkind to you," Mag said, something very like sympathy in her tone. "It seldom is, to the outcast and the oddity."

Igor swallowed. "Kind or cruel, I live here. And," he added, the thought only just occurring to him, "so do you."

Mag's expression soured. "As I said, my world has ended before. More times than I care to recount." She turned her head to the side and spat into the tepid water lapping at the ruins of her cottage. "But this time, at least, I shall dictate the terms of its unmaking."

Igor opened his mouth to refuse her offer, but before he could, Mag knelt, leaning heavily on her cane, and scooped a handful of that turgid river water into her palm. Her eyes shone faintly purple as she watched it trickle through her fingers.

"This time," Mag said softly, "I shall reshape it to my design."

"And that's what you're offering me?" Igor asked, almost as quietly. "The chance to . . . change the world? Make it more suitable for myself?"

"That and so much more." Mag's smile was almost dreamy. "To create a world free of want. Free of pain. One where we need not grow old, need not die. Where these fragile, fleshy forms are broken down to their constituent parts, remade into something sublime. Something . . . transcendent."

The violet gleam of magic in her eyes was joined by one of madness.

"Imagine," she said, rubbing her bad hip. "Never suffering hurt again, nor loss, nor any of the hundred other indignities of growing old. To be blessed with impervious bodies and unbreakable hearts."

Refusal danced on the tip of Igor's tongue, yet he could not voice it. What would it be like, he wondered instead, to live in a world conformed to his needs? One in which he was not a misshapen and poorly made creature, as the Doctor reminded him daily, but a majestic being as suited to his surroundings as the eagle was to the sky?

"Say I did help you." Igor told himself that he wasn't tempted, that he was asking purely out of scientific curiosity. "What happens to Grimalkin?"

An expression as brief and dark as a summer storm flickered over Mag's face. "Her long charade will end, and she will be returned to her true form. And rewarded by the King for her service, meager as it has been."

"And what about Cornelia?" Igor pressed. "Or Laura? The Doctor?"

Mag blinked. Evidently it wasn't a question she'd anticipated.

"They will be remade as well," she said slowly, as though this should have been self-evident. "Reforged by the Unsmiling King into shapes more pleasing to His eye. Perhaps," she added, "even given to those who have served Him better, to do with as they will."

She said this last with a rather solicitous smile. Igor wasn't sure which repulsed him more: that smile, or the sentiment behind it. Cornelia and Laura were his friends, not his servants or playthings. And the Doctor . . .

"One question more." Igor swallowed down his disgust. "Why?"

"Why remake the world?" Mag frowned. "I told you. To be free from pain and want—"

"I meant why the Unsmiling King? Why the Outside? Couldn't you get what you want from another realm, another power?"

"I might," Mag said thoughtfully. "Saints know that the Outside is quite a great distance from our world, metaphysically speaking. Doubtless it would be easier if I were to direct the Rite of Opening to a nearer realm."

"Why don't you, then?" Igor said, striving to keep his voice calm. Mag had just proven the theory which had brought him to Friar Bernhard correct: The Rite was not intrinsically tied to the Outside. It could be redirected. And even if the Above and its divine inhabitants would not answer the summons, anywhere Igor managed to open the portal to had to be better than the Outside. Except for the Below, of course.

"Nearer worlds are too similar to our own for my purposes." Mag's hands tightened about the skull that crowned her cane. "Oh, I've no doubt that one of the capricious lords of Faerie would turn our reality into a twisted mirror of itself, or that one of those rigid efreets would try to make this place as suffocatingly regimented as their brass city. But it would still be our world, thoroughly and unmistakably."

"And that's . . . a bad thing?"

"Look around you, Igor." Mag jabbed her cane towards the lights of Ravensburg, to the dockside bawdyhouses and taverns, then jammed it into the mud at her feet. "Pain is baked into this world. Suffering is woven into its fabric. Loss is—"

Her voice broke, and she rubbed furiously at her hip, as if trying to erase some invisible stain from her skirts. Igor moved to help her, but she waved him off.

"This world is broken," Mag murmured in a low voice, more to herself than to him. "Broken. So I will mend it from the atoms up."

She looked at him, her eyes shining with what Igor took at first to be madness, then realized with dismay was actually hope. If there was even a difference between the two.

"I think that I'm going to have to decline your offer." Igor edged away from the wreck of the cottage and gave Mag an apologetic smile, slipping one hand into his coat pocket. "I'm already gainfully employed."

"I see." Mag met his refusal with a flat, hard stare. "What a disappointment."

Violet light flashed in the fog as she thrust her cane at Igor, a jagged bolt of arcane energy spiraling towards him.

Just as Igor had anticipated.

He slipped in the mud as he threw himself clear of Mag's curse, hand flying from his pocket. He hurled the vial of highly combustible saltpeter he'd swiped from the apothecary directly into the path of the next blast of magic.

The resultant explosion was not large, at least compared to the many Igor had witnessed in his career. But the force of its shock wave was enough to press Igor deeper into the muddy riverbank, and to flatten the remnants of Mag's desolate cottage.

And, judging from the loud splash, to knock the witch herself clean into the river.

"Igor!" she called, coughing and spluttering somewhere in the fog. "Igor, wait—"

But Igor was already hauling himself up the riverbank and back towards town, his heart racing, his feet flying over the muddy cobblestones. His breath came in short, sharp gasps, a painful stitch stabbing at his side. Yet his narrow escape turned every lungful of air and every ache in his legs into something sweet, fleeting. Precious.

Mag had not been wholly wrong. Pain was a fundamental truth of reality, as immutable and inarguable as gravity. But her conclusion was flawed.

Pain was not a punishment. He should know, having suffered so many accidents and mishaps pursuing the Great Work, and bearing the scars to prove it. Nor was pain a sign of the world's fundamental brokenness.

Rather, pain was the price one paid for existing in this world. Pain was the cost of dwelling in a body that was equal parts perfect and flawed, mundane and miraculous. Pain was the promise that you were still alive, for only the dead were safe from it.

Perhaps Mag was right that a world free of pain *would* be better than the flawed one they dwelled in now, just as the Doctor's vision of a world of perfect humans might be an improvement over the current model. But Igor wanted nothing to do with the future she offered. Not when it came at so high a cost.

If pain was the price of living, then that was a bargain Igor gladly struck with every breath.

He sucked in another breath of sweet night air, thankful as he had never been for the ache in his legs and the stitch in his side, and ran on.

26

NOCTURNAL AFFAIRS

UPON RETURNING TO the waterfront, Igor ducked into Alexei's just long enough to slam his entire coinpurse onto the countertop, hoping it was enough to make up for his brief but necessary foray into shoplifting. Ignoring Alexei's startled questions about where they'd gone and what had become of Mag, Igor retrieved his shopping basket and its supplies, then drove the black coach back into the town center as quickly as the mares could trot. His one thought was to get back to the manor before Mag could. At least there he'd be under the Doctor's protection.

Fearing the witch might use her powers to pursue him, Igor wove through the maze of Ravensburg's winding side streets and narrow alleyways, eventually emerging onto a small, square park. There was a fountain at its center, where a trio of surprisingly toothsome bronze dolphins happily squirted jets of water from their mouths—though whoever had designed the fountain had likely never actually seen a dolphin, or possibly had conflated them with sharks. Through the curtain of falling water sprayed by the overly carnivorous cetaceans, Igor could just make out a pair of figures slouched together upon a bench on the park's far side.

He clambered down from the coach and cut through the park, hoping that whatever tryst he was about to interrupt hadn't yet grown too amorous—the more absorbed with each other the couple were, the less willing they would be to offer directions.

The park had a surprising number of trees, the better to keep off the light rain. They must have shielded Igor from sight as well, because the couple on the bench gave no indication that they'd noticed his approach. He was about to call out when their voices carried to him, just loudly enough to hear over the murmuring fountain.

". . . until I was nineteen," the larger of the two was saying, her husky voice matching her tall silhouette. Igor hesitated, surprised to recognize both as belonging to Laura. But of course, the vaudeville show must have ended hours ago.

"After that," Laura continued, "I moved from place to place for a time. Tried my hand at woodworking, forestry, farming. Even a bit of smithing, if you can believe it."

"Why shouldn't I?" Cornelia's reply was light and teasing as she rested a hand on Laura's arm. "Surely swinging a hammer is much like swinging an axe?"

"Wrong kind of smith," Laura said, shaking her head, though her white teeth flashed in the light of the waxing crescent moon. "I worked in precious metals."

"Silver and gold?" Cornelia teased, her hand traveling up from Laura's arm to cup her cheek. Igor glanced about the darkened park, seeking the best route to sneak away from what was clearly a private moment. He could retrace his steps, but the ground beneath the trees was littered with fallen branches, and it was a minor miracle he hadn't stepped on one already—

"Turns out I wasn't much of a silversmith," Laura said, not quite as teasingly. "I hope that you don't mind if all the jewelry I give you is gold?"

"Provided nobody was buried wearing it," Cornelia said. Beneath the shadow of the trees, Igor winced. She really *was* out of practice at this sort of thing, unless courtship fashions had changed so drastically that grave robbing was a suitable topic of discussion for young lovers.

"Certainly not," Laura said, but now there was a note of hesitation in her voice. "I . . . It doesn't bother you, does it? My profession, I mean."

"Why would it?"

"Some folk are unnerved at the thought of living so near a cemetery," Laura said. "Fearful of ghosts, I expect. Or disquieted at always having a reminder that they'll wind up on the other side of its bars someday."

"But you're not one of those."

"The dead make better neighbors than most folk give them credit for," Laura said. Igor blinked. Perhaps Cornelia was not the only one of the pair who was out of practice.

"They don't complain about how you dress," Laura continued, "or what your house looks like. They don't throw wild parties, don't show up on your doorstep demanding you repent your sins. The dead make for quiet neighbors, which are the best kind."

"Depends on the dead," Cornelia said, but from her tone Igor knew she was smiling. She leaned in, and Igor hastily turned away before the sound of lips smacking wetly together could reach him. He'd just have to make a run for it while they were distracted and hope neither of them recognized their fleeing hunchbacked voyeur—

"How lovely," came a thickly accented voice from the direction of the bench. Again, a voice Igor knew well, but this one tightened his throat and quickened his pulse.

"A young couple courting beneath the crescent moon," the Count said as Igor turned around again. He loomed in all his melodramatic glory above Cornelia and Laura as the pair hastily disentangled from their embrace. "And beside so quaint a fountain, too. The scene practically cries out to be painted."

"I don't know what you think you're doing, sir," Laura said, voice hot with anger as she came to her feet, looking the Count dead in the eye. "Sneaking up on women like—"

"Karl." Cornelia, too, stood, her gaze locked on her husband. "This isn't— I—"

"Karl?" Laura looked from Cornelia to the Count, sounding puzzled. "You mean this is the uncle you told me about?"

Igor frowned. Cornelia must have cast the Count in the role of the autocratic uncle instead of telling Laura she was married.

"Her uncle," the Count said, looking pointedly at Cornelia. Igor shrank farther into the shadow of the trees, fumbling in his pocket for his vial of garlic powder—and finding none.

"Yes," Cornelia said, not breaking eye contact with her husband, daring him to contradict her. "He's had guardianship of me ever since my parents' passing."

Where had it gone? Igor had been careful to keep garlic powder on hand ever since the Count's ambush. But he'd changed coats before leaving Ravenwald, the better to keep off the rain . . .

"A guardianship it seems you are outright eager to flout at every turn." The Count turned his attention to Laura. "You think to court my . . . niece, young lady?"

"Cornelia's of age," Laura pointed out, not knowing that this was true several dozen times over. "Capable of making her own choices."

"You don't need to defend me," Cornelia told her, rounding the bench to stand between her lover and her husband. "I sought her out, in fact."

"Did you, now," the Count said, his voice calmer than Igor had ever heard it, and all the more dangerous for that. "Planning on running away from home again, Cornelia?"

"Again?" Laura asked, puzzlement in her voice.

The coach, Igor realized. It was still parked on the far side of the square, the horses stamping restlessly under an overhanging balcony. He'd replenished his store of garlic powder while getting groceries only a handful of hours ago. If he could just make it to the coach . . .

"Oh, my Cornelia has attempted to"—the Count searched for a suitably disgraceful word—"emancipate herself several times over now. Sometimes with the pretense of taking a lover, as has so clearly worked upon you—"

"It's no pretense," Cornelia said. Even with her face in profile, Igor could see the worry in her expression. "Laura, I—"

"Like I said, Cornelia can make her own choices." Laura looked hard at the Count.

"You think so?" the Count asked softly, turning his gaze on Cornelia. His eyes flashed red, and when he next spoke, the words left a strange, metallic taste in Igor's mouth. **"Return home. Do not speak a word to a living soul until I bid you otherwise."**

Cornelia's back stiffened, her hands trembling at her sides. She gave Laura a pleading look, then retreated from the square one reluctant step at a time, until the fog swallowed her completely.

"Now," the Count said, turning to Laura. "As for you, young interloper . . ."

Igor made up his mind.

"Karl!" he shouted, running from under the trees in a stumbling jog made all the more awkward by the fist he'd kept plunged into his pocket. "Leave her be!"

The Count whirled, snarling at Igor with fangs extended and eyes aglow.

"Leave her alone," Igor repeated, bunching up the empty fist in his pocket and praying to whoever might be listening that his ruse would work. "You've already warned her off Cornelia. She doesn't need telling twice."

The Count's red eyes flickered down to Igor's pocket, then back to his face. Igor tried to compose his features into a mask of fierce defiance, which was hard to do when his legs were trembling like dry leaves in a hurricane. "So you *were* conspiring with Cornelia, after all."

"Call it what you like," Igor said, with a bravado he didn't remotely feel. "I was just trying to make her happy."

"I don't care whether she's happy," the Count snapped. "I care that she's *mine*."

A throaty growl behind him indicated precisely what Laura thought of that statement.

"I can see why Cornelia's so keen to leave," she said, her voice raspy and guttural. "Careful how you treat her, old man. Or I might decide to come pay *you* a call instead."

"I'm flattered," the Count said dryly, not ceding an inch. "But I would advise against calling upon either of us. It will be the worse for her if you do."

That gave Laura pause. "You would hurt her?"

"I would prefer not to have to," the Count said, his voice arctic. "But it seems she is in need of a firmer hand than I have given her, of late."

Igor had never craved garlic so badly before in his life, and not as an aromatic.

"Choose your lovers better in the future." The Count gave Laura a smile that was all teeth. "Other men will not be as forbearing as I when it comes to protecting their own."

Then he turned, cape fluttering behind him dramatically as he stalked into the fog. Laura growled and made to follow him, but was arrested by Igor grabbing at her sleeve.

"Don't," Igor said, his whole body trembling now that there was no ready outlet for his adrenaline. "It'll just make things worse."

"Worse?" Laura rounded on him, her calloused hands clenched into fists. "He's going to—"

"He won't hurt her," Igor said with a confidence he didn't truly feel. "I'll make certain of that, Laura, I promise you. But if you try anything on your own, the Count—"

Laura's nostrils flared. "I'm not afraid of him."

"You should be," Igor said quietly, eyes fixed on the fog. For all he knew, the Count might still be lurking there, listening. "I'll see to Cornelia. You just keep your head low."

"But I—"

"Have you ever had your home set aflame?" Igor asked sharply. Laura frowned, shook her head. "Because I have. Smoke's not a pleasant smell to awaken to, Laura."

"You think the Count would set my cottage on fire?" Laura asked, and Igor was guiltily relieved to hear apprehension in her voice.

"I think that's the least of what he might do," Igor said, looking about at buildings looming in the fog. "Find a tavern with a room for rent, at least for tonight. I'll send word once I know it's safe for you to go home."

Laura looked on the verge of argument, then swallowed it with a visible effort.

"All right," she breathed, not bothering to hide her chagrin. "I'm trusting you to keep her safe, Igor."

"I will," Igor promised, and hoped the Count wouldn't make a liar of him.

27

DOMESTIC DISPUTE

IGOR RODE BACK to Ravenwald as quickly as he dared. Soon—though not soon enough—the manor loomed before him in the darkness, flashes of light issuing from the upstairs windows. Igor threw himself from the coach as soon as it came to a halt, promising the horses that he'd unsaddle them as soon as he was able—as soon as he'd confirmed that Cornelia was all right.

He raced up the stairs, threw open the grand double doors, and only just avoided being hit in the face by a wooden chair.

"—stepping out on me after all this time!" the Count was shouting from the second story landing. He lifted a battered armoire as if it weighed no more than a loaf of bread and threw it at Cornelia, who blurred away. The armoire crashed against the wall behind where she'd been standing, reducing it to firewood.

Cornelia reappeared near the door. Snarling, the Count wrenched free part of the railing he'd been leaning against and hurled it. Cornelia dodged it as nimbly as she had the armoire.

"Stop," the Count said in the same tone of irresistible command that had sent Cornelia home, the same tone that had filled Igor's mouth with a coppery taste that made his teeth ache.

Cornelia froze, grimacing as the Count pointed a pale finger at her. **"Come here, dear one."**

Cornelia flashed her fangs even as her feet propelled her up the staircase. Igor followed, already reaching for the refilled vial of garlic powder.

"You stay there, hunchback," the Count said, fixing Igor with his scarlet glare. "Take one step up these stairs, and I'll order my lovely bride to drain you dry. As we should have done that first night you trespassed here."

"You wouldn't," Cornelia ground out, taking another unwilling step up the staircase. Her face was tight, drawn, as if each second she resisted the command laid upon her was exacting a physical toll. For all Igor knew, it was. "We had a deal, Karl. No preying on Igor or Grimalkin."

Igor blinked. Cornelia had never mentioned any such arrangement to him. But why else would the Count never have tried to feed upon the two most vulnerable residents of his home?

"That was before you violated the sanctity of our marriage," the Count snapped, his anger a mounting tidal wave. "With the support and encouragement of the hunchback, and likely the cat as well. Their lives are forfeit, as is our agreement."

"Do you really want to risk that?" Cornelia asked, her voice strained as she clung to the stairway railing like a drowning sailor clinging to driftwood. "Risk losing me forever?"

"Is that not your entire aim?" The Count's voice climbed to near hysteria. "To be rid of me? Of all that I have given you, these long years?"

"Try me, then, if you really think I'm bluffing," Cornelia said, and to Igor's alarm she gestured back at him, as if inviting the Count to take a bite. "Lay a hand on Igor, or on Grimalkin, and the next morning I will gladly walk into the sunrise."

The threat hung in the air between them.

“You’d—” Igor squeaked out, but the Count cut him off.

“I could command you not to,” he told Cornelia, lips peeling away from his fangs in a rictus too savage to call a smile. “Order you to remain within the manor walls every night. Forbid you to commit any act of self-harm, no matter how small.”

“You could.” Cornelia shrugged. “But your commands wear off within a few nights.”

“I shall remind you regularly, then.”

“By all means,” she said, sounding thoroughly unaffected. “Eventually you’ll forget, or leave a loophole wide enough for me to slip through and greet the dawn. I can afford patience far more than you can constant vigilance.”

The Count’s mustaches quivered. “You overestimate your value, my dear. I have had other brides before you.”

Cornelia’s face remained fixed, though a muscle twitched in her jaw. “Then I’m sure you’ll have no difficulty replacing me. One way or the other.”

The air hung thick with tension as the Count stared at his wife and Cornelia gazed levelly back. Igor hesitated at the foot of the stair, wishing he were armed with something more potent than seasoning.

“You would really court the final death?” the Count asked, his tone quietly disbelieving. “For the sake of a misshapen mortal, and a demon masquerading as a cat?”

“For my friends,” Cornelia corrected softly. “Yes.”

The Count stared at her, then growled in frustration and viciously slashed his hand through the air. Cornelia gasped and collapsed like a mannequin with its strings cut, teetering on the edge of the staircase.

Forgetting the Count’s threats, Igor rushed up the stairs and caught her before her head could hit the marble steps. Even if her vampiric nature meant such a tumble wouldn’t hurt her as badly as it might a mortal, he’d made Laura a promise.

“So be it,” the Count said, his voice chill with contempt. “I am off to hunt for my supper. As for you . . . perhaps a period of confinement and reflection will teach you your place."

"Confinement?" Cornelia croaked, feeling light as a feather in Igor's arms.

"And hunger," the Count added, smiling thinly. "If those combined are not enough to teach you proper gratitude, nothing will. **Do not leave the manor.**"

Then he was gone, leaving nothing but a faint blur in the air. Cornelia tried to sit up, but the effort seemed to cost her something, judging by the pain contorting her lovely features.

"Don't move." Igor brushed aside a red curl that had fallen into her face. "Are you hurt?"

"Woozy," she said, closing her eyes. "It'll pass in a bit. It's worse when I try to fight it."

"Thank you." Igor bent low over Cornelia. "For . . . for what you said. About how you've been protecting me, and Grimalkin."

"What I threatened, you mean," Cornelia said, smiling wanly.

"That." Igor nodded. "I think the Count even believed it."

"Of course he did," Cornelia said, closing her eyes. Her cold, slender frame trembled in Igor's arms. "I wasn't bluffing."

28

HUNGER PAINS

To Igor's immense relief, Grimalkin reappeared the following morning, still shaped like a cat—albeit one drenched from tail to whisker by the storm that had blown in just past dawn.

"I'm glad to see you again," Igor said, ushering her in through the kitchen door. "Especially looking like yourself."

"Oh, Mag kept me all slimy and tentacled for a day or so," Grim said, padding over to the fireplace. "But eventually she decided that it was more important to send me after the Eye of Anthomset than to keep punishing me."

"You could have said something to me before you went," Igor said, wrinkling his nose at the smell of wet fur. He returned to the kitchen stove, where he'd been preparing breakfast until Grim had scratched at the door, and cracked an egg. Spare watched from the kitchen counter, legs dangling off the edge. Their lack of a digestive system precluded them from eating, but they seemed to enjoy being present for meals nonetheless. "I've been worried for you, Grim. Especially after the Duke—"

"You needn't have been."

Igor wondered whether Grim's air of self-assurance was native to her or was something she'd practiced, the better to pass as the cat she clearly considered herself to be.

"Can't help myself." Igor picked up the saltshaker. Spare held out their hands eagerly, but Igor passed them the pepper grinder instead. Spare's enthusiasm for any new task often outstripped their capacity for restraint, and Igor preferred that his eggs have too much pepper rather than too much salt. "Where'd Mag send you, then?"

"In search of the Eye, naturally." Grim flicked her tail irritably. "She casts the bones every morning to see if they'll tell her where to find it."

Igor frowned down at the eggs, which Spare was enthusiastically burying under a small mountain of pepper. "Bones?"

"Her preferred method of divination," Grim said, stretching. "More detailed than a crystal ball, not as messy as entrails. Mostly they answer in riddles. The other morning they told her that the Eye is inside a head that never lived."

"Then it's probably not in a graveyard," Igor said, thinking back to their first encounter.

"It definitely isn't," Grim said. "Mag's interpretation was that the bones must have meant a headland—you know, cliffs right over the ocean?"

"We're a long way from the coast, though."

"I tried telling her as much." Grim flicked her whiskers in irritation. "But there are similar cliffs along the river here, in places, and she figures one of those might be the head in question. So off she sends me in search of a legendary treasure no one's seen since crusading times, up and down the river, in fair weather and in foul."

"She's been in a foul mood lately," Igor said. He flipped the eggs, then the bread toasting in the other pan, and told Grim about his encounter with her mistress the previous night.

"And you said no?" Igor was surprised by how taken aback she sounded.

"Of course I did," he said, frowning at her. "Why wouldn't I?"

"Well." Grim licked her paw, as she usually did when trying

to downplay her reaction to something. "I . . . can understand the appeal of wanting to be something you're not. To be turned into something less . . . misshapen."

Somehow the word stung less coming from her.

"Maybe it's a failure of imagination on my part, then." Igor shrugged his hunched shoulder. "I've always been the way I am. I don't *feel* misshapen, or that I don't belong in this world, no matter what the Do—what Mag said."

"No," Grim said, more sincere than Igor had ever heard her. "You're not."

"Thank you," Igor said. "And as it happens, I think I might have come up with a solution to our tentacle problem."

As he finished cooking the eggs and toast, Igor told her about his conversations with Friar Bernhard and Mag, and the plan he'd come up with. Grim listened attentively, her tail flicking as the fire dried her fur.

"So," she said once Igor had finished. "Your idea is to wait until Mag has found the Eye and begun the Rite, then wrest control of it from her so we can . . . open a portal to Above?"

"That's the idea." Igor nibbled his toast. "Way I see it, if there's an alien god looking to invade this reality, the best place to look for help is the one who's already in residence."

"Audacious," Grim said, which was high praise from her. Her tail flicked. "But that's all assuming she manages to find the Eye of Anthomset before the full moon. What if she doesn't?"

"Then we'll have to run for it." Igor had made up his mind about this on the drive back from Ravensburg. "You, me, Spare. Cornelia, if we can compel the Count to let her out of the manor. I'll have the coach loaded up and ready to flee Ravenwald while the Duke is distracted with Mag."

"And your Doctor?"

Igor nearly dropped his toast. He hadn't even thought of the Doctor.

"He'll come too," Igor decided, with more certainty than he

felt—the Doctor had a rather poor track record when it came to choosing between completion of his experiment and his bodily safety. "But that's if you and Mag *don't* find the Eye of Anthomset. If you do manage to, do you think the plan could work?"

"I suppose it could," Grim admitted, "provided that we manage to restrain Mag at the right moment."

"Exactly," Igor said through a mouthful of toast. "We redirect the portal and ask whoever's on the other side to keep it closed against the Unsmiling King and the Duke of Want."

"Hopefully whoever answers is willing to bargain," Grim said, but she could not hide an interested quiver of her whiskers. "You . . . Do you think they'd let me stay a cat?"

"That's the hope," Igor said, leaning back in his chair. "That, and find a way to release Cornelia from the Count's control. Things have gotten worse since you left."

By the time he'd caught her up on the latest development in Ravenwald's most unhappy marriage, breakfast was finished, and Spare had decided to amuse themself by inspecting the contents of the kitchen cabinets.

"So the Count's starving her?" Grim asked, arching her back. "Letting Cornelia go hungry while he drinks his fill?"

"Intends to, anyway." Elbow deep in the sink, Igor nodded. "Though Cornelia doubts he'll be able to fend for himself. By her account, he hasn't hunted on his own in centuries."

"And you're not worried about being stuck in a house with an increasingly hungry vampire?" Grim glanced towards the kitchen window, where rain pattered against the glass without any sign of slackening. "The roads will be useless until the weather clears."

"Hopefully that won't be long," Igor said, scrubbing the frying pan. "She fed last night, I guess, before she met with Laura."

"But she'll be hungry tonight," Grim remarked, watching as Spare opened a cabinet door so forcefully that an egg cup fell from one of the shelves and bounced off their head. "Sooner or later she's going to get thirsty enough that everyone in this house who doesn't already have holes in their neck is going to start looking delectable."

"Well," Igor said, bending to retrieve the fallen egg cup, "until we can come up with a more permanent solution, we'll just have to feed Cornelia ourselves."

"Igor," Grim said, gentle reproof in her voice. "I know you're a giving sort, but letting her drain you—"

"That's not what I'm suggesting," Igor said, cheeks flushing. "Look, there are other ways we could ensure that she gets blood while the Count tries to starve her out."

Grim lashed her tail from side to side. "Such as?"

"You've mentioned rats and mice in the walls," Igor said, gesturing around them with the egg cup. "Think you could catch a few and leave them in her coffin?"

"I could try," Grim said reluctantly. "Do you really think that would be enough to sustain Cornelia, though?"

"It's better than nothing." Igor set the egg cup back in the cupboard. "And the Doctor keeps a few liters in his study. Blood's a powerful alchemical ingredient."

"Well." Grim twitched her whiskers. "Sounds like we've got our work cut out for us."

"Best we get to it, then."

* * *

Igor had dwelled in Ravenwald long enough to become accustomed to the creaking of the manor's staircases. The sound had never given him pause until now, as he crept with greater than usual care up the long, winding stair leading to the upper floor, where the Doctor had converted one of the unused bedrooms into his alchemical laboratory.

Given the Doctor's possessive jealousy over the philosopher's art, Igor had been allowed to enter this room only a handful of times, and only while the Doctor was in residence. Still, it came as a rude surprise when he put his hand on the doorknob and found it locked.

"Must be to keep the others out," Igor muttered to himself, fishing in his coat pockets for his lockpicks. As the Doctor had alluded at dinner their first night, there was some crossover between the ingredients required for alchemy and for spellcraft. Nor would Igor have put it past Auntie Mag to attempt outright theft of the materials in question.

"Of course," he muttered, inserting a pick and gently probing for the first tumbler, "he'd do the same, if the shoe were—"

A short, sharp shock jolted through Igor's fingertips and up his arm, blasting him away from the door. He huffed out a breath as he landed hard against the opposite wall and slid bonelessly to the floor, his nose filled with the faint stink of ozone.

"Ouch," Igor croaked, watching as one of his legs kicked arrhythmically. Like the Doctor, he'd been electrocuted often enough to be familiar with the aftereffects, including the spasmodic twitching of the limbs. Groaning, he leaned his head against the wall and waited for his faculties to return to his control.

Pounding footsteps echoed up the stairs. A moment later the Doctor appeared at the end of the corridor, hastily stripping off a glove to reveal the brass gauntlet beneath.

"Got you, you conniving harridan!" he cried, but his words and footsteps both drew to an abrupt halt. "Igor?"

"Master," Igor croaked, jerking one hand in a wave.

The Doctor's gaze flicked to the door, then back to Igor. "You tried to break into my study?"

"I couldn't get in," Igor wheezed. "The door was locked."

"I knew that that would hardly serve as an adequate deterrent," the Doctor said, bending and picking up the dropped lockpick. "So I resorted to more direct means."

It took a moment for his meaning to penetrate Igor's hazy thought process. "You booby-trapped the door to keep *me* out?"

"Don't take that tone with me," the Doctor said severely. "After your misappropriations from the spare parts collection, you can hardly blame me."

"You don't trust me anymore." Igor's voice was small and strained, and not from the electrocution.

"I told you already," the Doctor said, his own voice still frosty, "trust takes time to re—"

Just then a tremor shuddered through the walls of Ravenwald, shaking the house so violently that Igor thought lightning must have struck the house.

But rather than fading away, the tremor intensified, drawing nearer. Igor pushed himself to his feet as from the far end of the corridor came a scrabbling, clawing, skittering tide of fur and fangs.

"Rats!" the Doctor hissed, adjusting a dial on his gauntlet. Igor hurried to his master's side, reaching him just before the horde of rodents barreling down the corridor.

Lightning flared from the Doctor's gauntlet, leaping out around him and Igor in a cage of crackling electrical arcs. Igor closed his eyes and clung tight to the Doctor's side, his nose filling with the acrid stench of ozone and the foul stink of frying rat.

They waited there, trembling, as the horde trampled past, clawing and scrabbling their way down the corridor. After a small eternity the tide of rodents slackened off, then disappeared down the very stairs Igor and the Doctor had ascended mere moments earlier.

"That was odd," the Doctor said, turning a dial on his gauntlet. The cage of electricity sputtered out of existence as he frowned down at Igor. "I wonder what caused—"

"Auntie Mag," Igor said, taking off after the tide of rodents. He reached the staircase just in time to see the last wormy tail disappear down the bottommost stair.

"Stairs," Igor groaned, and began his descent.

By the time he reached the ground floor, the walls had ceased their shaking, and the sound of the horde of rats had faded away, headed towards the southern wing of the manor, where the chapel lay.

"Igor!" Grim bounded towards him, barreled into his knees. "Are you all right?"

"Fine," he gasped, clinging to the railing. It had been a *lot* of stairs, and he wasn't fully recovered from being electrocuted. "All the rats—Mag's work?"

"Yes," Grim said. "She got it into her head that a mass sacrifice might be enough to power the Rite of Opening instead of using the Eye."

"Is it?" Igor asked, glancing towards the chapel in case something unspeakable and tentacled should come crawling from that direction.

"I doubt it." Grim sounded miserable. "This is my fault. I mentioned I was going hunting, and it gave her the idea—"

"Hey." Igor knelt and petted her with slow, reassuring strokes. "It's not your fault. You can't control what she does."

"Tell that to Cornelia," Grim said bitterly, though she pressed her head hard against Igor's hand. "I caught a few of them before Mag started calling them, but I doubt it'll be enough. Did you have any better luck?"

Igor shook his head. "The Doctor's locked up his alchemical supplies. I can't get to them."

"Well," Grim said, glancing at the rain sleeting against the nearest window, "hopefully the world won't end until after we've found a way to feed our vampire."

29

DARK AND STORMY NIGHT

THE WORLD DID not end that day, nor the next, though Igor soon almost wished it had.

Two nights into Cornelia's deprivation, Igor was startled from his dreams of drowning rats. He rubbed his eyes, uncertain whether he had dreamed the sound that had drawn him from his uneasy rest or it had been a part of his clawing, skittering nightmare.

The noise came again: a scratching at the door, so frantic and insistent that he found himself reaching for the knob, assuming he must have locked Grimalkin out of his little storeroom turned bedroom.

A lancing pain in his wrist forced him to withdraw his hand.

"Igor," Grimalkin warned, flexing her claws. "Don't."

Igor sucked in a breath, the pain jolting him into fuller consciousness. Grim was already here in his room, not outside scratching to be let in.

The scratching redoubled as he pressed his wrist to his lips, sucking the wet bead of blood Grim had drawn.

"Igor," came a low, whining voice from the other side of the door. "Igor, let me in."

"Cornelia?" Igor whispered.

"Igor," she repeated, her voice high and strained as he'd never heard it. "Igor, please. Let me in."

"Don't," Grim warned, leaning against him. Her body shivered, her ears pressed flat against her head, her tail trembling. "That's not her out there, Igor. That's her hunger."

"Hunger?" Cornelia's laugh was breathy, shrill. "Is this hunger, that curls its wormlike folds in my belly? Is this hunger that chokes my throat with dust? Is this hunger that tears my lips and bleeds my gums?"

As if to prove the truth of her words, there was a wet, tearing sound, and when Cornelia spoke again, her voice was ragged and muddled, as if she were speaking through a mouthful of raw steak. "Dry and dry and dry, a sailor drowning in a desert. Lungs full of salt, tongue made of sand. Open the door for me, Igor. Open the door, if you ever loved me."

There was no compulsion in Cornelia's voice, or at least none of the mystical sort the Count employed. Only the crazed and frenzied desperation of a madness born of suffering.

"I can't," Igor whispered into the dark, uncertain whether he spoke the words to Cornelia or to himself.

"Don't talk to her," Grim hissed, but she was interrupted by Cornelia's high and cackling laughter.

"Can't, shan't, won't," Cornelia shrieked in a manic singsong. "All I've done for you, and you deny me even a taste. Not a drop, Igor? And here I thought we were friends."

"We are," Igor said, unable to help himself even as Grim made a low growling sound.

"Some friend!" Cornelia growled in turn, the door shuddering in its frame as she pounded her fists against it, jostling the garlic bulbs Igor had hung there two nights ago. Igor flinched, fearing that any moment the wood would splinter and crack, but Cornelia's strength was not what it was when her thirst was satiated. "You enjoy this, don't you? Listening to me suffer, hearing me beg. Making me plead. As Karl does."

Igor closed his eyes, shook his head. There were some things he was not meant to hear, things Cornelia was in no state to share.

"Is that what you want, Igor?" Cornelia pressed from the other side of the door, mistaking his silence. "For me to be yours? I will, you know. If you let me in."

No, Igor's mouth said, but his throat was as dry as Cornelia claimed hers was, and he could not form the word.

"I can make you like me," Cornelia said, her voice softening, becoming something low and alluring. "I can make you young, Igor. Young, and beautiful, and strong. There is power in the blood, in what I am—what I have been made. Power that can straighten your spine, align your eyes, lengthen your legs. Open the door and I will fix you in all the ways you have been broken. Only open the door, and I will make you whole."

For a dark and awful moment, Igor was tempted—not by the promises, which he knew must be as empty as the threats which were sure to follow, but by the overwhelming need to silence that terrible, desperate voice that was a mockery of his friend's. His hand stretched towards the doorknob.

"Don't," came Grim's voice, soft as her fur as she climbed into his lap. Her body trembled, small and weighing next to nothing as she curled up in the crook of Igor's legs, purring fearfully.

Igor lowered his hand and stroked Grim from nose to tail. The slight weight of her held him down, held him fast, like an anchor to a storm-wracked ship. Grimalkin nuzzled her head against his hand, and Igor held her close, like a prayer.

They endured their friend's torment together through the long night, drawing comfort from each other as they awaited the sunless dawn.

30

HIGHWAYMEN

After days of foul weather, Ravensburg's streets brimmed with people eager to see the sun again, yet Igor could not help but feel that the black coach carried a black cloud with it as they trundled into town. This time there was no avoiding the scornful glances thrown their way. Or the rotten vegetables.

"What d'you suppose that was all about?" Igor asked, wiping a bit of tomato off his sleeve as the jeering pox-faced youth who'd thrown it shouted after them. "They don't think we caused the storm, do they?"

"They very well might," Grim said darkly. "At the very least, someone in town might've noticed lightning striking the manor, especially after you put that rod atop it."

"For science," Igor said, indignant on behalf of the Great Work. "Science can't summon rainstorms. At least not yet."

"Try telling them that." Grim hissed as someone threw a gourd at the coach. It exploded on impact, leaving a trail of pulpy vegetal gore down the wooden siding. "More likely the Count's been preying on townsfolk. Or trying to, if he's as bad at hunting as Cornelia claims."

Igor found that a much more distressingly plausible answer. Certainly it explained the dark glares hurled their way, not to mention the vegetables. He wondered how long it would take for the villagers to trade rotten tomatoes and moldy gourds for pitchforks and torches.

"How much longer until you and your Doctor complete your Great Work?" Grim asked.

"Maybe a week," Igor said, glad for a distraction from the dark turn his thoughts had taken. "The Doctor's nearly finished balancing the Subject's humors, and he's narrowed down his selection of heads to three possible candidates. Once those steps are done, it's just a matter of waiting for the next storm to blow in."

"For your sake," Grim said as they rounded a corner and found several Ravensburg youths armed with a market's worth of wilted produce, "I hope it comes sooner than that."

* * *

"I'm sorry to be making a habit of this," Igor said to Alexei, tossing a pail of water at the coach. "You're sure I can't pay you?"

"For helping to wash your poor carriage?" Alexei frowned at Igor from beneath the awning of the apothecary shop, understandably reluctant to expose his sensitive skin to the sun. "Is no trouble, my friend. I have soap in plenty, and as for water . . ."

He waved at the docks only a few yards away. Grim sat atop one of the wooden pylons, watching a pair of fishermen ply their trade with what Igor thought was a little *too* much interest.

"Thank you," Igor told Alexei, oddly moved by the small gesture of kindness. He picked up a sponge and began scrubbing at the carriage, washing away the vegetable stains. "Truly."

"No need." Alexei frowned as Igor scrubbed at a bit of surprisingly persistent gourd clinging to the side of the carriage. "Folk like you and me must stick together, you know."

"What sort of folk would that be?" Igor asked, glancing over his hunched shoulder.

"Folk who are different," the black marketeer said, gesturing at himself. "In appearance, maybe, or temperament, or any number of ways. It is not only because the light hurts my eyes that I conduct my business mostly at night, you know."

"I suppose not." Igor suddenly felt rather boorish. "Thank you again for meeting me today."

"Is also no trouble," Alexei said. "You are frequent customer, and you said it was an emergency. So I make exception."

"Thank you." Igor set down the sponge and wiped his hands on his trousers, then glanced about to make sure there was no one nearby who might overhear them. "And you're sure you have enough of the, ah . . . substance in stock?"

"Of course!" Alexei laughed, showing his white and even teeth. "Is hardly difficult to come by, after all."

"No," Igor admitted, "I suppose not."

"Now," Alexei said, "exactly how much blood are you looking to purchase?"

Igor looked steadily back at him. "As much as you're willing to part with."

* * *

As it turned out, Alexei was willing to part with a startlingly large quantity of human blood, all of it neatly bottled and stored in little wooden crates.

"Proprietor before me was hemophiliac," Alexei explained in answer to Igor's questioning look. "She required regular transfusions. When she moved away for her health, she left me the shop—and the blood. Truth be told, I have been wondering what to do with it."

As soon as the last bottle was loaded, Igor thanked Alexei and spurred the horses towards home, Grim sitting primly in her seat beside him. The afternoon was drawing on, and today's efforts would be rendered pointless if they didn't make it home well before sundown.

No more vegetables were thrown at the black coach, but the

day's troubles were not yet ended. Barely a mile out of town, they rounded a bend to find the road blocked by a trio of rough-looking men. Two of them had crossbows slung over their shoulders, while the third's rested in his hands.

"Good afternoon, gentlemen," Igor called, slowing the horses to a halt. Grim stood beside him, fur puffed out and tail quivering. "Would you mind terribly stepping aside so that we might pass?"

They did not answer at first, at least not in words. The nearest one stepped forward, shouldering his crossbow, while the others trailed behind him. All three were dressed in hunter's leathers, their unfriendly eyes fixed on the coach.

"You're the hunchback," the first hunter said, stepping closer as the others trailed him. Their leader, Igor surmised, though he was neither taller nor broader than either of his fellows. Perhaps he drew his authority instead from the length of his beard, which was braided and reached nearly to his belt. "The one who took up in the manor with that professor chap."

"Doctor," Igor corrected, keeping his polite smile fixed in place. These men had been in the Hairy Nag that first night, he recalled; he'd nearly collided with one of them when Grimalkin had attacked him.

He cleared his throat and did his best to sound unafraid. "Is there something I can help you with, gentlemen?"

"Might be there is," said another of the hunters, a burly fellow with fair hair and a badly sunburned nose. "This doctor of yours. He the sort who mends bones, treats sores, lances boils—that type of thing?"

"I'm afraid not," Igor said, hoping to hasten this conversation along to a peaceable conclusion. Curiosity from the locals was nearly as bad as hostility, sometimes even worse—particularly when he was carrying several gallons' worth of human blood inside the coach.

"Pity," the blond hunter said, scratching his armpit. "I've got a weird rash on my back that needs looking at."

"We've heard more'n enough about your rash, Dieter," the lead hunter said, rolling his eyes a little. "So what sort of doctor is he, then?"

"The experimental kind." Igor hoped that was vague enough to make them lose interest. He found it extremely doubtful that the three hunters were of a scientifically minded persuasion.

"Experiments like causing terrible storms?" asked the third and shortest of the hunters, whose beard looked like a dead opossum stapled to his face. "Weren't too long ago that you put up that pole atop the manor. Then all of a sudden it rains for days on end."

"I'm afraid you're mistaking correlation for causation," Igor said, and almost immediately regretted it as the hunters' faces darkened with mingled confusion and annoyance. He'd meant it to sound like the sort of learned pronouncement the Doctor often made, but he recalled belatedly that the Doctor's manner won him few friends.

"You're saying your doctor's experiments didn't cause the storm." The lead hunter nodded slowly. "What about the deer, then? His experiments have something to do with them?"

Baffled, Igor frowned down at him. "Deer?"

"Something's been scaring them off." The hunter gestured to the thick trees just beyond the road. "Ordinarily these woods are full of them, even if it's been storming like it has. But the past two nights there ain't been hide nor hair of them to be seen."

"Or *been* disappeared," added the shortest hunter, he of the dead possum beard. "Right, Josef?"

"Right," said the lead hunter—Josef, apparently. He adjusted his grip on his crossbow in a motion that might have been casual were it not so deliberate. "I'll ask you again, hunchback. Are you the one poaching our deer? Because if so, we're going to have to have a word about it with your boss."

Beside Igor, Grim let out a throaty growl, her fur standing on end. Igor opened his mouth to deny the hunters' accusation, then snapped it shut. He *was* responsible for the deer's disappearance. Just not in the way the hunters suspected.

Three nights Cornelia had been confined to the manor, yet the Count had been under no such restrictions. Each night he had ventured out in search of prey. By Cornelia's account, it had been decades since the elder vampire had actually done any hunting on his own. Igor could easily imagine it taking the Count only two nights of inept hunting to spook the local herds—perhaps even driving them away entirely.

None of which would have come to pass if the Count had not discovered Cornelia's courtship of Laura, which Igor had encouraged.

"I . . ." Igor started, trying to think of a convincing lie. Josef took a step forward, his crossbow still in hand.

"It's still a long ride to Ravenwald," he said, adopting an air of mock friendliness. "How about the three of us come with, keep you company along the way?"

"Oh," Igor said, paling, "that's not— I mean, I appreciate—"

"Don't want us riding with?" said Dieter, the big blond hunter, as he moved to flank the coach's side. "Too good for our company, is that it?"

"Of course not—"

"Or maybe," said Possum Face, rounding the other side of the coach and putting a hand on the door, "you're bringing something to the manor you don't want us to see."

"Don't!" Igor squeaked, even as his mind raced for a suitable explanation for why the coach contained enough human blood to fill several bathtubs.

But before Possum Face could open the coach and reveal its

sanguine contents to the world, a rangy shadow loomed from beneath the trees and stepped onto the road.

"Hunting season going so poorly you've decided to resort to highway robbery, Elmar?" Laura said, putting a hand on Possum Face's shoulder. He jumped and scurried away, retreating back up the road as Josef took a step forward.

"Josef." Laura nodded at the other two hunters. "Dieter."

"Laura," Josef said, an odd note to his voice. "This ain't any of your business."

"It is when you're threatening my friend." Laura squared her shoulders. Dieter and Possum Face—Elmar, Igor mentally corrected himself—shied away, but Josef merely stared at Laura, his expression unreadable behind his beard.

"You see any deer while you were off in the woods?" Josef jerked his head towards the forest. "I'm telling you, this little freak and his boss are doing something to the herds."

"You really haven't changed much, have you?" Laura gave Josef a sad, unfriendly smile. "Still blaming other folk for your own failures. Ain't Igor's fault that you've had a run of bad luck these last few nights."

"It ain't luck," Josef protested, glaring up at Laura. "The deer've up and disappeared. It's like someone went through the forest and dragged them all to the Below, one at a time."

"I'm no theologian"—Laura stroked the mane of one of the coach horses, which were growing agitated at the increasing tension between the humans around them—"but I don't think that deer are capable of the sort of sins that get folk dragged Below. And even if they were, I don't think Igor here is exactly equipped to do the dragging. No offense meant."

"None taken," Igor said, unable to disguise his relief at Laura's timely intervention.

"*Something's* doing away with the local game," Josef insisted, glaring past her at Igor. "And the only thing that's changed hereabouts since you moved to town is him and that creepy old doctor taking up in the haunted manor."

"Since I moved to town," Laura repeated, her tone growing less genial. "You accusing me of dragging your deer off now, Josef?"

"What if I was?" Josef said, and Igor had a sense that the deer were no longer the primary issue of contention. "You vanished awful quick, last time something was preying on the herds."

Laura winced, brushed a loose strand of hair from her face. "We were just kids back then. And the one thing had nothing to do with the other."

"No?" Josef asked quietly. "You left town practically overnight. I didn't even . . . You didn't tell me where you were going, or why."

Igor shifted uncomfortably in his seat. Behind Josef, so did Elmar and Dieter.

"There wasn't time." Laura looked down at her hands. "Everything happened so fast. I thought I—I thought I'd be back sooner."

"Instead of staying away a dozen years," Josef said bitterly. "Nary a word nor a letter, 'til all of a sudden your grandpa passes and you show up at the cemetery doing his old job. And you just expect you can talk to me like nothing ever changed?"

"Some things changed," Laura said quietly. "I did."

"Oh, I'm sure." Josef's mouth twisted into a sneer. "Picked up all sorts of odd habits, I don't doubt, gallivanting about in foreign—"

"Don't talk about things you don't understand," Laura growled. Even atop the coach, Igor shrank in his seat. "You have no idea, Josef. Where I've been, the things I've done, who I've—"

Her jaw snapped shut, but the damage had already been done. Josef stared at her, a look of naked hurt on his bearded face.

Laura's own face paled. "Josef, I didn't mean—"

"No," he said, shaking his head. "You're right. I don't know who you are, now. Just a stranger wearing the face of someone I used to know."

Laura swallowed hard but offered neither apology nor explanation.

"C'mon, Jo," Dieter said, taking his friend by the shoulder. On Josef's other side, Elmar did the same. "Let's go drown our sorrows at the Nag, eh? My treat."

"Fine." Josef nodded, shaking off his friends. One by one, the hunters filed past Laura and the coach, but when he drew level with Laura, Josef paused.

For a moment, the two of them just stared at each other. Then he leaned in, murmuring in her ear in a whisper pitched just loud enough for Igor to hear: "Word of warning, for the sake of what we used to be. One way or another, it's going to come out what the hunchback and his boss are up to in that big house. And once it does . . . you'd best think twice about standing in the way of those who'll put a stop to it."

He made to move past her, but Laura caught him by the sleeve.

"For your sake," she said, looking hard at him, "you'd best not be among them."

Josef scowled, then turned and trudged after his friends. Igor watched the hunters go, feeling it would be unsafe to speak until he was certain they were safely over the hill.

"Thank you," he said to Laura, once he was certain the huntsmen were well out of earshot. "That might've gotten ugly if you hadn't shown."

"Just happy I could help," she replied. "Sorry you had to see that. With me and Josef, I mean."

"Seemed like you two have a history."

"We do," Laura said. "Did. Back before I . . . We go back a long ways. Grew up together, played together as kids. Even thought we might get married one day, which is probably why he took my leaving so hard."

"He doesn't seem too thrilled at your return, either," Igor said, trying to cover his shock. Josef and Laura seemed so alike, he would have put money on their being distant cousins rather than childhood sweethearts.

"Didn't think I'd stay away as long as I did, I guess," Laura admitted, looking down at her hands. "T'be fair, neither did I."

"And now Josef isn't sure whether to treat you as a stranger or a friend," Igor finished. Laura nodded glumly.

"Small towns breed small minds, my pop liked to say," she agreed, forcing away her melancholy with visible effort. "That said, if you and your Doctor *are* experimenting on the deer, I'm going to feel like a right fool."

"We're not," Igor assured her. "What were you doing in the woods, anyway?"

"Oh." Laura glanced at the trees, as if they might know the answer better than she did. "I was, uh . . . out looking for firewood."

Igor raised an eyebrow. "Half a mile from your cottage door?"

"There's good timber out here."

"All of it still wet from days of rain."

"Dries off quick enough," Laura said, obstinately.

"You didn't bring an axe."

She blinked. "I didn't?"

"And you came from the wrong direction." Igor jerked a thumb over his shoulder. "You followed me from town?"

"I . . ." Laura scratched her shaggy head. "All right, fine. Might be I did."

"Because you're worried about Cornelia."

"'Course I am," Laura said, more anxious than bitter. "How is she? Has her uncle— If he's laid a hand on her—"

"He hasn't," Igor said, electing to omit the Count's furniture-throwing tantrum of the other night. "As for Cornelia, she's . . ." Not well, exactly. "Holding up."

Laura gave him a skeptical look. "Meaning?"

"Her uncle's confined her to her room without meals," Igor said, deciding against mentioning that the room in question was a crypt. Laura's eyes flashed, so he hastily added, "But I'm making sure she's fed. Whole point of my running into town today, in fact."

"Oh." Laura's fists unclenched, his posture relaxing fractionally. "That's . . . Thank you."

"She's my friend," Igor said. "Why'd you follow me, Laura? You could've spoken to me while I was in town."

"Oh. That." Laura offered one of the carriage horses her hand. The horse sniffed it, then allowed her to stroke her muzzle. "I . . . Well, let's just say that Josef and his crew aren't the only ones who've started wondering about you and your Doctor."

Oh. "You don't want to be seen with me." The realization stung more than Igor had expected. He was used to rejection, public or otherwise. Or at least he'd thought he was.

"It's not like that," Laura protested, as Grim pressed her shoulder against Igor's side. "Or . . . maybe it is like that, but not because I'm . . ."

"Ashamed to be seen in my company?" Igor was surprised by his own calm.

"Yes," Laura said, then flinched as Grim hissed at her. "I mean . . . look, I've been straight with you so far, haven't I? Kept your business in the graveyard between us, 'stead of calling the constabulary on you."

This wasn't quite the point in his favor Laura seemed to think it was, since even the constables in as rural a district as Ravensburg would quickly ascertain that Igor couldn't have plundered as many graves as he had without inside assistance. But he nodded for her to continue.

"Look, Igor," Laura continued. "Most folk 'round here never venture more than ten miles from where they were born. Makes 'em distrustful of what they don't know—*who* they don't know."

Grim let out a mewl of agreement.

"I'm familiar with the type," Igor said, and this time he felt the heat rising in his voice. "Just didn't think you'd be one of them."

"I'm—" Laura ran an agitated hand through her hair. "This is coming out all wrong. Look, did I ever tell you why I left Ravensburg in the first place? When I was twelve years old, I was—I got sick. Caught something black and bad, one night out in the woods."

"Was it contagious?" Igor asked, curiosity getting the better of him. He'd been immersed in the medicinal arts for long enough to develop a passing interest in virology.

"Very," Laura said after a momentary hesitation. "Not through the air, or just being around me, but . . ."

"Contact?" Igor suggested.

"Exactly." Laura looked down at her hands. "My pop was a jeweler, but after I was . . . after I got sick, I mean, he sold the shop. Traveled all over looking for a cure, even though it cost him everything he had. He died a poor man."

"I'm sorry," Igor said, and though he meant it, he wondered where Laura's tale was leading. "You found the cure, though?"

"I'd hardly have come back if I hadn't," Laura said, which was not quite an answer. "But now . . . folk remember me getting sick. Remember us up and leaving all of a sudden, practically overnight. Caused a stir back when, and again when I came back. Now they ain't sure whether they should treat me as one of their own, or like . . ."

"An outsider," Igor finished, none too sympathetically.

Laura winced, but nodded. "Suppose that's so."

"Suppose it is." Igor gestured with the reins. "Thank you for intervening, Laura. With Josef and the others. But I need to be getting back."

"Right," Laura said, stepping off the path with reluctance. "I didn't . . . I did mean it, you know. When I said you were a friend."

Igor had been about to spur the horses into motion, but something about her apologetic tone lit a deep-seated ember inside of him.

"So you'll defend me from the village yokels when we're alone in the woods," he said, looking down at Laura from the driver's seat, "but you won't be seen with me in town."

She flinched. "I didn't mean it like that—"

"Yes, you did," Igor said, more calmly than he felt. "I'm no expert on friendship, but I do know that you either stand by your friends or you don't. No matter who might be watching."

Laura opened her mouth, but no argument came forth.

"I'm going back to the manor," Igor said, nodding at the path ahead. "To help Cornelia."

"I'll come . . ."

"You won't." Igor allowed the heat burning in his chest to seep into his voice. Laura stepped back, off the road. "Cornelia will come to you when she's able to. When it's *safe* for her to come. But right now, the best thing you can do for her is to stay away."

Laura clenched her fists. "There has to be more I can do."

"There will be," Igor said, flicking the reins. The coach jerked beneath him as the mares started forward, eager to be off again. "One day—maybe one day soon—you might find you have to choose between Cornelia and the village."

Walking alongside the coach, Laura stared up at him. "But she's not—that is, she isn't—"

"Like me?" A dozen words whirled through his mind, each of them harsher than the last, all of them insults and accusations that had been hurled at him more times than he could recall, each harsher than the last. Hunchback, outsider, stranger, freak.

Monster.

Laura's silence told Igor all he needed to know. He snorted and flicked the reins, the horses quickly outpacing the gravekeeper.

"One day," Igor said again, calling over his shoulder as Laura fell behind the rolling coach. "The town, or Cornelia!"

Laura just stood there in the road behind him, looking lost.

Igor turned back, hands gripping the reins, eyes fixed on the road ahead. He had seen the light of torches in Josef's eyes, had seen the gleam of pitchforks in Dieter's unfriendly smile, had heard the shouts in Elmar's jeering voice. When the mob came—and it would come, Igor knew—those three would be at its forefront.

Where would Laura be?

"Hey," Grimalkin said, putting a paw on his arm. Igor looked down as she stared up at him, bright yellow eyes unblinking.

"Who are you," Grim asked, "and what have you done with Igor?"

31

GRIMALKIN STRIKES

IT WAS LATE afternoon by the time the black coach returned to Ravenwald Manor, loaded down as it was with its sanguine cargo. Igor, anxious to unload and get on with the grisly but necessary task of feeding a sleeping vampire, had spent most of the return journey rehearsing the plan in his head. Go down to the crypt—armed with a wreath of garlic, of course—pry the lid from Cornelia's coffin, and feed her straight from the bottles Alexei had so helpfully provided. Or, if that approach ran too high a risk, simply leave the bottles inside the coffin.

He was so wrapped up in his thoughts that he didn't realize someone was standing in front of the stables until the horses drew up short, one of them letting out a cautious snort.

"Hello, Igor," Mag said, looking up at him. She stood between the horses and the stable, which Igor had festooned with garlic wreaths to ward off the Count. "Have you given my offer any further consideration?"

Igor swallowed. "If I say no, are you going to try to curse me again?"

"A moment of pique." Mag waved her cane airily. "I'll admit I reacted rather poorly."

That was as close to an apology as he was likely to get. "My answer hasn't changed."

"Pity," Mag said in a voice which held none. "In that case, I'll thank you to return my familiar." She narrowed her eyes at Grim. "Who gave you permission to depart the manor?"

"Myself," Grim sniffed, as if that should be obvious. "You keep sending me out to search for the Eye, so I thought I'd spare you the trouble of telling me to and head into town on my—"

"Save it," Auntie Mag said brusquely, gesturing with her cane at Igor. "I'm not so easily led as this one's precious Doctor, nor as self-involved as that preening vampire. You've been shirking your responsibilities, Grimalkin."

Grim sat very still, her tail quivering. "You sent me out into a rainstorm. For *days*."

"And we have been stuck in this dreary little hamlet for *years*!" Mag shouted, grinding the tip of her cane into the dust at her feet. "Spending far too long searching for a relic that all portents and signs attest must be here somewhere. Those rains of which you complain are but the mildest manifestations of our King's displeasure. If we do not procure the Eye of Anthomset soon, He will visit sharper reminders upon us, in comparison to which the Duke of Want's ministrations shall seem a tender caress."

"Can't find something that isn't here," Grim said, flexing her claws. Igor winced at the thought of the damage that snags would do to the coach's upholstery. "I told you, the bones—"

"Are never wrong," Auntie Mag said, taking a step forward. "Today they told me, as clearly as they ever have, that the Eye is inside Ravenwald. Yet when I turn to you for aid, I find you are off gallivanting with the Doctor's hunchback."

Something about that comment rankled Igor, and not only Auntie Mag's refusal to refer to him by name, now that he'd so definitely declined her offer.

"So what?" Grim's tail lashed with agitation. "Are you going to confine me to the manor, as the Count did his bride? Or turn me back into a monster again?"

"Believe me, I am sorely tempted." Mag's scowl deepened. "But unlike that peacocking bloodsucker, I am more concerned with results than with bolstering my ego. Or did you really think I'd failed to notice how much you've been dragging your heels, even after the Duke graced us with a visit?"

"I told you," Grim said, though there was a faint thread of anxiety to her voice now, "I can't find something that isn't there—"

"Of course not, when you spend all your time *socializing*"—Mag spat the word out as a curse, thrusting her cane at Igor so hard that he flinched for fear that his next breath would be a froggy croak—"with creatures like this hunchback, or the Count's plaything. One might almost think you cared more about them than about our sacred duty to the Unsmiling King."

Igor's throat tightened, the memory of the encounter with Laura still fresh on his mind. How much worse would Grimalkin's rejection sting in comparison?

"I do," Grim said. One ear twitched, but the rest of her remained perfectly still.

Igor blinked, unsure if he'd heard her right.

Evidently Auntie Mag felt the same. "Do what?"

"Care," Grim said, flashing the swiftest of glances up at Igor, then back down towards her mistress. "About Igor, and Cornelia, and Spare. They're my friends, Mag."

"Friends!" Auntie Mag snorted. "Friends who're about to be washed away in the rising flood of the Unsmiling King's glory, I might remind you. Blessed to join Him in his munificence as he remakes this world and all in it as he deems—"

"No." Grim's fur fluffed out so that she looked twice her size, which was still quite diminutive. "Promise me that they'll be spared, Mag."

"Spared?" Mag stared up at her familiar, uncomprehending.

"You know." Grim made a waving motion with her paws. "From the tentacles and such."

Mag's mouth became a thin line. "You would deny our King's will?"

"Not so hard to do when He's still Outside," Grim pointed out. "Swear to me on your magic, Mag, that Igor and Cornelia and Spare won't be harmed when the Rite is complete and the door opens."

"You would make demands of the Unsmiling One?" Mag asked, disbelieving. "The King's will shall not be denied, Grimalkin. All shall enjoy His blessed torments and suffer His accursed joys, as He wills it."

"I'm making demands of *you,*" Grim clarified. "You are my mistress, as the King is your master. That obligation goes in both directions. You owe me for my work."

"Wages, I expect?" Auntie Mag threw a nasty glance Igor's way. He shrank back in his seat, wondering whether she and the Doctor had perhaps been conversing more than he'd realized. "Your own wing of the manor? Fresh tuna for dinner each night?"

"A scratching post would be nice," Grim said. "My friends' safety, Mag. Promise me that, and I'll bring you all the ephemera you could ever want, and spend all my waking hours searching for the Eye. But only if you swear on your power that they'll be kept safe when the Unsmiling King comes. Safe, and unchanged."

Auntie Mag's eyes flashed violet, as did those of her cane's skull handle.

"Ours is not to make demands of gods," she said. "Ours is but to do their bidding."

"Yours, maybe," Grim said, curling her tail about her legs. "I'm done."

The violet glow faded from Mag's eyes as she stared up, uncomprehending. "Done with what?"

"Working for you," Grim said, arching her back. "Until you

agree to my terms. Good luck completing the Rite without my help."

"Don't be foolish." Mag narrowed her eyes, yet could not hide the faint strain of desperation seeping into her voice. "The Unsmiling King is no kinder to turncoats than any other monarch. How do you think He shall repay you, once He claims this realm for His own?"

"Probably the same way He'll repay you for failing to manage your familiar," Grim said, tail lashing. "Now get out of the way before I have Igor run you over."

"You little ingrate!" Mag cried, and raised her cane.

Violet light suffused the world. Beside Igor, Grim let out a high, yowling sound, one that abruptly faded into a liquid burble. Igor glanced down at her, then wished he hadn't. Where the gray tabby had once been was a slimy, undulating thing that sent a lance of pain through his skull if he looked at it directly. He hastily averted his gaze, fighting to push away the impression of teeth and tentacles and too many eyes.

"Turn her back," he ground out, glowering down at Mag. His fists trembled as they gripped the reins.

"Or what?" The witch sneered up at him. "We both know she was bluffing about having you run me over."

"You're right," Igor said, looking from Mag to the looming shape of the manor, the westering sun shining off its eaves. "But the sun's going down, and there's an extremely hungry vampire in that house. If you don't change Grimalkin back into a cat this instant, I'll tear down whatever wards you've put up to keep Cornelia out of the chapel."

Mag snorted. "You'd do so at your own peril, hunchback. My wards would reduce you to something even more wretched than Grimalkin."

Beside him, the thing that had been Grimalkin made a moistly piteous sound.

"Guess I'll just have to blast the door down instead, then,"

Igor said, forcing himself not to look at the familiar's mind-bending true shape. "Or did you think that that gauntlet was the only weapon the Doctor has invented?"

Mag opened her mouth, closed it.

"Change her back," Igor said again, his voice hard. "I won't ask again."

Mag's face soured. "Fine."

Another wave of her cane, another burst of violet. The liquid burbling sound was replaced with the former angry yowling, and when Igor looked at the seat beside him he saw not an otherworldly abomination but a small gray tabby cat furiously grooming herself.

"Enjoy your playthings, Grimalkin," Mag spat. "But expect no mercy from the King or His servants when He hallows this world."

"He never has been the tolerant sort," Grim said, flattening her ears at her mistress. "Good luck finding the Eye without me."

Mag's lower lip trembled, and for a moment Igor was certain she was going to either burst into tears, or scream, or turn them both into monstrosities. Or perhaps all three.

Instead she turned without a word, her skirts rustling as she swept back towards the manor and her desecrated chapel. Igor looked down at Grim, grooming herself as if nothing unusual had just occurred—as if she had not just cast her whole life into disorder and uncertainty, for his sake.

He cleared his throat. "Are you—"

"Ready to take care of our vampire problem?" she asked in a too-bright tone, leaping nimbly down from the coach to land in the dust outside the stable door. "The sooner the better. Sun's not getting any higher."

A glance skywards confirmed that they still had at least an hour until it set, but Igor was unwilling to cut things that close if it could be helped.

"Grimalkin," Igor said, dismounting from the coach with somewhat more difficulty than Grim had. He unsaddled the horses and led them to their stalls, which remained festooned with wreaths of garlic. "If you want to talk—"

"I don't," Grim said shortly, fixing him with her yellow gaze. "I really don't."

"All right," Igor said, opening the coach door to reveal the bottles neatly arranged four to a crate. Above them, garlands of garlic hung from the coach's ceiling in thick rows, so many that any vampire opening the carriage door would be reduced to a wheezing puddle at the first whiff. "But—"

"Please," Grim said, her voice as small and soft as the kitten she'd never been. "Just . . . pretend you never saw that, okay? I don't want to see you looking at me and wondering whether what you're seeing is really me, or—"

"Grim," Igor said, "you're a cat."

Grim twitched her whiskers but otherwise turned absolutely still.

"A particularly mouthy cat," Igor allowed, "but that's all I've ever seen. All I ever will."

Grim closed her yellow eyes, very slowly, then opened them.

"Thank you," she said, then glanced up at the treetops. "We should get a move on, unless you've reconsidered becoming Cornelia's dinner."

"There's the Grimalkin I know," Igor said, smiling wanly. He selected a crate and heaved it out of the coach, tucking it carefully under one arm. In the late afternoon light, the bottles' contents looked less like wine and more like a particularly dark tomato soup.

"I feel like some sort of macabre milkman," he confessed as they trudged uphill to the manor.

"From henchman to milkman," Grim said, yawning. "Guess I'm not the only one in for a career change."

To that, Igor had no answer.

32

MARRIAGE COUNSELING

THE BOBBING LIGHT of the hooded lantern Igor held above his head cast long shadows on the crypt wall, flickering off the bronze placards inset into the cold marble. His footsteps echoed as he strode hesitantly towards the darkened coffins at the crypt's far end, footfalls accompanied by the soft clinking of the bottles under his other arm.

"Come on," Grim said, trotting up to the stone coffins, apparently wholly unbothered by the prospect that at any moment their lids might slide away and a ravenous vampire emerge. She hopped onto the coffin whose lid was carved in the Count's likeness, strode sedately up it, and sat down on its stone mustachios. "Let's not waste time. Sunset's not too far off."

"Right," Igor said, swallowing his fear as he set the crate of blood safely aside, then placed the hooded lantern in a wall niche he supposed had been meant for a funerary urn. He retrieved a crowbar from his coat pocket, then began to prize the lid from Cornelia's coffin.

Being a slab of pure stone, the coffin lid must have weighed as much as Igor did. But years of manual labor had bestowed upon him a strength greater than his stout frame implied.

Besides, he'd had plenty of experience at opening coffins.

The lid groaned, then lifted under his efforts. Taking great care, Igor slid it aside. Steeling himself, he peered inside the coffin.

Dressed in her customary white gown, Cornelia lay within, arms folded across her chest. Yet even in the dim lanternlight, the ravages of several nights' deprivation were readily apparent. Her face was drawn, her skin pallid and stretched thin across her skull. The red hair that pillowed her head was no longer lustrous but brittle, while her bloodless lips were peeled back from her dully gleaming fangs. Worst of all were her eyes, open but staring at nothing, clouded and glaucous as Igor had never seen them.

Until now, Igor realized, he'd never really considered what being a vampire truly meant. Certainly he had grasped the benefits of potentially eternal existence readily enough, even if he personally did not think such longevity worth the nocturnal lifestyle or the restrictive diet. But he'd never thought hard about what it meant to be a walking corpse, withered and decayed and forever thirsting.

"She's looked better," Grim remarked, peering into Cornelia's coffin.

Igor nodded, not trusting himself to speak. He picked up one of the blood bottles and held it over Cornelia's supine form, silently willing his fingers not to tremble as he fumbled with the cork. It came loose with a faint *pop,* discordantly loud in the still crypt. Igor looked down, half-expecting Cornelia to have been roused by the sound, or the smell. But she remained inert, a bloodless corpse.

"Sun's still up," Grim reminded him. "But it's not going to stay that way."

Nodding, Igor lowered the bottle to Cornelia's lips, the operation as precise and his hands as steady as any dissection he had performed. He pulled at her chin, opening her mouth and tipping the bottle so that its contents spilled onto her waiting tongue.

The signs of change began almost immediately. Oddly, Cornelia's hair was the first thing to revivify, brittle rust-colored strands growing red and curling and lustrous once more. Her fangs retracted to a more reasonable length, albeit still slightly longer and sharper than any human canines. Her lips and cheeks blushed rosily as she revived, her features softening and growing lovely once more.

Only when the bottle was nearly drained did the film clear from her eyes. She blinked, sputtered, seized the bottle from Igor's hands, and suckled from it until it was as empty as she had been mere moments ago.

"Easy," Igor said, taking the bottle from her as she sat up, blinking as if the lantern's dim light was painfully bright. "How are you feeling?"

"Thirsty," Cornelia answered, and Igor was relieved to hear that her voice was still her own, albeit raspier than usual—yet still a far cry from that horrid, maddened pleading that had haunted his door. "What . . . How did you—"

"The Count still won't let you leave the manor," Grim said, looking smugly down at the coffin she sat atop. "So we found a way to bring the blood to you instead."

"Clever," Cornelia said weakly, licking her lips. She glanced down at the crate Igor had brought, three bottles remaining. "Can I have . . ."

"Of course," Igor said, handing her another. "Here. Drink slowly, though."

Cornelia nodded, her throat bobbing as she greedily drained its contents, then licked the rim for good measure.

"Better?" Grim asked.

Cornelia shook her head, then winced.

"Haven't felt this bad after waking since last time I got drunk," she groaned, pressing her fingers to her temples. "And that was back when I was still alive."

"Here," Igor said, rubbing her back and handing her another bottle. This time Cornelia forced herself to sip slowly.

"You sure this one wasn't meant for the Count?" Cornelia asked, once she'd emptied it. "Four bottles, two vampires."

"We figured you'd have worked up a thirst." Igor didn't know whether Cornelia remembered prowling the manor, or how she had begged and pleaded and threatened and screamed at his door. For her sake, he hoped she recalled it only as a passing dream, or not at all.

"Besides," Grim said, still sitting atop the Count's coffin, "your husband seemed pretty confident that he could hunt for himself. Didn't want to deny him the opportunity."

"Meaning he's nearly as thirsty as I am," Cornelia said with grim satisfaction.

"Likely so," Igor agreed. "Listen, Grimalkin and I have a plan—"

"Igor's being modest," Grim said. "He came up with it all on his own."

Igor's heart warmed at the acknowledgment.

"As far as we can tell," he began, glancing at the coffin under Grim, "the Count hasn't had any success hunting for his own dinner, so he's probably as hungry as you are."

"Apparently he's been scaring all the deer out of the woods," Grim explained. "Not sure if he's resorted to preying on the townsfolk yet, but—"

"Karl's too much a coward to risk confrontation with anyone not already under his power," Cornelia said, frowning. "Unless he's *really* gotten desperate."

"He probably has, if he's gone as long without as you have," Grim put in.

Cornelia's frown deepened. "I've always been careful to take men who wouldn't be missed, when it came to feeding from the townsfolk. It wasn't only altruism that led me to become the Angel of Mercy. But I doubt we can trust Karl to be as discerning, or as careful."

"Best we leave before he wakes up, then," Grim pointed out, scratching idly at the lid of the Count's coffin.

"She's right," Cornelia nodded, turning to Igor. "So what's this plan of yours?"

"We wait him out," Igor said. "As you said, the Count's only going to get more desperate as time goes on. Meanwhile, we've got more blood we can feed you."

"Where did you—?" Cornelia started, then shook her head. "I suppose I'd rather not know. But what's to keep Karl from getting at this mysterious blood supply you've acquired?"

"Enough garlic to dissolve him into a puddle," Grim said, twitching her nose.

"But what good does that do me?" Cornelia asked. "Starving or not, Karl's still forbidden me to leave the manor."

"Bet his tune will change once he gets hungry enough," Grim said. "Which will leave you in the stronger bargaining position, since we'll have kept you fed."

"Bargaining," Cornelia repeated, comprehension dawning in her eyes. She looked at Igor. "You mean for a way out of our marriage."

Igor nodded. "Which do you think he'll choose, starving or setting you free?"

"A week ago I'd have said starving," Cornelia admitted. "But after these last few nights . . . you may be right."

"And he won't be able to compel you to hunt for him?" Grim's tail lashed across the stone likeness of the Count's mustaches. "The way he ordered you to stay in the manor?"

"The more complex the command, the more effort it takes," Cornelia said. "And even a simple hunt is a rather involved series of events. If Karl is in as bad a state as I've been, he'll lack the required finesse."

"So you just have to outlast him," Igor said. "Wait until he's desperate enough to agree to release you from your vows—"

"He won't, if I'm still his only means of feeding," Cornelia pointed out. "I'll have to teach him, before we can leave. But that would leave me back where I started, with him holding all the power in the relationship."

"There are lots of different kinds of power," Grim said, licking a paw. "Compelling people with your voice is one. Stabbing them with sharp bits of wood is another."

Cornelia turned to Igor. He stared steadily back at her, then nodded.

"You'd do it?" Her voice was soft. "Stake the Count?"

"It wouldn't be my first choice," said Igor. "But if you strike a deal with him and he goes back on it . . ."

He let the words hang there in the chill crypt air.

"Let's hope it doesn't come to that," Cornelia murmured. She shook her head, gave Igor a wan smile. "But it's got to be close to sundown by now, and you two need to get yourselves somewhere safe before the Count wakes up."

"No argument here," Grim said, leaping down from the Count's coffin. "We'll come back tomorrow with more blood, and the night after that, for however long it takes the Count to give in. Until then, just hold on."

"I will," Cornelia nodded. Then, to Igor's surprise, she folded him into a tight, quick hug.

"Thank you," she murmured in his ear.

"'Course," Igor mumbled back, blinking quickly. "It's what friends do."

Cornelia released him, looked from him to Grim and back.

"It is," she agreed.

33

SCABS

IGOR HAD RESOLVED to think of Spare as a person rather than a pet. Nonetheless, it was sometimes hard not to feel like the owner of a small but energetic dog whenever he took the chlorophyllic little cyclops outdoors for their daily time in the sun.

Early on, Spare had been content to spend these hours basking atop the manor roof, which had led Igor to learn the hard way that the little construct lacked any fear of heights. Rather than risk another near-fall, Igor had taken to letting Spare explore the relatively safer environs of the fenced pasture behind Ravenwald, though that too carried risks.

"You have to be more careful," he chided Spare after their third unsuccessful attempt to mount one of the grazing carriage horses. "It's a big world out there, and you're awfully small."

Spare made an indignant sound as Igor prodded their arms and legs with a careful finger, testing for breaks. He'd found none so far, but that didn't stop him from worrying.

The two of them sat in the sunshine, just past the manor stables, Igor atop a stool and Spare on an overturned bucket. On the far side of the pasture, the carriage horses grazed warily, ears flicking anytime one of Spare's meeping noises of complaint drifted their way.

"I didn't mean it like that," Igor said, shaking his head and wondering how long it would take for the small, headstrong monster he'd created to heed anything he said. Perhaps this *was* less like pet ownership and more like parenthood. "Just . . . You need to be more careful, all right? No more bothering the horses, or touching the hot stove, or running off on your own."

Spare grumbled incoherently.

"I know," Igor sighed as he completed his physical exam. "You think you know everything already."

Spare trilled an affirmative and hopped down from the bucket, then raced across the field, directly towards the horses.

"Why do I even bother," Igor muttered, following them. He'd not gone more than three paces when a shadow passed between him and the sun. He looked up and caught a glimpse of outspread wings and black feathers.

The shadow swooped low, talons stretching towards Spare. A second joined it, dropping from the sky.

"Spare!" Igor shouted, rushing towards his creation as a third black bird fell upon Spare, who shrieked and dived out of the reach of the grasping talons. The crows squawked and flapped away as Igor threw himself at them, flailing his arms and striking out indiscriminately. Feathers rained down around him, accompanied by outraged squawks as the trio of crows fled skywards.

"Are you all right?" he demanded, pressing Spare to his chest. Spare nodded their stubby head, eye peering past Igor as the trio of crows settled onto a dead tree nearby.

"That your boy, then?" one of them croaked at Igor, its diction throaty but thoroughly comprehensible. "Guess he takes after his mother, don't he?"

"Don't be daft, Ed," one of the other crows admonished, hopping along the branch for a closer look. There was an odd ruff of feathers about its neck, like a collar. "The little un's the spitting image of his old man, give or take an oculus."

"I could really go for an eyeball about now," the third and

largest crow added, fixing a beady black eye of its own on Igor. "Happy to oblige if they're looking to match."

"Not interested," Igor said, taking a wary step back, still holding on to Spare. A month ago, perhaps, he would have been surprised to find himself exchanging words with a corvid, but ever since moving into Ravenwald he'd found that his tolerance for the uncanny had increased tremendously. "But if you're hungry, there's a nice cemetery about a mile down the road . . ."

"Good to know." The first of the crows—Ed—bobbed its head, and Igor noticed a prominent scar across its beak. "But I'm afeared we've an appointment to keep, lads. No time to dawdle over a missed breakfast, even if the little green fellow does look a treat."

"Aye," the crow with the ruff said. "Maybe there'll be other dainty morsels in the house, though."

"House?" Igor asked, looking with alarm towards Ravenwald.

The first two crows launched from their perch, flapping away towards the south wing of the manor, their harsh caws echoing across the pasture. Igor held Spare tightly against himself as the biggest bird, still perched, continued staring at them.

"Be seeing you," it said at last, then flapped away after its fellows.

Spare chirped an interrogative.

"Yeah," Igor said, nodding his agreement. "I think it's best that we got inside."

* * *

"They're a flock of lickspittles!" Grim spat, her little feet pattering over the manor floors so swiftly that Igor hoisted Spare onto his shoulder to keep pace. "Bootlickers, blackguards, class traitors—"

"They're crows," Igor said.

"They *look* like crows," Grim corrected, her tail quivering angrily. "But they're familiars, like I am. More to the point, they're scabs."

"Scabs?"

"Strikebreakers," Grim hissed. "Mag's summoned them to do the work I refuse to."

That explained the crows' presence at Ravenwald, as well as the appointment they'd alluded to. "I didn't realize she could summon more than one familiar."

"She can't," Grim said, turning down the long corridor that led to the chapel. At its far end, the runes carved into its door glowed faintly but menacingly purple. "It took a considerable portion of her power to summon me in the first place. I don't think she could do it again, let alone three times."

That explained much of their contentious relationship, Igor supposed, as well as why it had taken so long for it to come to a head. "Then where did the crows come from?"

"They're mercenaries," Grim said dourly. "Hiring their services out to any witch who'd rather pay than invest so much of herself into summoning a familiar of her own."

Spare made an interrogative chirp.

"But *where* did they come from?" Igor asked, guessing at their meaning. He had been slowly learning Spare's surprisingly broad range of vocalizations, but the more complex the concept, the less certain he was of the translation. "The Outside, like you?"

"Worse," Grim said, drawing to a halt before the chapel door. "I can practically smell the brimstone on them."

Igor drew up so short he nearly tripped. Spare chirped with alarm, clinging to his shoulder.

"You mean to say," Igor said, pointing at the floor, "they came from Below?"

"That's your word for it," Grim said, one ear twitching in a feline shrug. "But yes. They're hellcrows, or I'm a puppy."

"Hellcrows," Igor muttered as Grim nosed the chapel door

open. He followed her inside, ardently longing for a simpler time when his biggest worry was a mob of angry luddites wielding farm implements.

Not that that particular worry had subsided entirely.

"Mag!" Grim yowled, trotting into the chapel with her tail raised, Igor and Spare trailing along behind her. "Margaret Devereaux! We need to talk!"

"I assumed you'd said your piece last night," Mag called from the altar, where she stood bent over a simmering cauldron lit from beneath with flames of an otherworldly magenta, stirring it with her skull-handled cane. "Or did you change your mind about quitting?"

"Not unless you've changed yours about granting my friends amnesty," Grim said. She leapt nimbly onto the altar and then onto a stool opposite Mag.

"Friends," came a croaking chuckle. "Ain't that cute?"

Igor craned his neck to see the trio of crows perched together on one of the chapel rafters, their heads bent low like eavesdroppers craning to catch every word.

"Yeah, ain't that cute, Gareth?" the largest of them said, nudging the one with the ruff around its neck. "Kitty cat cares about her friends."

"Wonder how much they'd care about her if they knew what she really looks like," said Gareth, to the others' croaking laughter.

"Hey, cat!" the largest crow said, ruffling its feathers on its perch. "You show them your tentacles yet?"

Grim pressed her ears back and hissed, which only caused the corvids to laugh harder.

"Watch out, Allan," said Ed, he of the scarred beak. "Kitty's got a temper."

Grim turned to Auntie Mag, her tail quivering with undisguised rage. "Make them leave."

"You're hardly in a position to make demands of me." Mag

turned to the shelves set against the wall, which were crammed with glass jars, each containing a silvery, glowing bit of ephemera. What sort of dreams they'd been harvested from and who had dreamed them, Igor couldn't say, but each of the ephemera was unique, and uniquely disquieting: a moth whose wings bore a pattern of blinking human eyes, a snail whose shell was a grinning skull, and a severed hand perpetually aflame, to name but a few.

Mag selected a jar containing what looked like a praying mantis made of bones, buzzing angrily against the glass. With a practiced motion, she pried the lid from the jar and threw the ephemeral into the cauldron, where it sizzled and dissolved with a smell like burning rubber.

"Maybe not," Grim said, hesitating. "But I'm worried about *you*. Please, Mag."

Perhaps it was the "please" that did it, or perhaps it was the hitherto unprecedented admission of care from her former familiar. Either way, Mag lifted her gaze slowly to the ceiling.

"Ed!" she called up. "Gareth! Allan! I need more ephemera."

Ed ruffled his feathers disconsolately. "What, right now?"

"This instant," Mag said snappishly. "A virgin's last kiss, a baby's first laugh, and the longing of a divorcée, as quick as you can find them. Now *go*."

The crows squawked their displeasure, which Spare answered by shaking a fist at them. Guffawing their croaking laughter, the crows winged out through one of the broken panels of stained glass, disappearing into the morning sun.

"There," Auntie Mag said, and resumed stirring the cauldron. "Consider that a courtesy, Grimalkin, in token of the work we've done together."

"How generous of you."

"I could call them back," she pointed out. "Now, did you just want to trade barbs, or was there something you wanted to say to me? Or perhaps some things you might want to unsay?"

Grim's fur rippled in what Igor recognized as an effort to restrain herself from further argument. "Does the Unsmiling King know that you're working with agents of the Below?"

"You of all beings should know that our dread sovereign has no preference as to how the Rite of Opening is completed," Mag said, eyes fixed on the simmering cauldron. Within, Igor glimpsed bits of something lumpy and disturbingly organic rising to the surface. "Only that it is completed. I need not remind you that His patience is not without limit."

"So you resort to infernal mercenaries?" Grim demanded. "They're not to be trusted."

"And you are?" Mag snapped. "You've made your own allegiance unquestionably clear, Grimalkin, and not to our lord and master. Without your aid, I am forced to seek it from other quarters."

Grim twitched her whiskers angrily.

"Why are they helping you?" Igor asked, hoping to defuse the growing tension. "I mean, if they're from the Below, why would they help you open a portal to the Outside? Wouldn't the Devil"—Mag snorted, but Igor pressed doggedly on—"or whoever it is that's in charge down there, I mean—wouldn't they take issue with their servants working with you to help the Unsmiling King conquer our world?"

"As we've seen," Mag said, glaring at Grim, "a familiar's loyalty is hardly ironclad. Those three may not be sworn to the King, but they'll help further His cause readily enough, for what I'm paying them. It's the same as what I promised dear Grimalkin, when she first entered my service."

"Which is?" Igor asked, looking from Auntie Mag to Grim, who became suddenly quite interested in the contents of the cauldron.

"Why," Mag said, smiling with all her teeth, "a place of lordship and dominion in the world to come, once the Unsmiling King has remade the place to His liking."

"You agreed to that?" Igor asked, a smile threatening at the thought of Grimalkin lounging upon a cushioned throne. But one look at her drooping posture and downcast eyes killed any mirth he might have felt.

"I didn't know," Grim said softly, not looking at him, "what it was like here. What *you* were like. If I had—"

"Then you'd have turned coat far sooner," Mag said, stirring the cauldron with renewed vigor. "But I am not heartless, Grimalkin. Return to my service, and I can still intercede with the King on your behalf. Provided you find the Eye of Anthomset before the crows do."

"They won't," Grim said, without conviction. "Please, Mag. You can't trust them."

"Nor can I you." The eyes in Mag's cane's skull handle flashed violet as she stirred. "As you've made abundantly clear. Now, if you don't mind, I've a potion to brew."

Grim stood, but did not jump down from the stool immediately.

"I could tell them, you know," she said. "The Unsmiling King's other servants. That you're collaborating with agents of the Below."

Mag stopped stirring. Slowly she lifted her cane from the cauldron and pointed it at Grimalkin.

"Two reasons you shouldn't do that." Her voice was deadly soft. "First, how do you think the Duke of Want will reward a renegade such as yourself?"

Grim's hair stood on end, but she offered no answer.

"Second," Mag said, turning her cane from Grim to Igor, who took an involuntary step back, "if I even suspect that you might be trying to contact the King's other servants, then the next bit of ephemera I order your replacements to collect will be a hunchback's screams."

Igor flinched. Grim hissed. Spare meeped.

"Fine," Grim spat, turning and hopping down from the stool.

"But I meant what I said, Mag. You can't trust those birds. Keep a close eye on them."

"Your concern is noted," Mag said. She returned her cane to the cauldron and resumed stirring. "Don't come here again, Grimalkin. The wards will be closed against you if you do."

Grim didn't dignify that with a response, only stalked down the long rows of pews without a backward glance, her tail held defiantly high.

"'Bye," Igor said to Mag, and hurried after Grim.

* * *

"So," Igor asked, once they were out in the hallway, the chapel door shut behind them. A glance back showed its glowing runes shifting position, reforming themselves into a new configuration of shapes that it hurt to look at. "What are we going to do now?"

"About what?" Grim asked, her tail swishing angrily.

"Our plan," Igor said, lowering his voice on the off chance that the crows might be loitering unseen about the rafters. "If they help Mag to find the Eye—"

"They won't," Grim promised, halting to peer up at him. "I hid it too well."

Igor blinked down at her. "*You* hid it? But I thought—"

"Why do you think it's taken Mag so long to complete the Rite of Opening?" Grim demanded. "I've been sabotaging her efforts for years."

Igor stared. "But she's— I mean, she was your—"

"Master?" Grim spat, turning the word into a curse. "Dogs have masters, Igor. I'm a cat."

"I know—"

"I *like* being a cat," Grim said, though for the first time she sounded uncertain—as if this were something she had long been afraid to admit to herself. "I like being a part of this world. The sounds, the smells, the food. I don't want to see it become like the place where I was before."

"The Outside," Igor said, nodding. "So you've been keeping Mag from completing the ritual all this time?"

"As best I could," Grim said miserably. "Knocking the wrong ingredients into her cauldron when she wasn't looking, filching ritual components so that spells go awry, that sort of thing."

"And hiding the Eye of Anthomset?"

"That too," Grim said, shouldering his leg. "When I finally found the Eye, I decided to hide it away someplace I hoped Mag would never find." Her yellow gaze shifted to the tall windows. "I think I hid it pretty well, but now that I'm not the one looking for it—"

"Grim," Igor said, crouching down to get nearer to her level. "We have a plan, remember? In case Mag finds the Eye. We prepared for this."

"A very stupid and risky plan."

"But one that *will* work," Igor countered, petting her. "One that'll stop the Unsmiling King and let you stay as you are."

"Instead of turning back into a monster." Grim looked shamefacedly down at her paws. "I didn't know, you know."

"Didn't know what?" Igor asked, frowning down at her.

"What it was like here," Grim said, as she had in the chapel. "The world, I mean, or the people in it. I thought they would be dull, interchangeable, like ants—"

"Grim," Igor interrupted. "It's all right."

"It's not," Grim said miserably, drawing to a halt and licking at her tail. "And I'm not . . . I mean, you've seen it, the way I really look—"

"I don't care."

Grim stopped grooming, blinked up at him. "You what?"

"I don't care," Igor repeated, kneeling beside her so that Spare could clamber down off his shoulder. "What you were

Outside, before you came here, or what your reasons were. That's not the cat I met in that tavern weeks ago. That isn't my friend."

He held out his hand to her in offering. Grim gave it a perfunctory sniff, then rubbed her face against his fingers.

"Thanks, Igor," she said. On her other side, Spare petted her with both hands, and she started purring.

"Don't mention it." Igor smiled down at her. "It's what friends are for."

34

MORNING CUPPA

A FEW MORNINGS LATER, Igor was rudely awoken by someone pounding frantically at the front door.

"I'm coming, I'm coming!" he shouted, bundling himself into the overlong lab coat that served as his dressing gown and hurrying down the foyer stairs. Neither the Doctor nor Auntie Mag was likely to answer, and Igor knew better than to awaken his master prematurely, especially when they were so close to completing the Great Work. The alchemical treatments had all been completed and applied, the Subject's head selected and sewn onto its neck, and an assortment of brains prepared for the night of the revivification.

Now all they had to do was wait for a storm.

Whoever was outside pounded on the door again, the sound echoing through the foyer. Hurrying across the marble floor, Igor opened his mouth to shout at whoever was on the other side to calm themselves. It came out as a yawn instead.

"Knocking harder won't make me come faster," he grumbled as the great oak doors rattled. Igor thought irritably of the ornate bronze knockers outside and wondered what sort of primitives resorted to using their fists instead.

Pausing only to retrieve a heavy brass candlestick, just as he had when Auntie Mag had first arrived on their doorstep, he opened the door a crack and peered out. "Sorry, but—"

It appeared that overnight someone had built a wall in front of the doors, one made of red-and-white-checked flannel. Igor craned his neck and saw that the flannel wall was topped with a mop of unruly hair. "Laura?"

"Igor." Laura's voice was rough and raw, oddly dry. "Can I come in?"

"I . . ." Igor hesitated, one hand tightening on the door, the other on the candlestick held behind his back. Not that he had any intention of braining Laura with it; for one thing, he almost certainly wouldn't be able to reach that high.

For another, Laura was a friend, or something like one.

"This isn't exactly a good time," Igor began, then trailed off as Laura sniffled. A further glance upwards revealed that the tall gravekeeper's eyes were red, her cheeks puffy. "I . . . Are you all right?"

"Not really." Laura fished a crumpled paper from her pocket. "Cornelia sent me a letter last night."

"She did?" Igor asked, faintly astonished. The Count had yet to release Cornelia from her confinement; either he'd gotten lucky on one of his forays into town, or he was simply too stubborn to come pleading to his wife to do his hunting for him. For her to have managed to get a letter from Ravenwald to Laura . . .

"Grim," Igor muttered.

"Not as much as you might think," Laura said, mistaking his meaning. She peered over Igor's shoulder. "She *is* here, isn't she? She mentioned that she and her uncle have been staying here upon your Doctor's good graces."

"She is," Igor hedged, seeing no need to inform Laura that their circumstances were in fact the reverse. But if she was here, looking for Cornelia during the daytime, then the relationship between the Doctor and the Count was far from the only thing

Cornelia was still keeping from her. "You can't see her, though. Cornelia's . . . taken ill."

Laura's face grew taut with anxiety. "Is it serious?"

"No," Igor assured her, racking his brain. "She just, err . . . fell into a swoon."

The heroines of the novels he liked to read in the rare days when he and the Doctor were between projects were always falling into a swoon, usually over trivialities ranging from reading distressing letters to not having enough pillows, or someone saying "no" too loudly.

"A swoon?" Laura repeated, sounding mystified.

"A bad one, too," Igor said solemnly. "Doctor says that she needs plenty of bed rest, and no disturbances while she recovers."

"Thought you said he wasn't that kind of doctor," Laura said, pushing a stray strand of hair out of her face.

Igor shrugged. "He's multidisciplinary."

"Oh." Laura looked forlornly past Igor, then down at her feet. "That . . . might be for the best, then. I didn't want to have to . . . Sorry to bother you, Igor."

She turned and shuffled disconsolately down the manor steps, broad shoulders drooping in a way that made her look like a sad, shaggy, flannel-clad mountain. A pang of guilt stabbed at Igor's heart as he watched her go.

True, his last encounter with Laura had not ended on the best of terms. But the tall gravekeeper was clearly sincere in her feelings for Cornelia.

And, Igor was forced to admit to himself, perhaps he had not been entirely fair to Laura when they'd last spoken, either. Having lived his whole life as an outsider, Igor couldn't begin to imagine how she must feel to find herself teetering on the edge between her community's acceptance and its ostracism. How, then, could he judge Laura for trying to straddle that divide, when he'd never been faced with such a choice?

"Laura," he called.

She halted, turning around as hope lit her bleary features.

"Would you like a cup of tea?" Igor asked.

* * *

"Nice setup you've got down here," Laura said, glancing about the manor kitchen approvingly. "Much homier than the rest of the place."

"Thank you," Igor said, rummaging in the cupboards for the tin of tea he'd bought from Alexei. "Do you prefer assam, or dragonwell?"

"Can't say I'd know the difference." Laura took a seat at the kitchen table. The chair groaned beneath her.

"Assam it is, then," Igor said, spooning a generous heap of black tea leaves into a strainer. "So. What was it Cornelia told you in this letter, if I may be so bold?"

"I'll spare you the gory details," Laura said—not without a touch of irony, considering their respective professions. She laid the letter flat upon the table, doing her best to smooth down its crinkles. "But the main thrust of the thing was that she's planning on running away from home. Or from her uncle, at any rate." She looked up at the ceiling, unaware that the Count's sleeping quarters lay in the opposite direction. "He's not . . . ?"

"Not here?" Igor shook his head as he retrieved the kettle from its shelf. "No, away on business until tonight."

"Pity," Laura said glumly. "Would've made today a fine day for her to get clear of him, if she weren't sick."

"Pity," Igor agreed, fishing a matchbook from a drawer. "But you don't seem too thrilled at the prospect of Cornelia's running away from home, and presumably into your arms."

"Well." Laura scratched her head. "By her own admission, Cornelia's never been on her own. She lost her parents young, and then that dreadful uncle of hers took guardianship of her."

"Cornelia's capable enough." Igor opened a cupboard and

scanned its shelves for sugar or honey. "And she's smart, and stubborn. She may surprise you."

"I've no doubt of it," Laura replied. Her chair complained as she leaned back, balancing it on two legs. "For what it's worth, I think she *should* live on her own."

"So what's the issue, then?" Igor asked, opening another cupboard. Spare's huge eye stared back at him from inside.

"She wants to move in with me."

"Gah!" Igor yelped, slamming the cupboard shut over Spare's inquiring chirp.

"It surprised me too," Laura admitted. "Especially coming so quickly on the heels of deciding to leave her only family."

"Naturally," Igor said, leaning back against the cupboard in what he hoped was a casual manner. From within came a faint thumping as Spare tried to push it open. "Would you mind checking in the pantry for the honey jar? I think I might've misplaced it in there."

"Certainly," Laura said, though obviously puzzled by the abrupt shift in topic. Her chair creaked as she stood from it and turned towards the pantry door. "What's it look like?"

"Blue with an orange stripe around the middle," Igor said, opening the cupboard door and hauling Spare out while Laura's back was turned.

"Go find Grimalkin," he hissed. Spare trilled a reply.

"What was that?" Laura called, voice muffled by the pantry.

"Kettle boiling!" Igor yelped. This assertion was proven true a moment later by the kettle's high whistle, steam shooting from its spout.

"Go on," Igor muttered, setting Spare down and giving them a gentle push towards the door. The cyclops threw him a resentful look but did as they were bidden, slipping out of the kitchen just as Laura emerged from the pantry.

"You sure there's a honey jar in there?" she asked, resuming her seat at the table as Igor lifted the kettle.

“Guess I was mistaken,” Igor said, pouring hot water over the tea leaves. “So, Cornelia wrote that she wants to move in with you?”

“Right.” Laura looked at the letter in the way most people regarded stinging insects. “I . . . don’t think it’s a good idea.”

“You don’t?” Igor was so surprised that he nearly dropped the kettle. “But I thought— That is, you two were getting on so well. I thought you liked her—”

“I did. I mean, I do. But . . . well, for one thing, we’ve only been courting a few weeks.”

“You’re afraid she’s moving too quickly?” Igor asked, feeling perversely grateful that he’d never felt the need for romantic companionship himself. From the outside looking in, it all seemed needlessly complicated—not to mention untidy.

“Yes,” Laura said, relief coloring her voice. “I . . . care for Cornelia, Igor. I really do. Which is why I think she shouldn’t take up with me, at least not yet. Not when she’s just getting out from under her uncle’s thumb.”

“Have you told her as much?”

“How can I, when you won’t let me see her?” Laura shook her head. “Sorry. That was . . . ungracious of me.”

“I’m used to it,” Igor said wanly as he poured the tea into their mugs.

“I’m sorry for that,” Laura said, sounding sincere. “I . . . Do you agree with me, Igor? That Cornelia’s taking things too quickly?”

“I honestly couldn’t say,” Igor said. “I don’t—that is, I’ve never . . .”

“Ah.” Laura surveyed Igor through the fragrant haze of steam rising from her mug. “Simpler that way, I suppose.”

“In some ways.” Igor took a sip of tea. It was still hot enough to scald his tongue, but he winced and swallowed it. “Not that my life lacks complications of its own.”

“Guess that’s true of everyone,” Laura said, blowing on her

mug. "And maybe I'm wrong. Maybe she's not just leaping from one thing to another, and she's moving at exactly the speed she needs to. But I don't know that I could live with myself if I were to wake up one day, years from now, and realize I'd taken advantage of that poor girl. You understand me?"

"I think so."

"Then will she . . ." Laura took a sip of tea, hesitating. "Do you think Cornelia will understand when I explain why I don't want her moving in?"

"I think you'd know the answer to that better than I would," Igor said, looking down at his mug. "What's the other thing?"

Laura's brows crinkled. "What other thing?"

"You said you'd only been courting a few weeks, for one thing." He sipped his tea. "Are there other reasons you don't want her to move in with you?"

Silence fell over the kitchen, save for the faint moaning of wind against the windows. Laura stared down at her tea, as if trying to divine some meaning in its leaves. "Do you have secrets, Igor?"

"Who doesn't?"

"Got me there." Laura let out a huffing little laugh. "I've got skeletons in my closet as well as my backyard. And if Cornelia . . . I'm not sure she'd look at me the same way if she knew."

"You might be surprised," Igor said. "Might even find she's got some skeletons of her own. And," he added, seeing the opportunity to throw Laura a bone, "if she's feeling fully recovered tonight, she can stop by the cemetery—"

"No." The legs of Laura's chair screeched as she pushed off from the table and stood to her full height, her head just shy of bumping against the ceiling. "She can't. Not tonight."

"Why not?" Igor asked, confused. "I mean, if you want to explain—"

"I can't," Laura ground out. "Tonight's no good."

"You have . . . other plans?" Igor asked, bewildered.

"No." Laura ran a hand through her hair. "Or . . . yes, sort of. I . . . Look, she can't stop by, all right? But tell her I'll try again in a few days."

"That might be too late," Igor cautioned, reviewing his mental calendar. Tonight was the night by which the Duke of Want had demanded that Auntie Mag complete the Rite of Opening or suffer their god's displeasure. Laura's expression crumpled, moving Igor to add, "But I'll tell her what you said."

"Thanks," Laura said, very quietly. "That . . . will have to be enough. I'll show myself out."

She turned, lumbering from the kitchen. Igor followed, not so much because he thought Laura would go seeking Cornelia if left unattended, but because he felt this a rather unpleasant note upon which to conclude their conversation.

Neither of them spoke as they strode across the foyer's marble floor. Upon opening the front doors, Igor was confronted with a blast of chill autumn air that swept a torrent of dry leaves into the manor. Beyond the treetops, a line of dark clouds brooded on the horizon.

"Looks like it'll storm tonight," Laura remarked, little knowing how the words sent an anticipatory thrill shuddering through Igor. "Stay safe, Igor."

"You too, Laura," Igor said, extending a hand.

"Thanks for the tea." Laura shook his hand with the firm but delicate grip of someone who knew not only her own strength, but its potential for harm. "And . . . I wrote this. For Cornelia."

She thrust a crumpled letter into Igor's hand, written in a scrawling hand untidy enough to rival Igor's own.

"Sometimes things make more sense written down," Laura said. "Hopefully this'll explain things to her better than I could. You'll see that she gets it?"

"I will," Igor promised. He could do that much, at least.

"Thank you." Laura nodded once, sharply, then turned and

departed. Igor watched her go, her tall form shrinking with each step she took as the brooding skies darkened overhead.

Igor closed the front door, shutting out the windy morning. "Spare?"

A trill answered him from startlingly nearby. Spare popped out of the umbrella stand by the door, blinking up at their creator.

"Let's head to the lab," Igor said, rolling up the sleeves of his overlong lab coat. "It's going to be a long day."

35

GATHERING STORMS

IT WAS.

They worked for hours without rest or interruption, save for those imposed by biological imperative. Igor's day was spent bent over the Subject, checking its stitches for any imperfections, or working up a sweat pedaling the stationary bike, generating enough charge to provide a brief spurt of life to a single limb or system. As tiring as his exertions were, they provided a welcome distraction from his steadily mounting anxiety over the deadline the Duke of Want had set for Auntie Mag. Spare scurried about the laboratory, occasionally catching dirty looks from the Doctor whenever he wasn't pointedly ignoring their existence. But this close to the Great Work's fulfillment, even he couldn't deny the usefulness of having an extra pair of hands to supply tools or fetch food and water whenever Igor's head began to spin.

By midafternoon, his feet ached too, but there was no helping that.

With the moment of scientific epiphany at hand, the Doctor threw himself wholeheartedly into every element of the Great Work. He practically danced through the laboratory, moving with the vitality and assuredness of a man a third his age as he adjusted the electrical conductors, inspected Igor's stitchwork, and performed the thousand other minuscule yet essential steps in the grand experiment to which he had devoted himself with such single-minded zeal.

As the wind clattered against the windows and the sky churned gray overhead, the Doctor's spirits rose. As they worked he whistled and hummed snatches of arias, even cracked jokes—and only a few at Igor's expense. Spurred on by his master's rare good humor, Igor pressed himself ever harder, reminding himself that things could be like this again, that things could always be like this. So long as he performed to these standards again, and again, and again.

This, after all, was his life's purpose, his meaning. The air heavy with the promised storm, his nose full of the acrid smells of formaldehyde and ozone, the howl of the wind and the Doctor's humming in his ears. The thrill of the universe's secrets lying in wait just beneath his fingertips, a consciousness ready to be unveiled by a single, perfect blast of lightning.

Igor had never been happier.

Yet even the most laborious of undertakings eventually reaches its conclusion, and there was only so much preparation to be done. Rain had fallen intermittently throughout the day, and the winds had never dropped below a gale, but neither wind nor rain had ever quite risen to a true storm—certainly not the titanic light show the Great Work required.

"Soon," the Doctor assured Igor when he finally broached the subject, a little after nightfall. The old scientist looked heavenwards, where they'd opened the observatory dome to permit a clear view of the gray clouds hanging heavy and underlit by the final rays of the dying sun. "Wind's picking up in the east. It'll be a long night, but we'll get our storm."

As if to confirm his assertion, a distant rumble of thunder announced its presence. Faint and far away, for now.

"Yes, Master," Igor said, doing his best to mimic the Doctor's gleeful grin. "Shall I—"

"Perform a final diagnostic?" the Doctor asked, unfurling a long roll of paper on which he'd scribbled the lengthy list of the body parts embedded within the Subject's flesh. "I'm so glad you asked!"

"Me too," lied Igor, who'd been about to suggest venturing down to the kitchen to fix them a repast. The last thing he'd eaten had been half an apple, some six hours ago. Nonetheless, he resumed his place standing over the Subject, double-checking its body parts against the Doctor's list. Spare joined him, standing on tiptoe to peer over the edge of the Subject's table.

"Lungs?" the Doctor called.

"In working order," Igor called back, having performed a trial run of the respiratory system only a few hours prior. "Heart, too."

"Refrain from calling out unprompted," the Doctor said, a bit of his old snappishness creeping back into his tone, "lest I lose my place and be forced to start anew. Fingers?"

"All ten accounted for and reasonably limber," Igor said, flexing each of the Subject's finger joints in turn.

"Kidneys?"

"Both of them," Igor said, poking the Subject's sides.

"I should expect so," the Doctor said, his eyes darting lower on the list. "Appendix?"

Igor hesitated.

"The appendix, Igor," the Doctor repeated. "The Subject does have one, yes?"

"I didn't think it needed one," Igor admitted, looking glumly down at the line of stitches running across the Subject's lower abdomen.

"You neglected to give our Subject an appendix?" the Doctor demanded, his lip curling in disgust as he tossed aside the list. "Need I remind you that our goal is the creation of the ideal human specimen? A masterpiece unlike any that has ever walked the earth before?"

"You told me once," argued Igor, a rare spark of defiance kindling in his breast, "that you didn't see the purpose of an organ whose only function was to be removed later—"

"That is quite beside the point!" the Doctor snapped, all trace of his former good humor disappearing. "Were you a composer, would you leave a break in the rhythm of the piece? Or a square of unpainted canvas in the middle of an otherwise perfect portrait?"

Igor clenched his teeth and shook his head. There was never any arguing with the Doctor when he got like this; only resignation to endure whatever diatribe was being hurled his way.

"Fortunately for the Great Work," the Doctor said, pushing his hair back from his brow with the air of a man struggling to remain calm, "there is still time to correct your blunder. Go fetch an appendix from the collection. With any luck, we'll be able to insert it and sew the wound shut again before the lightning strikes."

Igor nodded, not trusting himself to speak, lest he point out that it would be him doing the insertion and sewing, not the Doctor. Shoulders slumped, he headed towards the door, his mind racing as he tried to recall whether he'd even bothered harvesting any appendixes from donors over the last few weeks. He had always prided himself on his thoroughness, but his life had become so hectic of late . . .

"Not you," the Doctor said.

Igor turned around, one hand still on the doorknob, only to realize that his master had been speaking not to him, but to Spare. The little construct stood frozen halfway between Igor and the Doctor, huge eyeball flitting back and forth between them.

"Your creation stays here," the Doctor said, retrieving the list of organs from where he'd tossed it. "I can't afford to waste any more time, and it's good for another set of hands, at least. That appendix, if you please, on the double."

"Fine," Igor said, and slammed the door behind him.

* * *

No matter how hard Igor searched, no appendix materialized in the spare parts collection.

Half-frantic, he tore jars from the shelves, only to discard them when whatever briny organ they contained proved not to be the one he sought. He ransacked his carefully organized collection with growing desperation, leaving specimen jars scattered pell-mell across the cellar floor. Only when the wine racks were completely emptied was he forced to admit that he had not harvested a single human appendix in the entire time he'd dwelled at Ravenwald Manor.

He was teetering on the edge of despair when a distant growl of thunder sounded, loud enough and long enough to tremble through the wine cellar's sturdy walls. The sound which had presaged so many near-breakthroughs in the Great Work was a surprising balm to Igor's fraying nerves; a reminder that this was a problem with a fixable solution—provided that he act fast.

He just needed one appendix, after all.

The basement worktable on which Igor had brought Spare to life was still scattered with tools. He picked up a scalpel and contemplated the short, gleaming blade. Igor had made enough incisions in enough corpses to know precisely where to cut.

Besides, it wasn't as if he needed his own appendix for anything.

He had already given so much of himself for the Doctor. For the Great Work. What was one thing more, especially when that thing was so small, so insignificant, as Igor himself?

The thunder rolled again. Louder, this time.

Igor drew in a shuddering breath, slowly shook his head. Suddenly sickened by the gleaming steel, he shoved the scalpel into one of his coat's outer pockets, then trudged up the stairs. Silently, he resolved to tell the Doctor that the Subject would just have to do without this one inconsequential part. That even the greatest works of art were seldom wholly perfect, and that perhaps there was a sort of beauty to be found in imperfection itself.

That, though his master would never cease demanding, there was a limit to what even Igor could give.

* * *

The wine cellar was on the same side of the manor as the semi-detached observatory, which loomed against the gray sky and the blowing clouds as Igor approached, the wind tugging at his lab coat. He trudged along slowly, hoping the fresh air would help him think, give him the words to explain to the Doctor that they'd just have to—

His musings were interrupted by a screeching yowl, echoed swiftly by hoarse laughter and ruffling feathers.

"Grim!" Igor shouted. The gray cat was cowering against one wall of the manor, back arched and ears flat against her head, her fur fluffed to make her look three times her real size. The trio of crows fluttered through the air, cawing and jeering at her as she leapt at them, braying with laughter each time her raking claws missed them by inches.

"Grimalkin!" Igor shouted again, the scalpel suddenly in his hand again as he ran towards the four familiars, waving his arms. "Leave her alone!"

"Tell her to do the same for us, mate!" guffawed one of the crows—Gareth, Igor thought.

"Get them, Igor!" Grim yowled, coiling herself for another leap. "We have to stop them!"

The crows cackled again, fluttering out of reach as she sprang. One of them dived at Igor, black talons stretching towards his unprotected eyes. Yelping, Igor threw himself flat, a breeze ruffling the back of his neck as the crows flew through the space where he'd been standing. He looked up to see them winging away, their laughter drifting behind them as they banked sharply and were lost to sight behind the manor roof.

"Stop them!" Grim shouted, her tail lashing furiously as Igor pulled himself to his feet.

"I can't fly," he huffed. "What's going on, Grim? Why did they attack you?"

"You've got it the wrong way round," she said curtly, tail lashing the air. "Let's go."

"You mean . . . you attacked them?" Igor asked, puzzled.

"Yes!" Grim snapped, looking up at him with undisguised impatience. "There isn't time, Igor. They've figured out where I hid the Eye of Anthomset."

"But I thought you said it was someplace no one would ever find," Igor protested.

"I was wrong," Grim said. "It's inside the Count's head."

"What?"

"His statue's head," Grim clarified, nodding in the direction of town. "In Ravensburg."

"A head that never lived," Igor breathed, recalling the earlier riddle of the bones, how they'd claimed that the eye was inside Ravenwald. They just hadn't meant the building.

"Right," Grim said miserably. She began trotting southwards, towards the manor chapel. Reluctantly, Igor turned his back to the laboratory tower, wincing as thunder boomed overhead. "I was coming to look for you just now, when the crows found me and told me they knew. That they were on their way to tell Auntie Mag the truth, but that I could stop them if I cared to try."

"And you did?" Igor frowned down at her.

"What else could I do?" Grim demanded, looking up at him with pleading yellow eyes. "Please, Igor. You have to help me stop them. Have to keep Mag from going through with the ritual."

"She won't listen to me," Igor objected.

"I know," Grim said, and stood up on her hind legs to bat at his hand. The one holding the scalpel.

"Oh," Igor said, very softly. "*Oh.* I don't—"

"It's the world, Igor." If she were human she might have been on the verge of tears. "Please."

Igor had never cared overmuch for the world, which had always been swift to reject him. Nor did he much relish the thought of attempting to fight the canny witch and her trio of hellish helpers.

But Grim needed him. How many times had she helped him or Cornelia without ever asking for their aid in return?

She was asking now.

"Hold on," Igor said, doing an abrupt about-face and heading in the opposite direction, back towards the laboratory tower.

"Where are you going?" Grim asked, slowing to a halt behind him. There was naked hurt in her voice.

"The lab," Igor said, thinking back to their very first night in Ravenwald, when the Doctor had used the power of arcane science to ward off Auntie Mag's curses. "If it comes to blows, I want to be properly armed."

"Igor, there's no time!"

"There's always time," Igor said, stopping and kneeling so that she could catch up. "The crows are headed into town, right?"

"Yes, but—"

"And it'll take time for them to break the Eye out of the statue?"

"It will," Grim said slowly. "They'd have to revert to their true shapes, which will cause a panic in town . . ."

"But that gives us a chance to stop them," Igor pointed out, his excitement growing. "Then we take the Eye for ourselves and hijack Mag's ritual, just as we planned."

"A plan that's patently *insane,*" Grim protested, though she sounded more than a little impressed.

"Well," Igor said, "I do work for a mad scientist. I'll meet you at the stables, and we'll take the coach into town. All right?"

"All right." Grim looked anxiously over her shoulder, towards the south end of the manor, then back at Igor. "You promise you'll be right behind me?"

"I'll be there in two shakes of a cat's tail," Igor promised, causing the cat in question to wrinkle her nose disdainfully. He scratched her between the ears. "Promise."

"You'd better be," Grim said, pressing her head hard against his fingers before turning and racing along the manor wall, tail held high.

Igor stood and hurried in the opposite direction as swiftly as his mismatched stride permitted, grimacing as he reached the foot of the laboratory tower.

"Stairs," he muttered, and began climbing the winding steps corkscrewing about the tower's exterior.

The wind tugged at his lab coat, and he kept one hand on the stone facing for safety, until he finally reached the modest wooden door set into the observatory's side. Relieved at the prospect of escaping the elements, however briefly, Igor seized the laboratory door with both hands and threw it wide open. "Master, I— What are you doing?"

The Doctor stood over the Subject's worktable, a gleaming scalpel in one trembling hand. In his other, squirming and wriggling to break free, was Spare.

"As you can see, Igor," the Doctor said, ignoring Spare's frightened trills as he turned his gaze on his assistant, his lips splitting into a thin smile, "I've found our missing appendix."

36

TERMINATION, EFFECTIVE IMMEDIATELY

"PUT SPARE DOWN," Igor said, his voice trembling.

"I always cautioned you not to give these things names," the Doctor said, pursing his lips. "Not the Subjects, or the donors, or the horses. Names make it too easy to get attached—"

"Put them down!" Igor hadn't meant to shout the words, any more than he'd meant to point his scalpel at the Doctor.

Startled, the Doctor loosened his grip on Spare enough for them to wriggle free. Letting out a terrified shriek, they sprinted across the laboratory floor to hide behind Igor, peering fearfully at the Doctor from between his knees.

"The scalpel, too," Igor said, jabbing at the air with his own as the Doctor took another step forward. "Drop it."

"Why?" the Doctor asked, recovering the power of speech enough to sneer. The blade trembled in Igor's shaking hand. "I can hardly make the incision myself, Igor. You'll have to be the one to do it."

"No."

"No?" the Doctor repeated, cocking his head to one side, as if he'd never heard that single syllable uttered in his presence before. Never from Igor, at any rate.

"No," Igor repeated, reaching behind him with his free hand to put it protectively on Spare's head. "Spare's a person, not just a collection of organs."

"That's all anyone is," the Doctor said, wrinkling his nose. "I thought you knew that by now, Igor. A human being is just a machine made of meat, its organs and systems the cogs and gears. Or did you think it was some moral objection that led me to cease manufacturing donors?"

"Killing people, you mean," Igor said, no longer able or willing to defend the Doctor, through euphemism or otherwise. Not even to himself.

"How else?" The Doctor shrugged. "I stopped because of the attention it was drawing to our work, not because I had any qualms about bloodying my hands. Now kindly cease your theatrics. Time is pressing, and the longer you hesitate to unmake your squalid little cyclops—"

"Spare," Igor repeated, his hand tightening on Spare's quaking shoulder. "Their name is Spare."

Anger clouded the Doctor's features—not mercurial temper but real anger, deep and abiding. "It is a misshapen, misbegotten, ugly little thing! A creeping malformed idiot—"

"Look at what they've helped to do!" Igor's yell echoed off the laboratory walls as he jabbed his knife towards the Subject. "They sorted the organs, cleaned the instruments, even did a bit of the stitching—"

"None of which makes it any more than a tool!" the Doctor screamed, a string of spittle hanging from his lower lip. He raised his scalpel and took a step forward, and for a wild and terrifying moment Igor thought his master meant to stab him. Igor held his own scalpel in what he hoped was a warding posture, preparing himself for what promised to be history's least impressive knife fight, but the Doctor came no closer.

"Your little freak is of no more use than this blade in my hand!" the Doctor howled, pointing it accusingly at Igor. "And if you won't do as I say, *then neither are you*!"

The words hung there in the air between them, heavy and irrevocable. Igor stared at the Doctor, feeling an invisible hand wrap its cold fingers about his heart and squeeze. The Doctor stared back, his eyes wide and wild behind his goggles, chest rising and falling as though he'd just run a race.

"Move, Igor," he said, the words halfway between an order and a plea. Spare mewled softly.

Igor stood his ground. Not trusting himself to speak, he shook his head.

"Fine," the Doctor said, lowering the arm holding the scalpel. For the first time in longer than Igor could recall, the old scientist looked every one of his many years.

"Master," Igor said, all the hurt and anger and shame he felt supplanted by sudden concern. "I—"

"You're fired."

Igor stared at the Doctor. The Doctor stared back, gaze unwavering.

"I—"

"You're fired," the Doctor repeated, the words bringing a sharp stinging to the corners of Igor's eyes. "I no longer require your services."

"Master." Igor swallowed down the lump in his throat, blinked rapidly to keep his vision from blurring. "Master, I—"

"Go!" the Doctor screeched, hurling the scalpel at him. Igor flinched as it flew past his head to bury itself in the door behind him. "Get out of my sight and take your little abomination with you, before I decide to use you *both* for spare parts!"

He rounded on Igor, who shrank away. With his free hand the Doctor pushed up the sleeve of his lab coat, revealing the gauntlet he'd used to battle Auntie Mag to a standstill on that first night that seemed so long ago.

Igor scooped Spare into his arms and fled, out the door and into the night.

Lightning streaked across the sky above. The thunder tolled its mournful cry, and the first raindrops began to fall.

37

METAMORPHOSIS

HAD HE BEEN in a more coherent state of mind, Igor might have stopped inside the manor to gather his few belongings. But all his thought was bent on flight, on putting as much distance between himself and the Doctor as he could. On putting as much distance between *Spare* and the Doctor as possible. Never had the little cyclops curled in his arms felt more precious than it did in that moment, or as fragile.

His feet led him to the stables. In their stalls, the black mares whickered and pawed at the ground each time thunder rolled across the brooding sky.

Of Grimalkin, there was no sign.

"She must have gone ahead without me," Igor murmured, to Spare's agreeing coo. This supposition was all but confirmed when he mounted the coach and found the driver's padded seat torn open by an agitated pair of claws, down stuffing strewn everywhere.

Of course Grim had gone ahead to confront the crows herself rather than wait any longer for him. Of course she was more than capable of stopping the crows and foiling Mag's plan on her own. She hadn't needed his help after all. And if she didn't, and the Doctor didn't . . .

"What's the use of me?" Igor whispered to his boots, blurriness threatening his vision once again.

A soft tug at his sleeve, and an even softer *meep.* Spare gazed up at him, their huge eye wide with concern.

"Thank you," Igor said softly, his dejection not gone but pushed aside to make room for an upwelling spring of gratitude that he had made this strange, inquisitive, wonderful little creature.

Igor looked back up at the looming manor, its shadows long and brooding beneath the gray sky. He suddenly found he couldn't stand another moment in the shadow of this house, where his life had fallen apart just when it had been on the verge of finally coming together.

"We'd best be on our way, then," he said, climbing down from the coach. "We've a long road ahead of us, and it'll be easier if you ride."

Spare looked dubiously at him, then at the coach.

"Can't take it." Igor knelt, offering Spare a hand to climb onto his shoulder. "Or the horses. They're not ours."

Now that he was thinking a bit more clearly, Igor could no more bring himself to steal from the Doctor than he could to cut open Spare. Both were betrayals; similar in kind if not in magnitude. He only hoped that the Doctor would remember to feed and groom the mares. Sometimes the old man forgot that they were animals, not machines. As he did with people.

Besides, he thought as another roll of thunder echoed across the sky, it would be cruel to risk the horses in a thunderstorm. Neither of the faithful beasts deserved that.

Reluctantly, Spare climbed from the coach onto Igor's back, settling themself on the shoulder opposite his hump. Despite the added weight, Igor felt suddenly lighter. The wages the Doctor had paid him were already safely in the coin purse at his side, and he had no real possessions to speak of. Certainly none that were worth venturing back into the manor for.

"Let's go," he said to Spare, and set off down the lane leading away from Ravenwald and the memories it held. Spare bleated an interrogative, glancing over their shoulder at the manor.

"We'll write them," Igor promised. "Grim and Cornelia, once we've gotten to where we're going."

It would be easier to explain himself once time and distance had dulled the sting of rejection. Once he'd put himself together again.

He hoped they would understand.

Spare trilled another question, shifting so that they were looking ahead.

"I don't know," Igor admitted, having no fixed destination in mind. A smile spread across his face as he contemplated his options; the world spread out before him like an unfolding map, accessible as far as his feet could carry him. "Maybe someplace with a beach."

* * *

The storm blew faint, fitful gusts of rain as Igor trudged the long road to Ravensburg, prompting him to pull his coat's hood low over his face. He had a vague idea of going to visit Alexei's Apothecary, not for any alchemical ingredients—all that was behind him now—but in case the black marketeer knew of any smuggling captains looking to take on an extra hand. With his life upended, Igor figured there was no better time to pursue a change in career. He'd had enough of robbing graves for one lifetime, but thought that many of the skills he'd developed under the Doctor might be transferable to a similarly illicit profession.

He'd made it past the outskirts of town and was heading in the direction of the docks when he realized that the streets were uncharacteristically crowded, despite the intermittent gusts of rain and the perpetual fog. Nor could he miss the grim atmosphere; few of the townsfolk spoke, though many of them carried spades cradled against their shoulders, or hoes, or scythes.

Or pitchforks.

"Oh," Igor breathed, realization dawning. "Oh, no."

Spare mewled a question. Igor glanced furtively about, hoping that none of the townsfolk had noticed them, but all of their heads seemed bent in the same direction. Headed to the town square, watched over by the blind eyes of the Count's weathered statue.

Igor turned to retrace his steps, but the throng of people now pouring towards the square from every side made it a futile effort, like trying to swim against the tide. Igor gathered Spare in his arms, hoping that he looked like a parent holding his child close against the press of the crowd, and that nobody would scrutinize the child in question too closely.

A sharp crack rang through the fog, not loud enough or far off enough to be lightning, echoed a moment later not by thunder but by the thud of something falling to the ground. A flash of violet light seared Igor's eyes, suffusing the mists with a lavender haze.

All around him the crowd gasped, pressing themselves flat against the cobblestones as heavy wingbeats passed overhead, the croaking sound of corvid laughter drifting down in their wake—pierced by a high, angry feline yowl.

"Grimalkin!" Igor cried, fear washing away his self-pity in the light of cold clarity. For all her endless self-assurance, Grim was only one small cat. How could he have let her face the trio of hellcrows on her own?

Shame pushed him to his feet as the crows' laughter and Grim's yowls retreated, taking the violet light that must be the Eye with them. Heading back the way Igor had come, towards Ravenwald.

But there was no following them, not when the townsfolk too had risen to their feet, pressed so close about Igor that he could not fight against the human tide, only be swept along—in the opposite direction.

The current of bodies carried them to the town square. At its center stood the statue of the Count, now decapitated. A gap in the crowd showed its mustachioed head shattered near its feet, revealing the hollow where the Eye of Anthomset must have lain hidden all these years.

A familiar trio stood on the raised plinth beneath the headless statue, hastening the crowd's transformation into a mob.

". . . monsters and worse!" shouted Josef, his hunting leathers making him recognizable even through the drizzling rain. Elmar stood beside him, nodding his obsequious agreement, while the towering blond Dieter stood behind them both, thick arms folded across his chest. He pointed down at the remnants of the statue's head. "Demons in animal form stalking our streets! Kidnapping our friends and neighbors in the dead of night!"

Whispers of consternation greeted this proclamation, though Igor was relieved to hear they were not without a faint undercurrent of doubt.

"Men have gone missing from their homes for weeks now!" Josef continued, undeterred. "Good, upstanding members of our community. Mr. Falkner the banker, the lawyer Mr. Beckett, even our own good Sheriff Hertz—all vanished without a trace in the night!"

A ripple of murmured agreement spread through the crowd, heads nodding. Igor shifted uneasily; all three of the men named were amongst those he'd bribed weeks ago not to look into the goings-on at Ravenwald. Perhaps he should have paid greater attention to Cornelia's choice of victims.

"You all know that Ravenwald Manor is haunted," Josef continued. "Some of the braver of you have even ventured as far as its doorstep when you were kids, on a dare. But no one's looked inside for years, not since the old Countess and her entourage moved out back when my grandfather was young. Then that

Doctor moves in, and within weeks folk start disappearing, the deer have fled the woods, and demons in the shape of black birds attack the town itself!"

Heads nodded and villagers muttered angrily all around Igor. He shrank against the nearest building, lest the nascent mob realize that one of the objects of their ire was in their midst.

"The one hardly signifies the other," came a blessedly doubtful voice from somewhere near the front of the crowd. Friar Bernhard, standing with his hands folded across his chest, frowning up at the hunters. "All these goings-on occurring at the same time is strange, I'll grant. But the newcomers have given you no reason to accuse them, Josef."

"You've told me yourself that there's no such thing as coincidence, Friar," Josef countered. "Just as you told me that the servants of Below are ever seeking mankind's downfall." He pointed at the headless statue. "Surely you won't argue that a flock of birds could do *that*?"

"No," Bernhard admitted. "Those were certainly malign spirits, not mere birds. And . . ."

Oh, no. Igor's heart sank, and he cursed himself for his curiosity.

"And," Bernhard continued, hesitating, "the Doctor's servant did come to me, asking about summoning demons—"

A roar of inarticulate shock and rage rose from the crowd. Igor pulled his hood as low over his face as it would go and tried to stand as straight as possible.

"There you have it," Josef said with a satisfied grin. Friar Bernhard did not meet the hunter's eyes, instead looking down at his folded hands, brows drawn together in consternation. "The Doctor and his freak are consorting with demonic forces. To say nothing of the vampire."

Gooseflesh prickled Igor's arms in a manner that had nothing to do with the drizzling rain. Someone near the front of the crowd gasped so theatrically that he half-suspected Josef had planted them there.

"We've all grown up on stories of the first Count Ravenwald," Josef said, jabbing a finger down at the remnants of the Count's stone face. "Of how he sold his soul to the Devil for eternal life, only to be cursed with an everlasting thirst for blood. Until tonight, I thought those stories were just legends."

He stepped aside, gently pushing Dieter forward. In the glimmering torchlight, the big hunter's eyes looked reddened and puffy.

"Some of you may know," he said, his voice oddly hoarse. He paused, pressed a big fist to his mouth, cleared his throat. "That is . . . Ruth Dreyfuss, and I—we've been . . . well, I've been stepping out with her, these few weeks . . ."

He looked aside, blinking very quickly. Josef stepped in to fill the space.

"Dieter's been walking Ruth to and from her job at the Hairy Nag," he said, "ever since her uncle went missing earlier this month."

Igor frowned. Cornelia would never prey on Ruth, as she had on the uncle who'd been hitting her. Nor could she, with the Count having confined her to the manor—

The Count.

"We were walking," Dieter said throatily, having regained his voice, "not more'n an hour ago, talking about . . . I can't remember what. I said something that made her laugh, then all of a sudden someone hit me from behind. Knocked me down, as easily as if I were a lad half my size. The man who did it grabbed Ruth, and she swooned."

"Huh," Igor said. So it *did* happen.

"Then he . . ." Dieter's eyes turned downcast. As one the crowd leaned in, waiting. Josef placed a hand on his friend's shoulder, murmured something in his ear too low to catch. Dieter nodded, cleared his throat, lifted his shining eyes to the torchlight.

"He bit her," he said, ragged voice now shot through with anger. He jabbed two fingers at his neck. "Right here. I swear before all the saints, he was drinking her blood."

The crowd sucked in a frightened breath, a single animal with hundreds of mouths. Igor started inching along the building he was flattened against, eyes peeled for a break in the press of bodies.

"I got my feet back under me and tried to pull him off her," Dieter continued, "but the bloodsucker knocked me back down again. Last I saw of Ruth, he was carrying her off in the direction of the manor. *His* manor."

Dieter glowered down at the carven head of the Count, the intact half of his stone face and its drooping mustachios unmistakable even with the wear of rain and wind and time.

"The stories are true!" Josef shouted, spreading his arms wide and drawing the crowd's attention back to himself. "Count Ravenwald dwells in Ravenwald Manor, immortal and accursed. Asleep, until that Doctor and his freakish assistant came to loose him and his demonic servants upon us once again. And now they have taken one of our own!"

The crowd, never wholly quiet, now loudly voiced their dismay. A few feet from Igor, someone shouted: "We have to get her back!"

"We will!" Josef pointed to the person who'd shouted. Igor did his best to melt into the stone wall at his back. "We are the people of Ravensburg! Are we going to stand by while monsters stalk among us like wolves among sheep?"

"No!" someone else shouted.

"Are we going to allow them to take one of our own?" Josef demanded. "Or will you join me in rescuing Ruth Dreyfuss from unspeakable torment?"

Mingled shouts of both "No!" and "Yes!" echoed through the

square. The crowd was pressing closer to the statue of the Count, some of the most zealous of them banging the hafts of their farming implements against the ground. Taking advantage of this opening, Igor crept along the wall towards the road he'd taken into town.

"Are we going to wait to be devoured?" Josef pressed, his lips splitting into a feral grin. "Or are we going to take the fight to the monsters, and the mad doctor who unleashed them upon us?"

"Fight!" someone shouted, and the crowd—the *mob*—roared their agreement in wrathful unison.

"Then, my fellows," Josef yelled, raising his crossbow in one hand, "sharpen your knives, light your torches, and steel your hearts! We march on Ravenwald tonight!"

"Tonight!" the mob bellowed in one awful voice. Those carrying farming implements raised them like spears, while torches blazed into life like earthbound stars even as the last rays of daylight vanished from the gloomy sky.

Igor saw none of this. He had already slipped away from the crowd as it completed its terrible metamorphosis and was already loping as quickly as he could along the cobblestone street and back towards Ravenwald, Spare clutched to his chest, his heartbeat thudding with the knowledge that the angry mob would soon be on their heels. Fear lent speed to his ungainly steps as he ran to warn his friends. Hopefully to save them.

Or, should the worst come to pass, to die alongside them.

38

MOMENT OF TRUTH

RACING THE MOB though he was, Igor made one brief detour before returning to Ravenwald.

Night had truly fallen by the time he turned off the main road and onto the lane leading up to the cemetery. The storm had paused long enough to reveal an open patch of sky through which the moon shone, bright and full, allowing Igor to pick his way along the muddy path by its light. He counted this a mixed blessing; more rain would have slowed the mob's approach.

Not that a little thing like weather would be enough to deter their wrath entirely, of course. The mob's rage would only grow the longer they were kept from venting it, until it finally burst forth in a volcanic eruption.

The cemetery gates loomed ahead of Igor, their iron spikes gleaming dully beneath the moonlight. Locked, as was the front door of the cottage when he tried the handle.

"Laura!" Igor shouted, hammering on her door just as Laura had upon his only that morning. "Laura, it's me!"

No answer. Nor was there any light in the cottage windows, or even the telltale creaking of floorboards within. By all appearances the cottage was empty, its sole tenant having deserted it for the night.

Gone into town for a pint at the Hairy Nag, perhaps? Or—Igor's heart sank with sudden misgiving—had Laura made the choice Igor had pressed upon her earlier in the week and was even now marching towards Ravenwald with torch in hand?

"Laura!" Igor shouted again, a shrill note in his voice. Beside him Spare banged their tiny fists against the door, matching his yell with their own high trill. "Laura, open up if you're in there!"

They were answered not from inside the cottage but by a long, mournful howl that made the small hairs on Igor's neck stand upright. He'd heard that sound before, but never so close. This one sounded as if it were in the woods on the far side of the cemetery.

Igor waited, every muscle tensed, his heart beating so loudly he imagined he could hear its every thump against his ribcage. To his relief, no second howl answered the first. No pack of wolves lurked within the trees surrounding the graveyard, hungry to try a bite of hunchback now that the deer had fled their woods.

Not that Igor was any more eager to meet a lone wolf than a pack of them.

"Laura!" he called again, raising his voice so that it would carry through the door. If the gravekeeper was inside the cottage, and not marching with the townsfolk as Igor feared, she could not fail to hear him. "They're marching on Ravenwald. The townsfolk. A whole mob of them, all riled up by Josef and his friends. They're—they want to hurt us."

Spare cooed softly at his knee. Igor reached down and patted his creation's head, his eyes scanning the trees for a lupine silhouette, just in case.

"Not just me," Igor continued when none appeared. "The Doctor, too, and Cornelia. And Auntie Mag and Grimalkin, probably. They're coming for all of us, Laura. To set fire to the manor and string us up, each and every one. Cornelia included. She—"

The unseen wolf howled again, so close that Igor flattened his back against the door, his breath coming in fast, fitful gasps. Spare trilled and clambered onto his shoulder. Their three eyes peered into the dark, Igor wondering at the curious way the trees warped and distorted sound, befuddling the direction it came from.

It had almost sounded as if the howling had come from *inside* the cemetery.

"They think Cornelia's a monster," Igor continued, determined to relay the message he'd come here to deliver, praying to whatever saints or gods might be listening that Laura was inside her cottage after all. "And . . . well, maybe she is, a little bit. Maybe we all are. But that doesn't change the fact that they're coming for her. To hurt her."

No answer save the wind, blowing cold and chill as a cloud drifted across the moon, plunging the world into a darkness heavy with the promised storm.

"I know she hurt you," Igor continued. "And that you probably hurt her, too. That's what happens when people aren't honest with each other, even if they care about each other. But you'll never have the chance to explain yourselves if she—if they—"

He closed his eyes, trusting Spare would warn him if they were attacked. "I told you, that day in the woods, that you'd have to make a choice. Between us and the village. Between Cornelia and all the rest of them. Now's the time."

The wind whispered its agreement. Igor opened his eyes and saw that the rain had begun to patter down once more.

"I said just a minute ago that maybe we're all a little bit monstrous, and I think that's true. Of everyone, I mean. You, me, Cornelia. The villagers, the Doctor." He swallowed hard, blinking fast. "But . . . I think we're all a little bit saintly, too. I've stolen more hearts than I can count, Laura, and I don't mean that romantically. Hearts that belonged to murderers, or poets, or priests. But if I lined them up in a row, you couldn't tell whose was whose." He was almost sobbing now. "A saint's heart looks much the same as a sinner's. Virtue isn't innate, is what I'm trying to say. It has to be chosen, each and every night."

Igor stepped away from the door, raising his voice so that he could still be heard within the cottage. "Tonight, I'm choosing my friends. And maybe that means I'm siding with the monsters instead of the angels, but if I am, I can't say that it's the wrong choice. I hope you'll choose the same."

No answer came from within the cottage, nor from the surrounding woods.

"Come on," he said softly to Spare, putting his back to the graveyard. "Let's go save our friends."

Spare trilled their agreement, and the two of them set off back along the lane, towards the road and Ravenwald Manor.

Had either of them looked back, they might have caught a glimpse of gleaming eyes staring after them in the dark from between the bars of the cemetery that imprisoned it. Might have seen the shadow of something huge and furred and wolflike seize those same bars in clawed hands and wrench them apart, slipping out into the night after the hunchback's retreating form.

They did, however, hear its howl, long and mournful and hungry.

Igor and Spare fled into the night as lightning arced across the sky above them and the rains beat down.

The storm had come at last.

39

RETURN TO RAVENWALD

As Igor and Spare approached Ravenwald, the lightning now racing freely across the sky was answered by the unsettling, eerie purplish glow emanating from the stained glass windows of the chapel. Gooseflesh prickled Igor's skin as the distant chanting chorus of the Rite of Opening battled against the keening wind.

He reached Ravenwald's front doors to find them standing open, raindrops splattering the marble floor with every gust of wind. A burst of lightning revealed the long, uneven smear of dark red liquid trailing across the floor, winding its serpentine way from the entryway to the crypt doors.

"Ruth," Igor breathed, seized by a terrible, paralyzing indecision. Grim had failed to stop Mag from beginning the Rite of Opening, while the Count had dragged Ruth down to the crypt.

Whom to go to first? Which needed him more—the world, the cat, or the girl?

As he deliberated, Spare clambered down from Igor's shoulder. Before he could stop them, the little cyclops ran a finger through the bloody smear, then held it up for Igor's inspection. The next flash of lightning showed that the blood on Spare's fingertip was still glisteningly wet.

"Fresh," Igor said, relief and dread warring inside him. The Count must have beaten him to the manor by only a matter of minutes. Perhaps it was not too late.

"Ruth," Igor decided, trusting in Grim to keep herself safe until he could help her. He set off towards the crypt, his uneven stride certain and purposeful.

Trilling, Spare began tottering after their creator, but Igor restrained them with a hand on their shoulder.

"Find Grimalkin," he said, shaking his head. "Help her. I'll be along shortly."

Spare looked up at him, their eye narrowed dubiously.

"I promise." Igor gave his creation a reassuring smile. "Now go, and be careful."

Spare trilled skeptically, then nodded and set off in the direction of the chapel. Igor silently wished them luck.

Thunder rolled as he followed the trail of blood down into the vampires' crypt.

* * *

". . . time for your fits of pique!" The Count's voice echoed weirdly off the spiral staircase. "Even now, the witch is conducting her profane ritual upstairs, and this time she is certain to succeed. Neither of us should be here when that faceless *thing* intrudes upon our home again."

"So you're running." Cornelia's voice was dull and listless. "Of course you are. Never trouble Karl to do the hard thing, when there's an easy way out."

"I do *some* of the hard things," the Count was saying as Igor reached the crypt, squinting in the lanternlight. The vampires stood at its far end, the Count gesturing at Ruth's limp form draped across his stone coffin in a pose identical to the swooning heroines of Igor's novels. "I even brought you a snack, to sustain you on the journey. Now, hurry up and drink, before—"

Igor's foot caught on a loose bit of masonry, sending it skittering against the wall. The Count whirled, eyes flashing red. The air between them blurred. Pale hands seized Igor by the throat, choking the air from him.

"Hunchback!" the Count said, leering down at him. "How good of you to join us."

The lanternlight bathed the Count's features in stark relief. Days of futile hunting and vampiric hunger had taken their toll, reducing his formerly refined visage to feral savagery. Twigs and leaves tangled in his uncombed hair, now grown out to a ragged mane. His mustaches bristled at odd angles, and his rumpled clothes were filthy with mud and other, less identifiable stains. His skin stretched so taut across his skull that he looked more like a fanged skeleton than a man, eyes gleaming with red flame.

"All the better," he said, grinning down at Igor. Ruth's blood was smeared across his lips and chin. "The girl was delectable, but I had to leave enough of her for Cornelia. How good of you to slake my remaining thirst."

The air beside him blurred.

"What—" the Count started, turning.

Cornelia's fist caught him squarely in the jaw.

Igor went tumbling from the Count's grasp to land rudely against the marble, but the pain hardly registered. Scrambling on his hands and knees, he hurried away from the vampires and over to the coffins, where Ruth lay supine.

"Cornelia?" the Count frowned, rubbing his jaw. "You . . . struck me!"

Igor stood over Ruth, who looked unnaturally pale even in the dim lanternlight.

"You've done worse to me," Cornelia retorted, placing herself firmly between her husband and his intended victims. Igor bent over Ruth, watching the confrontation play out as he checked her pulse. Weak, but alive.

He wasn't too late.

The Count stared at his bride, as beautiful and vital and strong as she had ever been.

"How—" he started, then shook his head. "You are not starved at all, are you? You have been feeding, and not on rats and mice."

"Observant as ever," Cornelia remarked, matching the Count's movement as he attempted to sidestep her. "Leave them be."

Trusting in Cornelia's protection, Igor tore a strip of cloth from the hem of his lab coat and tied it around the punctures the Count's fangs had left in Ruth's throat, taking care not to restrict her airflow. Ruth's eyes fluttered open, looked blearily up at Igor.

"Hunchback?" she mumbled, her voice thready and weak.

Igor tried to smile, and to keep his voice from trembling. "Don't be afraid."

"I've had enough of your insolence, Cornelia," the Count said, his voice reverberating with that particular tone of command he held over her. **"Kill the girl and the cripple."**

Tensing, Igor turned, expecting to feel the sharp bite of Cornelia's fangs at any second. Instead she stood rooted to the spot, swaying like a tree buffeted by a gale, her shoulders heaving. A sharp, gasping hiss forced its way between her lips.

Cold fingers found Igor's, and he risked a glance downwards. Ruth had slipped her hand into his. He gave it a gentle squeeze.

"I said ***kill them***!" the Count screeched, and this time Cornelia's hoarse cry joined her husband's shriek. She fell to her knees, bracing herself on all fours against the cold marble. An unearthly shriek tore from her throat.

Unthinking, Igor went to her, pulling free of Ruth's feeble grasp to put his hand on Cornelia's shaking shoulder. Her skin was as cool as the marble beneath them. "Cornelia—"

She turned her face sharply to him, eyes shining red and

fangs fully extended, jaw opened wider than any human mouth allowed.

Igor did not flinch.

Slowly, with a great effort, Cornelia closed her mouth, her fangs retracting to their usual length. She turned her gaze back to her husband, the red glow fading from her eyes.

"No," she rasped.

The Count gnashed his teeth, fingers curling and uncurling as if he longed to wrap them about someone's neck. Cornelia stared back at him, and a deathly silence fell.

Then the Count's shoulders drooped, the wind gone out of his sails, taking his wrath with it.

"My dear," he said, waving a hand. "There is simply no time for this quibbling."

Cornelia let out a gasp as the command he'd placed upon her departed. Igor helped her to her feet.

"We must leave Ravenwald *now,*" the Count continued. "Before the witch can hand our home over to her dark god."

"That's not all you have to worry about," Igor said, seizing on a chance to drive the Count off bloodlessly—so to speak. "The townsfolk are marching on Ravenwald even now."

The Count bristled. "I see you and your Doctor have overstayed your welcome. Riling up the peasantry to march upon our door, I shouldn't wonder."

Igor hardly thought it was fair for the Count to lay the blame at their feet when it was his own ineptitude at hunting that had most agitated the townsfolk. But they were well past the point of argument.

"The townsfolk," Cornelia said softly, letting something slip from the sleeve of her gown. Laura's letter, Igor realized, which he'd slipped inside her coffin lid only that morning. It fluttered to the marble floor, the black ink spattered with pinkish tearstains. Near the bottom he could just make out the words I'M SORRY in jagged capitals.

"Is she with them?" Cornelia asked Igor without looking at him, her voice fragile.

"Of course your lover is," the Count said, not bothering to hide the smugness in his tone. "Did you really think your little courtship would last? That she'd never learn what you really are—or that when she did, she might overlook it?"

"I had hoped," Cornelia whispered.

Igor squeezed her arm, but she shrugged off his attempt to comfort her. He retreated to Ruth instead, gently easing her off the coffin and into a more comfortable position propped against it.

"All of this matters little, compared to the danger we now face." The Count schooled himself into calm with a visible effort. "Until we are safely away, I am willing to forgive you your indiscretions—"

"I don't want it," Cornelia whispered.

The Count's mustaches twitched. "What?"

"I don't want it," she repeated. "Your forgiveness, or the life you offer."

"I am trying to *save* you," the Count ground out. "We are caught between the fury of a brutish mob and the caprice of an alien god. We must flee, my dear. Now."

"To where?" Cornelia asked bitterly. "Another century in one of your other estates, watching you slip back into indolence as I fetch you prey and listen to your poetry? Is that all you have to offer, Karl? A return to the way things were?"

"This is the existence you chose—"

"I was a child!" Cornelia shouted, pinpricks of bright red showing at the corners of her eyes. "Or hardly more than one. I had so much life ahead of me, and you stole it all away! Just so you could have a trophy, a prize. A slave."

Igor flinched. Beside him, Ruth drew in a wheezing breath.

"You run away, Karl," Cornelia said, planting her heels. "I'm not going anywhere."

"Why?" the Count demanded, rather than answer her accusations. "Why stay now? When the lover you abandoned me for is likely among those marching on our home?"

"Maybe she is," Cornelia said quietly. "Don't you think that would be poetic, Karl, for her to be the one to put my torment to an end? For her to give me that which you've always refused me?"

"Cornelia, please." The Count's voice broke as he reached for her, but she stepped back, out of his reach. "I don't want to lose you—"

"I'm not yours to lose," Cornelia said. A particularly loud thunderclap rattled the crypt ceiling, shaking loose a rain of dust. Outside, the storm must have grown to truly titanic proportions. "Not any more."

The Count stared at her, his downturned mouth almost pleading. Asking without words for her to flee with him rather than stay to face certain doom at the townsfolks' hands. Cornelia met his gaze with the calm placidity of one who'd accepted her fate a long time ago.

"I could order you to come with me," the Count said, his mouth hardening into a thin line. "Compel you to obey my command to flee this place."

"You couldn't make me hurt Igor," Cornelia threw back. "Do you really think you can make me run?"

The Count's face turned blotchy with anger, but he didn't contest her refusal.

"You could stay," Igor said, drawing that red gaze. He gestured at Cornelia. "Stay and defend Ravenwald alongside us, I mean. With your help—"

"Help?" The Count's frown was a bitter slash beneath his mustaches. "This place is mine, hunchback. You and your master have resided here by my leave, but Ravenwald itself is mine to do with as I please. To fortify against the crowd of serfs marching upon it, or leave it for them to burn to ashes. My choice, either way."

"Then stay," Cornelia said quietly. "If you care at all about me, Karl, then stay and fight for us. Or were you lying when you swore to be my husband and protector?"

The Count went rigid, and on his face Igor read something that was, if not shame, then certainly its close cousin.

"We could die," the Count said, his voice quietly vulnerable. "The true death, I mean. Both of us."

"We might," Cornelia agreed softly. "Did you think becoming a vampire meant living forever?"

"That was rather the point, yes." The Count's countenance darkened as he glowered at his wife, and at Igor crouching protectively over Ruth. "But so be it. If you would consign yourself to oblivion rather than accept my salvation, far be it from me to interfere. Enjoy being Countess Ravenwald, my dear. You can rule over the ashes, for all I care. I am done with you."

The air where he stood shimmered, and a moment later the Count was gone, vanished like a bad dream.

"That's it?" Igor asked, looking about. "He's gone?"

"He is." Cornelia hugged her arms about herself, shivering. "As is his hold over me, I believe."

A wheezing sound drew both their attentions. Ruth was coming round, looking dazedly about the crypt.

"Where?" she asked in a croaking voice. "Where am . . . ?"

"You're with friends," Igor said, reassuring her as Cornelia knelt on her other side. Ruth looked wonderingly up at him, then at Cornelia. She blinked, her eyes coming blearily into focus as she gazed up at Cornelia. *At her Angel of Mercy,* Igor thought.

"I know you," Ruth whispered.

40

SO BELOW

"RUTH WILL BE all right," Igor reassured Cornelia for the third time as they rushed up the staircase. "The Count took a lot of blood, but not more than she can spare. She just needs rest."

They reached the foyer, where rivulets of violet light now swam across the ceiling, the air thick with a briny seaweed scent Igor knew only too well. Ravenwald's halls echoed with the eerie chorus of human voices and animal wails that presaged the coming of the Unsmiling King.

Nor was that the only danger which threatened. Through the tall windows and the open doors Igor could make out the faint glimmer of torches drawing nearer. The wind carried faint snatches of the mob's angry cries and cruel laughter as they advanced on Ravenwald, makeshift weapons in hand and fire in their hearts.

"We're out of time," Igor said, his mouth dry. The mob would be on their doorstep in a matter of moments, while in the chapel Auntie Mag was busy opening a portal to her eldritch god. Given his current run of terrible luck, Igor fully expected the Doctor's latest experiment would result in a Subject with a ravenous craving for human flesh, or something equally horrid.

"Not quite," Cornelia said, striding not in the direction of the desecrated chapel but towards the front doors, which Igor had left open in his haste. By now water was pooling on the floor, washing away the worst of Ruth's bloodstains.

Cornelia gazed through the trees, beyond which the marching line of torches was drawing steadily nearer. An odd, tight smile played upon her lips as she raised her eyes towards the raging heavens, the wind plucking at her long red hair.

"This old house has more defenses than you know," she told Igor. "And even if he didn't mean to, Karl just named me the new Countess Ravenwald."

A grinding, shuddering tremor shook the walls as something huge dropped from the manor roof to land beside Cornelia. It rose, shaking its horned head and unfolding its great wings, then turned its granite eyes questioningly upon its mistress.

Cornelia smiled at it, then at Igor. "You didn't think those gargoyles were just for show, did you?"

"Guess that'll teach me not to make assumptions," Igor said. "Listen. I don't want to leave you, but I sent Spare after Grimalkin—"

"Go, Igor." Cornelia cracked her neck like a prizefighter stepping into the ring, her eyes fixed on the line of torches drawing nearer. "Save Grimalkin and Spare. Stop Mag. I'll hold off the mob as long as I can."

Igor nodded, a thousand words hovering on his tongue. But all he could voice was a soft "Good luck."

"You too," Cornelia replied. A fierce grin lit her eternally youthful face. She looked more alive than Igor had ever seen her.

Thunder shook the manor as Igor turned his back on his friend and ran. His footfalls kept time with the arcs of violet light pulsing along the ceiling as he raced towards the desecrated chapel and whatever unholy horrors awaited within.

* * *

Igor had expected to find the chapel door shut against his entry, its warding runes glowing virulent purple against any intrusion upon the Rite of Opening. But either Mag had grown careless, or—more likely—Grimalkin had left the door open when she'd gone to plead with her onetime mistress for the fate of all reality. Whatever the case, the chapel door hung open like a mouth waiting to swallow him whole.

Igor tried not to take that as an omen.

"I'm coming, Grim," Igor said, and stepped over the chapel threshold.

The clattering of the scrimshaw trinkets hanging from the ceiling provided an arrhythmic accompaniment to the unearthly chorus and the feral cacophony issuing from the animal skulls mounted on the walls. Their dead gazes seemed to follow Igor as he stepped inside, feeling a vague sense of déjà vu.

Once again, Mag stood upon the altar, her head thrown back and eyes squeezed shut as she intoned the ritual words in the mind-itching Elder Tongue, moving her cane in steady circles above the silver ritual circle inset in the floor. Once again, a vortex of unearthly purple light swirled within its confines. Somewhere in those swirling depths, Igor sensed more than saw the movement of something huge, and old, and hungry. Like one of those ancient sharks who dwelled beneath the polar seas, cruising half-blind through the centuries of endless dark and numbing cold, slowly rising towards the distant light of the tiny human vessel that had caught its dire attention upon the distant surface.

Spare was nowhere to be seen.

Igor's gaze traveled past Mag to the shelves behind her, crammed full of silvery ephemera. There, sandwiched between idealist's despair and priest's shame, crammed into a copper wire birdcage much too small for her, sat Grimalkin.

"Grim!" Igor shouted, starting towards her.

A whisper of air on the back of his neck and the fluttering of wings were all the warning he had.

Igor ducked. A pair of black talons clawed the air where his scalp had been only a moment before. Croaking laughter and the flutter of feathers rang in his ear as Ed the hellcrow swooped past, Allan and Gareth following close on his tailfeathers. Igor lashed out blindly, batting them away.

"Look who came back to crash the party!" crowed Ed, settling himself atop a steer's skull affixed to the wall. Gareth and Allan joined him, landing on its horns. Igor realized that the crows must have been waiting atop the animal skulls when he'd entered, perched so motionlessly that his brain had dismissed them as taxidermies.

"Rather rude, Ed," Allan agreed, his words muffled by the fist-sized gemstone held in his beak. A thrill ran through Igor upon finally seeing the Eye of Anthomset, its dozens of facets catching and distorting the otherworldly light which filled the chapel.

"This is an invite-only affair," Gareth cawed, and dived at Igor again.

But Igor was already running, already moving towards the altar where Mag stood conducting the ritual that would end the world, sprinting as fast as his mismatched legs allowed.

Not fast enough.

Raking talons bit into Igor's back, slicing through his coat and tearing furrows across his shoulder. Igor's scream joined the unearthly chorus as the other two crows clawed at him, unbalancing him.

"Igor!" Grimalkin's voice, high and clear and more frightened than he'd ever heard her. Yellow eyes peered out from between the bars of her cage, ears slicked back against her head. "Igor, get out of here! You can't stop her, she—"

Auntie Mag, witch and devoted priestess of the Unsmiling

King, opened her eyes. They were a solid, glowing purple, exactly like those of the ivory skull atop her staff.

"Igor," she said, almost fondly. "Grim told me you would come. I'm rather glad you did."

Igor tried to push himself to his feet, only for bands of violet light to wrap themselves about his wrists and yank him rudely upward, until his toes dangled an inch off the chapel floor.

"After all," Mag grinned, her magic drawing him closer so that he hovered on the very edge of the whirling vortex, "it's not every day you get a front row seat at the end of the world."

Against his will, Igor glanced down at the portal swirling beneath his feet. This close, there was no way to miss the shadow of something vast lurking in its depths, a vague silhouette that was all tentacles and teeth and growing larger every moment.

"Mag!" Grim yowled over the maelstrom. "Igor hasn't done anything! Please, you can still let him go—"

"I can," Mag agreed, almost cheerily. "But I won't."

She raised both hands, one holding her cane, the other with palm upward. A flutter of wings, and Allan dropped the gemstone into her waiting hand.

"The Eye of Anthomset," she said reverently. The amethyst in her palm glowed and pulsed in time with the vortex at her feet. "The key to this world, for all those which lie behind."

Auntie Mag let go of the cane, but it did not fall. Instead it lengthened, becoming a pillar of smooth black stone, its base melding with the altar, the skull atop it hollowing itself to become a receptacle for the Eye, which Auntie Mag slotted carefully into place. Jagged arcs of mystical power dived from the gemstone into the vortex, which roiled and surged in answer.

Igor strained futilely against his bonds. There was no stopping the Rite once it had begun, but if he could only get his hands on the Eye, he might still avert the impending apocalypse . . .

Mag flung her hands wide, crying out in rapturous ecstasy:

"Come, Lord of Untruth and God of Blasphemy! Be welcome, Dour Prince! Enter in, Devourer of Worlds! Come, Unsmiling—"

A flutter of black wings, and the crows were upon her.

The violet light was snuffed from Mag's eyes as talons raked across her face, her cries joining those of the skulls mounted along the walls. Covering her face with her hands, she stumbled backwards, but the crows did not relent. Their wings flapped as they cawed, scratching and pecking at her furiously until she was driven to the floor. Gareth landed atop one of her arms, Allan the other, pinning her against the altar.

"Should have listened to your cat," Ed said smugly, alighting atop the black plinth that had been Mag's cane a few short moments ago. He opened his beak and nudged the Eye of Anthomset—not dislodging it, but shifting its alignment, very slightly.

The vortex beneath Igor's feet shuddered and roiled.

"We had a deal!" Mag screeched, struggling to sit up, but the crows' claws held her trapped in place. Only they were beginning to look less and less like crows. Unless there were crows whose heads sprouted curling horns, or whose backs arched and bodies writhed as new limbs burst from them like malign growths, serrated teeth jutting from their curving beaks.

"To help you complete the Rite of Opening, yes," Ed agreed, pecking at the Eye. He still looked for the most part like a crow, though a tumorous bulging beneath his feathers suggested that that would not remain the case for long. "But we never promised we'd open it to the Outside."

He nudged the Eye again. The vortex shuddered, then began swirling in the opposite direction, its light shifting from unearthly purple to bloody red. A blast of hot air scalded Igor's face, carrying with it the stench of sulfur and the sound of distant screams.

And within, as far away as the leviathan shape had been but

growing larger every moment, lurked something huge and horned and hungry.

"After all," Ed said, hopping down from the plinth and stretching the long, scaly limbs which had just sprouted from his chest, "where we're from is much more fun."

Igor looked away, not wanting to witness what the hellcrows' idea of fun looked like—just in time to see Spare clambering up the row of shelves behind the altar. They picked their way with surprising surety amongst the jars of ephemera, then reached out and unlatched Grim's cage.

"Thumbs!" Grim said appreciatively as the door of her prison swung open. She slipped out, stepping nimbly between the jars of ephemera lining the shelf to give Spare a quick, affectionate nuzzle.

Then, with a flick of one paw, Grim knocked the nearest jar of ephemera from the shelf.

It smashed against the ground, the silvery thing within writhing with its newfound freedom. Igor watched, his horror at the hellgate opening beneath his feet giving way to a sickened fascination as the ephemera squirmed and scuttled across the altar, towards Auntie Mag and the things that were no longer crows.

Another crash, and another, as Grim knocked more jars from the shelves with casual feline disregard. Spare let out an excited trill and joined in. The screams of the damned were drowned out by the shattering of glass as the construct and the cat cast dozens of jars from their shelves. A small horde of silvery beggar's wishes and curmudgeon's affections and other, stranger bits of ephemera teemed and surged across the altar, launching themselves at the crow-demons—there was no other term that fitted any longer—still restraining Mag.

Screeching, the demons recoiled, loosing their grips on Mag as they batted and clawed at their attackers. The awful sulfur smell became almost overpowering, as the ephemeras' slightest touch burned the demons' flesh—and now there were dozens of them clinging to the things that had been Ed, Gareth, and Allan.

Through the chaos, a gray shape leapt nimbly down from the shelves. Grim raced across the altar, tail held low and ears flat against her head, Spare running close behind her.

"Grim!" Auntie Mag howled, clawing her way out of the melee and pressing her back against the shelves, panting hard. One eye was swollen shut, the other a bloody mess, neither glowing any longer. "Stop them!"

Grim slipped between the legs of Ed, who still bore some vestigial corvid traits, though not the raking claws. Snarling, Ed grabbed at her, only to let out a pained shriek as Spare drove their scalpel into the demon's leg.

"Promise me my friends' safety, first!" Grim shouted over her shoulder as she leapt nimbly onto the plinth beside the Eye of Anthomset.

"Fine!" Mag yelled back, pressing against the shelf so hard that it looked as if she was trying to melt into the wood. An arm's reach away, the demons were stamping out the ephemera, each of which disappeared in a silvery flash as they succumbed to claw and talon and beak.

Grim settled onto her haunches. "From you, and the Unsmiling King, and any of his servants?"

"Yes!" Mag screeched, her hands twitching as she drew arcane sigils in the air, just as she had that first night in Ravenwald. The violet bands of her restraints vanished from around Igor's middle, dropping him painfully to the floor. "Now hurry and end it!"

Grim's tail lashed. "You agree to release me from your service, but not from this form?"

"Grimalkin!"

Grim licked one paw. "That's not a yes."

"Yes, yes, fine!" Mag was shrieking now, her face drawn as the hellcrows shook off the last of the ephemera. "Anything else?"

Grim thought about it. "A scratching post would be nice."

"As many as you want!" Mag screamed, and spat a bloody tooth at the purple sigils hanging in the air before her. It flashed, sealing the mystical binding she had made with blood, bone, and breath. "Do it, Grim!"

"You had only to ask," Grim said, and batted the Eye of Anthomset off its plinth.

All eyes in the desecrated chapel watched as the gem fell.

It hit the altar floor and bounced, glittering with hellish light as it sailed over the vortex. For a breathless moment Igor thought it was about to fall *into* those abyssal depths.

Igor reached out, and the Eye landed in his outstretched palms as neatly as if someone had placed it there. It was hot to the touch, and surprisingly heavy. For a moment he stared at it, entranced by its perfectly even facets, the way it shone with its own inner light—

"Igor!" Grim shouted. "The plan!"

"Right," Igor gasped, fumbling with the gemstone as he tried to work out how to use it. Was there some sort of trick to how it was held that would turn it away from the Below, or—

41

AS ABOVE

TIME DID NOT stop, exactly.

The vortex did not cease its roiling, nor the hellcrows their horrific transformations. Even Grim and Spare, standing alone upon the altar against the malefic trio, still moved. But all motions had been rendered slow, balletic, shorn of urgency. Color had drained from the world, rendering everything in stark gray monotone.

"Did it work?" Igor wondered—perhaps aloud, or perhaps in thought alone.

YES.

The answer was so immediate and clear in the muted world that Igor almost dropped the Eye—or would have, had his body been at all inclined to obey his brain. It seemed that he was not immune from whatever trance had overtaken the world.

"Err," he said, more certain now that he was thinking the words rather than saying them. He looked about at the slowed-down, colorless world around him. "Is this . . . the Above?"

NO came the answering voice. It was not quite male, not quite female—perhaps it was both, or neither. It occurred to Igor that Spare might possess such a voice, if they had one. *SAY RATHER THAT YOU HAVE KNOCKED UPON THE DOOR*

OF THE ABOVE. IT HAS BEEN ANSWERED, BUT NOT OPENED.

"Oh." Igor should have known that the Above was unlikely to share its more malevolent counterparts' desire to invade and reshape the world. "Thank you for taking the time to answer."

WE ALWAYS HAVE TIME, IGOR, the voice said, and this time it sounded more to Igor's ears like a chorus.

"Right," Igor said, looking down at his hands, which still held the Eye. "I suppose you know what I've come to you to ask, then? You being omniscient and all."

WE KNOW YOUR HEART, IGOR, the voices said, neither warmly nor accusingly, but with an absolute frankness that Igor found at once comforting and convicting. *BUT YOU STILL MUST ASK, ALL THE SAME.*

"I—" It was curious, feeling that his heart should be pounding a frantic tattoo in his chest when instead it thumped away at a fraction of its usual pace. "I've more than one thing to ask of you. Is that— Am I allowed?"

He expected outrage, exasperation, chastisement. Instead he felt more than heard a rich, tinkling laugh.

THE ANSWERS MAY NOT BE TO YOUR LIKING, the voices cautioned. *BUT YOU ARE PERMITTED TO ASK.*

"Cornelia," Igor said, figuring that if he was asking for a miracle, he might as well start with the biggest one. "Can you turn her human again?"

WE WILL NOT. Then, anticipating Igor's protest: *SHE CHOSE TO BE AS SHE IS. FOR ALL THE GRIEF AND HURT THAT LED HER TO THAT CHOICE, FOR ALL THE STRIFE AND SUFFERING THAT HAS FOLLOWED IT, THE CHOICE REMAINED HER OWN. WE WOULD NOT ROB HER OF IT.*

That made a bitter sort of sense, Igor supposed. Cornelia had been a vampire for far, far longer than she had been alive—to change her back would be a cruelty, not a kindness.

"I'm guessing that means you won't turn the mob away, either," Igor said. "Since they came here of their own free will and all."

NO, the voices agreed. *NOR SHALL WE TURN YOUR DOCTOR FROM HIS COURSE.*

"The Doctor?" Igor started, but forced that particular concern to the back of his mind. He turned to the altar, where Spare and Grim stood huddled together. "Grimalkin, then. Can you—will you make her a cat?"

SHE ALREADY IS ONE.

"What?"

GRIMALKIN HAS CHOSEN THIS WORLD OVER THAT OF HER ORIGIN, THIS SHAPE OVER THE ONE FORCED UPON HER. SHE IS AS SHE SAYS SHE IS, FOR THAT IS WHAT SHE BELIEVES HERSELF TO BE. AND SO WE BELIEVE HER IN TURN.

BUT TIME PRESSES.

Igor had the faintest sensation of something brushing his cheek, feathery as a kiss. It drew his gaze towards the altar, where Spare ducked in balletic slow motion beneath the demons' scything claws. Suspended in midair, Grim leapt away from Gareth's slavering fangs.

ASK, the voices commanded.

"Please," Igor whispered, the Eye weighing heavily in his palms. "Save my friends. Close the portal."

The answer came in a soft warmth upon his brow, less like a kiss than like an anointing. And with it, a deep and abiding sense of approval that filled Igor down to his toes, carrying with it the faintest, overlapping chorus of echoes:

THY WILL BE DONE.

* * *

Time resumed its normal course. Sound returned to the world, all yowling and screeching and otherworldly music, blasts of hot sulfuric air stinging Igor's nose.

The vortex gave a titanic shudder. The tremor shook the walls hard enough to send skulls crashing to the floor, shattering as easily as the ephemera jars had.

The wind howled, all the air in the room hurtling towards the vortex as it collapsed upon itself, whirling even more rapidly as it shrank, like an emptying drain. The demons that had been crows wailed their rage and their despair, clawing for purchase on whatever surface was nearest to hand. One by one, the wind plucked them and hurled them into the gravity of the collapsing portal to the world they'd come from.

"Never again!" shouted Ed, the last to be dragged screaming back to Hell. "Never! *Nevermore*—"

And then he was gone, as was the portal, and the wind. Only the sulfur smell remained as proof of what had transpired—that, and their wounds.

Igor stuffed the glittering purple Eye into one of his coat's inner pockets as he slumped against the nearest pew. Spare was at his side in an instant, cheeping an offer of help.

"I'm all right," Igor said, smiling down at the cyclops. "Nice work fending off those crows. You too, Grim."

"Took you long enough," Grim said, sauntering over. "I waited for you by the coach, but you never showed."

"I know," Igor said, wincing. "I'm sorry. The Doctor was going to cut Spare open, and then he fired me, and now there's an angry mob at the doors—"

"Never a dull moment with you, is there?" Grim asked, then rubbed against his leg to show there were no hard feelings. "Let's go deal with that angry mob, then."

Nodding his agreement, Igor started for the door.

"Wait!" Mag yelled after them. "You have to help me look for the Eye!"

Igor turned around slowly, folding his arms across his chest lest he rouse Mag's suspicions. "I like this world without tentacles, thanks."

"So do I," Grim agreed.

"You don't understand," Mag said, pushing herself unsteadily to her feet, leaning against the shelves in place of her cane. "The Duke of Want demanded that the Rite of Opening be completed tonight, the night of the full moon. If I don't finish it by sunrise—"

"Then he'll be rather put out with you, I imagine," Grim said, twining between Igor's legs. "It might be time to seek other employment, Mag."

Mag stared uncomprehendingly at her familiar. "Other employment?"

Grim licked her lips. "Or you could run. See how long it takes the Duke to find you."

Mag licked her lips in unconscious mimicry of her former familiar.

Then, hobbling a little without the use of her cane, she ran headlong down the rows of pews, shouldered past Igor, and disappeared out the chapel door.

"Guess I'm not getting that scratching post after all," Grim said.

"I'll make you one," Igor promised, bending down to pet her head.

"I'll hold you to that," Grim said. "Now, I believe you mentioned an angry mob in need of stopping?"

42

MONSTERS

IGOR HURRIED THROUGH Ravenwald's long corridors, Spare clinging to his collar and Grim darting along the walls beside him. With every step, the mob's cacophony of shouting voices, tramping feet, and clattering weapons grew louder.

They emerged onto the foyer to find the place in utter disarray. The great double doors lay flung open to the storming night beyond, one of them listing slightly off its hinges, the other hacked apart by the mob's axes.

The villagers teemed across the marble floor in a dark and angry tide. Their gleaming torches painted their wrathful faces in what Igor would have thought a hellish light, were it not for his extremely recent experience with the genuine article.

But where was Cornelia?

"The hunchback!" someone shouted, catching sight of Igor standing framed in the corridor, searching the crowd for a sign of his friend. "Get the hunchback!"

The crowd surged towards Igor. He took a step back, palms raised in what he already knew was a vain attempt to placate them. Spare trilled fearfully, leaping clear of Igor's shoulder as a reedy scarecrow of a man swung his scythe at them—

—only for it to be abruptly jerked from his hands by a pair of stone talons. Igor gawked as the gargoyle flapped low overhead, the mob collectively ducking to avoid being battered by its broad granite wings.

Nor was it the only one of its kind defending Ravenwald. Igor counted at least a dozen others swooping at the mob, forcing the townsfolk to remain on the defensive.

One of the villagers nearest Igor lashed at the retreating gargoyle with a long-handled rake, catching it by its stone tail. It turned clumsily in midair, wings beating desperately, but another villager hooked her hoe around its arm. Working together, they dragged the poor stone creature down to the marble floor, setting upon it with whatever tools they had at hand. Igor winced as a hammer blow sent one of the thrashing gargoyle's horns skittering across the marble.

It was not the only one of its fellows to have met such a fate. Igor reckoned there had been at least a score of such gargoyles adorning Ravenwald's roof. Now nearly half their number lay smashed, their scattered pieces strewn across the foyer, fallen in defense of their home.

Igor's heart twisted in sympathy as he glimpsed one goat-faced gargoyle's head lying against the near wall, its blank stone gaze seeming to peer mournfully at its body a few feet away. Though the gargoyles were unthinking automata, powered by the magic the Count had infused in his abode over the centuries, it was hard not to feel sorrow at their destruction.

A savage growl to his left drew Igor's attention. Cornelia stood alone between him and the nearest of the front windows, penned in by a crowd of villagers jabbing with their makeshift weapons to keep her at bay. For a moment Igor wondered why she didn't simply vanish from sight, before realizing that every one of the crowd's makeshift polearms had a small clove of garlic dangling from its business end.

Cornelia snarled, fangs extended, as she batted away the mob's probing pitchforks, red eyes darting about for any avenue of escape.

"Push her back!" shouted Josef, standing at the head of Cornelia's assailants, loaded crossbow in hand. "Get her in the corner so she can't run away!"

The crowd wordlessly shouted their agreement, prodding and pushing until Cornelia was trapped between their polearms and the wall. A flash of lightning through the nearby window lit her face, blazing red eyes and gleaming fangs doing nothing to hide her fear.

"Grim!" Igor shouted, shoving through the crowd towards Cornelia. "Take care of Spare!"

Grim's answer was swallowed by tolling thunder. Josef raised his crossbow, one eye closed as he took aim at the vampire cowering against the wall, his finger resting on the trigger.

Igor wasn't sure whether a crossbow would be enough to end Cornelia's vampiric unlife, but he had absolutely no scientific curiosity to find out. Letting out a wordless yell of his own, he charged forward, barreling through the mob. Lashing out blindly, he shoved Josef just as the huntsman squeezed the crossbow trigger.

A thrum filled the air, impossibly loud. A dull *thunk* followed.

Cornelia's gasp was short and sharp.

Dread seized Igor's heart as he turned his head, half unwillingly. Cornelia was pressed against the wall, her arms outflung. The crossbow bolt was buried up to the fletching in the peeling wallpaper, having missed her throat by inches.

Igor let out a relieved exhale as Cornelia pushed away from the wall—or tried to. Igor's relief turned to astonishment as he saw that the crossbow bolt had pierced the shoulder of her dress, pinning her in place.

"Hold her there!" Josef shouted, dropping his crossbow. His black boots stomped heavily across the marble floor as he produced a wooden stake from inside his coat.

"No!" Igor shouted, reaching for Josef. But he'd lost the element of surprise, and the grasping hands of the villagers seized him from all sides, arresting his movement. The shoulder of Cornelia's dress tore as she pulled free from the wall, but with the villagers pressing in on all sides, there was nowhere for her to run. Trapped, she hissed her defiance at Josef as he raised the stake in both hands.

Lightning flashed, revealing a hulking shadow looming on the other side of the tall window beside them.

Glass shattered as something huge and furred burst through the window, carrying the storm in with it. The crowd gasped and flinched away, their grip on Igor loosening enough for him to pull free, already reaching for Cornelia.

Josef hesitated, the stake still raised as he turned to look at the shadow looming over all three of them, huge and hairy and smelling incongruously of wet dog. A pawlike hand ending in wicked, curving black talons shot out and seized Josef by the wrist, bending his arm back with slow, inexorable might. The huntsman whimpered as the wooden stake slipped from his grip to clatter against the marble floor. Its owner joined it shortly thereafter.

With a low grunt, the shadow turned away from Josef, its gaze briefly landing on Igor on its way to Cornelia. There was something familiar about those brown eyes, though the muzzle and sharp yellow teeth were new.

"Cornelia?" it said, and though the voice was throatier and deeper than usual, Igor knew it immediately. "Are you all right?"

"Laura?" Cornelia stared up at the huge furry shape that was equal parts woman and beast. "What are you . . . doing here?"

Laura's ears—now distinctly canine—drooped. Her tail, which had burst through the seat of her ruined trousers, did similarly. "Apologizing, I suppose."

Cornelia gave her a slow once-over, starting with her clawed feet and working her way up to Laura's furry shoulders, from which the remnants of a plaid shirt still dangled. To her face, long-snouted and lupine but still, somehow, recognizably Laura. "You're a werewolf?"

A murmuration of alarm rippled through the crowd, though Igor surmised that all but the dimmest amongst them had already worked this out for themselves. Out of the corner of his eye, he saw that the battle had reached an abrupt cease-fire, gargoyles and villagers alike watching this bizarre reunion play out.

"Aye," Laura admitted, lifting her head. Her brown eyes met Cornelia's blazing red ones, flickered briefly down to the two long fangs jutting out from her upper lip. "Though I'm guessing there's a few things you haven't told me about yourself, either."

Cornelia gave her a wan smile. "I suppose we both owe each other some explanations."

"Laura?" Josef croaked, pushing himself up from the floor. "That's . . . It's you, isn't it?"

Laura turned slowly, another burst of lightning illuminating her werewolf form in all its furry splendor. Her lips peeled back from yellow fangs, causing the nearest members of the mob to shrink away in fear—a human smile mapped rather poorly to a wolf's face.

"Hi, Josef," Laura said, with a shy wave of her paw. "Dieter, Elmar."

The other two hunters nodded warily as they helped Josef to his feet. Josef shrugged them off, looking up at Laura with an expression somewhere between wonderment and disgust, though the longer he looked, the more it trended towards the latter.

"No wonder you left," he said, so softly that Igor barely heard it. Then, louder: "You're a monster."

A low, lupine growl echoed in Laura's throat as she took a step—not towards Josef, but putting herself between Cornelia and the mob.

"I know what I am," she said, lowering her paws. "I know what I become, once a month. It's the reason I left Ravensburg, all those years ago."

An illness she'd caught in the woods, she'd said. Igor supposed that was true, broadly speaking.

"It's the reason I keep to myself as much as I can," Laura continued. "Why I try not to stray from the graveyard, and why I lock myself inside its gates whenever the full moon comes around. But as to whether it makes me a monster"—she snorted in a decidedly doglike manner—"I'm not so sure. I used to think so, but now . . . a wise person told me that everyone's got the potential to be a little monstrous, or a little saintly. That it's a matter of our choices, not our natures. And I ain't never done no harm to no one in this room."

"Until now," Josef muttered, rubbing his wrist and shaking his head, sending shards of broken glass tumbling from his tangled hair.

"She's right," came a croaking voice.

The crowd parted as Ruth made her slow, staggering way through them. Her face was drawn and pale, her clothes bloody, but her eyes were bright and alert.

"Ruth?" Dieter's mouth fell open as he pushed his way to her. "Ruth! I thought you were—"

"I'm fine," Ruth said, though that did not stop her from leaning heavily against Dieter once he reached her. "Well. Maybe not fine."

Dieter swallowed hard. "The vampire. When it took you, I—we—"

"Rounded up a mob to come and burn down Ravenwald?" she suggested, looking about at the dozens of townsfolk with torches and farming implements in hand.

Dieter's cheeks flushed above his pale beard. "To save you."

"I'm flattered." Ruth pointed a trembling finger at Cornelia. "But *she* saved me."

The crowd's attention turned to Cornelia, standing warily beside Laura.

"The vampire?" Josef asked, not hiding his skepticism.

"She's not the one who took me." Ruth's golden curls bounced. "It was the other one. Count Ravenwald, I guess, like in the stories. He tried to make her drink my blood. Only she wouldn't do it."

The crowd looked expectantly at Cornelia. She grimaced back at them. "I didn't want to be a monster."

"You're not," Ruth said, pushing away from Dieter despite his protests, until she stood beside Laura and Cornelia. "It's not the ones who look monstrous you have to watch out for. The real monsters are the ones who look like you and me. The ones who know to hide their true selves behind an everyday mask rather than wear it openly."

"That's just what Laura admitted she's been doing," Josef shot back, jabbing an accusing finger at the werewolf, though he pulled it back just as quickly. "Hiding her true nature."

"Hiding herself away," Ruth corrected. "Because you made her—because we all made her. Made her feel unsafe to be herself around us. Made her think she had to hide who she is—what she is—in order for us to let her be part of our community."

She offered the towering werewolf a sad smile. "I'm sorry for that, Laura. We all are."

It seemed rather audacious for her to speak for the whole crowd. But to his surprise, Igor saw several heads bobbing their agreement.

"So Laura's not a monster," Josef said, though he sounded unconvinced.

"And neither is she." Dieter frowned at Cornelia. "But what about the other one? The Count?"

"You needn't worry about my husband," Cornelia said. "He's gone now."

"Husband?" Laura asked, sounding more like herself than ever.

"I'm sorry I didn't tell you," Cornelia said, taking her paw in one hand and giving a gentle squeeze. She turned, addressing the crowd. "He's the one who attacked Ruth, and who drove the deer from the woods. But he's gone now, and I don't think he's coming back."

"But you're a vampire!" Josef's voice climbed an octave. "You expect us to believe that your hands are clean? That you wouldn't drink each of us dry if given the chance?"

"She won't," Ruth said, looking reverently at Cornelia. "She's the Angel of Mercy."

A young man close to Igor gasped, while an older one looked guiltily away. On his other side, a woman in her later middle years closed her eyes, her mouth working in a silent prayer.

Josef scowled. "The Angel's just a folktale—"

"So are werewolves," Igor interrupted, pushing through the crowd to join Laura, Cornelia, and Ruth. As he did so, he caught a glimpse of Spare's eye peering out from inside a nearby vase, Grim sitting primly at its foot. "And vampires. It seems all sorts of tales are coming true tonight."

"The disappearances," came Friar Bernhard's resonant voice, the crowd parting as he strode forward. He glanced briefly at Igor, then at Cornelia. "Sheriff Hertz, Mr. Falkner, and Mr. Beckett. You . . . did away with them?"

Cornelia nodded. "Men in power are the most likely to abuse it, I find—and those nearest them the easiest victims. So I answered their prayers when no one else would, Friar."

"But I knew those men," Bernhard said, rubbing his tonsured head. "They came to church each week, invited me to dine at their homes. I know their wives, their daughters. I'd never have believed . . ."

"That," Ruth said quietly, "is exactly the problem." She

looked at Josef. "For all your talk, the only person who's protected anyone from real monsters is Cornelia."

"She's right," Friar Bernhard said. He lifted his gaze and his voice to the townsfolk surrounding them. "We have failed to see the monsters in our own midst, instead casting blame and doubt upon the outsider."

He turned to Laura, eyes lingering briefly upon Igor. Igor wondered if perhaps the friar could not sense, somehow, his own recent encounter with the divine.

"As Laura said"—Friar Bernhard's voice rang out in the clear, resonant tones of a practiced orator—"each of us has the capacity to choose for ourselves what we will be, regardless of our outward appearance. A man can be a monster—a werewolf a saint—a vampire an angel."

He spread his arms wide, one of them landing on Igor's shoulder. "For myself, I choose peace between myself and my neighbors. That choice lies before us all. I cannot make it for you. But I hope you will choose the same."

Igor waited, his every muscle tensed, trying to draw comfort from the friar's hand on his shoulder. Beside him, Cornelia clasped Laura's paw in both hands, while even Dieter drew Ruth close.

An older woman stepped forward from the crowd, her pitchfork held above her head. She tossed it at her feet, and it clattered as it hit the marble floor.

A few feet away, a sallow-faced farmer did the same. Soon the foyer rang with the sound of tools being tossed to the marble, as villager after villager laid down their arms, the fight gone out of them.

Igor had witnessed the transformation of crowds into mobs more times than he could recall, yet this was the first time he'd seen the process occur in reverse. The anger drained from the villagers as they disarmed themselves, no longer a unified seething force of rage—just people, as varied and complex and conflicted as any others. Sinners and saints, in equal measure.

More quickly than Igor would have believed possible, the crowd had fully divested themselves of their weapons. Only Josef remained armed.

"Jo," Laura said quietly. "It's over."

Josef looked up at the hulking werewolf, then back down at his crossbow. Unloaded, it was no threat to anyone.

"Fine," he snapped, and tossed it contemptuously aside. "Fine. You win."

Without another word, he stalked out of Ravenwald's doors and into the night, until he was lost in the storm. Inside, the villagers and the manor's inhabitants regarded one another uncertainly.

"So," Cornelia asked, a little awkwardly, "what happens now?"

"Now," replied Ruth, leaning on Dieter's arm as she surveyed the wreckage of the foyer, "we clean up the mess we've made of this place. It's what good neighbors do."

"Neighbors," Igor repeated, a slow smile spreading over his face. He rather liked the sound of that.

The other villagers nodded their agreement to this plan, albeit with varying degrees of enthusiasm. Several of them, apparently having grabbed brooms rather than pitchforks on their way to storming the manor, set about sweeping up the debris, while a man Igor recognized as the village stonemason ordered his apprentices to start collecting and sorting as many pieces of the shattered gargoyles as they could find.

"Well," Grim said, trotting over to where Igor stood beside Cornelia and Laura, Spare hurrying after her. "That went better than expected."

Igor nodded, wondering how many of the other violent mobs he'd fled from might have been deterred by an appeal to their shared humanity. Probably none; it had taken Laura's courage and Ruth's, and the judgment of the Angel of Mercy, and the pleas of Friar Bernhard, to pacify them tonight.

Blinding light flooded the foyer as a lightning bolt crashed down just outside, striking one of the trees standing nearest to the manor. As thunder shook the walls of Ravenwald, Igor became acutely conscious of the rain blowing in through the window Laura had smashed, and what it portended.

"The Doctor," he breathed, and took off across the foyer.

"Igor!" Grim trotted after him, twining between his legs in a manner that forced him to either slow down or fall. "Where are you going?"

"I have to get to the lab," he said, stepping gingerly over her. "The Doctor's up there, with the Subject. It was nearly complete when he fired me earlier—"

Grim's tail twitched in surprise. "He what?"

"It was him or Spare," Igor said as the little construct joined them, Laura and Cornelia following after. "Please, I have to talk to him."

"We'll come with you," Laura said, her tail wagging excitedly.

"No," Igor said, gesturing at the crowd of villagers helping to clean up the mess they'd created. From time to time one of them would glance nervously in their direction before looking hurriedly away. "You and Cornelia need to stay here. The more these people see of you, the more they'll realize they have no reason to fear you."

"Not *no* reason," Cornelia said with a fanged smile. "But you're right, Igor. You sure you'll be able to handle the Doctor alone?"

"Not alone," Grim said, leaning against Igor's leg and giving him a long, slow blink. On his other side, Spare trilled their agreement.

"Good luck, then," Cornelia said, bending and kissing Igor on the top of his head. Laura patted his shoulder gingerly, taking great care not to scratch him with those curving claws.

Not trusting himself to speak, Igor nodded his gratitude, then turned to push through the crowd, towards the laboratory.

"So this is it," Grim said, trotting along beside him. "You ready to help the Doctor complete his Great Work?"

"No," Igor said, his mouth settling into a firm line as lightning painted the world white. "I'm going to stop it."

43

THE GREAT WORK

RAIN POUNDED AGAINST the roof of the covered walkway leading to the observatory tower, howling winds whipping at Igor's coat. Each flash of lightning and roll of thunder sent a frisson of excitement through Igor, as if in echo of all the other times he had stood amidst a raging storm, the Doctor harnessing the power of the heavens even as he defied the natural order they had ordained.

Only this was a different sort of excitement that the thunder sent trembling through Igor's frame, fearfully anticipatory. Again he had the feeling of standing at a precipice, as he had when asking the Doctor for a wage atop the manor roof.

But this time, with Grim and Spare at his sides, flanking him like a miniature honor guard, he no longer feared falling.

He seized the laboratory doors with both hands and flung them open wide. "Doctor!"

He'd borne witness to the scene before him countless times. The Subject lying inert atop its slab at the center of the laboratory, its every perfect muscle and grafted limb upon display, a sheet modestly covering those bits Igor had least enjoyed stitching. The roof open to the stormy sky above, through which arcing lightning crackled across the clouds obscuring the full moon.

The twin conducting towers thrumming with ambient power, like a pair of racehorses champing for the starting gun.

"About time you came back, Igor!" the Doctor shouted, laying down a trail of electric cables from the conducting towers towards the Subject. "I was beginning to fear you'd actually meant what you'd said about quitting."

"Quit—" Igor frowned, wrong-footed. "You *fired* me."

"I think I'd recall firing my assistant," the Doctor said, stopping when he reached the Subject and attaching the cables to the electrodes affixed to its cranium. "I knew you'd come back, although I admit I'd expected you to tire of your fit of pique more quickly. You can't imagine how tedious it was, having to insert the Subject's brain by myself."

"I can, actually," Igor said, frowning at the uneven row of staples across the Subject's forehead where the Doctor had sealed its cranium shut. He reached back, making sure Spare was safely behind him. "What about its appendix?"

"Don't think I've forgotten about that," the Doctor said, his expression souring. "Alas, our Subject will have to do without, at least until it's ambulatory. We can insert one then."

Igor blinked. "You want to put a new appendix in the Subject while it's conscious?"

"They get taken out all the time," the Doctor said, shrugging as he opened one of the Subject's eyes, examining it. "Can't be that difficult for you to put a new one in."

Of course the Doctor expected that Igor would be the one to do it. He'd been responsible for every grafted limb and stitched-together organ, from harvesting them to selecting them to installing them. For all his grand plans and his supposed vision, the Doctor had contributed relatively little to the Great Work, save for the alchemical concoctions Igor was beginning to suspect had been kept from him not on account of their complexity, but because they were the only part of the process in which the Doctor could claim the greater skill. Certainly his trembling hands and impatient demeanor meant he could never achieve the precision of stitchery to which Igor had devoted so many painstaking hours.

From its grafted toes to its carefully selected skull, the entire Subject was Igor's creation as much as it was the Doctor's.

Which meant that what became of it was also Igor's responsibility.

Lightning streaked across the sky, illuminating the Doctor's familiar manic grin.

"It's nearly time," he said breathily. "Go and man the lever, will you, Igor? I don't fancy being electrocuted again."

Neither did Igor, for that matter, but that wouldn't have occurred to the Doctor.

"No," Igor said, shutting the laboratory doors behind him. The sound of their closing caused the Doctor to look up, fixing Igor with his full attention for the first time since his arrival.

"No, what?" The Doctor narrowed his eyes. "We really haven't time for more of your attention seeking, Igor. Not when we're on the verge of creating a scientific miracle—"

"You're creating a person," Igor corrected, fists clenched at his side. He walked slowly into the room on his uneven legs, holding the Doctor's gaze. "A thinking being, with its own thoughts, its own wants, its own feelings."

"I don't recall your ever objecting before," the Doctor said, and gestured to where Spare stood hovering near the door, no doubt wary after their last encounter with the Doctor. "Particularly when you've already made your own."

"You're right," Igor admitted. Behind the Doctor, Grim jumped soundlessly onto a worktable covered in alembics and vials. "I should have considered the consequences before I brought new life into the world. Which is why I'm asking you to do the same."

He drew to a halt at the foot of the Subject's slab, the Doctor standing at its head. Their creation lay stretched out between them, as did all their years and work together.

"Igor." The Doctor's voice was low, nakedly pleading. "All this time we've spent in pursuit of the Great Work. And now, after trials and tribulations beyond count, it finally lies within our grasp."

"And what happens," Igor asked, "once it's done?"

"Done?" the Doctor asked, befuddled. "I— Well, there will be further experimentation, of course. Tests to determine the Subject's physical and mental capacities, gauge its—"

"What happens to the *person* we've made!" Igor found he was shouting. He swept his hand over the body upon the slab, which he knew more intimately than any lover's—just as he had known all its predecessors. "Who will clothe it, feed it, care for it? Who will teach it speech, or how to be among people, or right from wrong? Will you, *Master*?"

"I . . ." The Doctor's mouth worked soundlessly as he sought for an answer, finding none.

"That's what I thought." Igor looked down at the Subject. The broad, strong features of the face the Doctor had chosen for it looked strangely vulnerable in repose, the mouth hanging half-open in a way that was almost childlike. "I used to be jealous of them, you know. Our Subjects."

"Jealous?" the Doctor asked, bewildered. He looked down at the Subject's wide, perfectly formed shoulders, then touched a hand to his own, as if to assure himself that his back was still unhunched. "I suppose I can see—"

"Not of that," Igor said, heat creeping into his voice. "Of the attention you gave them. How your whole life—our whole lives—revolved around them. Because I knew that one day the Great Work would be complete, and you'd have your perfect Subject, and then what use would you have for me?"

"Don't be absurd," the Doctor said, his voice climbing almost to a wheedle. "There would be other experiments, of course."

"That's just it." Igor moved to the Subject's slab, brushing his fingers delicately along the stitches where he'd so painstakingly sutured wrist to forearm. "I should have realized all along. Even if they *were* your perfect human being, you were only ever going to treat our creation as a test subject. Something to be measured and prodded at and experimented on, at best."

"In the name of *science,*" the Doctor said, as if science were a god whose invocation justified all manner of sins. Then he frowned, his scientist's curiosity piqued by Igor's last words. "'At best'?"

"At worst," Igor said, lifting his hand and his gaze both from the Subject, "you'd treat them the way you do me."

Behind their goggles, the Doctor's eyes bulged.

"You—" he started, taking a step forward, then let out a yelp as Spare interposed themself between them, slashing their scalpel wildly at his ankles. Igor rounded the Subject's slab and gently pulled each of the electrodes from its head, one by one.

"Don't—" the Doctor started, sidestepping Spare and grabbing at Igor, but before he could lay a hand on his assistant, the sound of glass shattering filled the laboratory.

"Oops," Grim said, and knocked another vial from the worktable.

"Don't!" the Doctor yelped, darting a step towards her, then hesitated, looking back at the Subject.

Too late. Igor had peeled the rest of the electrodes from the Subject's head, severing any connection between it and the conductor towers. He retreated several steps, well out of arm's reach, holding up the bundle of cables with the electrodes still dangling from them.

"It's over, Doctor," Igor said softly. He felt no satisfaction at the words, only a quiet emptiness. "No more experiments."

Shock twisted the Doctor's features, swiftly giving way to

anger. Apparently having no use for the remaining stages of grief, he tore the insulating leather gloves from his hands, revealing the brass clockwork gauntlet he'd used to battle Auntie Mag to a standstill weeks before.

"Put those back, Igor," he said, pointing his gauntleted hand at his former servant. "Or it'll be your appendix—"

The rest of his threat was drowned out by the world exploding.

Or at least that was how it felt. Gooseflesh erupted over every inch of Igor's skin, his hairs standing so sharply on end it felt like they were trying to escape his body, the air thickening with the heavy stench of ozone.

The world turned white as the lightning bolt struck the laboratory—not the lightning rod outside, but the lab itself, snaking down through the open roof as if hurled directly by some wrathful god.

Time seemed to slow as the Doctor's head jerked upwards, the blinding lightning shining in his eyes. One hand drifted downwards, outspread fingertips resting lightly on the Subject's head as if in benediction.

The other hand, the one with the metal gauntlet, reached heavenwards to catch the lightning.

"Master!" Igor shouted, reaching for him, but the force of the bolt striking so near was enough to knock him backwards. He stumbled, craning his head to see lightning pulsing through the Doctor's thin frame, traveling down his arms and into the Subject's inert body.

The Doctor laughed, or perhaps he screamed. Perhaps both.

The lightning stopped, the blinding light slowly receding with it. Igor winced, rubbing his eyes with his free hand to clear his vision of spots.

The Doctor stood over his Subject, statue-still, his fingers no longer twitching. Wild white hair stood out in all directions, singed at the ends, its stench mingling unpleasantly with the ozone stink.

"Did it work?" he asked weakly, then collapsed to the floor.

"Master!" Igor was at his side in a moment, all strife and animosity pushed aside as he stooped over the fallen Doctor to help him up. "Master, are you—"

A groan filled the room, deep and croaking and groggy, like someone rudely awakened from a long sleep and none too happy about it.

On its slab, the Subject stirred, then sat bolt upright. Its broad naked back was crisscrossed with scars and stitches.

Igor stared at his handiwork, the old familiar frisson of excitement shuddering through him once again. "It's—"

44

ALIVE

"I *DID IT!*" the Doctor shouted, clambering unsteadily to his feet. "At last, after all these years, my genius bears fruit!"

The fruit in question let out another groan, shifting so that its legs hung over the slab's edge. Igor stared at the face he had spent countless hours laboring over, subtly transformed by the animation of life within its muscles, feeling and thought working behind its dark eyes.

The Subject lifted its arms, inspecting its hands with obvious curiosity, turning them this way and that. A pang of protective feeling pierced Igor, just as when he'd created Spare. He started for the Subject, only to be shoved rudely aside by the Doctor.

"Perfect!" he crooned, rounding on the Subject. His gaze roamed appraisingly up and down its broad torso. "Skeletal system sufficiently supportive of the musculature, and seems to have full range of motion. Though further inspection—"

The Subject's face, already creased in confusion, drew into a flinch as the Doctor grabbed its arm and began testing its fingers, bending them first one way and then back the other. "A bit stiff, perhaps, but—"

The Subject jerked its hand from the Doctor's grip, then slapped him with it. Already unsteady from the lightning strike, the Doctor teetered, and would have fallen entirely had the Subject not shot out its other hand. The fingers Igor had painstakingly stitched together wrapped around the Doctor's throat, tightening as the Subject lifted the Doctor off the floor.

"Gah!" the Doctor croaked, thrusting his gauntlet at the Subject, but no blast of energy issued forth. The lightning had fried its workings.

"Gah!" the Subject bellowed back, squeezing tighter. The Doctor's legs kicked helplessly inches above the floor, a frightened gurgle issuing from his throat.

"Hey!" Igor called, then lowered his voice. "Hey, you."

Still holding the Doctor aloft, the Subject turned its head to him, naked animal panic written across its features. Again, Igor was reminded of Spare's awakening, and how their first reaction had been not dissimilar.

"It's all right," Igor said, gentling his voice and holding his palms up as he took slow steps towards the Subject. "I know you're confused right now, and scared, and that you have no idea what's going on. But you don't have to be afraid."

"Gah?" the Subject asked warily.

"It's a confusing, scary world you've come into," Igor continued, drawing closer, though not yet quite within arm's reach. "But there are people in it who will care for you. Take care of you. I am one of them."

A familiar weight shimmied up Igor's leg and torso, then settled onto his shoulder. Spare trilled a greeting to the Subject, waving a green hand cheerfully at their much larger cousin.

Perhaps recognizing a kindred spirit, the Subject waved back—albeit with its free hand. The other still held the Doctor, whose face was turning purple.

"Spare is another person who will care for you," Igor said, gesturing at them. "And we are only two. There are so many more out there, waiting to meet you. People who will love you, if you give them the chance to. More than you can imagine, err—"

Igor realized belatedly that it would have been helpful of the Doctor to have given the Subject a name, but before he could think of one, a loud, throaty purr filled the air. Grim twined between the Subject's legs, nuzzling her head against its shins demandingly.

"Kitty!" the Subject bellowed in uncomplicated delight, Grim's affection sparking some trace memory within the folds of its gray matter. It dropped the Doctor unceremoniously so that it could squat down and pet Grim with both hands. Her purring intensified as she arched her back under the Subject's touch, which Igor was relieved to see was quite gentle.

"And that's Grimalkin," Igor said, nodding at her and taking another step forward, so that he was within arm's reach of the Subject. He pointed at the cat. "Grimalkin, or just Grim."

The Subject recoiled, gathering a complaining Grim into its arms and holding her against its chest, no doubt fearing that Igor meant to take her from it.

"She's a friend," Igor said, making no sudden movements as he pointed at himself. "And so am I. Igor."

"Igor?" the Subject repeated dubiously. Igor nodded.

"Igor. Friend." The Subject looked down at Grim, still purring in its arms. "Grim friend?"

"That's right," Igor said, as Spare trilled in his ear. "And Spare."

"Spare friend," the Subject said, sounding pleased with itself.

"Ugh," the Doctor wheezed from his place flat on his back on the floor.

The Subject threw Igor a quizzical look. "Ugh friend?"

"No," Igor said, shaking his head and turning to the Doctor, who was struggling up onto his elbows.

"Igor," he said, his voice coming in short wheezes. "Restrain the Subject, posthaste."

"I don't think they're a threat," Igor said, as Spare clambered down from his shoulder to inspect the newest addition to their odd little family. He turned away from the tableau as the Subject tried petting both Grim and Spare at the same time. "Provided you treat them kindly, anyway."

"Igor," the Doctor said, swallowing hard, "please. As your employer—"

"Actually," Igor said, "I'm done."

The Doctor blinked. "Done?"

"Done with being ignored," Igor said. "And with being disregarded. With belittled, bullied, mocked. With having my work taken for granted, my achievements downplayed. I have slaved for you, bled for you, nearly died for you. Without complaint, or recompense, or even a word of thanks, for *years.*"

Something stung Igor's eyes, and he blinked rapidly. When his vision cleared, it was to see the Doctor looking at him with an expression he couldn't place.

"So you blame me," the man Igor had called Master said, his voice flat, "for your misery?"

"Only half as much as I blame myself," Igor said. "I let you treat me this way. Told myself that you didn't mean it when you called me broken, misshapen, ugly. But no more. I'm done, Doctor. Find someone else to take your abuse, because I won't any longer."

"Abuse." The Doctor's voice stiffened, as did his spine. "I took you in when no one else could stand the sight of you. I taught you a trade. Gave you a *purpose.* Fixed your tongue, if you'll recall. If it weren't for me, you'd still be a slobbering, gibbering half-mute no one could comprehend, let alone care for."

Not long ago, those words would have struck Igor like a blow. Now they washed off him, robbed of their power by the sounds at his back: Spare's excited trills, the Subject's soft coos, Grim's gentle purring.

"You cured my lisp," Igor said, running his tongue over his

teeth, "so that it'd be easier for you to understand me. Not that you ever did. Or will."

He took a step back. The Subject's heavy hand landed with surprising gentleness upon Igor's shoulder, resting lightly on his hump. Spare wriggled from the Subject's grip to hug their creator's leg, while Grim's purring doubled in volume.

"I've had enough of being your henchman, Doctor," Igor said.

The Doctor stared up at him, uncomprehending. "What do you mean?"

Igor smiled beatifically down at him.

"I quit," he said.

EPILOGUE

"HOLD STILL," IGOR chided his latest patient. "I've finished connecting the tendons, but if you don't keep still while I finish closing the suture, something might tear."

"Sorry," said the zombie lying upon the slab where Igor had painstakingly stitched together another, significantly more amalgamated corpse six months ago. "It just tickles a bit."

"That'd be the nerve endings connecting," Igor said, keeping his eyes focused on his needle as he sewed a new arm onto the exposed humerus poking out from the zombie's tattered sleeve. "I can give you something to dull the sensation, if you'd like. Spare?"

Spare trilled as they looked up from their worktable on the far side of the lab, where they were busily grinding some bitter-root leaves into a fine powder using a mortar and pestle. Strewn across the worktable was a wide collection of alembics, vials, and cylinders in which numerous alchemical concoctions were in various stages of decanting. The Doctor had left behind many scribbled notes and alchemical treatises following his hurried flight from Ravenwald.

Some days he still expected to awaken to the Doctor pounding on the front doors of the manor, demanding Igor pack up his laboratory equipment and accompany him as he embarked upon some new Great Work—transmuting lead into gold, perhaps, or unlocking the secret of spontaneous human combustion. But the Doctor had vanished in the middle of the night, taking the black coach and its horses with him—though these had turned up not five miles down the road, the coach having gotten stuck in a particularly deep puddle. Boot prints in the mud indicated that the Doctor had continued on foot, away from Ravenwald and out of Igor's life without so much as a farewell or a word of thanks.

Perhaps that had always been too much to hope for, Igor supposed. Not that it lessened the sting of that departure—fractious and one-sided as their relationship had been, its abrupt dissolution still left a hole in Igor's heart, heavy with the weight of things left unresolved. But with each day that passed, the loss hurt a little less, the friendships he'd formed slowly filling the space that that absence had left.

"A numbing tincture, please," Igor said, smiling at Spare, who chirped their assent and began measuring a dull green liquid into a syringe.

"Now," Igor said, returning his attention to the zombie, "I understand that your arm isn't the only reason you've come to visit us here at Ravenwald, Mr. Widdershins?"

"That's right." Widdershins the zombie nodded, an action that caused his jaw to hinge lopsidedly open at one side. Sighing, he slotted it back into position with his free hand. "Sorry. Damned thing always does that."

"I can take a look at screwing it more securely into place," Igor offered, resuming his stitchwork as his partner tottered over holding a syringe above their head. "Thank you, Spare. You were saying, Mr. Widdershins?"

"Well," Widdershins said, his eyes following Spare as the construct clambered onto the slab behind him and inserted the syringe into his stump of an arm, just above where Igor was attaching the new limb. "Word travels, as I'm sure you know. Suffice to say that you lot started quite a stir in the community, dealing with your masters the way you did."

Igor didn't bother asking what community he meant. In the half a year since the Count, the Doctor, and Auntie Mag had all been driven from the manor on the same night, Ravenwald had played host to more than a dozen unexpected guests, from a gaggle of ghouls to a mournful banshee. Diverse as they were, these visitors had one thing in common: All were in the service of masters who treated them with less respect than they ought to have done. All sought to advocate for themselves and their rights, with the guidance of those who had done so first.

Namely Igor, Grim, and Cornelia.

"So you're here on behalf of your . . ." Igor trailed off, uncertain what the polite term was for a plurality of zombies.

"Horde," Widdershins said, which was what Igor had suspected it might be. "Though there are only six of us. We're in the service of the Dark Lord Farrow, dreaded necromancer and dark prophet of the Reaper."

Igor pulled tight another stitch. "Can't say I've heard of him."

"His titles are mostly self-bestowed," Widdershins confided. "Anyhow, he's about as demanding and ungrateful a master as you could imagine. Always ordering us to terrorize villages or tear heroes limb from limb, with nothing in the way of compensation for our labor, or restitution made for lost parts."

"I know the type," Igor said, finishing the last stitch and tying off the dangling thread. "So, you've come seeking the Union's help?"

"We have," Widdershins said again, with another nod vigorous enough to displace his jawbone. He jammed it back into place before continuing. "Well, as I've got the most intact vocal apparatus, the rest of the horde nominated me to come and see if you might be able to . . ."

He gave a vague wave of the arm Igor had just finished stitching, then stared down as he realized.

"Shinbones!" Widdershins swore softly, moving his new fingers experimentally. "That's quite something, Mr. Igor."

"Just Igor," Igor assured him. "How does it feel? Like new?"

"I honestly wouldn't know," Widdershins said, slowly clenching and unclenching his fist. "Thank you. I—"

The laboratory door groaned ominously open, reminding Igor that he needed to oil its hinges. Into the room stepped the towering figure Igor had helped usher into the world half a year past, the faint scars left by Igor's stitches still visible around his neck and wrists. He was dressed in a pair of trousers Igor had knitted himself and a flannel shirt Laura had donated, and a pink apron.

"Igor?" inquired the final Subject he and the Doctor had collaborated on. "Supper's ready downstairs."

"Thank you, Kitty," Igor said, smiling at him. "We'll be down momentarily."

"I'll have the table set," Kitty said, beaming and turning about, exiting the way he'd entered. Igor winced and promised himself that he'd oil the doors as soon as dinner was over.

"Kitty?" asked the zombie, looking as though he'd have raised an eyebrow if he'd possessed any.

"He named himself," Igor said, shrugging. "It was his first word. It stuck."

Widdershins grunted. "Suppose I'm not one to cast stones in that regard. Now, about the necromancer . . ."

"You've come to the right place," Igor assured him, putting a hand gingerly on the zombie's shoulder. "But as Kitty said, supper's waiting. We can discuss the details of your plight while we eat."

"You sure?" Widdershins's face contorted into the nearest thing to a frown his lopsided jawbone allowed. "Not that I don't appreciate the hospitality, but I've got a rather particular palate."

"We anticipated as much," Igor said, rising and striding to the door. "And Kitty's been dying to try out a new recipe, ever since he found out you were paying us a visit."

* * *

"Brains!" Widdershins exclaimed, his jaw hinging dangerously to one side as Kitty removed the metal cover of his dish with a flourish to reveal the mass of gray matter beneath.

"Cervelle d'avocat," said Kitty, who'd become nearly as facile with languages in his six months of consciousness as he had in the kitchen. Igor had been only too happy to impart his culinary knowledge to the newest member of the Ravenwald household, and he had little doubt that Kitty would surpass him before the year was out.

"I supplied the body," Cornelia confided across the table to Widdershins, swirling the goblet in her hand.

The new Countess Ravenwald had been swift to repair not only the manor, but its relations with its neighbors. Evidently the Count had left a significant store of wealth secreted beneath the crypt, which Cornelia had immediately put to use restoring the manor to its former grandeur, as well as establishing several charitable ventures in Ravensburg, including an orphanage and a food bank, with the help of Friar Bernhard. In light of these good deeds, the townsfolk had quickly become accustomed to having a vampire for a neighbor; Igor had even heard it opined on his trips into town that, bloodsucker or not, the new Countess was far less of a parasite than your typical aristocrat.

No one had heard from the Count since the night of his departure, though rumor had reached them of a dangerous but sloppy killer plaguing the streets of Chernodrang, some two hundred miles to the north, whose victims often bore wounds on their throats. If those killings were the Count's handiwork, Igor suspected that the good folk of Chernodrang would root the vampire lord from their midst sooner rather than later.

"You missed a spot, dear," Laura said as Cornelia set down her goblet. She gingerly dabbed the corner of her lover's mouth with a napkin, wiping away the faint smear of red that had gathered there.

Though she still dwelled in the little cottage beside the town cemetery, Laura had been approached earlier that year by the newly created Ravensburg town council, of which Ruth Dreyfuss was a founding member. In recognition of her unique attributes, they had offered Laura the role of gamekeeper for the forests surrounding Ravensburg, ensuring that the deer population remained at a manageable level. Laura had made the transition from gravekeeper to gamekeeper quite well, in no small part because the town council turned a blind eye if some of the culled deer wound up in the crypt of Ravenwald Manor.

"Thank you, love," Cornelia said, giving her a brief peck on the cheek. Blushing furiously, Laura lowered her attention to her plate, and the extremely rare steak Kitty had prepared for her.

"Are we ready to start?" Igor asked.

"Almost," Grim said, trotting into the room with her tail held high and a silvery fish hanging from her mouth. She leapt nimbly onto the top of her scratching post.

"Where did you get that?" Igor asked, bemused, as she dropped the fish and settled her paws on top of it.

"Mag might be gone," Grim said, "but she left that silver circle in the chapel floor."

Like the Count and the Doctor, Auntie Mag had disappeared into the night, never to darken Ravenwald's doors again. The manor's inhabitants had been surprised when, several months later, a courier had arrived with a letter and a package. The former had been from Mag to Grim, who'd refused to let the others read it once they'd used their thumbs to open it for her, but she had accepted the scratching post contained by the latter after reading it.

Laura furrowed her brow at Grim, now seated atop that same scratching post. "So you use an interdimensional portal to . . . summon fish?"

Grim licked her chops. "I'm a cat."

"And also vice chairperson of our local chapter," Igor reminded her, giving her an affectionate scratch between the ears. He looked from her to Spare, climbing onto the table beside him, to Cornelia and Laura holding hands atop the table, then to Kitty, just taking his seat beside Widdershins and watching the zombie's every bite of the brain he'd so painstakingly prepared for their guest.

Igor smiled wide, suddenly overcome with gratitude at the fellowship he'd had a hand in forming. Of the family they'd made together, in this manor house that was now their home.

He cleared his throat. Eleven eyes turned his way, giving him their full attention.

"As presiding chairperson of our local chapter," Igor said, smiling, "I hereby call this meeting of the Henchpersons' Union to order."

ACKNOWLEDGMENTS

Much like stitching together an amalgamated corpse sourced from various body parts, writing a book is a messy, disjointed, and occasionally grisly process. This one could not have been brought to life without the hard work of many hands, and as Igor and his friends amply demonstrate, all labor deserves recognition. To wit:

This book could not have been written without the enthusiastic guidance and wisdom of my agent, Brent Taylor, who not only fully supported this book's gleefully absurd premise, but whose sharp insights helped iron out a rather uneven and episodic narrative into the coherent story you've just finished reading. I also hold the dubious distinction of being Brent's first client ever to receive a publication offer while actively boarding a plane, or to have accepted said deal in an airport Chili's.

I owe an equally huge debt to my editor, Gabby Colangelo, whom I clicked with from the first moments of our introductory call. It's an incredibly special gift for an author to get to work with an editor who understands the book at its most fundamental level, who loves both the humor and the emotional heart of the story you're telling, and who gets your decade-old meme references. Gabby's insights and suggestions consistently enhanced and elevated Igor's story, and I'm so grateful to her for helping to shape *Henchperson's Guide* into its final form. Thank you for everything, Gabby, and I'll see you in the ball pit.

Thank you as well to the rest of the team at Penguin Random House for your work making this book the best it can be: Dan Denning, Caro Perny, and Taylor Noel in Marketing & Publicity; Scott Shannon, Jennifer Hershey, Kim Hovey, and Kara Cesare at Bantam; Saige Francis, Ted Allen, Angela McNally, and Jo Anne Metsch in the Managing Editorial & Production Editorial departments; and to Scott Biel and John Viet-Triet Hoa Nguyen for the incredible cover art.

I owe a particular thanks to Angela Cowan and Nicole McKeon, both of whose real-time feedback through this book's development were instrumental in keeping me going. You guys are (Chris Traeger voice) *literally* my ideal readers. Thank you as well to MK Calderini and Re Gwaltney for giving this book some much-needed early feedback.

Lauren Thoman and Sarah Brown: I'm so glad you guys were the only other introverts in the room at that mixer, and I can't imagine a better start to a beautiful friendship than going tipsy book shopping together. Thank you, Lauren, for being a constant voice of reason and experience in the crazy world that is publishing, and to Sarah for keeping me updated on the latest drama in fandoms I'm not part of.

Chase and Adelyn Trautwein: Thank you for being the sweetest readers, biggest advocates, and dearest friends. If writing a book is like running a marathon, the two of you were there to cheer this one on at every mile marker. Let's go take some Oktoberfest selfies soon.

Thank you to Andrea Stewart for being a mentor and a role model in this industry, and for paying it forward. You're my hero.

Thank you to Emily Krempholtz for paving the way, and for our shared adventures in beekeeping.

Thank you to Liz Griffin for being my Dragon Con buddy—

we've come a long way from waiting in line for a Jim Butcher panel together, and I can't wait to see where we go next! And speaking of Dragon Con, thank you to the Shadow Alley Press crew for taking a chance on an unknown, and asking me to make my first book into a trilogy.

Thank you to Mom, Megan, Cody, Scott, Maggie, and Bre for letting me steal fifteen minutes of Cody and Maggie's wedding weekend to tell you all the big news of my book deal in person. (Fear not, gentle reader: The rest of the weekend was indeed about the happy couple.) This book is about found family, but I count myself beyond lucky to have had an amazing one from the start.

Thank you to the friends who've believed in me from the very beginning: Caitlyn Trousdale, Colin Howell, and Lindsey Boren. I would never have even tried to write a book if it wasn't for you.

The last and greatest thanks of all goes to Megan, who in addition to being my favorite person in the world is also an incredibly sharp, insightful, and patient reader. Thank you for laughing at my jokes, cuddling our cats, hashing out plot arcs and character dynamics over morning walks, and occasionally talking sense into me whenever I get too into my head. I love you so dearly.

AUTHOR PHOTOGRAPH: CHLOE RAVINA

MARSHALL J. MOORE is the author of the *Son of a Sailor* cozy fantasy trilogy, the *Rites of Resurrection* epic fantasy trilogy, and more than thirty published short stories. His story "Red Lanterns" won second place in the Baen Fantasy Adventure Award Short Story Contest. When he is not writing, or talking about writing, you can find Marshall teaching Muay Thai or reading at his home in Atlanta with his wife, Megan, and their two cats, Delilah and Furiosa.

marshalljmoore.com
Instagram, TikTok, Facebook,
Threads: @marshalljmooreauthor

ABOUT THE TYPE

This book was set in Hoefler Text, a typeface designed in 1991 by Jonathan Hoefler (b. 1970). One of the earlier typefaces created at the beginning of the digital age specifically for use on computers, it was among the first to offer features previously found only in the finest typography, such as dedicated old-style figures and small caps. Thus it offers modern style based on the classic tradition.